# Blood and Silence

# Blood and Silence

## The Origins of Will Anderson

*A rookie learns fast: the badge won't save you.*

W Mark Harrington

## Dedication

For my family—my first and last line of defense.
For the ones who answer when the radio crackles and
who walk into chaos while others turn away.
For those who hold the line, unseen and uncelebrated,
standing between order and the dark that never sleeps.
For every man and woman who's worn the badge with
honor,
judged by those who'll never know the cost,
who'll never see the evil you face
or the silence you carry home.

You're the reason the line still holds.
May God continue to watch over you.

## Disclaimer

*Blood and Silence* is a work of fiction inspired by the realities of law enforcement. While procedures, investigations, and terminology may reflect authentic experiences, all characters, names, and events are entirely fictional. Any resemblance to actual persons, living or deceased, or to real cases or agencies, is purely coincidental. Certain elements have been altered or dramatized to preserve confidentiality and enhance narrative impact.

## Content Warning:

This novel contains depictions of violence, trauma, and crimes of a graphic and psychological nature that may be distressing to some readers. These scenes are portrayed with respect for victims and the realities faced by those who serve in law enforcement. Reader discretion is advised.

# Table of Contents

# Preface

This story began long before the first page was written—before Will Anderson ever walked into a crime scene or faced the shadows that would come to define him.

*Blood and Silence* isn't about heroics. It's about survival—what the job does to those who wear the badge and what it takes to keep showing up when the world stops believing in you.

I spent more than two decades in law enforcement. I saw the best of it—and the worst. The people I served beside weren't perfect, nor did they claim to be, but most showed up when it mattered, often without thanks and sometimes at great personal cost. Their courage, their flaws, and their quiet exhaustion are the pulse beneath these pages.

This book doesn't glorify the work—it honors the reality: the noise, the politics, and the toll of holding a line against wrong and evil most people never see, or even know exists.

To those I've served beside, thank you for showing me what resilience looks like.
To my family, thank you for your patience and love through the long nights and quiet mornings.
And to the readers who walk this road with Will—thank

you for understanding that the silence after a call can be louder than the chaos that came before.

If *The Demon of Oakhaven* showed the man shaped by darkness, *Blood and Silence* shows how he first stepped into it.

— **Mark Harrington**

*"All that is necessary for the triumph of evil is for good men to do nothing."*
— Edmund Burke

*"We sleep safely in our beds because rough men stand ready in the night to visit violence on those who would do us harm."*
— George Orwell

# Prologue: Badge

The badge didn't sit right.

Too clean, too gold, too new. It felt like stolen valor, earned, maybe, but not here. The collar scratched worse than sand in a flak jacket. He told himself to *sit still—breathe, watch, listen—*calling on muscle memory from his Army days.

But the badge on his chest wasn't a rank patch, and this squad car wasn't a Humvee. He'd endured worse in the desert, sure, but at least his flak jacket hadn't tried to choke him.

This was a police cruiser. And Sergeant Joe Donovan—his Field Training Officer—wasn't here to babysit. He was here to see if Will could sink or swim.

Will shifted slightly. His brand-new boots gave a soft squeak against the rubber floor mat. Again. The third time in five minutes. Each squeal felt like a klaxon announcing: *Rookie. Rookie. Rookie.*

Beside him, Joe Donovan sat unmoving behind the wheel. One hand was draped over the steering wheel, as if it had been glued there for days. The other wrapped around a stained white travel cup that might once have said "Best Dad" or "#1 Cop"—the print had long since vanished under the patina of years. The dark lenses of his aviators gave away nothing. The man looked as if he had been carved from the dashboard itself—gray, cracked, and unfazed.

The cruiser crawled through the streets of Summit Falls' East District, slow as a hearse. Bars on liquor store windows. Graffiti clinging to roll-down gates like scars. Apartment buildings leaned on each other like old drunks trying to stay upright. A mural of civil rights leaders faded under layers of grime, a half-visible face watching them pass. A pit bull on a rusted chain blinked at the cruiser without interest.

Will's breath fogged the window. He shifted again. Squeak.

Joe sipped his coffee. No words. No glance. Just silence thick enough to gum up the gears.

Will cleared his throat. "Sir, uh... Sergeant Donovan."

A pause. Then, flat: "What."

"I just wanted to say I appreciate being assigned to—"

"Don't." Another sip. No inflection. "Learn the streets. Then maybe I'll care what you say."

Will shut his mouth. His cheeks went hot. The speech he'd practiced in the mirror—*honored to serve, grateful to learn from the best*—died on his tongue.

They kept rolling.

Will's eyes flicked to the radio. Static buzzed softly. He caught their reflection in the glass of a storefront: one man upright and squared off, the other hunched slightly forward like he was still waiting for permission to be here.

This wasn't how his first shift was supposed to feel.

The radio crackled.

*10-37... suspicious person.* Will's gut tightened. First real call. First chance to prove he wasn't just some academy grad with shiny boots and textbook answers.

*"Unit 2-4, we've got a 10-37. Possible match for last week's phone store robbery. Male, dark hoodie, pacing near Eastland and Brooks. Caller says he looks twitchy, possibly armed."*

Joe's hand moved. Calm. Controlled. He picked up the mic. "2-4, en route."

He dropped it into the cradle. Flicked on the lights. Red and blue exploded across the windshield. Reflections painted their faces like masks.

Joe finally turned his head toward Will.

"You're up, boot."

Will blinked. "Me?"

Joe didn't blink. "You see a third guy in the backseat?"

"No, sir."

"Then get your ass ready."

The cruiser surged forward. Tires hummed against cracked pavement. Streetlights buzzed overhead, though it wasn't yet dusk. Will felt the weight of the vest against his chest, the radio on his belt, the sidearm that still felt like borrowed authority.

He spotted the suspect—a wiry man in a dark hoodie, moving fast but not quite running. Head twitching side to side. Hands shoved deep into the front pocket.

Joe slowed the cruiser. "You see the hands. Always the hands."

Will nodded, throat dry. His hand hovered near the door handle. He stepped out. His legs felt both weightless and heavy.

The man turned as Will approached, eyes sharp, shoulders tensed.

"I'm just walking," he said, voice tight. "You ain't got cause to touch me."

Will raised a hand, unsure if it was to calm or to warn. "Sir, I need to speak with you. Please keep your hands visible—"

The man didn't wait.

"I see what this is," he snapped. "You think I'm dumb?"

Then he ran.

"Shit—" Will bolted after him. Vest bouncing. Boots hammering pavement. Every step rattled his bones.

The alley swallowed them both. Narrow. Dark. Smelled like oil, rot, piss. Trash bags slumped against walls like collapsed bodies. The suspect juked right at a fork.

Will hesitated.

*Do I call it in? Do I chase?*

He had seconds—less than seconds—and his brain locked up, gears grinding.

That second cost him everything.

He turned the corner. Empty.

Just a chain-link fence. Dumpster. Shadows. A single shoe. A plastic bag flapped in the wind like a ghost trying to escape.

Will bent forward, hands on knees. His pulse throbbed in his ears. No movement. No footsteps. Just the ringing silence of failure.

Will heard Joe's boots hitting pavement behind him—slower, more deliberate. Not old, but not sprinting either. "The knees don't bounce like they used to," Joe had said once. However, he always seemed to arrive just in time.

Joe appeared, calm as ever. Not winded, not surprised. He scanned the alley with the same expression you'd give a burned microwave dinner.

"Didn't call it in," Joe said.

Will straightened, chest heaving. "I... I thought I could get him."

"You didn't."

"I froze."

Joe exhaled through his nose. He rubbed his forehead like he was scrubbing the moment from memory. Then he nodded once. "Yep."

He turned and walked away.

They drove back in silence. No sirens. Just the low hum of the engine and the weight in Will's chest. The city outside blurred past: rusted signs, cracked sidewalks, empty bus benches.

At the garage, Joe shut off the engine. Didn't get out. The fluorescent lights buzzed overhead.

"Get your notebook," he said.

Will blinked. "Sir?"

"You wanna be a real cop, you write things down. Mistakes especially."

Will pulled out the black leather-bound notebook from his breast pocket. It still smelled like the bookstore. He opened to the first page. Blank. Too clean.

"Walk me through it," Joe said. "Step by step."

Will's voice was thin. "We got the call. 10-37. Eastland and Brooks. Suspect in a dark hoodie. Acting suspicious."

Joe held up a hand. "You rolled up. He had his hands in his pockets. What'd you do?"

"I told him to stop."

"And when he ran?"

"I chased."

Joe shook his head slowly. "You went cowboy. No backup. That's how rookies get buried. Ever do anything in the Army alone?"

Will looked down. The badge on his chest felt heavier than ever.

Joe's voice was lower now. Not cruel—just real. "You think you're ready to take a life?"

Will hesitated. "Only if I have to, sir."

"Good. Means you're not a psychopath. But you'd better be ready to make the decision. Fast. Before someone else makes it for you. You don't get to hesitate, Anderson."

Will swallowed hard. "Yes, sir."

Joe opened the door. Paused. Looked back at him. "You get one hesitation, rookie. That was yours."

He stepped out, leaving the door open behind him.

Will sat in the cruiser alone.

The badge didn't shine so bright now.

He looked down at the notebook. Pressed the pen to the page.

**Notebook Entry**

*Eastland & Brooks*

*First chase. Froze. Didn't call it in.*

*Lesson: You get one hesitation.*

*That was mine.*

*It won't happen again.*

## Think

It started with shouting—ragged, sharp, the kind that cut through walls and windows. By the time Will and Joe pulled up on Grafton Street, the whole block was awake. Porch lights flickered across cracked siding. Curtains shifted. A woman in a nightgown stood on the opposite curb, clutching her phone like a lifeline, bare feet on the pavement.

Apartment 3-B. Top floor.

"Domestic disturbance," Joe muttered as they climbed the stairwell. His boots hit the steps with heavy, deliberate thuds—like war drums. "Never know what you're walking into. Sometimes it's yelling. Sometimes it's knives. Always think 'what if' in these situations, be prepared."

Will's hand hovered near his holster. Old instincts stirred. Clearing rooms in Kandahar. Breathing slowly when the glass shattered nearby. But here, the hallway smelled of boiled cabbage. Doors stood half-open. Toddlers stared with wide eyes. Civilian eyes. Collateral damage wasn't an option. His stomach tightened.

"Understood," he whispered.

Joe's tone flattened. "Don't understand it. Respect it."

They reached the door of 3-B. A crash from inside—then silence. The kind of silence that made Will's pulse slam against his vest.

Joe knocked hard with the side of his fist, fast and deliberate. "Summit Falls PD. Open the door."

Fumbling at the lock. The door creaked. A woman appeared—early thirties, hair in a messy bun, mascara streaked like smoke. The tank top stretched at the collar, revealing the top of her bra on one side. A cut fresh on her lip. Her voice shook. "He's in the kitchen."

Joe's voice was steady as stone. "Ma'am, stay right here."

They stepped inside. The apartment reeked of stale pizza and booze. Baby toys littered the carpet. Something dripped in the sink. A family photo hung crooked on the wall, the father's face fractured by a spiderweb crack in the glass.

A whimper. Will turned his head. A toddler clutched a blanket in the hallway, eyes like saucers. The mother's hands trembled as she tucked the child behind her.

"He's drunk," she whispered. "Thinks I'm sleeping with someone else. Won't take no for an answer."

Joe cut his eyes to Will. Quiet. Stay sharp.

In the kitchen: a man. Six-two. Shirtless. Chest heaving. Fists clenched. A gold chain swung against his bare skin as he turned. His knuckles were red, raw from a wall—or worse.

Joe raised his hands, his movements calm and deliberate. "Sir. Let's talk. Nobody needs to get hurt tonight."

The man's eyes flicked to the woman in the hall. His voice cracked between rage and disbelief. "So you called them? What'd you tell them? That I hit you? That I'm the bad guy?"

"Let's not make this worse," Joe said evenly.

"Worse?" His jaw locked tight. "She's the one screwin' around, and I'm the villain? Paying all the bills so she can blow the neighbor and whore around while I'm at work. And I'm in the wrong. Fuck that!"

Will's hand brushed his cuffs. He stepped in. "Sir, let's step outside—"

"Bullshit." The man's voice dropped, darker now. "You're a damn fool if you think I'm gonna let you parade me out like some damn animal?"

Then he moved.

The table flipped in an eruption of glass and wood. A chair clattered across the tiles. He bolted through the back door like he'd planned it all along.

Joe barked, "Nobody needs—"

But Will was already moving.

The fire escape rattled under his boots. Night air slapped his face. The suspect vaulted down landings two at a time, then hurled himself off the last flight into the alley. Will chased, ribs jolting with every impact.

They hit pavement. The man sprinted toward a chain-link fence. He climbed. Fast. Desperate. Will grabbed for the bars, hauled himself up—

Impact.

A shoulder slammed his ribs. Pain burst through him. A fist cracked his jaw. He crashed onto gravel. Blood filled his mouth. The alley spun sideways.

Bootsteps thundered. A shadow loomed. Will threw a wild punch, connecting with something solid. Pain screamed through his side. His arm wrenched, pinned. Breath stolen.

The man's face hovered above his. Twisted. Sweat dripping. In his hand, the jagged neck of a broken bottle caught the alley light, sharp as teeth.

Will's fingers clamped his wrist. They grappled, muscles burning, glass inches from his throat. His grip slipped.

*He's going to kill me.* Flashed in Will's mind.

"Move, rookie!"

Joe hit like a freight train. The man slammed into a dumpster with a clang that rattled the alley. Metal groaned. The suspect crumpled. Joe pinned him, cuffed him, one knee grinding into his back.

Then Joe's eyes cut to Will. Longer this time. Measuring.

"Still breathing?"

Will coughed, nodded. His hands shook uncontrollably. He pressed them to the ground to stop the trembling. His ribs screamed with every breath.

Joe turned away before Will could read what passed over his face.

Will slumped against the wall, lungs burning, jaw throbbing. The stink of rot and motor oil coated his tongue. His chest felt too small for air.

Joe looked down at the cuffed man, then back at Will. "You run fast, kid," he said. "But you think slow."

They hauled the cuffed man toward the cruiser, as he cussed them, cussed at her, telling the whole neighborhood that he was gone and she's open for business. Spitting blood and rage as they tossed him in the back and slammed the door. Still yelling something muffled that Will couldn't hear, nodding his head as if he was having a one-sided conversation and winning the argument.

Joe opened the door. "One, Nobody cares, Two, nobody can hear you through the glass, so sit there and remain silent, or keep talking so everything you say can be used against you in court. I'm sure that will help her out more than you. So pipe down."

The man just slumped over in the seat, "Hurry up then damnit, get me downtown and get these cuffs off me, ya damn bastard!"

Later, in the cruiser, after booking the wife beater, silence pressed heavier than bruises. The dash glowed faintly red and blue from the remnants of long-forgotten lights.

Will touched his ribs, winced. "I didn't want to freeze again."

Joe's jaw tightened. His hands gripped the wheel. "You overcorrected. A dead cop still counts as a mistake."

Neither spoke again until they rolled into the garage. The engine clicked as it cooled.

"You good?" Joe asked.

Will nodded too fast. "Yeah."

"You're not." Joe didn't press. He left it there.

In the locker room, Will peeled off his vest. His shirt clung to blood and sweat. The mirror showed a swollen eye, a split lip, and a uniform shirt shredded. Fluorescents buzzed overhead. The stink of bleach stung his nose.

He sat on the bench for a long time. His notebook lay heavy in his hand.

Finally, he flipped to a clean page. Pen scratched.

### Notebook Entry
*Grafton Street:*
*Domestic gone bad. Rushed in solo.*
*Out of position.*
*Almost didn't come home.*
**Lesson: Patience and backup beat ego.**

13

## Glass

Will had testified in court before—quick, procedural stuff. A statement here, a timeline there. But this case was different. Messier. A burglary gone sideways, with the DA's office pushing hard to make it stick. Which meant prep. In person. Ravenwood County Justice Center.

He arrived at 0900 sharp, the courtroom was opening to the public at the other entrance, and his badge was clipped neatly to his chest. The uniform felt stiff, like it hadn't softened since the academy. Sleep had been fitful. The foot chase in the alley still looped through his head: the suspect's eyes, the turn, the silence after. Mistake or lesson? Both.

The Justice Center didn't smell like the precinct—no coffee, no sweat, no oil-stained floors. Here it was lemon polish and quiet ambition. Clean glass walls and brushed metal signs made everything feel transparent, even when it wasn't.

Security waved him through. A receptionist, more interested in her phone than the badge on his chest, pointed him toward back offices. Frosted glass panels lined the hall, names etched in tidy black. One stopped him cold:

**Kristen Dalton, Assistant District Attorney.**

A flicker of memory sparked. Not just from the file. College. Ravenwood University. Tuesday nights. *Constitutional Law.* Will had sat in the back, quiet, still carrying the desert in his posture. She'd sat up front. Always two steps ahead of the lecture.

He knocked.

She looked up. Black blazer, dark jeans, hair twisted up like she hadn't had time for anything else. One AirPod in. Coffee half-forgotten at her elbow. A yellow legal pad scrawled with neat handwriting rested beside the file he'd delivered earlier.

"Will Anderson. Thought that name was familiar," she said, recognition in her voice, sharper now, but there.

He blinked. "Kristen... Dalton. From Constitutional Law?"

She tugged the AirPod free. A smile flickered. "You, I remember. Always first out the door, the second class ended. You were there for a while, then—poof. Gone."

"Yeah," he said, rubbing the back of his neck, a little sheepish. "Transferred to UNC Chapel Hill for a bit. My family is nearby in North Carolina. Finished out with a psych degree."

Her brow lifted. "Psychology? Not the direction I had you pegged for."

He shrugged. "I almost went to law school after. Thought about it more than once. But..." His grin tilted wryly. "I figured the courts already had enough lawyers.

15

Somebody had to keep writing the reports you guys get to tear apart."

That earned him a laugh, the kind that tugged her shoulders loose.

"And you're still underselling yourself," she said.

"And you're still rewriting the syllabus," he countered, smirking.

"And now you're the one delivering clean casework to the DA's office. Funny how that works." She gestured to the chair opposite. "This report's yours?"

He nodded.

"It's solid. Clear. Most cops write like they're allergic to punctuation."

A corner of his mouth tugged upward. "Army taught me to get to the point."

She flipped a page. "And you still sit like you're expecting incoming fire."

"Not the worst way to get through a courthouse."

### Courtroom, Trial Day

By morning, the trial was underway. The air inside was cooler, tighter—wood polish, old paper, nerves. Will shifted in the witness chair, the uniform collar digging into his neck. The defense attorney's questions came clipped, meant to trip him: *Were you certain of the ID? Wasn't the alley dark? Could you see the suspect's hands?*

Kristen objected twice, her voice calm, surgical. She didn't glance at him often, but when she did, it was just a nod—steady, quiet assurance: *You're fine. Keep going.* He clung to that like armor until the judge finally called recess.

## Lunch Break

Kristen caught up to him by the courtroom doors. "There's a Cuban place two blocks over. Fast, cheap, won't kill you. You in?"

Will blinked. "Sure. You're the boss today."

They stepped into Ravenwood's government district. Noon bustle. Suits on phones, coffee carts, a saxophone wailing faintly from a corner. The Cuban place was wedged between a bail bonds office and a dry cleaner. Tile floors, handwritten menus, roasted pork, and garlic heavy in the air.

They ate outside at a metal table. Traffic rolled by. The city noise filled the space between words.

Kristen peeled the paper back from her sandwich. "So. Summit Falls. You like it?"

Will chewed a bite of plantain. Swallowed. "Depends on who I'm partnered with."

"Still with Donovan?"

He raised an eyebrow. "You know Joe?"

"Everyone knows Joe. He's either a legend or a cautionary tale, depending on who you ask."

Will smirked. "He's both."

She laughed. Genuine. Not courtroom-tight, just easy. The sound surprised him.

"You still think about South Raven?" he asked.

She rolled her eyes. "Only when I get court flashbacks."

"Same. Except I had sand in my boots half the time. Army never really washed out."

"You always wanted to be a cop?" she asked.

He hesitated. "Didn't know what else to do after the Army. Tried school. Thought about law. Didn't have the stomach for debt. Or lectures."

Kristen studied him, thoughtful now. "I remember you. You always left class the second the professor dismissed us. Never lingered."

"Didn't think anyone noticed."

"I did."

A pause. Longer. Comfortable.

Back at the courthouse steps, she scribbled her number on the back of a card. Handed it to him. The loop of the *K* was deliberate.

"Text me if you ever want to run another case by me. Or grab lunch. Or coffee."

He tucked it into his pocket, surprised by the slight flutter in his chest. "Yeah. I will."

## That Evening

End of shift. The sun dipped behind rooftops, shadows stretching long across the cracked streets. Will sat in the cruiser a moment longer after signing off, letting the silence settle.

His ribs still ached from too many jolts against the wrap of the vest, his notebook was filled with more mistakes than wins, and the stink of stale coffee clung to his hands. Another day of beat work that felt heavier than it should.

He leaned back, eyes closed, trying to remember why he'd wanted this so badly. Why did he think the badge would feel like a purpose instead of just a weight?

Then his phone buzzed.

Kristen Dalton: *Court is canceled for tomorrow. Still want that coffee?*

Will stared at the screen, the corner of his mouth lifting before he realized it. A shift full of grit and disappointment, and now—something good.

His thumbs tapped the screen.

*Yeah. I'm in. Name the time.*

### The Coffee Shop

The next morning, Will arrived early. Not in uniform—gray button-down, jeans. He sat near the window, his hands wrapped around a cup that was already cooling. He'd been in shootouts with steadier nerves.

The door jingled. Kristen stepped in. Hair down. No blazer, no folder. Just a dark green sweater, jeans, and a leather bag slung over one shoulder. Softer, but no less sharp.

Will blinked. Yesterday had been all blur—folders, arguments, focus. Here, with morning light slanting through the glass, she looked different. Striking in a way that sneaks up on you. High cheekbones. Raven-dark hair. Eyes so blue they cut through the haze. Her accent slipped Southern when she said, "Morning." Polite, but steel-threaded.

"You're early," she said, sliding into the chair opposite.

"You said 8:30. Ex-military. We treat time like it bites."

She chuckled. "Fair enough." She waved at the barista, who nodded like they knew her order. Local.

"So," she said, leaning forward on her elbows, "what'd you think of court?"

"Honestly?" He shrugged. "Felt like basic training. Everyone shouting, no idea what half of it meant, and somehow it ended with paperwork."

Her laugh was open, unguarded. "It went better than you think. Some officers freeze up. You didn't."

"I did in the alley."

She tilted her head. "And you learned from it. Most don't admit that part."

Their drinks arrived, hers black. He raised a brow. She smirked. "Grew up on gas station coffee. Cream tastes like plastic now."

They drifted into easier topics: bad cafeteria food, Ravenwood's impossible street names, neighbors who played music too loud. Kristen laughed as she admitted, "I know I had seen Beaufort on pages all my life, but I called it *BOH-fert* for my first week on the job. The clerk looked at me like I'd just confessed to a crime. Apparently it's *BYOO-fert*. I blame my law professors for that."

Will chuckled. "South Carolina, yeah. But drive a couple hours north and cross into North Carolina, it really is *BOH-fert*. Locals will swear you're wrong either way, or try to fight ya."

Kristen smirked. "So technically I wasn't wrong. Just... misplaced."

"Story of every rookie's life," Will said. "I had one who thought '10-33' meant bathroom break. Radioed it in as if it were code for 'urgent pit stop.' Half the county thought we had an officer down."

Will found himself watching her hands as she talked, how her fingers tapped her cup when she thought, how her smile curled when something genuinely amused her. He told himself it was professional curiosity. He knew better.

Kristen, meanwhile, found herself more at ease than she'd expected. Outside the courthouse, Will was quieter. Thoughtful. He didn't fill the silence for the sake of it. There was steadiness there, under the nerves. It settled her in a way she hadn't felt in a while.

Eventually, she glanced at her phone. "I've got to be back in court by ten. Two plea deals and a motion to suppress. Fun morning."

"Sounds thrilling," he said.

She stood and shouldered her bag. Paused. "This was nice. Not just the coffee."

"Yeah," Will said. "It was."

For a second, her expression sharpened like she might say more. Instead, she smiled. "I'll text you. Don't ghost me, Officer Anderson."

He grinned. "Wouldn't dare. You'd subpoena me."

She laughed—bright, real—and left with the bell jingling behind her.

Will sat back down, coffee still warm, chest lighter than it had been in weeks.

### Notebook Entry

*Trial Day — Ravenwood County. Kristen Dalton.*
*She remembered me. Lunch. Coffee.*
*Asked questions that mattered. No armor. No act.*
*She gave me her number. She texted first.*
*Her laugh hit different.*
*Told myself I wasn't looking for this.*
*Maybe I lied.*

## Beat

Another week of field training had crawled by, and the radio was quiet. Too quiet.

Will knew better than to say it out loud. In the Army, you never tempted fate by calling a patrol calm—never gave the gods of war an excuse to remind you they were listening. Same rule here. You called it quiet, and the gods of the radio would punish you, raining chaos down on whatever peace you'd carved out.

He shifted in the passenger seat, notebook balanced on his knee, pen hovering above the page. His ribs still ached from the alley fight. Every pothole, every speed bump reminded him of the bruises hidden under his vest. He wanted to drum his fingers against the notebook, but stopped himself. Joe didn't tolerate fidgeting.

For some reason, Joe always drove. Other trainees said their FTOs let them take the wheel on day one. Joe hadn't mentioned it once since they started. That was his way: no explanations, no sympathy, no "you'll heal up." Just another shift. Another street.

The cruiser prowled through the East District like a shark, slow and sure. Storefronts slid by: a bodega with sun-faded soda ads taped to the glass, a barber shop with a mural of Dr. King peeling off brick, a laundromat where half the neon letters sputtered. **UNDRY.**

Joe lifted two fingers in a lazy salute toward the barber shop. The barber—old man with steady hands, razor flashing in the chair—nodded back without missing a beat.

"You know half this job?" Joe muttered, eyes scanning the street.

Will blinked. "Sir?" He was already scribbling a crooked question mark in the margin of his notebook.

"Being a metronome."

Will frowned. "Metronome?"

"Same beat. Every day." Joe took a sip of his coffee. "People hear the sirens when shit blows up, but it's the rhythm that keeps the street alive."

Will chewed on the words. "The rhythm."

Joe shot him a glance, brief and sharp. "Kid, if it were all chases and shootouts, we'd all be in the ground. Ninety percent of this job is routine, boring shit. You keep the beat steady so folks don't forget the world's still turning."

Will nodded slowly, jotting it down. *Keep the beat.* He didn't fully get it yet, but he knew better than to press Joe twice on anything.

Joe pulled the cruiser into a narrow space in front of a corner store. Fluorescent light flickered through dusty windows. Inside smelled of bleach and stale chips.

Mr. Alvarez, the shopkeeper, had a white-knuckled grip on the shoulder of a boy no older than thirteen. The kid's backpack sagged open, stuffed with candy bars, chips, and sodas.

"He was stealing!" Alvarez barked, jabbing a finger toward the boy. "I caught him shoving things in!" His voice climbed in pitch, outrage burning hot.

The boy's eyes darted between Will and Joe—wide, wet, panicked. His knees trembled, jaw tight like he was holding back tears.

"Empty it," Joe said, voice flat, unimpressed.

The boy fumbled with the zipper. Candy bars spilled across the counter with a clatter.

Alvarez's voice turned rapid-fire Spanish, frustration spilling fast and sharp. His hands carved angry shapes in the air.

Will stiffened. His academy training whispered: theft = arrest, paperwork, juvenile hall. He stepped forward. "We should—"

Joe crouched, bringing himself eye level with the kid. "What's your name?"

The boy swallowed. "Marcus."

"Marcus, you know what happens if I haul you downtown for this?"

Marcus's chin dipped, barely. "Juvie."

"Worse." Joe's voice softened, but it had weight. "You get a jacket. A record. Then every cop who sees you for the rest of your life? They see a thief first. Kid second. That's a weight you don't want."

Marcus's mouth opened, then closed. He stayed silent, eyes fixed on the floor.

Joe turned to Alvarez. "You want the candy back, or you want the paperwork?"

The shopkeeper huffed and snatched the bars into a box. "He cleans. Then he goes."

Joe plucked a broom from the corner and shoved it into Marcus's hands. "Sweep every aisle. Don't stop till Mr. Alvarez says you're done."

Marcus clutched the broom like a pardon. "Yes, sir."

Back in the cruiser, Will frowned. "That's it? No arrest?"

Joe sipped his coffee. "You think the system fixes everything? That kid's hungry, bored, or both. He pays it back, Alvarez gets a clean floor, and nobody learns to hate us. Call it a win. Officer discretion."

Will sat with that, wanting to argue, but the words wouldn't come. Joe's certainty had a weight that silenced questions.

He jotted in his notebook: *Not everything's cuffs. Sometimes it's just keeping the beat.*

The rest of the shift played out in smaller beats, like notes in a song:

A drunk passed out in a doorway, reeking of gin. Joe nudged him awake with his boot. "Go sleep it off somewhere that doesn't scare old ladies." The man mumbled curses and stumbled into the darkness of the night.

A little girl with pigtails and tear-streaked cheeks wandered alone. Will crouched, softer voice this time, coaxing her name out. Relief slammed into him when her frantic mother sprinted up and scooped her close. Will looked back—Joe gave him the slightest nod. Approval.

A shop owner vented about kids tagging his walls. Will stood in the cramped store for fifteen minutes, saying almost nothing. Just listening. When they left, Joe muttered, "Sometimes the job is being the ear, not the fist."

By sundown, Will was starting to hear it—the rhythm Joe talked about. Ninety percent routine. Quiet beats that didn't make headlines but kept the city breathing.

For the first time since he'd clipped the badge to his chest, Will felt steady. Like maybe he was learning the song.

Then the tricksters of the radio shattered it. Emergency tones blaring their sing-song notes, then on cue, the dispatcher sang out her chorus.

**"All Units, Possible shots fired, block of Drexel and Maple. Units respond."**

Joe flicked the siren. Red and blue lights painted the street in strobing colors.

"Here's your ten percent," Joe muttered, foot pressing harder on the gas. "Hang on."

Will's stomach dropped. His bruised ribs tensed against the seatbelt. The rhythm snapped like a guitar string.

He shoved the notebook into his pocket, gripping it tight like a charm as the city blurred past.

**Notebook Entry:**
*Ninety percent routine. Ten percent chaos.*
*Don't chase the chaos.*
*Keep the beat. That's the job.*
*Last night of FTO, finally get to go solo.*

## Collision

Days later, it was supposed to be a quiet shift. Friday nights usually meant the worst of Summit Falls—booze, bruises, and regret stacked on top of each other—but tonight had been eerily uneventful. Will was halfway through a stale vending machine sandwich in the precinct break room, the bread rubbery and the meat gray around the edges, when dispatch crackled:

*"Unit 2-4, possible assault on a female at Boone's Tavern. Multiple subjects are involved. One female is possibly injured. No mention of weapons. Medical en route, standing by for the scene to be secured. Officers respond Code 2."*

Will tossed the sandwich into the trash, grabbed his jacket, and was out the door in less than thirty seconds flat. His pulse was already ticking faster. Mind playing through the "what if" scenarios.

### Boone's Tavern – Downtown

Moments later, the street pulsed with red-and-blue strobes, painting the brick buildings like a warning sign. Boone's wasn't known for elegance. It was known for cheap whiskey shots and bad decisions that spilled onto the sidewalk. By the time Will pulled up, two units were already angled in front, doors open, radios hissing. A knot of people gathered outside, buzzing with adrenaline, half with phones raised to record, the other half with cigarettes shaking between their fingers.

Inside was chaos.

Chairs overturned, a stool snapped clean in two, glass crunched under Will's boots. Neon beer signs flickered like faulty heartbeats, lighting the wreckage in sickly colors. EMTs crouched near a corner booth, voices urgent, working over someone out of sight.

But Will's eyes locked on the far wall.

Kristen.

She stood with her back against the wall, flanked by two friends. One tall and blonde, fury painted across her face, sequined tank catching the light with every angry gesture. The other, shorter, curvier one, holding a napkin to a bleeding lip, wore a green halter top darkened with smudges from the scuffle. They looked like women who'd dressed for fun, not for a police report. And Kristen—her hair half-fallen from the neat twist she'd started the night with—anchored them, one hand on each of their shoulders. Her deep blue wrap dress was stylish but understated, cinched at the waist, with a long coat open around it. Boots with modest heels gave her an edge without the wobble. Discipline in every line of her frame. Except for the red mark blooming high on her cheekbone.

Not bleeding. Just raw. But it made Will's stomach drop.

He crossed the room fast, weaving past the chaos.

"Kristen," he said, voice low but urgent. "What happened? Are you alright?"

Her eyes found him. Dazed, yes, but clear. "I'm fine. I think." She blinked twice, steadying herself. "Got clipped when the guy shoved his way out. Elbow maybe. Dumb luck."

Will lifted his hand, tilting her chin gently. Her breath hitched, eyes closing for a beat as if bracing herself. The swelling was already starting. She winced but didn't pull away.

"You should sit," he murmured.

Kristen shook her head. "It's not that bad." She nodded toward her friend with the napkin pressed to her lip. "She's the one who got grabbed."

His jaw tightened. "Tell me everything."

Kristen's voice tightened, her words clipped but heated. "He grabbed Melissa's ass. Twice. The first time, she pushed him back and told him to stop. He came right back—grabbed her again, then shoved his hand up her skirt. That's when another guy stepped in, pulled him off, and then fists started flying. I tried to get her clear, and I caught a stray shot in the process."

Will followed her gaze. At the bar, two officers were cuffing a red-faced man with blood smeared down his shirt and a swollen eye. His curses filled the air, venomous and slurred.

"You want to prosecute?" Will asked.

Kristen's lip curled. "Oh, Mel will absolutely want to. He's going to love seeing me again in court."

Will smirked despite himself, but his eyes lingered on the red mark blooming across her cheek. In the low light, it stood out sharp against her skin, raw and already threatening to swell. "You sure you don't want medical? A cold pack from the EMS truck outside? That's going to leave an impression in the next few days."

Kristen exhaled slowly, though her breath hitched at the end. "I'll ice it when I get home. Promise. With a glass of wine to dull the sting."

She tried for lightness, but the faint tremor in her fingers betrayed her. Her hand was still resting against his sleeve, almost without thought, the brush of her knuckles steady as if contact was the only thing tethering her to the moment. The warmth of it sank through the fabric, and Will felt the weight of her trust—unspoken, fragile, but real.

Her eyes flicked away, scanning the chaos of Boone's like she needed the noise to cover her own unsteadiness. Broken glass glinted on the floor, EMTs bent over another patron in the corner, and yet here she was, holding onto his arm as if this were the only solid ground in the room.

Will didn't move. Didn't shrug her off or shift away. He let her stay anchored, even though part of him knew the touch meant more than she realized in the haze of adrenaline.

Against the far wall, another man sat calmly on a stool amid the wreckage. Broad-shouldered, buzz cut, his T-shirt spattered with someone else's blood. Bruising under one eye, lip split, but posture steady.

Will walked up beside him. "You the one who stepped in?"

The man wiped blood from his mouth with the back of his hand. Nodded once. "My name is Brad Jones. I saw what was happening. Couldn't let it slide. Got him off her, warned him. He swung first. I finished it." His voice was low, even. "Sick bastard."

Will studied him. "You did what you had to. Defending someone—especially in her situation—doesn't get you in trouble."

The man squinted back, sizing him up. "Military?"

"Army."

He patted his own chest with a closed fist. "Marines."

Will let out a short laugh. "That explains the overkill."

The Marine's teeth flashed through a blood-smeared smile. "Explains why I'm still standing and he's not."

Will clapped him lightly on the shoulder. "Fair enough. I appreciate you stepping in."

The Marine nodded once. "Would've done the same for my sister. Or yours."

Later, when the cuffs were secure, the statements taken, and the crowd drifted into the night, Kristen leaned against the brick wall outside. The air was cool, carrying the faint smell of fryer grease and spilled beer. Her arms crossed tight, the long coat wrapped around her, hair falling loose across her cheek.

Erin was fussing with her phone, calling a ride, her voice tight with frustration as she argued with the app about wait times. Melissa kept pressing her lip with a napkin, muttering angrily about men. "Grab a drink, they grab your ass. Try to stand up for yourself; they throw punches. Every damn time…"

Kristen didn't say anything, just pulled her coat tighter, the bruise on her cheek throbbing under the night air.

Will stepped up beside Kristen, hands deep in his jacket pockets. The cruiser's lights flashed faintly across her cheek, illuminating the bruise.

"You sure you're okay?" he asked.

She sighed, breath clouding in the cold. "Just tired. Adrenaline's wearing off." Her eyes met his, steady. "And yeah, sore. But it's Boone's. You know what you're signing up for after ten."

He raised a brow. She smirked faintly. "It's actually good earlier in the night. Food, drinks, decent crowd. Then the bottom shelf crowd shows up, and…" She gestured toward the broken stool inside.

Will chuckled. "Dinner and a show?"

Kristen tilted her head, a smile playing on her face. "Speaking of dinner… I think I'm still owed one. Proper dinner. No fistfights. No uniforms."

His smile warmed. "Tomorrow?"

"Pick me up at seven." She pushed off the wall, rejoining her friends without waiting for an answer—like she already knew what he'd say.

Will stood there, watching her go, pulse steady now but chest lighter than it had been in weeks.

**Notebook Entry:**
*Boone's. Bar fight. Kristen's friend was assaulted.*
*Kristen was bruised in the chaos.*
*Marine stepped in—good instincts.*
*Kristen says she still wants that dinner.*
*She was looking for me. Again.*
*Dinner's on. This one might mean something.*

## Almost

The next evening, Kristen's bedroom looked like a boutique after closing, discarded dresses draped across the bed, shoes abandoned in pairs, one gold earring lying lonely on the nightstand. Underwear changes with the different outfits, lying across the bed.

The first dress she'd tried on, a slinky black sheath, had felt too severe. *Like I'm heading to a boardroom, not a date.*

The second, a fluttery floral wrap, made her look, she decided with a wince, as if she were on her way to brunch with her aunt.

The third, a sparkly silver number, shimmered under the lamp but whispered desperation. *Like I'm auditioning for attention.*

In the end, she chose a deep emerald dress that skimmed her figure without clinging, elegant but not fussy. When she caught her reflection, she allowed a small smile. *This feels like me, only a little braver.*

From the perfume tray, she lifted two bottles, hovering between them. The sharp, citrusy one reminded her of confidence, but it felt like armor. Instead, she dabbed on the softer jasmine scent, something warm and secret, a fragrance that wouldn't shout but might make him lean closer.

By 6:52, she was pacing. Her bare feet brushed against the cool wood floor, heart tugging faster with every glance at the clock. She caught herself smoothing the skirt of her dress again, palms damp, as though the fabric might betray her nerves.

Then the headlights swept across the curtains. The clock read 6:55. Her stomach tightened.

When the doorbell rang, she nearly jumped. For a second, she thought of letting it ring again, collecting herself, practicing her smile, adjusting her dress. But she couldn't make herself wait.

She opened the door.

Will stood there, framed by the evening air, his dark jacket cutting a sharp contrast against the fading light. He tucked his hands into his pockets, a small smile forming, but his eyes stayed on her, soft and searching. And in that moment, Kristen felt as though the jasmine had done its job after all, the space between them was already charged.

The door slowly swung open to the wall, and for a beat too long neither of them spoke. Will stood there, framed by the fading light, his jacket crisp, his smile small and uncertain.

Kristen felt her breath catch, but then she remembered. Shoes. Her toes curled against the cool wood floor.

"You're early," she blurted, tilting her chin in mock reproach, though her pulse was fluttering.

Will's mouth curved, not quite a grin. "Couldn't help it. Guess I didn't want to risk keeping you waiting."

Her cheeks warmed. "Well, you did," she said, stepping back quickly. "By about five minutes. And I'm not even wearing shoes yet, so—come in, but don't laugh."

He chuckled softly, obeying as the jasmine scent drifted with her as she hurried to the small bench by the door. She slipped her feet into a pair of nude heels, fingers fumbling just slightly with the straps.

"See?" she muttered, glancing up at him, self-conscious. "Still a work in progress."

His eyes swept over her—not hurried, not unkind, just intent. "Looks pretty finished to me," he said quietly.

Her hands stilled on the buckle. The words lingered between them longer than they should have. She managed a laugh, though her throat felt dry. "You're trouble, you know that?"

"Only five minutes' worth," he answered, smiling now. Then he gestured toward the street. "Shall we?"

The night air was cool as Kristen stepped outside, the faint click of her heels on the walkway too loud in her ears. Will walked beside her, not touching, but near enough that she felt the warmth of him anyway.

He opened the passenger door, waiting. The courtesy made her chest tighten in a way she hadn't expected. She slipped inside, the emerald fabric of her dress whispering against the leather seat. When he closed the door, she breathed in the scent of his cologne, a clean fragrance with a darker edge, and tried to will her pulse to slow down.

A moment later, he slid in behind the wheel. The engine hummed to life, a low, steady sound. For a stretch of seconds, neither of them spoke. The silence wasn't empty; it was charged, filled with the soft brush of her perfume mixing with his cologne, the muted rhythm of the turn signal, the unspoken awareness of how close they were.

Finally, Will glanced at her, his smile faint, almost hesitant. "So... was that the perfume I interrupted? Or the shoes?"

Kristen chuckled, though the sound caught in her throat. "Both. But you only saw the shoes." She turned her head toward the window, though her lips curved. "The perfume's more... subtle."

He let the words linger before replying. "Not that subtle."

Her heart jolted. She didn't answer, not right away. She only smoothed her skirt over her knees again, aware of the way his gaze flicked briefly from the road back to her.

The city lights blurred past, each one a small flare against the dark. Kristen sat back in her seat, pulse finally beginning to steady—though not entirely. Something about the quiet between them felt less like absence and more like promise.

The car slipped into the city's glow, and soon Will eased into a quiet side street. He parked in front of Ember & Ash, a place Kristen had only ever noticed in passing. By day, its brick façade blended into the block, understated, but at night, its windows glowed amber, promising warmth. Through the glass, she caught glimpses of white tablecloths and candle flames flickering low.

Will rounded the car to open her door, and she stepped out, the faint clip of her heels softened by the hush of the evening. A doorman greeted them, and the moment they stepped inside, the outside world dimmed away.

The restaurant lived up to its name—walls of dark wood, shadows like velvet, the air carrying a faint scent of oak smoke. The hum of conversation blended with the soft murmur of a piano tucked somewhere out of sight. Glassware gleamed like stars scattered across each table.

Kristen slipped out of her coat, suddenly aware of Will's hand brushing briefly at the small of her back as the host led them forward. It wasn't a claim, just a touch meant to guide—but the heat of it lingered long after his hand fell away.

Their table was tucked into a corner, lit by a single candle that cast an unsteady glow across the linen. When she sat, Kristen found her fingers playing absently with the edge of her napkin, her nerves refusing to settle.

Will's eyes found hers across the table. He didn't speak right away, letting the silence stretch, as though the candlelight itself were a language. When he finally did, his voice was quiet but sure.

"You look beautiful tonight."

Kristen's throat tightened. The compliment was simple, almost ordinary—but in his tone, it felt like something rare. She lowered her eyes for a moment, smiling faintly as she reached for her water glass. "Thank you. You clean up pretty well yourself."

He chuckled, and the sound mingled with the low notes of the piano. The candle between them flickered, and Kristen thought—not for the first time that evening—that the jasmine had done precisely what she hoped: it had brought him closer, without a word.

The host slipped away, leaving them with menus and the soft glow of the candle. Kristen ran her fingertip over the embossed lettering, though she wasn't really reading.

"Everything looks good," she said, glancing up. "I might just have to close my eyes and point."

Will's lips curved. "That's one strategy. But if you end up with the squid ink pasta, don't blame me."

She tilted her head, pretending to study him. "So you're decisive, then?"

"Not always," he admitted, leaning back in his chair, the candlelight catching faintly in his eyes. "But when it comes to dinner, yes. It's high stakes."

Kristen laughed softly, the sound easing something in her chest. She rested her chin lightly on her hand. "And what's the safe bet tonight, then?"

"The ribeye," he said without hesitation. Then, after a pause: "Or... whatever you're ordering."

Her pulse skipped. She shook her head, smiling into her menu. "That's either very charming or very lazy."

"Why not both?"

Their waiter appeared, taking orders and retreating again, leaving them in the hush of candlelight. Kristen toyed with the stem of her water glass, aware of Will's gaze more than the murmur of the room around them.

"So," he said at last, voice low. "Do you always try on four dresses before dinner, or was tonight special?"

Her mouth parted, surprised, then closed again as warmth rose to her cheeks. "You noticed?"

"I noticed you weren't quite finished when I showed up," he said gently. "But honestly..." His eyes lingered on her, steady. "I can't imagine the other three topping this one."

The air between them thickened, and for a moment Kristen forgot about the menu, the waiter, even the room. She only felt the flicker of the candle, the brush of jasmine rising faintly from her wrist, and the quiet promise in his words.

Their drinks arrived first—Kristen with a glass of wine, Will with something darker, bourbon neat. She swirled her glass, watching the candlelight ripple through the red.

"So, bourbon," she teased, arching a brow. "Trying to impress me with your rugged taste?"

Will chuckled, lifting his glass. "It's not about rugged. It's about simplicity. Fewer choices, fewer regrets." He tipped the rim toward her wine. "And you? Choosing elegance?"

She smirked. "Choosing courage."

He blinked at that, surprised, then laughed softly. "Fair enough."

The waiter returned with their plates—her salmon, his ribeye—and soon the air was filled with the scents of seared butter and herbs. For a while, conversation drifted light: disastrous travel stories, a shared laugh over Kristen's memory of nearly missing a connecting flight because she was hunting down a cinnamon roll, Will's confession that he once wore mismatched shoes to a job interview.

But then the laughter settled, replaced by a quieter hum between them. Kristen rested her fork down, watching the candle flicker low.

"Do you always arrive early?" she asked, her tone gentler now.

Will leaned back, studying her for a moment before answering. "Not always. Just when it matters."

The words slid into the silence like a secret, and Kristen felt the heat rise to her cheeks again. She looked down, tracing the edge of her napkin.

She wanted to say something light, but what came out was softer: "I wasn't sure what to expect tonight. I almost... talked myself out of it."

Will tilted his head, voice low. "And now?"

She met his gaze, candlelight reflected in his eyes. Her lips curved, though her chest was tight. "Now I'm glad I didn't."

For a moment, neither of them moved. The sounds of the restaurant—clinking glasses, low laughter, the hush of the piano—seemed to fall away. Then Will smiled, slow and sure, as if the night had just begun.

Dinner wound down with slow sips of wine and the shared silence of two people reluctant for the night to end. Kristen found herself laughing more easily, leaning in closer, and—when she wasn't careful—watching the way Will's eyes softened when he listened.

The waiter returned, clearing their plates with practiced ease. "Would either of you care for dessert tonight?"

Kristen hesitated. She didn't speak, but her glance at the menu betrayed her.

Will caught it instantly. "Only if you want it."

Her lips curved. "That's not an answer."

His smile was easy, confident. "I think something sweet wouldn't stand a chance against you. With the way you're built, your metabolism could burn through a bakery."

The compliment hit deeper than she expected— playful, yes, but laced with sincerity. Her cheeks warmed, and she didn't look away this time.

"Fine," she said, a spark in her voice. "Cake it is. But you're sharing."

Will chuckled, low and steady. "Wouldn't dream of doing otherwise."

They split a slice of flourless chocolate torte, rich and dense, its sweetness softened by coffee. Kristen teased him for taking the larger bites, and he countered by pointing out how she'd scraped every last streak of raspberry sauce from her plate. Their laughter was quieter now, the kind that settled into the chest and lingered.

When the check came, he slid it off the table without a word. Kristen opened her mouth to protest, but he just shook his head. "Next time, you can fight me for it."

*Next time.* The phrase settled between them, warming her more than the wine had.

The waiter whisked away the last of their glasses, and soon they were stepping back into the night. The city air was cooler now, carrying the faint scent of rain on pavement. Kristen pulled her coat tighter, heels clicking softly against the sidewalk.

Will walked close beside her, not touching, but near enough that she felt his presence in every stride. Their breaths clouded faintly in the air, mingling as they spoke.

"That place was beautiful," she said.

"You were the one who made it beautiful," he replied, quiet but certain.

She glanced up, startled, caught off guard by the steadiness in his gaze. For a heartbeat, she forgot how to breathe.

They reached the car, and Will paused with his hand on the passenger door handle. For a moment, he didn't open it. Instead, he turned toward her, closer now, the glow of the streetlamp tracing the line of his jaw.

Kristen's pulse hammered, her fingers tightening on her coat lapel. The jasmine she'd dabbed hours ago still clung faintly to her skin, rising in the cool air between them.

For a breathless second, it seemed inevitable that he would reach for her hand, or tilt forward, closing the space the candlelight had started to burn away.

But instead, he exhaled, slow and steady, and opened the door for her. His restraint was almost more charged than a kiss.

Kristen slid inside, her heartbeat wild, and as he rounded the car to join her, she couldn't help the thought that threaded through her: *The night isn't over. Not yet.*

The drive back was quieter, but not uncomfortable. Kristen rested her hands in her lap, stealing glances at Will in the glow of the dashboard lights. His focus on the road, the strong line of his jaw, the way his fingers tapped once against the steering wheel—it all made her chest tighten.

He didn't fill the silence with small talk. Instead, the car held the low hum of the engine and the faint overlap of their breaths. The kind of silence that felt like it belonged only to them.

When he pulled up to her building, the street was hushed, tucked beneath the soft gold spill of a single lamppost. The SUV's engine idled for a beat before Will turned the key and killed it, leaving only the ticking of the cooling motor and the faint hum of the city in the distance.

For a moment, neither of them moved. The world felt sealed inside the vehicle—warmth trapped in the cabin, faint traces of leather, and the clean scent of polish mixing with her jasmine perfume.

Kristen turned toward him, her fingers brushing the clasp of her coat. The small, nervous movement sounded louder in her own head than it should have. "Thank you... for tonight. It was—" She hesitated, because *nice* was too small, too ordinary. Her throat tightened. "More than I expected."

Will's eyes met hers in the dim light. Steady, unreadable at first. Then he leaned a fraction closer, his

47

voice pitched low, velvet against the quiet. "That sounds like a good thing."

Her pulse kicked, heat rising in her cheeks. "It is."

The space between them shrank until she felt the pull of it in her chest. The air was warm with the mingling of their breaths—hers quick, his slower, bourbon-softened. Will didn't rush, didn't close the gap in a single motion. He lingered there, as though giving her time to decide if she wanted the distance erased.

Kristen's hand shifted against her coat, halfway to reaching for him. She faltered. Close enough now, she could count the flecks of gold in his eyes, could feel the ghost of his breath on her cheek. The lamplight caught in the windshield, casting faint shadows across his jawline, sharpening the inevitability of the moment.

For one suspended heartbeat, it felt certain—that kiss, the one that had hovered since the first candle at Ember & Ash.

Will's smile flickered—small, quiet, there and gone. He leaned back, easing the tension by degrees, and his hand slid to the door handle. With practiced ease, he pushed the heavy frame open. Cool night air rushed in, brushing against their skin like a sudden exhale.

But he didn't step out. Not right away. He just angled toward her, one arm resting on the door, holding it open with a quiet deliberateness—as if the gesture itself meant something more—a kind of intimacy, wordless and patient.

"Goodnight, Kristen."

Her chest tightened, caught in the space between relief and longing. She gathered her coat around her and slid from the seat. Her heels tapped softly against the pavement as she stood and adjusted her jacket, tugging the lapels closed against the bite of the autumn air. Will had already stepped away—circled the hood—and stood waiting near the open passenger door, the streetlamp above cutting him into bronze and shadow, outlining the sharp angles of his frame.

Kristen walked the short path toward the stoop of her townhouse, each step echoing softly on the concrete. She felt his gaze follow her—a quiet, watchful presence pressing gently between her shoulder blades. It didn't unsettle her. If anything, it grounded her.

At her door, keys in hand, she paused. Turned.

Will stood by the curb, one hand braced casually on the SUV's roof, his figure half-lit, half-shadow. He didn't call out. Didn't move closer. He was just there. Present. The faintest smile tugged at his mouth—something between goodbye and something unsaid.

Her pulse jumped. "Goodnight, Will."

She slipped inside. The door clicked shut behind her, locking the cool outside air away—but not the moment. Not the feeling. Her heart was still racing. Through the thick silence of the house, she heard the low growl of the engine, then the soft crunch of tires pulling away.

But even long after he was gone, Kristen could still feel the weight of what almost happened. The near-miss. The hesitation that hovered like a held breath.

She leaned back against the door, one hand finding the edge of the wood for balance. Her breath stuttered in her chest. The house was still. Her pulse was not. The echo of his smile. The space he'd left behind. The warmth of his nearness. The pause before restraint.

It all lingered—soft and persistent—like candle smoke curling in the air after the flame is gone.

She touched her cheek, where the heat still burned, and let the truth settle.

*Almost.*

# Cherry

A few shifts later, the radio crackled to life, sharp against the low hum of the cruiser. *"Unit 2-4, check on an unresponsive female, Crown Motel. The caller states that the door to Room 214 is open. Female subject visible from the hallway. No movement. Medical is staging nearby—waiting for officers to clear."*

Will keyed the mic, his voice steady. "2-4, copy. En route."

The Crown had a reputation, and not a good one. Weekly rentals, neon that buzzed louder than the guests, and a steady stream of calls that never made the evening news.

When he pulled into the lot, the motel's sign sputtered in pink and blue, casting sickly light over cracked pavement and sagging balcony rails. A pair of bystanders lingered near the office, smoking and watching as if waiting for the night's entertainment to unfold.

Will took the stairs two at a time, boots thudding against rusted metal. The radio hissed faintly on his shoulder, the words "unresponsive female" looping in his head.

The dark, and half-lit hallway smelled of stale smoke and industrial cleaner, the kind that never quite covered

51

what it was meant to. He slowed near 214. The door hung slightly open, and the chain lock, undamaged, was dangling. From the threshold, his flashlight beam cut across a pair of discarded high heels—red, scuffed, too bright for a place like this.

Inside, the room was cold, the kind of chill that clung to the skin. The bedspread was twisted, half-dragged to the floor, its faded floral comforter bunched like a crumpled shroud beneath it.

A Will surveyed the room. The woman lay sprawled across the mattress, her bare, naked body discarded as though she had been tossed there. Her blouse hung in tatters, one sleeve stretched and knotted around the headboard post. Across the room, her skirt had been flung into the corner, the seam ripped clean apart. Her underwear clung limply to her ankle, the waistband torn down one side as if ripped in a single violent motion.

The violence was written into the room itself. Buttons littered the carpet like dropped coins. A lamp lay sideways on the nightstand, its shade dented, the bulb flickering against peeling wallpaper. Near the bathroom door, a smear of dark red was dragged across the wall, a silent testament to struggle.

Her face told its own story. Lips split and bleeding, her skin marred with bruises, and a deep gash at her temple—blood cascading down like a curtain of paint. Whoever had done this hadn't just killed her; they had destroyed her with rage, with anger, with a twisted hunger for power.

And when it was over—when there was nothing left to take—he had positioned her body, with intent, not hidden, not covered. Displayed. As though she were an exhibit, stripped of dignity, left behind as a message for everyone to see.

Will's gaze caught on the arrangement of her limbs. Her right arm had been lifted above her head, bent at the elbow, her hand resting near the crown of her hair. The left was drawn across her torso, hand to elbow, as if she had been placed in a parody of repose. A circular burn mark by some unknown object was etched on her stomach by her navel.

It wasn't natural.

The killer had positioned her—angled her body to showcase her nudity, to leave her exposed in the most degrading way possible. Her legs were spread, pillows propped under her to lift her hips, not carelessly but intentionally, placed so that the intimacy of her body became part of the display, the damage inflicted on her unmistakable. The blouse sleeve tied to the headboard made it look staged, almost theatrical, as if she were being offered up instead of mourned. Wrists and ankles bore the marks of removed restraints, the signs of struggle cutting into the flesh, rubbed raw. A note on the corner of the bed, not there by mistake, poised as if it were the exhibit label for a piece of artwork on display in an art gallery. Will read the note that had been scribbled in sloppy lettering to himself,

*Her suffering was her cleansing.*

*Her screams are the proof of sin.*

*Only in silence was she worthy of love.*

To anyone walking in, it would be impossible to ignore the intent. She wasn't just left behind—she was *arranged*. Exploited even in death for what she had been in life, her profession twisted into a final humiliation.

Will's jaw clenched. He could almost feel the killer's message in the room: *She was just a prostitute. This is all she was worth.*

And it made his stomach turn.

Will swallowed hard, stepping closer. The recognition that he knew her—the jester tattoo on her inner thigh.

*Cherry.*

In life, Ivy Cole had looked like any other twenty-something you might pass on the street. You wouldn't have guessed, at first glance, that she used her body to scrape together enough money to feed her habit. She carried herself with a confidence that was almost disarming—shoulders squared, chin lifted, lipstick always sharp as if to defy anyone who pitied her.

Once, leaning against his cruiser with that sly grin, she had teased Will about her fake breasts, telling him she could let him touch them for free, *"no charge for you, officer."*

She'd laughed at her own joke—throaty, sharp, like gravel wrapped in silk—while he shook his head and told her, as he always did, that there were resources out there, people who could help her.

She never listened. *"I'll never get off this street,"* she'd said once, eyes cutting sideways as if daring him to contradict her. *"I'm chained to it for life."*

That was Ivy. But everyone else called her Cherry. The girls on Seventh had given her the nickname for her fire-red lipstick and that rasping laugh she wore like armor whenever a client tried to short her.

She had another trademark, too. When Will parked too long on her block, she'd hike up her skirt without warning, sometimes revealing she wore nothing at all beneath it, other times just a thread of a thong. She'd moon him with a wicked grin. *"Can't arrest me for showing my backside,"* she'd taunt, quoting the statute word for word before he could even open his mouth. Then, as if to drive the point home, she'd sometimes tug her top, flip it up, and bare her breasts at him, unbothered and unashamed, daring him to react. Sometimes yelling, "Invitation still stands!"

*"Ivy, but no one calls me that anymore,"* she'd told him the first time he pressed her for her real name. *"Clients like simple. So—Cherry."*

Now, staring at the way her body had been left, Will felt the cruel irony bite deep. The killer had stripped her down, arranged her like an exhibit, exploiting in death what she had once turned into survival. And though the others in the room would only ever see "Cherry, another dead hooker," Will saw Ivy—the woman behind the nickname, the woman who had once stood grinning in the glow of his cruiser lights, teasing him like she wasn't afraid of anything. Replaying her broken dreams of a small apartment far from the strip, a dog she'd always wanted, a name she wouldn't have to change to feel safe in a life that hadn't yet been stolen from her before she could reach it.

Now her mouth, once painted bright, was slack and empty.

His flashlight beam caught on ink above her inner thigh—a faded jester, the kind done cheap and fast. He remembered noticing it when she perched on the curb one night, skirt hiked high, giving him grief for "scaring off her job security." That jester, fitting to her personality, burned itself into his mind's eye now, a mark of who she'd been before someone decided to erase her.

Boots thudded behind him. Officer Diaz leaned into the doorway, his partner Clark close at his shoulder. Diaz whistled low. "Jesus. Another working girl. Happens sooner or later. They play with fire, they get burned."

Clark shook his head, scribbling into his notepad. "She probably knew the guy. They almost always do. No point in wasting sympathy."

Will turned sharply, his voice low but edged. "She deserves the same attention as anyone else. She was a person. Someone's daughter, maybe someone's mom. She mattered."

The words came out before he realized he'd spoken them, the same ones he'd heard on a Bosch episode a few nights back. Everyone matters, or nobody matters. At the time, it had sounded like TV wisdom—gritty, scripted. But now, standing over Ivy's body in the Crown Motel, it didn't feel like fiction. It felt like the only truth worth holding on to: everyone deserved the same treatment for the sake of justice.

Diaz raised a brow, smirking. "Rookie, you're gonna drown if you let every case get under your skin. These women make their choices. You'll learn."

Before Will could respond, two detectives arrived, Harris and Lowe, both gray at the temples, coats half-buttoned, coffees in hand. They looked tired before they even entered the room.

"Scene secure?" Harris asked, already scanning without really seeing.

Will nodded, jaw tight. "Yes, sir."

As the detectives moved past, Lowe caught Will's words to the uniforms. "Don't romanticize it, kid. Give it a couple of years, and you'll get the hang of it. You can't carry every lost cause on your shoulders."

Will's fists clenched at his sides. "With respect, sir, she's not a lost cause. She's a victim. Name is Ivy Cole, and she deserves justice like anyone else."

Harris sighed, muttering as he pulled a camera from his bag. "Stay in your lane, Anderson. Patrol the streets, answer your calls. Leave the cases to us."

But Will didn't move. His eyes stayed fixed on Ivy—on Cherry—on the ink of the jester against her skin. The echo of her laughter came back to him, stubborn and unbroken.

And in that moment, Will made himself a quiet promise. No matter what the others said, he would remember her name.

The memory of her laugh—sharp, unbothered, too alive—stayed with Will long after he left the hotel room. He couldn't shake the image of her blouse sleeve tied to the headboard, the cruel echo of the way she used to moon him with a grin, daring him to write her up. It gnawed at him, the thought of Cherry reduced to just another file number in a stack of unsolved cases.

So the next night, he found himself on Seventh again, easing the cruiser to the curb where the girls worked the block. The cold bit through their thin skirts and fishnets, but their eyes were as sharp as ever, sizing him up.

"Cherry been around lately?" he asked one of them, keeping his voice low. "You see who she was with the night before?"

The woman—blonde wig, arms folded tight against the wind—studied him for a long moment before shaking her head. "Guys come and go. Hard to keep track." But her eyes flicked sideways, toward a cluster of girls farther down the line. Word traveled fast out here.

Over the next few nights, Will asked again, carefully, never pushing too hard. A few admitted Cherry had left with someone they didn't recognize, a man in a dark truck. No one could give a plate, no one was willing to say more. Still, the fact that they answered at all told him they trusted him enough to share scraps.

But scraps were enough to draw attention.

Three days later, a lieutenant called him into the office, the blinds half-drawn, the desk cluttered with reports. Lieutenant Nash didn't look up right away.

"Anderson," he said, his tone clipped, "I'm hearing you've been poking around down on Seventh. Asking questions about that girl."

Will kept his shoulders squared. "Ivy. Cherry. She was murdered. Somebody knows something. I'm just trying to—"

Nash cut him off. "You're a patrolman. Your job is to drive that beat, answer calls, and keep the lid on the pot. Homicide belongs to the detectives. Vice says one of their Confidential Informants heard you sniffing around. That ends now."

Will's jaw tightened. "Sir, with respect, she deserves more than—"

"You heard me." Nash's voice hardened. "You want to keep that badge, you stay in your lane. Let the detectives handle it."

Will left the office with the words burning in his chest, heavy as a stone. *Stay in your lane. Forget her.*

But as he walked back into the hum of the precinct, the only thing he could see was the smiling jester tattoo inked on Cherry's thigh, and the way her body had been left like a message. He knew he couldn't just let it go.

### Report Excerpt – Officer W. Anderson

Victim identified as *Ivy Cole*, known on the street as "Cherry." white female, 26 year old, located deceased at Crown Motel, Rm. 214.

Signs of violent struggle present: torn clothing, scattered personal effects, and blood spatter near the bathroom wall. The blouse sleeve was tied to the headboard post in a manner suggesting restraint. Wrists and ankles showed abrasions. The victim's body was arranged post-mortem, positioned deliberately with legs spread, pillows placed to elevate the hips. Circular burn mark consistent with branding observed on the abdomen.

A handwritten note was located on the corner of the bed, positioned intentionally, with the following text:

*Her suffering was her cleansing. Her screams are the proof of sin. Only in silence was she worthy of love.*

The scene appears to be deliberately degraded and staged for display. The arrangement implies a ritualistic or symbolic purpose. The victim was not hidden but presented to be discovered.

Crime scene and detectives contacted to respond. No further information at this time. Case notes attached. Case remains open/active.

## Restraint

Kristen had invited him over for dinner, nothing elaborate—roast chicken, a bottle of red, candles flickering low on the table. She'd texted him earlier, *"No restaurants, no noise. Just us."*

When Will arrived, the smell of garlic and herbs filled the apartment, warm and grounding. He handed her his coat, but his eyes didn't brighten the way they had at the restaurant. There was a heaviness on him, a shadow that trailed in with him.

"Rough day?" she asked, setting plates on the table.

He shook his head, brushing it off. "You don't want to hear about that. I don't want to bring work into this."

Kristen tilted her head, catching his gaze until he couldn't look away. "But work is part of you. And if I'm inviting *you* here, Will Anderson, then I want all of you. Even the parts you think I can't handle."

For a moment, he just stood there, glass of wine in hand, torn between holding the line and giving in. Finally, he exhaled, sinking into the chair across from her.

"Someone I knew," he said quietly. "She was killed. And the way it happened—what it meant—" His throat tightened. He shook his head. "I can't stop seeing it."

Kristen's chest ached at the rawness in his voice. She reached across the table, her hand brushing over his, waiting for him to pull away. He didn't.

"She mattered to you," she said softly.

He nodded, jaw clenched. "But to everyone else, she's just another dead prostitute. They say I'll get used to it in a few years. That I'll stop caring." He laughed bitterly, no humor in it. "I don't ever want to get used to it."

Kristen rose, moving around the table. She slid onto the bench beside him, her thigh brushing his, the warmth of her body grounding him in a way nothing else had all day. He turned slightly, surprised, but she only slipped her hand into his, holding it steady.

"You don't have to," she whispered. "Not with me."

Her closeness, her insistence, broke something loose in him. He turned toward her, their faces inches apart, the candlelight painting shadows along her cheekbones. For a long moment, he breathed her in—the jasmine clinging to her skin, the softness of her hair brushing his shoulder.

Then, slowly, he leaned into her warmth. Not a kiss, not yet—just the press of his forehead against hers, a silent surrender.

Kristen closed her eyes, letting the moment wrap around them. And in that quiet space, she allowed herself to draw closer still, her arm slipping around him, holding him in the way he didn't yet know he needed.

And then she lifted her chin ever so slightly.

Her lips brushed his first, tentative but sure, a question whispered into the space between them. For half a breath, Will froze, caught between pulling away and giving in. His hand tightened around hers, knuckles whitening.

And then something inside him broke loose.

The kiss deepened suddenly, no longer gentle but raw, hungry, as though he'd been holding it back for far too long. His free hand cupped her cheek, sliding into her hair, while his other arm wrapped tight around her waist, pulling her against him with a low, desperate sound.

Kristen gasped softly, her fingers fisting in his shirt as she clung to him, her body molding to his as if she could hold the storm itself. The bench beneath them groaned, the edge of the table rattling faintly when her hip pressed into it. The candles flared in their holders, shadows leaping across the walls, flickering wild in rhythm with their uneven breaths.

His mouth left hers only to trail down her jaw, hot and unsteady, finding the curve of her throat. Kristen tilted her head instinctively, shivering at the press of his lips, her pulse racing beneath them. Her hands slid up his chest to his shoulders, nails grazing through the fabric, grounding him even as she urged him on.

"Will—" she breathed, the sound half warning, half plea.

"I shouldn't—" his words rasped against her skin, though his lips didn't leave it, torn between restraint and need.

Kristen's reply came soft, steady, her lips brushing his temple. "Then don't stop."

The words unraveled him. His grip on her waist tightened, pulling her closer still, until there was no space left between them. The taste of wine lingered on her lips, and the scent of jasmine rose thick around him, dizzying and intoxicating. For a heartbeat, he let himself drown in it, his body answering what his mind told him to resist.

But then—he pulled back, just barely, forehead pressed hard to hers, breath ragged. His hands trembled where they still held her.

"If I stay—" he began, voice hoarse, "I don't know if I'll be able to stop."

Kristen's heart pounded so hard it hurt. Her thumb brushed his jaw, her voice low and certain. "Maybe I don't want you to."

He closed his eyes, pained by how much he wanted to believe her. He kissed her once more—fierce, claiming, like a man taking one last sip of water before the desert— and then tore himself away, rising to his feet as if distance were the only thing that could keep him tethered. He allowed her hand to fall away as he pushed himself toward the door. Kristen followed.

At her doorway, he turned back, eyes dark, lips still swollen from her kiss. "Kristen..." He shook his head, jaw working, words failing him. Finally, he settled on the only thing he could trust himself to say. "Goodnight."

The door shut behind him, and Kristen leaned back against it, her chest heaving, lips tingling. She knew with a sharp, undeniable certainty: the next time they were together, neither of them would stop.

Kristen leaned back against the door after it closed, her palms flat against the wood, her chest still rising too fast. The apartment was silent now except for the soft ticking of the clock on the mantel and the faint hiss of the candles burning low.

She touched her lips with the tips of her fingers, as though she could still hold the shape of him there. Will Anderson. Solid, steady, stubborn—and yet so deeply human it ached. He carried the weight of other people's pain like it belonged to him, like he couldn't put it down even when he wanted to.

*He didn't want to stop,* she thought, the memory of his voice rough in her ear. *He only did because he felt he should.*

Kristen blew out the candles one by one, their smoke curling into the dim apartment, the room falling into shadow. She gathered the plates she'd set so carefully earlier, half a meal left untouched, and placed them in the sink. Her body moved through the motions, but her mind was elsewhere—still at the table, still on the bench, still pressed against him, remembering the way his hand had trembled when he held her.

In the bathroom mirror, she caught her reflection. Her cheeks were flushed, her hair mussed from his fingers. She let out a quiet, almost disbelieving laugh. *What are you doing, Kristen?* she asked herself. But the truth was already there: she couldn't stop thinking about him, not even if she tried.

By the time she slipped into bed, the sheets cool against her skin, her mind was still circling him. The storm in his eyes. The way he tried to shield her from his darkness, even though it was that very honesty that pulled her closer.

She lay back, staring at the ceiling in the dark, and whispered into the silence: "What kind of man are you, Will Anderson?"

Her heart already knew the answer. The kind who carried too much. The kind who wouldn't look away, even when everyone else did. The kind who kissed like he was fighting for air.

She pulled the blanket over her, exhaling slowly. And even as her eyes closed, she could still feel the press of his mouth on hers, the echo of his breath on her skin. Sleep came slowly, but when it did, it carried his name with it.

# Morning

Kristen woke slowly, tangled in sheets that still held the faintest trace of jasmine from the night before. For a moment, in the hazy quiet, she half-expected to find Will sitting at her kitchen table, shoulders hunched, eyes shadowed but steady. But the apartment was silent, the only sounds the hum of the fridge and the patter of a neighbor's shower, along with her singing through the wall.

She pulled herself upright, the ache of sleep still clinging to her limbs, and padded barefoot across the cool floor. In the bathroom, she twisted the shower tap until steam began to fog the mirror. The hot spray hit her skin, loosening her muscles, but her mind refused to quiet.

When Kristen slid off her shirt and tossed it to the floor, the tug at her still-sore jaw pulled her straight back to the bar—and to Will. The memory of his steady hand guiding her through the crowd lingered sharply in her body.

Stepping out of her panties, her hand brushed down her thigh, and the contact made her remember the warmth of her leg pressed against his on the bench. Even now, her skin tingled where their bodies had touched, as if the imprint hadn't faded overnight.

Later, after her shower, she let the towel slip from her body in a slow cascade. For a moment, she stood still, her hand trailing across her hip, her waist, remembering the way his fingers had pressed there, strong and trembling at once. A shiver ran through her.

She dressed slowly, tugging on her jeans, the denim hugging close. As she fastened the button, she thought of his hand gripping her shirt, how tightly he'd held her as if letting go would undo him. Sliding into a blouse, her collar brushed her neck, and she felt again the heat of his mouth at her throat, the soft rasp of his breath as he whispered he shouldn't.

At the mirror, she ran the blow-dryer through her hair, watching her reflection shift and change in the glass. The flush on her cheeks, the softness in her eyes—it wasn't just from the steam of the shower. It was him. Will Anderson.

She set the dryer down and braced her hands against the sink, staring at herself for a long moment. *Girl, you are in trouble,* she whispered under her breath.

Because every motion, every thought, circled back to him.

New feelings simmered in her chest—heady, dangerous, impossible to ignore. She was already in deeper than she'd realized. And for once, she let herself enjoy it, a slow smile curving across her face.

Across town, Will Anderson sat on the edge of his unmade bed, lacing his boots with hands that had trembled half the night. Sleep had been fractured, restless, haunted not by the job this time, but by Kristen.

He kept replaying it—the press of her thigh against his, the jasmine rising in the air between them, the moment she leaned in and kissed him first. The way her hand had gripped his shirt like she was afraid he'd disappear if she let go.

*You should have stopped sooner,* he told himself. *You should have walked away before you kissed her back.* But the truth gnawed at him: he didn't want to stop. And that scared him more than anything.

He ran a hand through his hair, exhaling hard, trying to shake her from his thoughts. But then he saw her again in his mind, sitting beside him at the table, candlelight softening her cheekbones, her eyes steady on his when she said he didn't have to carry it alone.

For a beat, he let himself linger in the memory.

Will had just finished lacing his boots when the call came in. His phone buzzed, a blocked number. He almost ignored it, but something in his gut made him swipe.

"Officer Anderson?" The voice was thin, shaking.

"Yeah. Who's this?"

A pause. Then: "It's Tonya. From Seventh. You gave me your card... when you were asking about Cherry."

Will's pulse quickened. "What happened?"

Her words came out broken, jagged. She said she'd gone with a John to a motel off the strip, nothing unusual. But once inside, he had slipped his belt free and looped it around her throat. He pulled until the world narrowed and went black.

Before she lost consciousness, she remembered what he said. Over and over.

*"Stay quiet. I'm taking your sin away. Give in to your sin. Let it out."* His voice was low, chanting like a preacher. *"Repent. Pain is necessary."* Each phrase was punctuated by his fists, by the tearing of her clothes, by blows that left her ribs aching and her skin burning.

Her voice cracked as she forced the words out. "I thought he was gonna kill me. I was sure of it. He was choking me, raping me, and beating me, repeating those lines over and over. I remember hearing the banging on the wall next door."

When she came to, she was propped up on the bed. Pillows arranged behind her back like she was some exhibit. Her blouse was in tatters, her skin welted and bleeding, branded with some metal object, bleeding and bruised. The door was wide open. Left that way on purpose One of the other girls found me.

"He wanted me seen," she whispered. "Like he was showing me off. Making sure anyone who looked would know what I was."

Will's jaw clenched hard, his grip on the phone white-knuckled.

"You need medical treatment," he said.

"No." Her answer was sharp. "I don't want an ambulance, no ER. Just... bandages. The bruises will heal. I'm not letting anyone stick me with needles or run tests."

"Tonya—"

"I'll only talk to you, Mr. Anderson. Not the others. Not vice. Not detectives. Just you."

Will exhaled slowly. He knew what that meant. Breaking protocol. Crossing lines. But he also knew the alternative—her silence—meant the man who had brutalized her would vanish back into the night.

"Where are you?" he asked.

She gave him the motel name, voice barely above a whisper.

Will grabbed his jacket, sidearm heavy at his hip. As he jogged down the stairs, he thumbed his radio. "Dispatch, this is Unit 2-4. Be advised, responding to a possible assault victim at the Crown Motel, Room 116. The victim is requesting me specifically. Notify the zone unit to assist, but keep medics staged unless requested. Copy?"

"Copy, 2-4," dispatch replied.

He shoved the radio back on his belt, jaw tight. Whatever he was walking into, he knew one thing: Tonya trusted him—and him alone. And the words she repeated—the sermon of violence—echoed Ivy's death too closely to be a coincidence.

### Crown Motel – Room 116

The door was cracked; although the lock was intact, it outwardly appeared functional. Previously, it had been busted as if someone had kicked it in and didn't bother fixing the frame afterward. A red "No Vacancy" sign buzzed behind Will as he approached, the hum of fluorescent lights crawling over his nerves.

He knocked once, low and firm. "Tonya. It's Will Anderson."

A pause. Then the door creaked open an inch.

Her eye met his through the gap. Swollen. Purple. Lips split. One arm held the door, the other clutched a towel like armor.

"You alone?" she whispered, her voice raspy.

"I am." He kept his voice soft. "I called in medics, but they're staged. You say the word, I'll wave them off."

Her jaw clenched. "They'll ask questions." She swallowed hard, trying to talk.

"I'll answer them," he said. "But not unless you want me to."

Another pause. Then the door opened.

The room was dim and suffocating—curtains drawn, the air stale with the scent of blood and motel cleaner. The smell of fear hadn't left. It never did in rooms like this.

She shuffled backward into the room, towel wrapped tight, body trembling in places she couldn't control. Will's breath caught in his throat.

She was wrecked.

Finger-shaped bruises circled her wrists and arms, like someone had gripped her hard enough to brand her with their rage. Scratches raked across her ribs in angry red slashes. Her split lip trembled—not from cold, but from the aftermath of screaming, sobbing, maybe both. Blood crusted in a thick, tar-dark pool around her eyebrow and cheek, her hair matted, sticky, tangled like it had been dragged through glass.

Ligature marks encircled her throat—raw abrasions that looked like a collar had rubbed her skin raw. Her eyes were bloodshot, wide, and wet with trauma, and the scatter of tiny red pinpricks on her face—petechiae—dotted her cheeks like freckles that didn't belong. Capillaries, Will's mind noted mechanically. Ruptured from strangulation. Forensic guys would confirm it later, but he didn't need them. He'd seen enough to know.

He stepped in and shut the door gently, the soft *click* sounding far too loud in the silence.

"You bring what I asked?" Her voice was hoarse, fragile but defiant—like she was still trying to stand on what was left of her dignity.

Will reached into his jacket, pulling out a small kit—bandages, antiseptic, gauze. Not department-issued. Just the kind of things he'd started carrying after the alley fight his first week on patrol. Just in case.

He held it out.

She nodded once, eyes shimmering. "Thanks."

"Can I help?" he asked, carefully.

"No," she snapped, too fast. Then, quieter, almost ashamed: "But... stay."

He dragged the only chair in the room into the corner, positioning it where she could see him but still have her space. He sat, hands loose in his lap, resisting the urge to fidget. The air in the room was hot and stale, and the stink of bleach barely masked the metallic scent of blood. He stared at the torn curtains, the cigarette burns on the carpet, the cheap plastic lamp bolted to the nightstand—anything but her body. Not out of squeamishness. Out of respect.

She moved slowly, wincing with every step, every touch of the alcohol to her wounds. Her hands shook as she worked. She flinched at her own touch. But she didn't cry.

Not yet.

"He said I was dirty," she murmured, voice cracking like brittle glass. "Said I had to bleed it out." She stared at the peeling wallpaper as if it might give her the words. "Said that's what he did to the last one. Said he 'cleaned her.'"

Will went completely still. His stomach turned, a cold knife of understanding sliding between his ribs. Cherry.

Tonya didn't see his reaction. Her gaze was vacant, a thousand yards deep. Like she wasn't in the room anymore.

"He said... she screamed at first, but then she just laid there." Her voice faltered. "He said she finally understood. And that's when he loved her most."

Will rose slowly from the chair, every muscle tense beneath the fabric of his shirt. His heart pounded against the inside of his chest, but his hands stayed steady—muscle memory from deployments, from learning how to act calm when every cell was screaming.

"He said that, exactly?" he asked.

She nodded, silent tears sliding down her bruised face.

Will crouched beside the bed. He didn't touch her—couldn't. She was brittle as glass, cracked in places the eye couldn't see. But he came close, voice low, steady, just enough to cut through the fog clinging to her like smoke.

"Tonya, listen to me," he said. "That man has done this before. What happened to you—it's not your fault. He's not going to stop. But you survived. That means something."

For the first time, she met his eyes.

"Will you find him?" she whispered.

"I swear to you," he said, and his voice nearly broke. "I will."

Her breath hitched like a sob, but no sound followed. Just a tremor. Then: "Then I'll tell you everything."

## Magnolia

What followed didn't feel like a statement—it felt like a confession. Will just sat and listened to her story.

Through a raspy voice from being strangled and tears, the words came like a flood.

"As soon as the door shut, I didn't even turn around. His belt slipped over my head, and he choked me from behind, pushed me face-first on the bed, and held me down with all his weight, and ripped off everything I had on. Like the harder he jerked on my clothes, the louder he laughed. He would punch me, and when I went to block him, he would rip at something else. I didn't have that much to take off, but he pulled it, ripped it. When I tried to stop him, he would hit me again.

He said that he was soon going to love me. He just... kept going. Violating me. I couldn't fight back. Couldn't breathe." Her voice was unraveling now, thinned out by pain and panic. "I heard someone banging on the wall, yelling at him to shut up. But he just laughed, and it got more violent. Forced me down. Pulled the belt tighter. I think he got off on knowing someone could hear." Her hands trembled so hard she dropped the gauze, let it fall.

She curled inward, voice splintering. "I started to black out. White specks. I saw them. Floating. Like stars. I felt something hot. Burning me. I couldn't move. I thought I was dead. I have had rough dates before, but this was different. It was like he got off on causing pain. I gave up, I just knew I was going to die, and there was nothing I could do. I saw my whole life flash before my mind's eye; you know what they say, it's true. Then everything went black.

I woke up and felt like I was on display, with pillows propped under me, the door open, and one of the other girls standing there, as if it were another day in the Falls. She buried her face in her hands and collapsed to the floor, her back sliding off the bed like she was trying to sink into the ground itself. She dry-heaved, her body wracked with tremors. As the towel slipped, Will saw it: a scorched, angry circle burned into her skin just above the navel. The mark looked deliberate, as if it were branding.

She didn't care about modesty now. She crawled back to the bed, curled up on the edge, then laid down on her side, sobbing quietly, one arm curled over her ribs as if trying to hold herself together.

Will wanted to scream. Instead, he whispered.

"I'm still here, Tonya. I want to hear your story."

Her breath hitched. Then, in a voice nearly too soft to catch: "He was white. Late thirties, maybe early forties. Muscular, but not bulky. Gloves. Wore gloves the whole time." She closed her eyes like she could still feel the rubbery sensation. "Dark green truck. Older model. Smelled like smoke. And bleach."

Will jotted everything down in his notebook, fingers flying. The pen felt too small for the weight of her words. His knuckles whitened as he wrote.

She went on, voice flat now. "He talked slowly, calm even, not excited. Like a preacher. Every time he hit me. Every time he pulled the belt. He called it a sermon. Said my body was the altar." Her lip curled in disgust. "He said pain would 'set me free.'"

Will flipped to a new page. "I need your real name for the report," he said gently.

She hesitated. Her hands tightened on the towel in her lap. Then she let out a small, bitter breath.

"It's Magnolia Truelove."

His pen froze. She added, "People used to call me Maggie."

"It's a beautiful name," he said.

"Doesn't feel like it fits anymore," she whispered. "Haven't felt like a Magnolia in a long time."

He didn't push.

After a long pause, she added, quieter: "Tonya was someone I knew, back in college. She was wild, flirtatious, fun to party with, brave... unafraid. I borrowed the name. Thought maybe it'd make me braver too."

Will swallowed hard. The walls of the motel room seemed to close in, every word a nail in the coffin of whoever this man was.

When she finished, her shoulders sagged like someone had removed her spine. She looked up, bloodshot eyes searching his face.

"You believe me?" she asked, voice barely audible.

Will met her gaze without hesitation. "I believe every word."

She nodded once, slowly. "Then find him... before he makes someone else into a sermon."

"Ok, but I need to tell you something," he said carefully, crouching beside her again, not wanting to break the fragile trust she'd just given him. "I have to call in the forensic unit. This whole room is a crime scene. We need to preserve it, document it, and collect any evidence he left behind, prints, DNA, and trace evidence. It's the only way we build something the court can't ignore."

Her eyes widened, panic flashing. "Wait—what? I can't—" Her voice cracked. "I don't have any clothes, Will. Nothing. I can't walk out there like this."

"You won't," he said, voice low and steady. "I'll get you something clean. Right size. Whatever you need. You won't have to talk to anyone you don't want to. No uniforms, no questions unless you're ready."

She hesitated, then pulled the towel tighter around her, as if it could shield her from the world. Her chin trembled, but she gave a slight nod. "Okay. ... don't leave me like this."

"I won't," Will said. "I promise."

When she finally finished speaking, her shoulders sagged like someone had removed her spine. She looked up at him, bloodshot eyes searching his face.

"You believe me?" she asked, voice barely audible.

Will met her gaze without hesitation. "I believe every word."

She nodded once, slowly. "Then find him... before he makes someone else into a sermon."

### Outside the Crown Motel – Minutes Later

The cold air bit at his face as Will stepped into the night. His radio buzzed—Unit 3 had arrived, checking the perimeter. Medics staged at the end of the lot, waiting for his word.

He keyed the mic. "Victim declining medical at this time. I'll follow up at the precinct with a full report. Have forensics sweep Room 116. I'm heading back with a statement."

"Copy that, 2-4."

But he didn't head back.

He got in the cruiser, started the engine, and pulled out his phone.

Not his department phone. His personal one.

Kristen's name lit the screen.

She picked up on the second ring. "Will?"

"I need a favor," he said, still staring at the Crown Motel in his rearview mirror. "I've got a survivor who talked. This guy matches Cherry's case, almost word for word. I need someone who won't bury this. Someone who'll actually listen."

Kristen's voice sharpened, already in motion. "Come by the office. I'll call the DA investigator and flag this for priority review. If there's overlap, we'll find it."

Will exhaled slowly. "Thanks. I owe you."

"You don't," she said. "Just bring me everything."

He hung up, heart still pounding. The night was far from over.

The killer had a voice now. A pattern. A name waiting to be carved from silence.

And Will had a promise to keep.

The motel lights buzzed behind him, casting long shadows as Will jogged to the cruiser. The Crown logo flickered overhead like a dying neon halo.

He drove fast, not lights-on fast, but *I've got no time to waste* fast—his eyes scanning storefronts as he reached the main strip. A late-night 24-hour drugstore blinked in the distance.

RiteSmart – 12:46 a.m.

He ducked into the store under cold fluorescents, grabbing a plastic basket by instinct. He didn't know her exact sizes, but he'd paid attention—people like him always did.

He hit the basics first:

A pair of soft black sweatpants with a drawstring.

A loose gray hoodie.

Clean underwear and a sports bra. Medium.

A pack of socks.

Travel-size shampoo and body wash.

Hair tie.

A bottle of water.

Lip balm.

He paused near the feminine hygiene aisle. Grabbed a small pack, just in case.

When he hit the counter, the cashier raised an eyebrow but said nothing. Will didn't offer a badge. Just paid cash, stuffed everything into the plastic bag, and was halfway to the exit when his phone buzzed.

JOE DONOVAN

He answered without breaking stride.

"Yeah?"

Joe's voice came low and sandpaper-rough. "Heard your call to dispatch. Are you working on a sexual assault?"

"Yeah," Will said. He slid behind the wheel, dumped the bag on the passenger seat, and started the engine. "Victim's a known street contact. Survived an attack that mirrors Cherry's murder. Word-for-word. Preacher talk, burn mark, belt around the neck. Left her displayed."

A pause.

Then: "You sure?"

Will nodded even though Joe couldn't see him. "She described details we never released. The sermon lines.

82

The staging. Same mark on her abdomen—same pattern. She said he told her what he did to the last one."

Joe let out a slow breath. "Jesus."

"I've got her in the room still. Cooperative but wrecked. I told her I was getting her clothes. Forensics is en route."

"You call Homicide yet?"

"I'm calling you," Will said. "*You* call Homicide. Tell them to get someone over to the Crown, Room 116, now. They want this guy, they need to treat this like the second attempt, not a separate case."

Another pause.

"Copy," Joe said. "You want me on-site?"

"No. Stay where you are. I'll bring the statement straight to Kristen once she's dressed and safe."

Joe didn't argue. "Good work, kid."

Will hung up, pulled the cruiser into gear, and turned back toward the motel.

The Crown's red sign was still flickering when he pulled into the lot.

Bag in hand, he walked fast.

He had a promise to keep.

### Crown Motel – Room 116

The air was thick and sour when Will eased the door open again. The neon glow from the parking lot cut through the blinds in slanted stripes, crawling across the room like prison bars.

Tonya hadn't moved. She lay balled on the mattress where he'd left her, no towel, no covers, just bare skin marked by the aftermath. Her arms wrapped around her knees as though she could fold herself small enough to vanish. The bruises stood out like ink stains, dark rings circling wrists and ribs. The burn on her stomach looked raw in the dim light, angry red, as if it were still whispering smoke.

Will set the plastic bag on the dresser and crouched low so she could see him without having to lift her head.

"I got what I could," he said softly, pulling out each item one at a time: gray sweatpants, black hoodie, new underwear in plastic, socks. Plain, simple. "Should be close to your size. Shampoo, soap. Lip balm. Nothing fancy."

Her eyes flicked to the pile, dull at first, then sharper. "You didn't have to."

"Yes," Will said, steady. "I did."

She sniffed, a sharp wet sound, then pushed herself up slowly, wincing at the movement. For a moment, Will expected her to ask him to turn away. Instead, she reached for the hoodie, tears streaking silently down her cheeks, and pulled it over her head without hesitation.

Will shifted his gaze toward the corner, giving her the space she deserved. "I'll turn around," he murmured. "You don't need me watching while you—"

"Don't," she cut in, sharp despite the rasp in her voice. Her hands trembled on the hoodie in her lap. "Every man

I've ever been with looked at me like I was nothing, or worse, they looked right through me. If you turn away now, you're just one more. I don't need privacy, Will. I need proof I'm still here. Don't let me be alone in this."

The words stopped him cold. Slowly, he turned back, meeting her eyes, letting her see he wasn't going anywhere.

The words landed heavily in his chest. He nodded once and forced himself to meet her eyes as she tugged the hoodie down, every movement stiff with pain. Her breath caught when the fabric brushed the burn on her stomach. She swallowed the sound, like she'd swallowed a hundred others.

The sweatpants came next. She eased them up her bruised legs, tears dripping freely now, streaking her hollow face. The simple act of clothing herself seemed to cut deeper than the blows she'd taken. When she was done, she stuffed the unopened underwear and socks back into the bag and curled into the hoodie's sleeves like she was trying to disappear inside.

Will's voice stayed low. "You need medical treatment. Just let EMS check you. Let them clean the burns and make sure your ribs aren't broken."

"No." She shook her head hard, stringy hair swinging. "No hospitals. No nurses with needles and forms. I'll get a friend to help me clean up."

"Tonya—" He stopped, catching himself, then steadied. "You're not evidence. You're a victim. And you survived. That means something."

Her chin lifted, trembling, eyes glassy. "Find him," she whispered. "Promise me you'll find him."

"I will." The words came like a vow. "I swear to you."

For the first time, she studied him. Really looked. Her voice rasped. "Why? Why do you care about some low-level street walker when every other cop would've left me in the gutter?"

Will's jaw worked. "Because you're not 'some street walker.' You're a person. You've got a name. You've got someone, somewhere, who misses you. And you matter. Don't let anyone make you believe differently."

Her face crumpled. The sob tore out of her, raw and shaking. Through it, words scraped free: "Don't call me Tonya anymore, she's dead. Call me Maggie. Please."

Will swallowed hard. "Maggie," he said.

She nodded, tears streaking, then whispered: "I want to go home. Back to Indiana. Will you help me? Please."

Before he could answer, she moved toward him, slow and uneven, then wrapped her arms around him. Her body shook with the effort, her face pressed to his chest. "Thank you," she whispered. "But you better get that son of a bitch."

Will tightened his arms around her, just enough for her to feel steady. "Count on it."

That's when he saw it, sticking out from the sheet crumpled on the floor, the same style handwriting on a card.

*They are nothing until they bleed.*
*Only in blood do they earn a name.*
*Marked and silenced, loved, they belong to me.*

The word *Marked*, caught Will's attention. Marked. Like livestock. Like he owned them. Son of a bitch thought pain and branding them made them his.

Footsteps echoed in the hall—heavy, measured. Voices carried. Will straightened, guiding her back gently toward the bed.

"They're here," he said. "Stay, let me talk to them first."

By the time he stepped into the doorway, his face was steel again. Cop mode.

Two homicide detectives stopped just short of him, one lifting his brows. "Anderson. Why the hell are we here on a live victim? Thought this was a DOA."

Will met their eyes without blinking. "You're not looking at just another assault. You've got a serial rapist on your hands. One who likes to kill women. And she's the only one who's seen him and lived to tell it."

The hallway went quiet.

Will didn't flinch.

By the time the crime scene techs packed up their kits and homicide finished their last photos, the Crown Motel room looked stripped of life. Detectives Harris and Lowe had Maggie out in the parking lot within minutes of arriving—standard procedure. She'd balked at their first questions, barely lifting her head, voice frayed.

Now she sat in the open door of Will's cruiser, hood pulled low, her frame swallowed by the black hoodie, face bearing the signs of abuse. She hadn't said much since they'd brought her outside. Didn't look at Harris when he tried, politely enough, to ask who she'd been with. Didn't flinch when Lowe suggested taking her downtown. Just stared at the asphalt, arms folded tight across her ribs.

"I don't want to talk to them," she muttered finally, her voice sandpaper-thin. "Not right now. I'll talk to you, maybe later... but not them. They're typical asshole cops."

Harris sighed, trading a glance with Lowe. "We'll need a statement eventually, Officer Anderson. She can't stay silent forever."

Will nodded, jaw set. "Understood. Right now, she's in shock. Give her some space."

The detectives walked off in low conversation with each other. Will stayed by the door, keeping his frame in the gap so Maggie didn't feel on display.

She shifted slightly, her eyes finally meeting his. "Can I go? Please. I don't... I don't feel like talking tonight."

Will hesitated. Protocol said keep her close, funnel her downtown for processing, maybe even protective custody. But looking at her—drawn in, shaking, hanging on by threads—he knew pressing her now would only break her further.

"Yeah," he said softly. "For tonight. But I'll check in on you."

Her shoulders sagged, relief softening her face just a fraction.

### Back of the Courthouse – 2:17 a.m.

Joe Donovan was already waiting, leaning against the unmarked door with a paper coffee cup in his hand. He gave Will a long look, then glanced at the woman trailing behind him—small, bruised, hood drawn low. Joe gave a single nod. *You did right, kid.*

Inside, the fluorescent lights buzzed overhead, too bright, too clinical. A clerk's office during the day, but now it was quiet, chairs stacked against the wall, a first-aid kit cracked open on a desk—the smell of coffee, paper, and antiseptic filled the air.

"Sit," Joe said softly, gesturing to the chair. His voice had none of the gravel it usually carried on the street.

Maggie lowered herself slowly, hands stuffed in the sleeves of the oversized hoodie Will had bought. She sat stiff, like the chair itself might betray her. Will knelt at her side with the kit, damp gauze in hand. He cleaned the dried blood from her cheek. She flinched at the sting but didn't pull away.

"You're fine," he murmured. "Just a scratch. Hold still."

Joe handed him a packet of closure strips, and Will carefully pressed them across the gash above her brow. His hands were steady and practiced, but his eyes remained gentle. By the time he was done, Maggie looked less broken, more human again.

The door opened. Kristen stepped in, hair pulled back, suit jacket still on despite the hour. She looked at Maggie, then at Will, her gaze lingering on him longer than usual.

"I'll take her statement myself," Kristen said, pulling out a notebook.

Will stepped back. Maggie lifted her eyes, studying the woman across from her, weighing whether she was safe.

"You can trust her," Will said.

Maggie's head snapped toward him and slowly turned back to Kristen, and then she spoke, her voice rough from being strangled but gaining strength with each word.

"He believed me," Maggie said, nodding at Will. "Didn't treat me like trash. Didn't brush me off. He stayed."

Kristen tilted her head. "That shouldn't surprise you. He's a cop."

Maggie gave a hoarse laugh that broke into a cough. "Yeah, that's the thing. I've hated cops most of my life. To them, we're not people—we're problems. Arrests. Paperwork. Half the time they don't even look at us, unless it's to sneer, or... try to get something out of us or from us." Her eyes shimmered, jaw trembling. "But him? He looked at me like I mattered. Like I wasn't just another busted up whore bleeding on a bed. He seems like he doesn't buy into that whole *'you can't rape a whore'* bullshit. He's... different. "Will shifted uncomfortably, hands in his pockets, but Maggie wasn't done.

"He brought me clothes," she said, voice cracking. "Sat with me while I cleaned my cuts. Didn't try to fix me, didn't judge me. He just... stayed. Do you know how rare that is?"

Kristen's pen hovered over her notebook, forgotten for a beat. Her gaze flicked to Will again, softer now.

Maggie noticed it: Kristen's glance at Will. Even bruised and shaking, she managed a crooked smile. "You'd better scoop him up," she rasped. "Before some other damsel in distress figures out what kind of white knight you've got walking these streets."

Kristen blinked, caught off guard. A flush rose in her cheeks before she smoothed it over with her professional veneer. "Let's focus on your statement, Maggie."

Maggie dragged the frayed sleeve of the hoodie across her eye, voice rough but steady. "I'll tell you what happened... but don't pretend you didn't hear me. I saw it in your eyes when you looked at him. A girl knows, the same way I saw it in his eyes when he swore he'd find that bastard. His eyes didn't lie, and neither do yours. So don't wait too long. Guys like him... they don't come around twice."

Kristen clicked her pen once—sharp, decisive, like a gavel striking wood. "Noted," she said evenly, gaze dropping back to the page. "Now—start from the beginning, Maggie. Every detail."

But her pen hovered a fraction too long before it moved. Maggie caught it. So did Will. From his place against the wall, he felt the ground shift under him. Kristen's mask slipped—just a flicker of warmth, something personal—and it hit him harder than he expected. His chest tightened, like he'd walked into a room where the air was suddenly thinner. He told himself it was nothing. Just a look. Just heat in her cheeks. But his gut didn't buy it.

He shifted his weight, jaw tight, eyes darting to the floor. The Army had trained him for chaos, for bullets and blood and panic. But not for this—for the way a single glance could knock him off balance worse than any firefight.

Kristen cleared her throat, softer now, as if steadying herself. "Go ahead."

For the first time since Room 116, Maggie's posture shifted. Her shoulders straightened. Her chin lifted. Like maybe, just maybe, she believed she wasn't invisible anymore.

Maggie started, "I'll tell you what I told him, but nothing on paper, not now."

**In Will's Report (Formal excerpt):**

Victim identified as Magnolia Truelove, 28-year-old, white female, known locally as "Tonya." Subject declined medical treatment at the scene. No written statement recorded, the victim declined out of fear. Forensic unit dispatched to Room 116. Victim's description of suspect matches M.O. from previous homicide investigation (Cole, Ivy). Another ritual note left by the suspect. Recommend priority review. Case open/active.

## Pattern

The courthouse was silent when Will finally stepped out into the night, his boots echoing on the concrete steps. He drew in the cold air, but it didn't settle him. His notebook felt heavier than usual in his pocket, the weight of Maggie's words—and Kristen's look—dragging against his chest.

Behind him, the door clicked shut, sealing Maggie in with the DA's office. She'd be placed with a counselor and a safe bed for the night. That was the plan. But Will knew better than to trust plans.

Joe leaned against the cruiser at the curb, hands in his coat pockets, steam curling from his breath. His eyes tracked Will the way they always did, sharp and unreadable. "So," he said. "Our mystery preacher's got a survivor now."

Will slid into the passenger seat, the engine rumbling beneath them. His jaw flexed. "Don't call him that."

Joe's brow arched. "What, preacher doesn't fit?"

"He's no preacher." Will stared out the windshield, voice low, raw. "Preachers save. They guide. This bastard? He destroys. He twists it. He's a... false prophet. A butcher dressing up his sickness in sermons."

The word hung in the cab, heavy as gunmetal. False Prophet.

Joe let it settle, then gave the faintest nod. "All right then. False Prophet it is."

The city blurred by as they pulled into the street, neon bleeding against wet pavement. Joe finally spoke again. "This isn't just a freak with a taste for working girls. He's building something. A pattern. And if we don't break it, you'll be zipping up another body bag by the end of the week."

Will's grip tightened on his notebook. He could still see Maggie clutching the hoodie, her voice raw when she said, *Guys like him don't come around twice.* Except she hadn't been talking about the killer. She'd been talking about him.

And Kristen... she'd heard it too.

Will pressed the heels of his palms into his eyes, forcing focus. The case came first. Always the case. But his gut told him, this was bigger than a case. This was a hunt. And somewhere out there, the False Prophet was already choosing his next sermon.

### Summit Falls PD – Roll Call Room, Three Nights Later

The roll call room buzzed with the hum of vending machines and the rustle of paper reports. Fluorescent lights flickered overhead, casting the whole place in a jaundiced glow. Will followed Joe inside, both of them still shaking off the cold night air.

On the duty sergeant's desk sat a stack of bulletins, the top one stamped *Fusion Center Distribution.* Bright red

lettering ran across the header: **INFORMATIONAL –
SERIAL ASSAULT/M.O. MATCH.**

Joe grabbed it, his brow furrowing as he scanned. "Hell
is this?" He flipped the page toward Will.

Will skimmed the first few lines. Summit Falls PD had
pushed out a bulletin to surrounding agencies—details
stripped down, no names or crime scene photos, just
enough to show the pattern: women assaulted in motels,
restrained with improvised bindings, branded, and
staged. A calling card left behind with scripture-like
phrases.

Joe's jaw worked. "Looks like somebody in
communications did us a favor." He held up another
stapled sheet, a faxed response tagged *Oakhaven PD*.
"County forwarded this. They've got a case last fall—body
dumped behind a truck stop. Same damn burns, same
kind of note. They're asking if we want to compare."

Will's stomach tightened. Oakhaven was forty miles
south, a quiet little town, not without its big city
problems that spilled over. Close enough for a night drive.
Close enough for the False Prophet to stretch his sermons.

Joe studied him, then shoved the paper into Will's
chest. "You're the one who's lived in these files. You saw
Cherry. You talked to Maggie. You know the details better
than anybody. Follow up."

Will nodded, the paper crumpling slightly in his grip.
"I'll reach out. See what they've got."

Joe leaned back against the wall of the Sergeant's Office, arms crossed, watching him like he was measuring his resolve. "Careful how far you stick your nose in, kid. This isn't just our backyard anymore. We stir too hard, homicide's gonna scream jurisdiction. But..." He paused, the corner of his mouth twitching into the ghost of a grin. "You've got instincts for this one. Run with it."

Will glanced back at the bulletin, the words *marked and silenced* burning into him all over again. Different town, different victim, same hand.

The False Prophet was already spreading his gospel.

### Summit Falls PD – Detective's Office, Later That Night

Will went upstairs to see if any of the detectives were in. This time of night, every once in a while, one of them could be working late. Not this night. Will walked in, and the motion lights lit up the room, a faint click and a hum from each as they sprang to life with a spray of light. Will sat at the empty desk up front, the fusion bulletin and Oakhaven's fax spread in front of him. He drummed his pen once, then picked up the phone and dialed the number scribbled at the bottom of the report.

After two rings, a gravel-thick voice answered. "Rogers."

"Lieutenant Dan Rogers?" Will asked.

"Yeah. Who's this?"

"Officer Will Anderson, Summit Falls PD. I'm following up on the response you sent about a case similar to ours."

There was a pause, then a sigh that sounded like it carried a year's worth of weight. "Yeah. I figured somebody would call. You got a minute?"

"I've got all night," Will said.

"Good. 'Cause this one still sticks under my skin." Rogers's tone hardened. "The victim was a college kid. Twenty-one. Her name was Tammi Warner—her street name was 'CandyCrush.' Miami girl, nursing program at Ravenwood University. She and her roommate ran a little hook-up service out of their dorm. Real quiet operation—students and townies paying cash. We didn't even know it existed until after she turned up dead."

Will's jaw clenched. "How was she found?"

"Truck stop just off I-20. Dumped behind a dumpster like garbage. But it wasn't random. She was staged. Body propped up, clothes ripped, legs arranged—pure humiliation. The roommate came clean about the side hustle once her friend went missing. Said Tammi left for a 'date' that night. Never came back."

Will scribbled notes, pulse quickening. "Any injuries consistent with restraint?"

"Yeah. Wrist bruises, ligature marks around the neck. And one more thing..." Rogers's voice dropped. "She had a brand. Circular, about the size of a silver dollar, burned into her abdomen. ME said it was inflicted while she was still alive. She would've felt every second of it."

Will's grip on the pen whitened. "We've got that here as well. Same spot. Same type of burn."

"That's not all." Rogers exhaled. "We found a note at the scene. Stuck to the back of the truck stop wall using the victim's blood as glue. Shaky handwritten block letters, scripture-like. Said she was claimed. Said pain was proof of love. It was short, but it was sick. Sounds like the same kind of scripture-like message you described in your bulletin."

Will's chest tightened. "So he's done this before. At least once. Maybe more."

"Yeah. The problem is, the case went cold. No DNA, no prints, no trace. Guy's a damn ghost. Checked her phone, her laptop, her roommate's devices. Nothing. Whoever she was meeting, he left no footprint. No texts, no emails, no messages. Like he never existed."

Will leaned back, staring at the wall, his notes blurring. "What about witnesses at the truck stop?"

"Dead end. Cameras had blind spots. Nobody saw a damn thing. My gut says he beat the hell out of her, then killed her somewhere else, and dumped her there after staging the scene. He wanted her humiliated, not hidden."

Silence stretched. Will finally said, "This lines up with what we've seen. The branding. The scripture. The staging. It's the same guy."

"Then you've got a live one," Rogers said, his voice rough. "I envy you. Ours was nothing but a body bag and a cold file. If your girl survived, get every damn word she remembers. 'Cause it sounds like he's not gonna stop."

Will stared down at his notes, Maggie's face flashing in his mind. *Marked and silenced. They belong to me.*

"I will," he said. His voice came out like a vow. "I'll find him."

Will set the receiver back in its cradle, his knuckles still tight around the plastic. The notes in front of him were a mess of ink—dates, names, places—but the through-line burned clear.

Joe stepped into the doorway, coffee in one hand, expression unreadable. "That Rogers?"

Will nodded, rubbing the bridge of his nose. "Yeah. Said their case went cold. The victim was a twenty-one-year-old college girl. Tammi Warner. On her socials, she went by *CandyCrush*. Nursing student at Ravenwood. She and her roommate ran a hookup service. Met guys off-campus for cash."

Joe's brow furrowed. "And?"

Will's voice flattened. "She was branded. Same spot. Same burn. And they found a note—stuck to the wall in her blood. Said she was claimed. Pain was proof of love."

Joe's jaw tightened. "Mother of God..."

Will flipped the notebook toward him, the scrawled lines barely legible. "He staged her, too. Propped, humiliated. Just like Cherry. Just like Maggie, if she hadn't fought through it. Only difference is, Tammi didn't walk away."

Joe took a slow sip of coffee, studying the page, then set the cup aside. "So he's not just ours. He's mobile, been active for a while."

Will nodded grimly. "Rogers thinks she was killed somewhere else and dumped at the truck stop. Cameras were useless. No DNA, no digital footprint. Guy's like a ghost. Guess he changed to more private settings with the rooms."

Joe leaned against the desk, folding his arms. "Ghosts don't leave scripture. They don't burn sermons into skin. He wants to be known, Will. He wants to be recognized. You don't mark your victims and stage them like exhibits unless you're building something bigger."

Will's gaze dropped to the bulletin again, the words blurring into a single idea: *False Prophet.*

"He's spreading his message, so-called anti-sermon," Will said quietly. "Cherry. Maggie. Now we know of Tammi. He's been doing this, and he is not gonna stop until someone silences him."

Joe's eyes met his, steady and cold. "Then it better be us."

### Summit Falls PD – Conference Room, Night Shift

The air was different the second Will and Joe walked in stride. The captain had requested their presence. The bullpen buzz was gone, replaced by the low murmur of voices leaking from the conference room at the end of the hall. When they pushed the door open, Will stopped short.

Every chair around the long table was full—homicide detectives, a vice sergeant, county deputies, even someone from state fusion. Laptops glowed, maps spread wide across the table, red pins stabbing motel locations like wounds. At the head sat Captain Nate Archer, jaw tight, eyes sweeping the room like he'd been waiting for this storm to break.

Joe muttered under his breath, "Well, holy hell."

Archer gestured them in. "Anderson. Donovan. Good—you're here. Sit."

They slid into the two empty chairs at the far side. Will's gaze flicked over the case boards—Cherry's photo tacked in the corner, Maggie's blurred medical stills from his phone while EMS patched her up, and now a fresh sheet with *Oakhaven PD – Tammi Warner (CandyCrush)* scrawled across the top.

Archer cleared his throat, the low rumble cutting through the buzz of papers and keyboards. The room stilled.

"You've all seen the fusion bulletin," he began, voice steady but edged with steel. "As of tonight, Summit Falls PD is officially partnering with the county and Oakhaven. This is now a joint task force."

He let the words settle, his gaze sweeping across the table.

"Dan Rogers will be joining us from Oakhaven tomorrow. We have a serial offender moving across jurisdictions—violent assaults, homicides, staging, scripture-like notes. We don't know his endgame. What we do know is that he's escalating."

Archer's eyes found Will. "Anderson, you've got the most insight on our two most recent cases. That puts you closer to this thing than anyone else. So, for the time being, you're drafted up to the big leagues."

He shifted his gaze toward Joe. "Donovan's coming with you. He's been around long enough to know how predators like this think. You'll need that experience."

Silence followed—tight, expectant. Every detective at the table knew the air had shifted. This wasn't just another case anymore. This was war.

A homicide detective, Lowe, leaned forward, pen tapping against his legal pad. "Anderson—you were first on scene with Ivy Cole. You've spoken to the survivor, Maggie. You also followed up with Oakhaven on their case. Bring us up to speed."

Will laid out what he knew. Cherry's staging, Maggie's survival and statement, the burns, the scripture left behind. Then Tammi Warner. Twenty-one. Nursing student. Branded alive. A note written in blood, claiming her through pain. Dumped and humiliated.

When he finished, Lowe snorted, leaning back in his chair. "That's a hell of a story, patrol. But you're connecting dots with a Sharpie. Different counties, different victims, no DNA. How do you know this isn't just two psychos doing the same thing?"

Will met his stare, steady. "Because he brands them the same way. Circular burn, abdomen, while they're still alive. Because he stages them the same way. Exposed. Humiliated. Because he leaves scripture every time, his twisted sermon in blood or ink. That's not a coincidence. That's pattern."

Another detective, Harris, chimed in. "Survivors misremember. Trauma does that. You sure Maggie's not just latching onto what she heard after Cherry's case hit the wires?"

Will shook his head once. "She gave me details that weren't public. The exact phrases he used. The belt. The cadence of his voice. I heard it from her before I heard it from anyone else. That's not misremembering. That's surviving."

The room went still. Even Joe, arms folded in his chair, gave the faintest twitch of a nod, like *steady, kid.*

Then Lowe tried again. "So what do we call him? Can't keep saying 'our mystery preacher.'"

Will's jaw tightened. He let his eyes sweep the board—Cherry, Maggie, Tammi Warner—before looking back at them. "He's not a preacher. Preachers save. They guide. This bastard twists faith into a weapon. He destroys. He marks them, silences them, and calls it holy." He let the silence stretch, then said it plain:

"He's a False Prophet."

The name settled over the room like a shroud.

Archer leaned forward, voice carrying more weight than the detectives' skepticism combined. "You heard him. From here on, he's the False Prophet. That's how we'll refer to him in every case file, every interagency call, every report. Clear?"

The room murmured assent. Even the homicide guys who had pressed Will earlier said nothing more, their eyes shifting back to the board.

Will sat back, notebook closed in his lap, the word echoing in his head like a vow.

The hunt had a name.

As the meeting broke, Archer caught Will's eye across the table. Just a flicker—a subtle nod, the kind only a soldier would recognize. Approval without ceremony. Trust without words.

For the first time since Cherry's body in Room 214, Will felt like someone else believed him.

The conference room emptied in slow drifts of footsteps and shuffling papers, but Will lingered. The case boards still glowed under the fluorescent lights—faces, maps, photos of bruised wrists and torn motel curtains pinned in neat rows of horror. His own notes sat closed in his lap, heavy as a weapon.

False Prophet.

The name clung to him as he walked out into the bullpen. Detectives peeled off toward coffee pots and ringing phones, voices already shifting back to routine. But for Will, nothing about this was routine. He felt it in his chest—the same tension he'd carried on patrol in Afghanistan before a raid: the silence that wasn't silence at all, but the moment before the breach.

Outside, the night was cold enough to sting. He lit a cigarette, something he hadn't done in months, the smoke harsh in his throat. He thought of Maggie in that hoodie, Kristen's steady gaze across the table, Rogers's voice on the phone calling Tammi Warner nothing but a cold file.

Maggie was alive. That mattered. But the False Prophet was still out there, choosing his next sermon.

Joe's voice broke the quiet behind him. "You know what you've just done, right? You didn't just give him a name. You put a target on your back."

Will exhaled smoke into the dark, eyes fixed on the horizon. "Good. Makes it easier for him to find me."

# Armor

The bar was hot and noisy, the kind that seeped into Will's shirt and clung like sweat. Kristen's friends had staked out a corner booth with three empty pitchers and a lineup of shot glasses that multiplied every round. Will kept his back to the wall, one beer steady in his hand, eyes scanning habitually even as he pretended to watch the game on the TV above the bar.

Kristen wasn't pretending. She was alive tonight—laughing with her girls, hair loose around her shoulders, eyes brighter than he'd ever seen. Every so often, she'd cut a glance across the booth at him, and it was the kind of look that made him forget every boundary he'd drawn.

By the time they stumbled toward the curb, the birthday girl—Lilly—was the loudest of the bunch, arm slung around Kristen's neck, shoes dangling from one hand. "Where's my knight in shining armor?" she slurred, squinting at Will. "Oh wait. Kristen's already got him."

The rest of them chimed in like a pack of sirens, teasing, laughing, shoving Kristen toward him. "Come on, Anderson, carry us all home," one said. Another added, "Bet he's got the stamina."

Kristen just rolled her eyes, cheeks flushed with more than alcohol. Will didn't rise to the bait, but he felt the heat of it all the same—the way their laughter turned him into a spectacle, the way Kristen's hand tightened on his arm like she was both embarrassed and proud.

Back at Kristen's apartment, the night unraveled fast. The girls raided her kitchen like it was a stage, pulling open cupboards, finding more liquor, tequila, and a Bluetooth speaker thumping bass through the walls. Lilly climbed onto the counter first, hair wild, hips swaying to the beat as she laughed and peeled her sweater over her head.

Then another followed. And another. One by one, they turned the counter into a makeshift runway, dancing like they were in some private strip club, daring each other louder with every turn. Clothes flew—jackets, scarves, heels kicked aside.

Will leaned against the doorway, caught between disbelief and an unwilling thrill. He shouldn't have been watching, but the room didn't seem to notice him. They were in their own world, laughing, shrieking, their eyes only on each other.

That's when he noticed it.

As Lilly spun, skirt hitching higher than she knew, then with a flip she had it sliding down her leg and with a flick of her ankle the skirt went flying, a loud cheer erupted from the pack, a tattoo flashed on the soft inside of her thigh—a white lily, petals etched just above the crease where leg met hip. The mark was subtle but deliberate, like a hidden badge of belonging.

And when the other girls joined in and started their show,  Will noticed a pattern of a rose inked in the same place. Then a tulip. Then an orchid.

Each of them bore a flower, hidden just out of sight unless they wanted it revealed, just inside the crease of the thigh, easily hidden under a bathing suit, but not tonight.

Will's jaw tightened. It was more than friendship. It was a bond, a club. A sisterhood. And Kristen was one of them.

"Don't look so shocked," Kristen whispered suddenly, at his side, before he realized she'd left the group. Her breath was warm against his ear. "They forget you're here. That's how it always is when it's just us."

Then she took his hand, fingers lacing with his, and pulled him down the hall.

Her bedroom door clicked shut, cutting off the bass and shrieks. The quiet pressed in around them. She pushed him back against the door, kissing him hard, urgent. He kissed her back—helpless against it—until he pulled away, breath ragged.

"You're drunk," he murmured. "You don't know what you're doing."

Her eyes lit, sharp and unyielding. "Don't patronize me. I am an adult, Will. I know exactly what I want." She pressed closer, lips grazing his jaw. "A white knight. And I've waited too damn long for him to ride into my life." Her smile curved, wicked. "So take me now, Sir Anderson. Take off your armor and treat this damsel in distress like a hostile witness before we miss out and court gets adjourned."

Something inside him cracked. He kissed her again, deeper, hands sliding over her waist, tugging at the hem of her blouse. She let him, gasping, tugging his shirt free in turn.

When he peeled her skirt down, that's when he saw it.

A daisy, small and delicate, inked just inside the crease of her thigh, tucked where her bikini line began—hidden until this moment.

His breath caught. Kristen's smile widened as she watched his eyes find it. "Now you see," she whispered. "Now you know."

He swallowed hard. "Daisy."

"Mine," she corrected softly. "Always mine."

And then there was no more hesitation. They tumbled onto her bed, their clothes scattered carelessly on the floor, while outside, the girls screamed and sang, keeping their party alive.

In here, though, it was fire and surrender, armor stripped at last.

The apartment smelled like stale vodka and perfume.

Will woke first, the light pale against the blinds, the muffled throb of a headache building even though he hadn't drunk much. He lay still for a moment, listening—

soft snores, a cough, the creak of pipes as someone flushed the bathroom down the hall.

Kristen stirred beside him, hair a tumble across the pillow, one arm slung loosely across his chest. Her breathing was slow, steady, but even in sleep her fingers flexed as if she wasn't ready to let go.

Will brushed a strand of hair back from her cheek. He thought about last night—the counter, the laughter, her pulling him into the bedroom with fire in her eyes. The daisy inked into her thigh, small but defiant, a secret she'd chosen to give him.

He kissed the top of her head, then carefully slipped free to pull on his jeans.

The living room was wreckage.

Two of Kristen's friends were passed out on the couch, tangled together in a heap of limbs and throw blankets. Another was curled on the floor with a pillow hugged to her chest, lipstick smeared across her chin, a label of some sort stuck to her bare bottom. Apparently, she lost the contest. The birthday girl, Lilly, was still on the counter—flat on her back now, one arm flung dramatically over her eyes, an empty tequila bottle standing tall like a trophy beside her.

Clothes were everywhere. A bra hung from the lamp. Someone's dress was draped over the TV. A single high heel stood upright on the coffee table like a drunken monument.

Will ran a hand over his jaw. He'd seen worse crime scenes. Barely.

A groan came from the couch. "Water..." one of them croaked.

Will found a pitcher in the fridge, filled a couple of glasses, and set them out on the counter. When he turned, Lilly cracked one eye open and spotted him.

"Ohhh, Sir Will," she slurred, voice rough from smoke and shots. "Did our hostess survive her knight in shining armor?"

Will shook his head, but before he could answer, Kristen's voice floated from the hallway. "Alive and well. Thanks for asking."

She appeared barefoot in his t-shirt, hair messy, cheeks flushed in a way that wasn't just sleep. She padded past him, grabbed a glass of water, and handed it to Lilly with mock ceremony.

"Drink, Your Majesty," Kristen teased. "Queen of the Counter."

The others laughed weakly, groaning at the sound of their own amusement.

Will leaned against the counter, watching Kristen as she herded her friends toward recovery—handing out water, offering aspirin, pulling a blanket over the girl on the floor. She moved with ease, like this chaos was second nature, but every so often her eyes flicked to him.

Soft. Knowing. His.

When the girls finally collapsed back into silence, Kristen slipped close, brushing her fingers against his. "Stay," she whispered, too quiet for anyone else to hear. "Don't run off yet."

Will turned, looking down at her—at the curve of her smile, at the glint of the daisy just visible where her t-shirt hem rode high. His chest tightened.

"I wasn't going anywhere," he said.

Her hand squeezed his. "Good."

And for the first time in a long time, Will realized he didn't want to.

When the chaos dulled again to half-hearted snores, Kristen slipped close and brushed her fingers against his. "Come back to bed," she whispered, too low for anyone else to hear. "Please."

Will followed her down the hall, the muffled bass of the girls' laughter finally gone. She shut the bedroom door, shutting the world out with it.

Kristen climbed back onto the bed, pulling him with her. The morning light softened her face, catching on her hair, on the faint bruising at her jaw from the bar fight days ago. She studied him in silence, her hand resting warm against his chest.

"Do you regret it?" she asked finally, her voice quiet but steady.

Will's stomach knotted. He cupped her cheek, brushing his thumb over her skin. "No," he said, and the word came out like a vow. "Not for a second."

Relief flickered in her eyes, followed by a smile—small, but so sharp it pierced him. She shifted closer, lips brushing his jaw.

"Good," she murmured. "Because I don't either."

Her hand trailed down his chest, over the hard plane of his stomach, and Will realized there was no armor left. Not between them. Not anymore.

And for the first time in years, that didn't terrify him.

For a long time, they just stayed tangled together, the world muted to nothing but the rise and fall of each other's breathing.

But Kristen's apartment wasn't built for silence.

By mid-morning, the muffled thrum of voices filtered through the bedroom door—groans, laughter, the rattle of a cabinet being opened too hard. Kristen sighed, pressing her forehead against Will's shoulder.

"They're alive," she muttered.

"Unfortunately," Will said, making her laugh into his skin.

When they finally emerged, the living room was in full recovery mode. Veronica had found a box of cereal and was eating straight from it; Lilly was nursing black coffee as if it might save her life, and Amber and Gina were sprawled in various states of disarray, trading battle stories from the night before.

The apartment smelled like stale wine and burnt coffee by the time Will and Kristen emerged. Kristen's hair was pulled back in a loose knot, his T-shirt hanging on her frame; Will trailed after her, boots in hand, still blinking against the light.

The living room looked like a battlefield: bottles toppled, heels scattered, a pair of panties draped across the lamp. Veronica Ruiz—Rose to her friends—sat curled in a blanket burrito on the couch, scrolling her phone between groans. Amber Collins, better known after a few drinks as Tulip, had taken over the cereal box, eating it dry by the handful. Naomi Park, Orchid in their little circle, sprawled across the rug like a cat, nursing her coffee. And on the counter sat the birthday girl herself, Lillian Harper, Lilly, far too chipper for someone who'd led the charge into oblivion the night before.

The second they spotted Kristen and Will, silence hit. Then Lilly raised her mug high.

"Well, well, well. *Sir Anderson* emerges from the boudoir," she sang, her grin wicked. "Kristen, honey, you should've warned us you had a knight in actual shining armor."

Veronica cackled. "Forget armor—did you *see* the way she dragged him out of here last night? I thought the doorframe was gonna splinter."

Amber chimed in through a mouthful of cereal. "Pretty sure it did."

Kristen's cheeks burned. "Grow up."

"Grow up?" Naomi purred, stretching lazily, her oversized tee sliding to reveal the orchid inked high on her thigh. "Sweetheart, you've been holding out on us. Never said your boy could actually *slay*."

The room dissolved into howls. Kristen groaned into her hands.

Will, deadpan as ever, just said: "For the record, she threw me against the door."

That shut them up—before they erupted again. Lilly nearly choked on her coffee, Veronica banged her mug on the table like a gavel, and Amber shouted, "Go, *Daisy!*"

The word froze in the air.

Kristen stiffened, her gaze cutting sharply to Will. He didn't miss a beat—arched brow, faintest hint of a smile. Daisy. He hadn't forgotten.

The girls, oblivious, just kept laughing, chanting "Daisy, Daisy, Daisy" until Kristen groaned and stormed toward the kitchen, tugging Will with her by the wrist.

"You're enjoying this," she hissed under her breath.

"Little bit," he murmured, low enough only she could hear.

Her eyes flicked up to his, soft despite her embarrassment. "Well, get used to it, Sir Anderson. My friends don't forget. And neither do I."

Will glanced back at the living room—at Veronica's bare legs sticking out of the blanket, at Amber still strutting around in just panties like she'd forgotten he was even there, at Naomi stretching on the rug without a care in the world. None of them seemed bothered by modesty in the least, not even with him standing right there.

Kristen followed his look and smirked. "That's their power, Will. They don't give a damn what you see. Drives men crazy—and that's the point."

Before he could answer, a sing-song voice cut in.

"Damn right it is," Lilly said, grinning as she hopped down from the counter in nothing but her tank and panties. She sauntered over, peeled the panties off without hesitation, and pressed them into Will's stunned hand. "Here, Sir Anderson. Be a dear and fetch me a clean towel. Birthday girl needs a shower."

Kristen nearly choked, smacking a hand over her face. "Lilly!"

But Lilly wasn't finished. She yanked her tank off in one quick motion and tossed it over Will's shoulder like he was staff. Then, bare-breasted and grinning, she leaned in close, gave Kristen a playful wink—and smacked her hard on the butt.

Kristen gasped, whirling around. "LILLY!"

The room erupted—Veronica howling into her blanket, Amber spitting cereal in laughter, Naomi clapping like it was a performance.

Unbothered, Lilly just strutted toward the hall, hips swaying deliberately. "Don't keep me waiting, butler!" she called over her shoulder. "Queen needs her shower."

Will stood frozen, the lace in one hand, the top sliding down his arm. Kristen snatched both away, cheeks flushed with fury and embarrassment, though her lips betrayed the faintest twitch of a smile.

"Don't let her fool you," she muttered, glaring after her friend. "They'll tease you to death if you let them. But me?" Her eyes found his, sly and certain. "I'm the only one you need to worry about."

## Sermon

The conference room smelled of stale coffee and dry-erase markers, a far cry from the wreckage of Kristen's apartment. With a new schedule on the task force, Will, with coffee in hand, sat forward in his chair, elbows braced on the table, eyes fixed on the case board that now stretched across an entire wall.

Ivy Cole.

Tammi Warner.

Maggie Truelove.

Brookhaven Jane Doe.

Four pins, red string threading them together across counties, across months.

Captain Archer tapped the board with the butt of his marker. "That makes four. Oakhaven, Summit Falls, Ravenwood, and now Brookhaven. He's mobile, he's organized, and he's escalating."

The homicide sergeant, Lowe, muttered, "So what's the endgame? Guy's not leaving DNA, not leaving prints. Hell, he's not even leaving tire tracks. He's a ghost."

"No." Will's voice came before he realized he was speaking. The room turned to him. He swallowed, steadying. "He's not a ghost. He wants us to see his work. That's the point of the sermons, the brands, the staging. He's building something, and every victim is a chapter."

119

The door banged open. A broad-shouldered man in a county windbreaker stepped in, carrying a file box like it weighed twice its size. His face was rough-hewn, eyes lined from years in the job.

"Sorry I'm late," he said, voice gravel. "Traffic on 26."

Archer straightened. "Lieutenant Rogers. Glad you made it."

Will felt a jolt. Rogers. The voice from the phone.

The Oakhaven lieutenant dropped the box onto the table with a heavy thud. "Files on Tammi Warner. CandyCrush. Every interview, every photo, every lead that went nowhere. If this son of a bitch is yours now, then maybe you'll have better luck than I did."

The room went still as he cracked the lid, pulling out manila folders swollen with paper. The photographs slid across the table—Tammi's staged body, the burn, the blood-written note.

Will forced himself to look. He had to.

Rogers' eyes found him. "You Anderson?"

"Yes, sir."

"You're the one who called me." Rogers leaned back, arms folded, measuring him. "A lot of rookies wouldn't have picked up the phone. You did. So tell me—what makes you so sure this is the same guy and not two psychos with the same sick habits?"

Will met his stare, steady. "Because it's not just habits. It's ritual. He brands them the same way, stages them the same way, and writes scripture every time.

Different county, different girl, same sermon. He's not experimenting. He's preaching."

A long silence hung over the room. Then Rogers gave a slight nod, like a soldier recognizing another who'd been under fire.

"All right," he said. "Then let's hunt him together."

Before Will could answer, Lowe leaned back in his chair, arms crossed, pen tapping against his legal pad. "That's assuming we're even talking about the same guy. It could just be two creeps with the same kinks. Seen it before."

Rogers' head snapped toward him, eyes narrowing. "You ever seen *this* before? A twenty-one-year-old girl branded alive, dumped behind a truck stop with scripture written in her blood? Because I have. I zipped her into the bag myself. And I'll tell you right now—this isn't a copycat. It's the same hand. Same sick sermon."

Lowe didn't flinch. "All I'm saying is, we don't have DNA. No prints, no trace. You're hanging this whole task force on gut feelings and theatrics."

Rogers slammed a folder down so hard the pens rattled. "It's not theatrics when you're the one knocking on a mother's door to tell her that her kid's never coming home. This case went cold because we didn't connect the dots soon enough. I won't watch you fools make the same mistake."

The room went tight, everyone holding their breath.

Archer cut in, voice low but sharp. "That's enough. We're not here to measure egos, we're here to stop a killer." His gaze flicked between Rogers and Lowe like a commander separating two soldiers. "Lowe, you want evidence? Fine. Anderson and Rogers will find you evidence. Until then, we treat this as one offender. Clear?"

Lowe muttered something under his breath but scribbled in his notes. Rogers eased back into his chair, jaw tight, eyes still burning.

Will sat between them, notebook closed in his lap. He could feel the weight of both men, one daring him to prove it, the other demanding that he not fail.

And somewhere out there, the False Prophet was already writing his next sermon.

Archer let the silence stretch, then leaned forward, planting both hands on the table. "Enough posturing. We've got women dead, one who barely survived, and a predator who thinks pain is scripture. We move now. Priority is evidence, patterns, and territory. Rogers, Donovan, Anderson—you're lead on victimology. Find the overlaps. Work the timelines. If he's mobile, there'll be a trail: motel registries, truck stop cameras, credit card hits."

He looked at Joe next. "Coordinate with vice. Map every working girl tied to those motels in the last six months. Quietly. No grandstanding. If he's shopping victims on the street, the girls will know before we do."

"Copy," Joe said, scribbling notes.

Archer turned to Rogers. "You've got the truck stop. Re-pull the surveillance, even if it's garbage: re-interview staff, night drivers, anyone who might've seen something. Anderson goes with you. He's got the survivor's words fresh in his head—might catch what you missed."

Rogers gave a sharp nod. "Understood."

"And Lowe," Archer said, his tone harder now, "since you're skeptical, prove us wrong. Investigate cold case files within a fifty-mile radius. Look for matches—burns, scripture notes, staged displays. If it's not the same offender, you'll have the chance to say 'I told you so.' Until then, we proceed like it is."

Lowe's pen froze mid-scratch. He gave a tight shrug, but said nothing.

Archer's gaze swept the room one last time. "We build a task force because a predator like this doesn't stay in one jurisdiction. He's crossing counties, maybe states. He's not a ghost, he's a pattern—and patterns leave trails. Find me his trail."

Chairs scraped back as the room broke into motion. Rogers scooped up his folders with a sharp movement, already muttering about pulling maps. Joe tucked his cigarette pack into his pocket and clapped Will on the shoulder. "Hope you got some gas in the tank, kid. We're about to burn rubber."

Will's hand closed around his notebook, knuckles white. Maggie's bruised face flashed in his mind. Cherry's tattoo. Tammi Warner's photo. All strung together by the same sick hand.

False Prophet.

The hunt had begun in earnest.

The highway south was a ribbon of wet asphalt, the rain from earlier still clinging to the blacktop. Will sat in the passenger seat of Rogers's dented Crown Vic, the heater blowing stale air that smelled faintly of old coffee and cigar smoke. The Oakhaven lieutenant drove like he did everything else—hard, unflinching, and without wasted words.

For the first half-hour, silence ruled. The wipers squeaked across the windshield. Rogers kept one hand on the wheel, the other nursing a Styrofoam cup that had been refilled too many times.

Finally, Rogers spoke. "You remind me of me, Anderson." His voice was gravelly. "That's not a compliment."

Will glanced over. "How so?"

"You still believe every victim matters. Still think you can fix it. That kind of thinking—" Rogers shook his head— "will get you chewed up and spit out by the job. Ask me how I know."

Will didn't blink. "Maybe it'll chew me up. But I'd rather that than turn cold."

Rogers barked a humorless laugh. "That's what I said twenty years ago. You think you're different. You're not."

Will tightened his jaw. "Or maybe you just stopped being different."

The car went quiet again, the tension heavier than the engine's hum. Rogers's knuckles whitened on the wheel, but he didn't fire back. Not yet.

An hour later, the neon glow of the truck stop rose on the horizon—half-lit signs, diesel rigs lined up like sleeping beasts. Rogers slowed as he turned into the lot, his eyes scanning every corner with the weariness of a man who'd done this a hundred times.

"Back here," he said, pulling behind the row of dumpsters. The headlights swept over the cracked pavement, the stains that never washed out. Will could almost see it—the staged body, the humiliation painted in blood. His stomach turned.

Rogers killed the engine and leaned back, watching Will carefully.

"This is where I zipped her up. Tammi Warner. Twenty-one years old. Still had her college ID in her bag. You ever tell a girl's mother she was dumped like garbage?" His voice flattened. "You think you've got fire in your gut now, but wait until you see that look in her eyes."

Will swallowed, chest tight. "I don't need to see her mother's eyes. I saw Maggie's. And Cherry's. That's enough."

Rogers studied him for a beat—something unreadable in his gaze, half challenge, half respect—then opened his door.

"Come on."

The air outside hit like rot—diesel, grease, and wet pavement. The truck stop lights flickered overhead, casting a sodium haze across the back lot. They walked behind the dumpsters, boots crunching gravel, past a dark stain on the concrete that hadn't washed out. Not after the rain. Not after the bleach. Not after time.

Rogers stopped, arms folded tight, gaze fixed on the ground.

"This is the spot," he said. "Where he left her. Legs propped. Arms posed. Head tilted like she was waiting for a eulogy."

Will stood beside him in silence.

Rogers didn't look over. His voice came quietly, but not softly.

"I've seen this too many times. The motel girls. Lot lizards. And even the college kids selling a piece of themselves between classes. They act like they're in control. Like the cash gives them power. But when it goes bad, they all say the same thing: *I didn't know it would get this far. Well, at least the ones who report it.*'"

Will's voice was steady. "It's not an invitation."

Rogers exhaled, slow and steady, like the thought had weight.

"Maybe not to you. But to men like him? It's not just an invitation—it's a signal flare. They walk into the dark like they belong there. Like they *were made* for it. And when the world finally sees what they've done... everyone acts shocked, like they didn't know the fire would burn, like the devil is real and they finally admit that he just claimed another soul."

He paused. The silence that followed wasn't hesitation. It was a calculation.

"You think that makes him a monster. I think it just makes him honest."

Will stiffened. "You sound a hell of a lot like the son of a bitch we're trying to stop."

Rogers finally looked at him. Something flickered behind his eyes—something not quite gone, but far from whole.

"No," he said. "I sound like someone who's spent twenty years cleaning up the mess after men like him—and starting to wonder if maybe the only difference between predator and prey is who gets caught first."

Will didn't answer. The quiet between them stretched long, taut as a wire.

Rogers turned away, started walking again, then stopped—halfway to the lot's edge. His voice carried back, cool and sharp.

"You want to catch this guy?" he said. "Stop judging him long enough to understand him. You can't stay on your white horse and hunt a man like this. You've got to think like him. Get inside his rituals, his timing, the why of it. You need to crawl into his head and sit with the filth until it starts making sense."

He turned back toward Will, eyes glinting under the flicker of the overhead lights.

"That doesn't make you like him. It just means you're willing to go farther than the last cop who failed."

Will stared at him, jaw tight.

"And what happens," he said slowly, "when you go so far in you can't find your way back?"

Rogers didn't blink.

"Then you hope like hell you picked the right devil to chase."

He said it without flinching. No hesitation. No irony. Just flat truth, spoken like scripture.

Rogers took a slow step forward, boots crunching glass or gravel—Will couldn't tell.

"Girls like Tammi..." Rogers said. "They roll the dice every night. Meet strangers in dark places. Ignore their gut, because the money's good, or the loneliness is worse. And when it turns bad, they act as if they're surprised. But maybe some of them... maybe they want to be seen. To be marked. Proof they were here."

Will's jaw clenched. "You think they asked for it."

"I think they asked to matter," Rogers said flatly. "And sometimes pain is the only way the world pays attention."

Silence dropped like a shroud.

Rogers turned toward the gas station, nodding toward the smudged glass door.

"Manager's inside. Still got some of the old tapes boxed up."

He started walking.

Will followed, slower, his thoughts turning heavy.

Because for a moment—just long enough to count—he hadn't been sure who Rogers was anymore.

Inside, the air was thick with the smell of stale coffee and bleach. A tired night clerk pointed them toward a back office with a flick of his pen.

In the corner, a stack of dusty VHS tapes leaned against the wall, marked by year and month.

Rogers dropped a thick case file onto the desk in front of Will. "Fresh eyes," he said. "Tell me what I missed."

Will flipped the first page. His pen moved fast, sharp, ink soaking into the paper like blood into cloth.

The hunt for the False Prophet had just stretched its roots deeper.

### Summit Falls PD – Parking Garage

Later that shift. The structure hummed with silence. Just the low whine of a fluorescent light overhead, flickering like it couldn't decide whether to live or die. The scent of motor oil, cold rain, and old concrete clung to everything. Will leaned against the trunk of his cruiser, arms folded, staring at the far wall like it owed him answers, catching his breath.

The city hadn't quieted. Not really. Sirens still flared in the distance, half-muffled by the thick air. Somewhere above, a gull shrieked like it had taken a wrong turn into the wrong town.

Footsteps echoed behind him—measured, deliberate.

Joe Donovan.

He appeared from the stairwell, a Styrofoam cup in one hand, steam curling from it like smoke from a dying fire.

"You look like a man who found something in the dark and wished he hadn't," Joe said.

Will didn't look over. "Maybe I did."

Joe came to a slow stop beside him. The two stood in quiet for a moment, the kind only men in this line of work knew how to keep. The kind that held weight, not awkwardness.

"You wanna talk about it," Joe said finally, "or are you gonna brood like a protagonist with a dead partner?"

Will let out something between a breath and a scoff.

"It's Rogers."

Joe didn't respond. Just sipped his coffee. Let it hang.

Will pushed off the car slightly, fingers curling around the lip of the trunk.

"We were going through Tammi Warner's file and pulling old surveillance. Talking timeline. And out of nowhere he says, 'Maybe this guy's just doing what the system's too afraid to.'"

Joe blinked once. Then again. "That's what he said?"

Will nodded once. "Like it was casual. Like it wasn't insane. Just that these girls shouldn't have expected not to get burned by the devil type thing."

The words hung there. Joe stared off toward the far end of the garage, into nothing. Will waited.

Then, finally: "You think he meant it?"

Will didn't answer right away. "I think he's tired. Broken in ways he won't admit. And when a man like that starts seeing purpose in a killer's work, even for a second, yeah, I think he meant it, almost as if he were in his shoes and agreed."

Joe exhaled, the kind of breath that came after you saw a name on a toe tag that shouldn't have been there. "That's not just cynicism. That's rot."

"Yeah." Will's voice was low. "And it's spreading."

A silence fell between them again, thicker now.

"You think he's involved?" Joe asked quietly.

Will shook his head. "Not like that. Not the boots-on-the-floor kind of involved. But his head's somewhere dark. And if he keeps sliding, we won't see the difference between him and the bastard we're chasing."

Joe sipped his coffee, but his hand was tenser now. "You report it up, you'll get labeled emotional. You know that, right? 'New kid with a savior complex.' They'll bury it. Might even bury you."

"I'm not reporting it," Will said. "Not yet. I'm watching. That's all."

Joe nodded slowly, like that was the answer he'd hoped for. Then he looked over at Will, something sharp but steady in his eyes.

"Just don't look too long, kid. Men like Rogers? They've stared into the fire so long they stopped seeing the burn. And if you walk too close to that heat, it'll scar you before you know it."

Will didn't respond.

He just watched the lights of the city blur in the reflection of his cruiser's paint, the distorted red and blue bleeding together like old bruises. Inside the trunk was the evidence kit. Maggie's file. A notebook thick with ghosts.

Joe started walking away, footsteps fading. But his voice drifted back.

"You see a man trying to justify pain, you don't give him rope. You cut it."

Will stood there long after he was gone.

Alone with the silence. With the shadows.

And with the dawning realization that the most dangerous sermon might not come from the Prophet...

But from a man who carries a badge just like his.

## Lessons

Moments like this made Will think of his father, because Rogers sounded nothing like him. His father had taught him that every life mattered, especially those that others wanted to overlook.

Will could still hear his father's voice on nights when silence pressed too close. Not the clipped tone of an officer giving orders, but the steady, weathered voice that carried truths harder than any badge or gun could hold. His father hadn't lectured him into becoming a man. He had carved lessons into Will's life, each one arriving in a moment that burned itself into memory.

**Always tell the truth, even when it's hard.**

He was nine the summer the baseball cracked through Mr. Hanley's window. Will had tried to hide it, cheeks burning as he swore it wasn't him. But his father saw through it immediately. He didn't raise his voice; instead, he knelt in front of Will, looking him dead in the eyes.

"Son, a man who lies to escape trouble builds a cage around himself. Every lie is another bar. Sooner or later, that cage closes."

The guilt hit harder than any punishment. That night Will confessed, and while his allowance vanished for weeks paying for the window, he never forgot the mix of shame and relief. The truth hurt — but it also set him free.

**Do the right thing, even when no one is watching.**

Years later, riding home in the patrol car after practice, Will saw his father pull over suddenly. No sirens, no call on the radio. Just a fallen tree limb across a dark stretch of road. His father stepped out, hauled it to the ditch, and brushed his hands clean.

"No one saw that," Will pointed out when he slid back behind the wheel.

His father gave him a look. "That's the point. Character isn't about applause. It's about responsibility. Someone else might've hit that branch and never made it home."

Will never forget the quiet weight of that lesson — how rightness mattered most when no one was there to reward it.

**Stand up for what's right, even when you are the only one standing.**

That one came from the schoolyard. Will had watched a smaller boy named Chris get shoved around, laughed at by a circle of older kids. Will's stomach twisted, but he didn't step in. Not that day. He carried the guilt home until his father caught the look on his face and coaxed the truth from him.

"Were you afraid?" his father asked.

Will nodded.

His father placed a rough hand on his shoulder. *"Courage isn't about not being afraid. It's about standing up anyway. If you wait for the crowd to back you, you'll wait forever. One person's voice — one person's stand — can change everything."*

The next time, Will didn't hesitate. He stepped forward, fists clenched, voice trembling but steady. The hit came hard and fast, knocking the breath from him — but he stayed on his feet. And in that bruised, breathless moment, he understood: he could stand alone and still matter.

There was never a third time. Because when Will walked up after that, he wasn't alone. Three other boys rose with him, their defiance shoulder to shoulder with his. For the first time, Will felt what his father meant — that one person's stand could give others the courage to rise.

That younger kid would eventually become his good friend, enlist in the Army after graduation with Will, and become one of his greatest friends in life.

**Courage is not the absence of fear.**

Will's father showed this truth not with words but with his own scars. There were nights he came home pale and shaken, eyes haunted by things he never spoke aloud. Yet every morning, he put the badge back on and walked out the door. "Fear is natural," he told Will once. "But courage is when you do what's needed anyway. If you wait to feel brave, you'll wait your whole life."

**Compassion is strength, not weakness.**

For all his hardness, Will's father had a tenderness that surprised people. Will remembered the night he came home with a shivering puppy zipped inside his jacket, rescued from an alley. "Being tough doesn't mean being cruel," he said, setting down a bowl of milk. "The strongest men I've known were the ones who knew when to show mercy." Watching his father stroke the trembling creature's fur, Will realized that strength wasn't just in fists or firepower. It was in kindness.

**Discipline and accountability.**

The lessons weren't always gentle. When Will forgot chores or slacked off, his father never barked but never let it slide, either. "Every action has consequences," he would say. "Good or bad, they're yours to own. Excuses won't change that." Will learned early that failure wasn't final — but running from responsibility was.

**Service before self.**

And woven through it all was the quiet example of service. His father didn't speak about sacrifice often, but Will saw it: late-night calls that pulled him away from dinner, weekends lost to double shifts, shoulders bowed from carrying more than his share. "We don't just wear the badge," he said once. "We serve the people behind the doors. Never forget that."

**If good men do nothing, evil prevails.**

That was his father's refrain, spoken in countless ways across countless nights. Sometimes, after shifts where he came home carrying more sorrow than he could shake. Sometimes after funerals, when he spoke less and stared more. The words weren't just a warning. They were a charge, a torch passed down.

Now, years later, Will felt those lessons like a compass in his bones. Truth, integrity, courage, compassion, discipline — they weren't just principles his father taught. They were the marrow of who he was. And every time he stood at the edge of fear, or temptation, or silence, he heard his father again:

*Always tell the truth. Do the right thing when no one's watching. Stand up, even if you stand alone. Be brave, be kind, be accountable. Serve others before yourself.*

The world was full of shadows, his father had said. But shadows only grew when men refused to bring the light.

And Will had promised himself long ago: he would never let the dark grow on his watch.

## Lines

### The Whetstone Grill – 7:14 p.m.
### Two Nights After the Task Force Briefing

The lighting was low—amber bulbs in black wire cages, flickering over exposed brick and weathered wood. The Whetstone wasn't fancy, but it was far enough from the precinct that nobody knew them by name.

Kristen sat across from Will, one arm draped casually over the back of her chair, her glass of red wine untouched. She was in black again—jacket hung over the backrest, hair down for once, loose around her face. She looked like she belonged here. Will felt like he was still carrying the cold stink of crime scenes and motel rooms in his collar.

They hadn't said much since the waiter left. Just sat, letting the clink of silverware and murmured conversations around them fill the space.

Kristen finally broke the silence.

"So... funny thing."

Will looked up from his water.

She grinned. "I got assigned to a new interagency task force this morning."

He raised a brow. "That so?"

"Yeah." She leaned in slightly. "Some real sick bastard making his rounds across the state. Calls himself the False Prophet. You heard of him?"

Will chuckled, low and dry. "Maybe once or twice."

Kristen blinked. "Wait—don't tell me—"

Will nodded, easing back in his chair. "I'm on it. Been on it since the Cherry Cole case. Pulled in deeper after Maggie. Didn't realize they looped the DA's office into the formal task force yet."

Kristen's smile tilted. "Guess we're coworkers now."

Will shook his head. "God help us."

She raised her glass. "To professional boundaries we're about to ignore recklessly."

He tapped his water against it. "Cheers."

They both drank, and the mood softened. But Kristen was watching him now, more closely.

"You okay?" she asked. "You seem... I don't know. Off."

Will hesitated. Then sighed.

"I wasn't going to bring it up tonight. Wanted this to be... normal."

Kristen's brow arched. "This is *us*, Will. Normal doesn't exist."

He smiled faintly. Then leaned in, elbows on the table, voice low.

"Rogers."

Her face shifted. "What about him?"

Will looked around—not paranoid, but cautious. Then he spoke.

"I've been partnered with him on parts of the case. Pulled him in from Oakhaven. He's got history with the

Tammi Warner file. Knew it cold. But... Kristen, I'm telling you—something's off."

Kristen didn't interrupt. Just listened.

"He talks about the Prophet like he's a known variable. Not a suspect. Not a monster. Like a... constant. Something he understands." Will shook his head. "He said the difference between predator and prey is who gets caught first."

Kristen blinked. "That's a hell of a quote."

"That's not even the worst of it." Will's jaw flexed. "He told me the only way to catch this guy was to stop judging him and start thinking like him. And the way he said it... It didn't sound like a theory. It sounded like regret."

Kristen sat back, her wine forgotten. "You think he's involved?"

"I don't know," Will admitted. "But I think he's too close. He talks like a man who stopped seeing victims years ago. Like he understands the sermon."

Kristen looked down at her menu, but didn't read it. Then: "You know if you go after him without proof, they'll eat you alive."

"I'm not going after him," Will said. "Not yet. But I'm watching. He's deep in this, whether he knows it or not."

She was quiet a long time.

Finally, she said, "Do you want me to request reassignment?"

Will looked at her, startled.

Kristen met his gaze, steady. "If this is going to get messy—"

"No," Will cut in. "I don't want you off the case. Hell, I need someone I trust on it."

A beat.

Kristen nodded, then smirked faintly. "Good. Because I wasn't going to let you hog the False Prophet without me anyway."

That made Will laugh, and the tension eased slightly. For a moment, the case slipped to the edges of the booth. The lights felt warmer. The world felt smaller.

Kristen leaned in again, eyes softer now. "For the record, I was hoping this was just dinner. No files. No trauma. Maybe some awkward flirting."

Will grinned. "There's still time."

"Don't make promises, Officer Anderson."

He raised his hands. "Wouldn't dare."

But underneath the banter, the shadows lingered. Rogers' words. Maggie's eyes. The Prophet's scripture.

Will no longer knew where the line between work and life was.

He only knew that whatever was coming next—it was already too close to stop.

## Misread

### Summit Falls PD – Task Force War Room

Three days later, the walls buzzed with quiet tension, stale coffee fumes thick in the air. Case files cluttered every surface. Four names now lived on the board. Three confirmed. One—until recently—anonymous.

Will sat forward in his chair, pen tapping his knee as Kristen flipped through a newly arrived file. Her brows were pulled tight, lips a hard line. She didn't look up when she spoke.

"Brookhaven Jane Doe has a name now. Avery Howell. Twenty-two. Originally from Illinois. Dropped out of Ravenwood University in her junior year. No record, no priors. But she had a brand."

She turned the page, laying down a faded autopsy photo. A burn mark, circular and angry, just above the navel.

Will leaned closer. "Same shape?"

Kristen nodded. "Same shape. Same placement. Same burn pattern—deliberate, controlled, inflicted while she was still alive."

Joe folded his arms. "What else do we know?"

Kristen flipped another page.

"She was found three months ago in Room 214 of the Crescent Palms Hotel. High-end boutique place—

Brookhaven's version of luxury. The room was pristine. No broken furniture, no signs of struggle. She was lying on the bed, nude, body carefully positioned. No visible bruises, no ligature marks. Nothing that screamed 'homicide.' Wrote the burn off as something accidental."

Will frowned. "Staged to look like an overdose?"

Kristen nodded again. "That's how they logged it. Body temp, lack of trauma, the setting—it all read accidental at first glance. Officers assumed she was a high-end escort who'd had a rough night with a client. ME suspected a possible opiate OD. But tox came back clean. No heroin. No fentanyl. No alcohol. No sedatives. Just caffeine, trace amounts of THC, and—"

She held up a page. "Nicotine. That's it."

Rogers let out a low breath. "So the body told a story the evidence didn't support."

"Exactly," Kristen said. "But there's more."

She flipped to the scene photos—grainy stills from the hotel staff's phone, taken before the official unit arrived.

Will's eyes locked on the image.

The bed was perfectly made beneath her. Avery lay across the white sheets, arms at her sides, legs straight, as if placed with care. A studded black leather collar ringed her throat. Not tight. Not cutting. Just there.

"She was wearing it when they found her," Kristen said. "They cataloged it as part of her... lifestyle. One of the reasons the scene was never pushed up the chain. The staff told officers she'd checked in alone and had been quiet. Cleaning crew thought she was asleep until she didn't move."

Joe's voice came low. "So they made assumptions."

"They always do," Kristen said. "Room contained BDSM gear—cuffs, straps, even a flogger—but nothing used. No prints on the restraints. They were *displayed*, not active. On a side table, neatly arranged."

Will's brows pulled together. "Staged like a prop set."

Kristen flipped to the last photo. A crumpled white card, half-stepped on, lying near the foot of the bed beside a pair of thigh-high boots. The words were faint—partially smudged, possibly trampled.

*The body is the altar. The obedient are sanctified in silence.*

Will stared at it. "That's new."

Kristen nodded. "Variant of the message. Still scripture-adjacent. Still matching pattern. But they missed it. Thought it was a client's kink note. The evidence technician logged it under 'miscellaneous clutter.' It was found days later in a secondary bag, marked for discard."

Rogers shook his head slowly. "Unbelievable, freaking amateur hour."

"They never ran it for prints. Never photographed the reverse side. We don't even know who handled it first—officer or hotel staff."

Joe's jaw worked. "So they wrote her off."

"Completely," Kristen said. "Until the ME flagged the burn. Even then, the connection was slow. Only when

Tammi Warner's case came through Oakhaven did someone at Brookhaven PD pull the Howell file back up."

Will's pen tapped against his boot. "You said she was a student. What happened?"

Kristen pulled a final sheet and slid it across the table.

"Avery Howell. third year, Ravenwood University. Studying marketing. GPA was solid. Then, out of nowhere, she drops out. No disciplinary action. No financial aid issue. Just walks."

Will read the summary. His gut twisted.

"She started a website," Kristen said. "Online persona: *HowellYouWantMe.* She made her own branding. Subscription paywall, tiered access. Photos, custom content, video calls. Then, quietly, she began meeting select clients in person. Invitation only. Vetted through the site's private backend. Payment in crypto. No trail. And she was making real money."

"How much?" Joe asked.

Kristen tapped the bottom of the page. "Quarter of a million last fiscal year. On track for double that when she died."

Silence settled over the room like dust.

"She didn't need school," Will murmured. "Didn't need anyone. She built something from nothing, and no one was looking for her when she vanished."

Rogers' voice came like gravel. "Until she showed up naked in a hotel room, wearing a collar and no pulse."

Kristen folded the file closed. "She wasn't seen as a victim. She was dismissed. And the man who put her there knew she would be."

Will stared at the board. At the card. At the empty eyes of a girl whose name had arrived too late.

"She wasn't just overlooked," he said. "She was planned. Picked because the world wouldn't look twice. And he made sure of that."

Kristen's tone was razor-sharp. "Which means this wasn't early. This wasn't sloppy. This was strategic."

Will's hand tightened around his pen.

The Prophet wasn't improvising anymore.

He was orchestrating.

"All right," Archer said. "Let's put this together."

He pointed to the first pin, holding a green laser pointer in his hand.

"Ivy Cole. Known as Cherry. Summit Falls. Staged in a motel. Burn mark. Sermon note."

The marker moved down.

"Tammi Warner. Twenty-one. Oakhaven. Nursing student, moonlighting with a hookup service. Branded while alive. Note written, stuck to the wall with her blood. Dumped at a truck stop."

The next pin.

"Maggie Truelove. Crown Motel survivor. First, to describe his sermon in detail. First to give us the cadence, the gloves, the voice. She lived."

Finally, Archer rapped the marker against the new name.

"Avery Howell. Brookhaven. Found nude on a boutique hotel bed. Branded while still alive. Wearing a studded collar. No signs of beating or restraint. The room was staged to suggest an overdose. Tox came back clean. Scene was botched—note cataloged as clutter, likely stepped on before collection. Three months later, ID finally confirms who she was. Online alias: *HowellYouWantMe.* Ran her own website. Explicit content, subscriber tiers, private meetups. More money than she'd ever make with a degree."

Kristen added, "Locals dismissed her. Assumed high-end escort OD'd on her client's watch. No one questioned it until the ME flagged the burn mark. By then, the evidence was degraded."

Joe muttered, "So she vanished into their filing cabinet until we shook it loose."

"Exactly," Kristen said.

Archer's jaw tightened. "And now we see the pattern." He drew a line across the board, stringing each name together.

"Different backgrounds. Different counties. However, every scene has three key elements: the brand, the staging, and the sermon. He's refining it. Less noise. Less trace. He's learning how to make his gospel invisible."

The room fell quiet again.

Will sat forward, pen pressed to paper, his voice barely above a whisper. "He's not just choosing victims anymore. He's curating them."

Rogers leaned back in his chair, arms crossed, eyes hooded. "Or he's proving a point. To himself. To us. Maybe both."

Archer didn't answer that. He capped the marker with a hard click.

"Four women. Three dead. One alive. From here on out, everything runs through this room. We don't get another cold case. Not again."

The board loomed heavy, names bleeding into red string.

- *Ivy Cole (Cherry)*
- *Tammi Warner (CandyCrush)*
- *Maggie Truelove (Tonya)*
- *Avery Howell (HowellYouWantMe)*

Four sermons.

The Prophet was still preaching.


**Two Weeks Later**

The board hadn't changed in fourteen days. Same four names. Same red string. The only thing new was the ring of coffee stains bleeding into the case files and the half-dead marker left uncapped on the table.

Bang on doors, watching video footage from local businesses, street light cams, interviewing witnesses, nothing new.

Kristen dropped another folder with a sharp slap. "Ravenwood professors. Roommates. Classmates. No one remembers Avery Howell doing anything but studying and leaving. Not one mention of strange dates or mystery cars."

Archer pinched the bridge of his nose. "What about the website clients?"

"Crypto payments, scrubbed through three different services. No trail," Kristen said. Her tone was flat, exhausted.

Joe leaned back in his chair, a toothpick rolling between his teeth. "Tammi's roommate clammed up again. Still swears she didn't know who Tammi was meeting that night. Either she's scared or she's playing dumb. My money's on both."

"And Maggie?" Archer asked.

Will answered that one, jaw tight. "Same as before. She's still in Indiana with her sister. Still refuses protective detail. Says she hasn't seen anything out of place. Every time I ask if she remembers something new, she shuts down."

Silence fell heavily over the room.

Rogers finally spoke, voice low and flat. "I told you. You're looking for a ghost. He doesn't exist until he wants to. And when he does, it's already too late."

Will shot him a look. "That's not an answer."

Rogers didn't flinch. "It's the only one that fits."

Archer broke the tension with a sharp tap of his marker against the board. "We're not done. Run me the rest."

Kristen flipped another page. "Tammi Warner's family? Still grieving. Parents think she was killed by some random john, not a serial offender. They don't want to believe their daughter was targeted because of her side work. They shut me down every time I push."

Will added, "Ivy Cole's mother won't even open the door anymore. Says she's given her statement twice. She won't say another word unless it's about burying her girl."

"Which leaves us with?" Archer asked.

The room stayed quiet.

Rogers stood, pacing toward the board. He tapped each photo with a finger. "Four women. Four sermons. We retraced every step. Talked to their families, their friends, their professors, their roommates. All we've got is silence." He turned, eyes dark. "Maybe that's the point. Maybe silence is his sermon."

Kristen bristled. "Or maybe you like the sound of him too much."

Rogers didn't answer.

Archer slammed the marker down on the table. "Enough. The Prophet doesn't get to bury us in paperwork and call it victory. We continue to press—cross-referencing motel registries. Pull every Ravenwood dropout in the last three years. I don't care if you have to knock on every door in Brookhaven—somebody saw him. Somebody heard him. And when they do, I want us there first."

Chairs scraped. Files shuffled. But the energy was low, the kind of tired that seeps into bone.

Will stayed seated, staring at Avery's photo. Her eyes bright in an old headshot, lips painted into a smile meant for her audience. She'd built a world, and it had been erased in a single night.

He whispered it under his breath, too low for anyone else to hear.

"He's always two steps ahead."

## Political

### District Attorney's Office – Summit Falls

That afternoon, the DA's corner office overlooked the courthouse steps, glass windows streaked with the gray wash of early spring rain. Inside, file towers leaned against the walls like tired soldiers.

Kristen sat across from DA Harold Lanning, legal pad balanced on her knee. He was older, hair thinning, tie loosened, his hands folded on the desk with the patience of a man who'd heard every plea twice already.

Kristen leaned forward. "I want clearance to travel to Indiana. Maggie Truelove is with her sister in Muncie. She's the only surviving witness we have. We were never able to obtain a full, sworn, written statement, and she's the only one who has heard his voice. She described his cadence, his gloves, his words. That's evidence we can't leave half-finished."

Lanning sighed, rubbing at his temple. "Kristen—"

"No," she cut in. "Hear me out. She was traumatized. I get it. But she's stable now. And she trusts Will Anderson. If I bring him, we can get the full picture. This man's ritual, his speech, every phrase she remembers—it could be the thread that ties these women together in court. Right now we're chasing shadows."

"Kristen—"

She pushed harder. "She's crucial. You know it. Without her, we've got no face, no voice. Just corpses and scripture."

The DA leaned back in his chair, eyes heavy. "You're not wrong."

"Then—"

"But," he said firmly, cutting her off, "it's not happening."

Kristen froze. "Excuse me?"

Lanning steepled his fingers. "Budget's already stretched thin. We've got capital trials coming up. Homicide's screaming for funds. And I've got three different councilmen asking why we're pouring hours into prostitutes when the city's backlog is still stacked with gang cases. You want me to authorize two prosecutors and a police officer to cross state lines on the county's dime? Not a chance."

Her jaw clenched. "So politics over justice. That's the game."

"Careful," he warned, voice low.

Kristen leaned forward anyway. "She survived. That means she matters more than anyone. If this goes to trial and we don't have her voice on record, every defense attorney in the state is going to gut us alive."

Lanning's expression softened for a fleeting second, then hardened again. "I agree with you. But my answer's the same. Drop it. Focus on what you can control."

Kristen's throat tightened. She nodded once, curtly, then rose to her feet. "Understood."

She left the office with her pad clutched tight enough to crease the cardboard.

**Task Force War Room – Later That Day**

The mood was the same as it had been for days: tired, restless, quiet. Will was flipping through Avery Howell's file again when Kristen walked in, dropped her pad on the table, and said flatly, "I asked the DA for clearance to go to Indiana. Talk to Maggie face to face."

Joe looked up from his cigarette. "And?"

Kristen's laugh was sharp, humorless. "Shot down. Budget. Politics. Pick your excuse. Doesn't matter. The one woman who can describe this bastard in detail, and we're leaving her to rot because the city doesn't want headlines about taxpayer dollars chasing hooker cases across state lines."

Will's pen froze above his notebook. "She's not a hooker. She's a victim."

Kristen met his eyes. "Try telling that to the DA."

Silence fell across the table.

Finally, Archer spoke. "We move forward. We've got four names on the board. We work with what we've got."

Kristen sank into her chair, bitter heat still in her chest. She didn't say what she was thinking. That Maggie Truelove might be the difference between catching the Prophet and watching another girl get branded.

Will glanced at her from across the table. He could see it in her eyes—the wheels hadn't stopped turning.

If the DA wouldn't authorize the trip, Kristen was already considering how to do it anyway.

### Summit Falls PD – Parking Garage – Late Afternoon

The garage was half-empty, concrete echoing with the drip of rainwater through rusted pipes. Will was leaning against his cruiser, jacket collar up, when Kristen's heels clicked across the floor. She stopped a few feet away, arms crossed, her breath showing white in the cold.

"I should've expected it," she said. "The DA doesn't stick his neck out for cases like this."

Will studied her quietly. "You knew he'd say no."

"I hoped he wouldn't." She let out a sharp breath, shaking her head. "Maggie is the only one who heard his sermon. The cadence, the words, the way he twisted them. That's not just trauma—it's evidence. And we're leaving it half-buried because the county wants to save face."

Will straightened, stepping closer. "What are you really saying, Kristen?"

Her eyes lifted to his, steady but burning. "I'm saying I don't care what the DA thinks. I'm saying Maggie matters more than their budget meetings. And I'm saying if someone doesn't go to her, we're going to lose the only living piece of this case."

Silence hung. The hum of the sodium lights above them filled the space.

"You'd go without clearance," Will said finally.

Kristen didn't flinch. "Would you?"

Will looked away, jaw tight. He thought of Maggie curled up on that motel bed, whispering Don't call me Tonya anymore. He thought of the burn mark still raw on her stomach. He thought of her tears when she begged him to promise.

"Yes," he said. Quiet. Absolute. "I would."

Kristen's shoulders eased, just a fraction. She stepped closer, her voice dropping low. "Then maybe we don't wait for permission. Maybe we should stop asking and do the job."

"You know they always say, It's easier to ask for forgiveness than permission," Will interjected.

Their eyes met, the air thick with what wasn't being said. Not just about Maggie. Not just about the Prophet. About trust. About lines that blurred every time they stood too close.

Will nodded once. "If we go, we do it clean. Quiet. No paper trail."

Kristen gave a faint smile that didn't reach her eyes. "Guess it's a good thing I've got practice bending rules."

She turned toward her car, heels echoing sharply against the concrete. Before she slid inside, she looked back at him over her shoulder.

"Think about it, Will. Because the longer we sit here spinning our wheels, the closer he is to writing his next sermon."

Then she was gone, taillights bleeding red across the wet floor.

Will stayed rooted, the promise to Maggie still heavy in his chest.

He already knew his answer.

## Star

Two days later, at Summit Falls Roadside Inn, the call came in at 4:32 p.m.

The maid's scream still lingered in the hallway when Will and Joe ducked under the tape. Two uniforms ushered her away, leaving silence in their wake.

Inside, Room 12 was colder than it should've been, curtains pulled tight, neon bleeding red through the gaps. The air carried the scent of copper and cheap perfume, clinging heavily to the walls.

The woman was lying on the bed.

Nude. Early twenties. Face beaten until it was nearly unrecognizable, one eye swollen shut, lips split. Rope, bright red, deliberate, bound her wrists to her ankles behind her back, forcing her body into a grotesque arc. The brand was there, seared into her stomach, skin blistered around the angry circle.

Cuts traced parallel across her breasts and thighs, shallow, deliberate, like punctuation. Between her legs, the violence was unmistakable. Not just rape. Display. Humiliation written across flesh.

Homicide detectives Lowe and Harris lingered near the dresser, both pale but trying not to show it. Lowe muttered, "Sick bastard's putting on a show."

Will crouched near the bed, pen scratching across his notebook. His voice came low. "No. He's writing another sermon."

Joe's gaze swept the room, landing on the card propped against the lamp. He slipped it into an evidence sleeve before reading it aloud:

*The flesh is nothing until it is torn.*
*The blood is nothing until it stains.*
*The soul is nothing until I mark it mine.*
*In silence, she can be loved.*

"Damn," Harris muttered, shaking his head.

But Will was already staring at the mirror.

The victim's lipstick had been dragged across the glass in jagged, frantic letters, the tube left twisted on the counter.

**STOP YOUR HUNT.**
**THE RIGHTEOUS MAN DOES HIS WORK.**
**TO INTERFERE IS SIN.**

The words glared back at them, dripping red in the dim light.

Lowe let out a sharp exhale. "So now he's preaching to us. Hell of an escalation."

Joe glanced at Will. "What do you see?"

Will's jaw tightened. His pen pressed harder into the page until the ink blotted. "I see a man who thinks this is a war. And he just made it personal."

**Summit Falls PD – Records Division**
**7:19 p.m.**

The fluorescents buzzed overhead, their hum matching the churn of the old database terminal. Will sat forward, eyes burning as he typed, Joe leaning over his shoulder with a Styrofoam cup gone cold in his hand.

"Try catalog search," Joe said. "Tattoo index."

Will logged in, keyed in search *parameters: butterfly, crescent, moon, star.*

Clicked the search box.

The screen flickered, loading... then stopped on a result.

First, the standard booking photo: a young Latina, early twenties, chin lifted with weary defiance. Eyes rimmed dark, hair pulled back.

Then the secondary file: a close-up photograph cataloged at intake. The ink clear as day—crescent moon, star cluster, butterfly perched on the curve. Below it, the description field:

Tattoo, left side, behind the ear. "Star cluster w/ crescent moon + butterfly."

Will exhaled, tension leaving in a sharp hiss. "That's it."

Joe squinted at the file header. "Name?"

"Lena Morales. Twenty-three. Street name Star." Will clicked through, scanning. "Two prior arrests—solicitation and possession. Last booked eighteen months ago."

The printer spat out both images: her face and the tattoo detail. Will pulled them free, the paper still warm.

"Victim confirmed," he said, voice flat. "Lena Morales. Alias Star."

Joe stared at the tattoo photo for a long beat before tucking it into the file. "Pin her up."

Minutes later, in the war room, the board shifted.

Ivy Cole.

Tammi Warner.

Maggie Truelove.

Avery Howell.

Now, Lena Morales.

Another string. Another nail in the Prophet's sermon.

## Summit Falls PD – Task Force War Room
## 9:04 P.M.

The board glowed under tired fluorescents. Five names now, pinned in a row, red string cutting between them like scars.

*Ivy Cole.*

*Tammi Warner.*

*Maggie Truelove.*

*Avery Howell.*

*Lena Morales.*

Her booking photo—flat, defiant eyes—hung beside the close-up of the tattoo, the crescent moon and butterfly frozen in ink.

Captain Archer stood at the head of the table, arms braced against the edge. "This isn't escalation. This is a declaration. The branding, the staging, the mirror message? He's not whispering anymore. He's shouting. And he's daring us to shut him up."

Joe tapped the card evidence sleeve with his pen. "Wants us to know it's personal. He's dragging us into his sermon."

Kristen leaned forward, voice taut. "Then we need Maggie more than ever. She's the only one who heard him. The only one who can tell us how he speaks, how he moves, what he sounds like when he breathes down someone's neck. That's leverage. That's courtroom gold."

Rogers gave her a sideways look. "Or it's another dead end. The girl is already broken. Push too hard, you'll lose what little she's holding on to."

Will's jaw tightened. "She's stronger than you think."

The room simmered in silence until Archer's desk phone rang, sharp and jarring. He snatched it up.

"Archer."

A pause. His face shifted, brows furrowed. "Yes, sir. Understood." Another pause. "I'll make it happen."

He hung up, turning back to the room.

"That was the DA's office—change of orders. The word's out about the lipstick message. Media's circling. They want a clean survivor statement on record before the press makes her a ghost."

Kristen straightened, eyes narrowing. "Meaning?"

"Meaning," Archer said, "they want Maggie re-interviewed. Formal. Full transcript. And they want one of ours in the room when it happens."

Joe leaned back, smirking. "Let me guess who they asked for."

Archer's gaze landed on Will. "Anderson. You'll accompany Kristen and another ADA to Indiana. Tomorrow morning. They are coordinating with local agencies as we speak."

Will's pen froze above his notebook. Kristen shot him a glance, something unreadable flickering in her eyes—part relief, part warning.

Rogers barked a humorless laugh. "So two weeks ago, she didn't matter. Now she's their golden ticket."

Archer didn't flinch. "Doesn't matter why. Orders stand. Pack your files, Will. Wheels up at nine."

The board loomed behind them, five names, five sermons.

And one survivor is waiting in Indiana.

A few moments later, the room was still buzzing after Archer hung up. Files shuffled, pens scratched, Lowe and Harris muttered at the far end. The board loomed over them all—Ivy, Tammi, Maggie, Avery, and Lena—five women strung together by a red thread.

Kristen's phone buzzed on the table. She glanced at the screen, then stepped toward the corner. "It's the DA's office," she murmured.

She answered low, half-turned from the others. "Kristen Dalton."

A pause. Her face didn't move, but her eyes sharpened.

"When? ... Why now? We've been asking for weeks."

Another pause.

"Understood. Yes. We'll leave tomorrow."

She hung up slowly, sliding the phone into her jacket pocket.

Will was already watching her. "What changed?"

Kristen gave a bitter little smile. "The Prophet scrawled on a mirror. That's what changed. It's not about Maggie—it's about headlines. They don't want the press saying the DA ignored the only survivor while women keep turning up dead."

Will's jaw flexed. "So Maggie's just damage control."

Kristen nodded once. "And if she can't hold it together for them? They'll bury her again. Pretend she doesn't exist." She hesitated, lowering her voice. "Part of me wonders if we're doing her a favor... or if we're handing her over for slaughter."

Will leaned closer, his voice steady. "We'll protect her. Whatever the DA's angle, Maggie's ours. We don't let them use her and toss her aside."

For a moment, Kristen's eyes softened. Then she exhaled, straightened, and the moment was gone. "Flight's at nine. Pack light."

## Indiana

### Summit Falls Regional Airport – 7:41 a.m.

The terminal was half-awake, a wash of humming fluorescents and the faint sting of burned coffee drifting from a kiosk that hadn't seen fresh pastry in hours. Travelers shuffled toward security, scarves and jackets pulled tight against the stubborn spring chill leaking through the glass doors.

Will stood by the gate, duffel strap across his chest, scanning out of habit. Kristen Dalton leaned against a row of plastic chairs, hair tied back, coat buttoned high, her gaze fixed on the tarmac where a commuter jet rattled in the wind.

Her phone buzzed. She answered, listened a beat, and her posture went rigid.

"What?" Will asked as soon as she ended the call.

"Shelby's out," Kristen said flatly. "Other ADA on this trip. Claimed she came down with a stomach bug this morning."

Will raised a brow. "That's convenient."

Kristen's mouth twisted into a humorless smile. "Convenient, or political. Either way, she's not getting on this plane."

"So it's just us."

165

"Just us," she echoed. Her tone was clipped, but something softer flickered behind it—relief, maybe. Maggie wouldn't be sitting across from a panel of strangers. She'd have Will, and Kristen, and no one else.

The gate attendant called boarding. They walked the narrow ramp side by side, cold air pressing in the farther they went. Outside, the silver fuselage crouched on the wet tarmac, propellers ticking as they spun up.

Kristen tugged her coat tighter, her voice low. "Less oversight means less cover if this goes sideways."

Will adjusted his grip on the duffel. "Or it means she actually talks to us."

Their eyes met briefly before she climbed the metal steps into the belly of the plane.

Will paused once, scanning the gray horizon as the rain started again, thin needles against the glass. Then he followed her inside.

The door shut behind them with a heavy thud.

Indiana waited.

Just after takeoff, the plane rattled like it had been held together with duct tape and prayer. Thin sunlight cut through the scratched window beside Will, catching dust motes in the air. Below, endless patches of farmland stretched flat, stitched together like a quilt under the gray sky.

Kristen had the aisle seat, legal pad balanced on her lap. She'd been scribbling bullet points since takeoff—

questions, details from the case board, things Maggie might have left unsaid. But the ink had slowed, and now she just stared at the page, her pen resting idle.

"You're gonna burn yourself out before we even land," Will murmured.

Kristen gave a tired laugh. "Says the guy who's been running on fumes since this started."

He shrugged, shifting against the cramped seat. "I'll nap."

"You? Sleep on this death trap?" She tilted her head toward the shuddering ceiling panel.

"Afghanistan taught me to sleep anywhere," he said. "Even when the roof's rattling over your head."

She studied him for a beat, then closed her pad with a sigh. "Sometimes I wonder if that's what makes you so good at this. You don't flinch where the rest of us stall out."

Will didn't answer right away. His eyes stayed on the fading horizon. "Doesn't feel like a gift. Feels like scars I never got stitched."

The silence that followed wasn't heavy—it was tired, but shared. Kristen leaned back, letting her shoulders sink against the thin seat cushion. After a long moment, she shifted, resting her head lightly against his shoulder.

Will froze at first, unsure if it was accidental, but her voice came low, certain. "Just for a minute. Wake me before we land."

He let out a slow breath, relaxing into the seat. "Yeah. I got you."

Her breathing steadied, softening until it matched the hum of the engines. Will stared out at the flat gray sky, notebook clutched loosely in his hand, the weight of Maggie's words and the Prophet's sermons still pressing down.

But for the first time in weeks, he didn't feel alone in the fight.

### Muncie Regional Airport – 11:32 a.m.

The commuter jet touched down with a squeal of tires and a lurch that jolted both Kristen and Will awake. Outside the scratched glass, the Indiana sky was pale and washed-out, the land mostly flat as far as the eye could see.

They grabbed their bags, stepped into the chill air, and crossed the tarmac to a waiting rental car. The drive from the airport was quiet—two-lane roads cutting through fields gone fallow, barns sagging under the weight of years. Will handled the wheel. Kristen watched the horizon, pen tapping absently against her notepad.

Neither said much. The silence felt like the calm before impact.

### Maggie's Sister's House – 12:47 p.m.

The little ranch house sat at the end of a cracked driveway, shutters peeling, wind chimes clinking against the front porch rail. A weather-beaten Chevy pickup sat under the bare maple tree out front.

Jill Moore, Maggie's older sister, stood in the doorway as they walked up the path. She was tall, plain-featured, her hair tied back in a severe bun. Her arms folded tight across her chest. She knew they were coming, but her eyes made it clear she disapproved.

"She's been better," Jill said flatly as Will and Kristen approached. "Don't stay long. She's just starting to settle."

Before Will could answer, movement behind her caught his eye. Maggie pushed past, thin but fierce, her hoodie sleeves swallowed over her hands. The moment she saw Will, her breath hitched.

Then she was moving out the doorway, across the porch, into his arms.

Her sobs came hard, tearing, raw. She clutched him like a lifeline, her face buried against his chest. Will froze for half a beat, then wrapped his arms around her, steady and solid.

"I didn't think you'd actually come," she whispered through broken breaths.

"We promised," Will said softly.

Maggie pulled back just enough to look up at him, tears streaking her face. Her eyes flicked to Kristen, then back to Will. "I need to talk. I changed my mind. I saw the news about what he did in South Carolina. I can't sit here and hide while he's still out there. I need to get it all out."

Her voice trembled, but her jaw set. She tugged at the hem of her hoodie, yanking it up.

The angry circle scar burned red against her pale skin, still healing, still raw.

Her voice cracked, but the steel underneath was undeniable. "I want to help you keep your promise. I want you to catch the bastard who did this to me."

Will's throat tightened. He nodded once, steady. "Then we'll listen. Every word."

Kristen stepped closer, her hand brushing Maggie's arm lightly, support without crowding. "Let's go inside. Start from the beginning. No rush, no pressure. Just us."

Jill shifted uncomfortably in the doorway, her disapproval warring with something softer. Finally, she stepped aside.

The three of them crossed the threshold together, Maggie between them, still clutching her hoodie as if it could shield her—but her eyes burning with the need to finally be heard.

### Maggie's Sister's House – 1:14 p.m.

The living room was small but neat, the kind of space that felt more like Jill's order than Maggie's presence. A crocheted blanket folded sharp across the couch back. Family photos lined the shelves—graduations, school plays, none of them recent.

Maggie sat forward on the edge of the couch, hoodie sleeves twisted in her fists. Will took the armchair across from her, notebook balanced on his knee but unopened. He laid a digital recorder on the table and hit record.

Kristen sat close, not crowding, her legal pad on the coffee table between them. Jill hovered near the kitchen, arms folded, pretending to fuss with a glass of water while keeping one ear turned.

For a long moment, nobody spoke. Maggie's breath came shallow, her eyes fixed on her hands. Then she lifted her chin, voice raw but clear.

"You changed my life." Her gaze flicked between Will and Kristen. "Both of you. You don't even know it."

Will's jaw tightened. "Maggie—"

"No. Let me say this." She swallowed hard, tears burning at the corners of her eyes. "Before that night, I'd already decided how I was gonna go out. I thought the streets would kill me. Or the drugs. Or some john who didn't care if I lived through it. And part of me was okay with that. Like it was all I was worth."

Her voice cracked, but she pressed on. "But you... You stayed. You believed me when no one else would have. And you—" she turned to Kristen, "—you looked at me like I wasn't trash. Like I still mattered. You might've actually saved me from the road I was set on. You two may have saved my life."

Silence stretched, heavy and fragile. Kristen blinked hard, her throat working before she found words. "You did that yourself, Maggie. You survived."

171

Maggie let out a bitter, brittle laugh. "Survived. Yeah. That's what I call it." She yanked her hoodie up, exposing the angry ring of scar tissue seared into her stomach — red and raw against skin gone almost translucent. "But it doesn't heal. Not really. It burns every time I look in the mirror, like he's still laughing."

Her voice trembled, but she didn't stop. "I've got all the other scars from him. I see him in my sleep. I can smell him. Feel him. Hear him. That laugh..." She shuddered. "It's like he's still here."

Her hands trembled as she let the fabric fall back into place. "And the worst part? I keep remembering things. New pieces. Like my mind's been keeping them locked up until now."

Will leaned forward, voice low but steady, anchoring her with his gaze. "He's not here anymore, Maggie. He can't touch you now. What he did—what he tried to bury—you're stronger for dragging it into the light. So tell us what you remember."

Her eyes flicked past him, unfocused, dredging from somewhere deep. "His smell—" she faltered, pressing her knuckles to her mouth. "Not cigars. Not normal smoke. Something cheaper. Sharper. I can't get it out of my nose."

She rubbed her arms like she could still feel it clinging to her. "His hands were rough. Not just calluses—like they'd worked rope. Or leather. And his face..." She shivered. "He had this half-shaved look like he started to shave and didn't finish. Bristles on one side. Smooth on the other. I'll never forget how that felt when he leaned close."

Will's pen hovered, the words carving deep into the page.

"And his eyes," Maggie whispered. "Dark. Brown. Almost black. And when he looked at me—" She broke, tears spilling fast now. "When he looked at me, I knew I was already gone."

Kristen reached across the coffee table, covering Maggie's hand with hers. "But you weren't."

Maggie squeezed back like a drowning woman clutching a rope. "No. Because something else happened. Something I didn't tell you before."

Both Will and Kristen froze.

Maggie's voice dropped, the tremor in it sharp enough to cut. "When we were in the truck... before he attacked me inside... he made a phone call. I thought it was nothing at the time. Just noise. But now, now I think he was talking to someone. Another man."

She glanced between them, eyes hollow, haunted. "He told him he was *busy,* that he'd call when he was done with his *work.*" She swallowed, the word hanging heavy in the air. "The way he said *work*... it came back to me."

Her voice cracked as she finished. "I think I was the work. And I think that other guy knew exactly what he meant."

The air in the room shifted—thicker, colder.

Will's chest tightened, pen digging into the paper. "You're saying he has a partner."

Maggie nodded, trembling. "I don't know how else to explain it. But it wasn't random. It was like... like there was someone else waiting on the other end of that call. Someone who understood."

Kristen's knuckles whitened against the pad of her legal pad. "That changes everything."

Will closed his notebook carefully, the weight of her words pressing down like stone. He looked Maggie dead in the eyes.

"You did the right thing telling us. You're not alone in this anymore."

Maggie's shoulders sagged, the last of her strength spilling out in sobs. Kristen moved to her side, sliding onto the couch and wrapping an arm around her. Maggie leaned into her, shaking.

Will sat back in the armchair, the notebook heavy in his lap. His mind was already moving, threads connecting, the circle widening.

The False Prophet wasn't preaching alone. Which meant what they'd seen so far wasn't the message — it was only the introduction.

The interview wound down slowly, the weight of Maggie's words still thick in the air. Kristen's notes lay scattered across the coffee table, pages filled with jagged handwriting. Will closed his notebook, but his pen stayed clipped in the spiral like he wasn't ready to let it rest.

Maggie leaned back into the couch, sleeves swallowed over her hands again. She wiped her cheeks, then looked between them with something sharper than tears in her eyes. A glimmer.

"You two..." she said softly, a crooked smile tugging at her lips. "I saw it the night you found me. Back in that motel room. The way you looked at each other."

Kristen blinked, caught off guard. "Maggie—"

"No, listen." Maggie sat up a little straighter, her grin widening through the tears. "I told you then, didn't I? Not to let him get away? Guess I was right."

Will shifted uncomfortably in his chair, rubbing the back of his neck. "We're here for the case, Maggie. Not—"

"—Oh, don't give me that cop voice," she cut in, laughing through her hoarse rasp. "You can stare down killers but blush like a schoolboy when someone notices your girl? Good for you, Will. Good for *both* of you."

Kristen's cheeks warmed, but the smile she tried to hide gave her away.

When it was time to leave, Maggie stood with them at the door. She hesitated only a second before stepping forward and wrapping her arms around Will again, holding him tight. Her voice muffled against his chest.

"I'll never forget you," she whispered. "You gave me my life back."

Will hugged her back, steady, careful of her still-healing scar. "Just don't let anyone take it from you again."

She pulled back, eyes wet but mischievous now. "And hey, if you and Kristen don't work out, I can always move back down to South Carolina. I'll save you a seat."

Kristen choked on a laugh as Will's ears turned red. Maggie pivoted, wrapping Kristen in a quick hug, her voice playful.

"I'm just messing with you. He's your knight, and I hope you two never part. Hang on to this one, rare breed. You deserve some happiness after all this hell."

Kristen squeezed her hand, voice thick. "So do you, Maggie."

Jill lingered in the doorway, arms still folded, but her eyes had softened. She watched as her sister's laughter—fragile but real—filled the threshold for the first time in months.

As Will and Kristen stepped back into the Indiana afternoon, Maggie leaned against the doorframe, scar hidden beneath her hoodie again, but strength written plain in her smile.

For the first time, she looked less like a victim. And more like a survivor.

### Muncie – 6:12 p.m.

The sun was setting as Will guided the rental into the parking lot of a business-class hotel, the kind with brick siding, a uniform lobby, and a glowing neon vacancy sign that buzzed softly in the dusk.

Before they went inside, Will pulled out his phone and stepped away from the car. He dialed Joe.

The old detective picked up on the second ring. "Anderson."

"It's me." Will's voice was low, steady. "We just left Maggie's."

Joe grunted. "How'd she hold up?"

"She's stronger than I expected. Gave us more than we had before." He glanced toward Kristen, waiting by the trunk. "Joe... she remembered things. His smell—strange cigarettes. Half-shaved face. Rough hands, like rope or leather work. Dark brown eyes."

"Good," Joe said. "Details help."

Will swallowed. "That's not all. She said he made a phone call while she was in the truck. Talked to another man. Told him he was busy with his 'work.'"

The line went quiet. Then Joe's voice came sharp. "Work. Jesus. You think he meant her?"

"She does. And she thinks the other guy knew exactly what he meant."

A long pause. Then Joe exhaled, rough as gravel. "Listen, Will... keep that part to yourself for now. It could be something, or it could be her fear twisting the memory. If we throw it to the room and it doesn't hold, they'll tear her apart—and you with her."

Will's jaw tightened. "So we sit on it."

"For now," Joe said. "Bring me everything else. We'll regroup at the board."

"Copy," Will said.

He hung up, slipped the phone back in his pocket, and joined Kristen inside.

### Hotel Lobby – 6:31 p.m.

The place was warm and sterile, with fake ferns and the smell of lemon cleaner. The clerk slid key cards across the desk, smiling with professional detachment.

"Two queens, third floor. Rooms 312 and 314," she said.

Kristen thanked her and scooped up the cards. Once they were in the elevator, she shot Will a sidelong glance.

"Guess Maggie wasn't wrong about you having options," she said, lips quirking.

Will blinked. "Options?"

"You know—if we don't work out, you've always got a backup plan in Indiana." Her grin widened as the elevator dinged.

He groaned, rubbing the back of his neck. "She's never gonna let me live that down, is she?"

"Not if I have anything to do with it," Kristen teased, bumping his shoulder as they stepped into the hall.

They reached their doors. Will slid his key into 312, Kristen into 314. But when the locks clicked, they only carried their bags into one room.

Will dropped his duffel by the dresser, Kristen kicked off her heels, and the weight of the day finally seemed to lift.

"Just so you know," Will said, pulling off his jacket, "if anyone asks, we definitely used both rooms."

Kristen smirked, curling onto the edge of the bed. "Oh, absolutely. Full use of both. We're very responsible professionals."

Their laughter filled the small space, easing the shadows that had followed them all day.

### Next Morning – 7:18 a.m.

Will woke to the pale light seeping through the hotel curtains, thin and gray against the carpet. For a rare moment, the world was still. Kristen lay beside him, hair spilling across the pillow, her breathing slow and steady. No Prophet. No task force. No murder boards or evidence bags. Just warmth, just breath, just her.

He let himself watch her for a moment longer before easing out of bed. By the time she stirred, he'd already showered, the coffee pot gurgling in the corner.

By eight, they were checked out, travel mugs in hand, their bags stowed in the trunk of the rental. The morning air had a bite to it, dew still clinging to the edges of the windshield.

Will slid behind the wheel, turning the key until the engine coughed to life. He glanced sideways at Kristen.

She was already watching him, her cup cradled in both hands.

"Back to South Carolina," he said, voice even.

Kristen sipped her coffee, her eyes sharp but tired. "Back to the hunt."

Will turned onto the main road. The horizon stretched flat and endless before them—miles of asphalt between them and the plane unspooling like a sermon waiting to be delivered.

Neither spoke. The silence wasn't heavy, just steady, carrying them toward whatever came next.

### Over Ohio – 11:02 a.m.

The commuter plane shuddered hard enough to rattle the ice in plastic cups, and Will's coffee nearly sloshed over the rim. He steadied it, jaw tightening as the turbulence passed. Across the narrow row, Kristen sat stiff-backed, pen idle above her legal pad. The page was mainly blank—just a handful of words scribbled, circled, then abandoned.

Will tilted his head toward her. "You've been quiet."

Kristen didn't answer right away. Her eyes lingered on the paper like she was staring straight through it. Finally, she said, "I've been thinking about Maggie's memory. The phone call."

Will turned slightly in his seat, studying her profile in the dim cabin light. Her jaw was set, her lips pressed thin. "You don't think it's real?"

Her head lifted, sharp now, eyes meeting his. "No—I think it's real. Too real. But not the way it sounds." She lowered her voice, her words almost lost under the hum of the engines. "The Prophet doesn't share his sermons. Not with another man in the room. But a call? That feels different."

Will's brow furrowed. "Different how?"

Kristen leaned back, her gaze flicking to the scratched oval window, farmland rolling like a patchwork quilt below. "I think he was checking in. Reporting. Like someone already knew what he was about to do, and he wanted them to hear it. To confirm it."

A knot twisted in Will's gut. He shifted in his seat, lowering his voice. "An accomplice. Rogers said something about it being two before we connected the assaults as ritual. Trying to dismiss it as two psychos with the same sick habits?"

"Not with the acts," Kristen said firmly, shaking her head. "That's all him. But in knowledge? Absolutely. Someone listening. Approving. Maybe even pushing. That's worse, Will. Because then he's not just killing for himself—he's performing for an audience."

Will stared at her, unsettled by the certainty in her tone. He turned toward the window, his reflection caught in the scratched Plexiglas. The farmland slid past in endless green and brown squares. "If you're right, then someone out there knew about Maggie before we ever did. Knew while it was happening."

Kristen's voice softened, but the steel remained. "Exactly. And if we bring it up now? Half the task force will call it paranoia. They'll say trauma distorted Maggie's memory, or that we're chasing shadows."

Will gave a slight nod, the echo of Joe's voice heavy in his head: *keep that part to yourself for now.*

Kristen lowered her voice. "Better to keep it between us until we have proof. It changes nothing either way."

For a long beat, the only sound was the drone of the engines.

Will studied her, the way she didn't flinch under the weight of her own words. He felt the vow form in his chest before it ever left his mouth. "Between us."

Kristen held his gaze, then gave the faintest nod. Her shoulders relaxed a fraction, but her fingers never loosened around the pen.

The plane jolted again, making the overhead bins creak. Neither of them moved.

Will's eyes returned to the farmland below. Kristen closed her pad and let it rest in her lap.

Both of them knew the war room would only hear half the truth.

The other half—the darker half—would stay locked between them, for now.

**Summit Falls PD – Task Force War Room**
**Mid Afternoon**

The plane ride was unremarkable. Walking into the war room, it smelled of burned coffee and dry-erase fumes, with the hum of old fluorescent lights filling the silence. The board dominated the far wall, five names strung together with red thread, photographs staring out with flat, frozen eyes.

Will and Kristen stepped in, travel-weary, files clutched under their arms. Archer looked up from the head of the table, arms braced wide. Joe leaned back in his chair, toothpick rolling slowly across his teeth. Rogers sat hunched in the corner, arms folded, watching with that sharp, unreadable stare.

"Well?" Archer asked. "How'd it go with Maggie?"

Kristen laid her pad on the table, then set down a flash drive and a legal-sized envelope. "We took a full sworn statement. Written and recorded. Audio files on here, hard copies inside."

Joe nodded once, confirming. "They called me before they left Indiana. Said she gave more than she ever has."

Will opened his notebook, flipping to fresh pages. "She did. Confirmed details we had before—the cadence, the gloves, the sermon-like phrasing. Added more this time: strange-smelling cigarettes, rough hands like rope or leather work, half-shaved face, dark brown eyes. All of it is consistent with a man who wants to be remembered."

Joe's brow furrowed. "And she gave it willingly?"

Kristen nodded. "She wanted to. She's stronger than people give her credit for."

Will didn't add the rest. Not yet. The phone call. The second voice. That stayed locked between him and Kristen.

Archer leaned forward, marker tapping against the table. "That's more than we had before. We'll get it logged, circulated. Maybe someone will bite on the cigarettes or the grooming detail. Good work."

Kristen's gaze flicked toward Will for a heartbeat—silent confirmation that their private vow held. The war room would hear the safe version. Not the whole truth.

Across the table, Rogers finally spoke. "Doesn't change anything. You can dress him up with smells and stubble, but at the end of the day, he's still a ghost. And ghosts don't leave trails."

Will's jaw tightened. "Maybe not. But Maggie's still breathing because he slipped once. If he did it once, he'll do it again. We just need to catch it."

Rogers leaned back, expression flat. "And pray it's not too late by the time he does."

Archer cut the tension with a sharp clap of the marker. "Enough. File your notes. We've got five names on the board, and I'm not adding a sixth."

Silence fell again, heavy, broken only by the rattle of the air vent.

Will glanced at Kristen, her face unreadable as she scribbled on her pad. He wondered if she was replaying Maggie's words the way he was—the call, the other man, the idea of someone listening in the dark.

Neither of them said it out loud. Not yet.
The war room would only hear half the truth.

## Lamb

**Two Days Later, 5:42 p.m.**

The parking lot reeked of old fry grease and diesel, the flickering neon VACANCY sign buzzing like a fly trapped in glass. Squad cars boxed in the entrance, their strobes splashing the stucco walls with red and blue — a failing heartbeat pulsing against a motel that had seen too many of these nights.

Will ducked under the tape first, Joe right behind him. Lowe and Harris stood stiff near the dresser, pale but posturing, notebooks in their hands that hadn't been opened. They kept their eyes on the floor more than the bed. Rogers lingered in the corner, arms folded, his expression shadowed, eyes scanning the scene with the stillness of a man cataloging instead of recoiling.

The air inside was colder than it should have been. The curtains were clamped shut against daylight, incense sticks burned to ash in a chipped glass on the nightstand. The cloying sweetness fought with copper, but only managed to make the stench worse, as if the Prophet wanted them to choke on both.

The girl was on the bed.

Nude. Early twenties. Her skin looked waxy under the humming fluorescents, as if it had already begun surrendering to the room. Her arms were bent cruelly behind her back, wrists cuffed to her ankles, contorting her body into a grotesque kneel. The forced arch of her spine made her look displayed rather than discarded — a mannequin for a sermon no one wanted to hear.

Her lips were split wide, underwear jammed between her teeth, blood dried in a black crust that traced her chin and throat.

Her face was pulp — nose broken flat, cheekbone collapsed, one eye swollen shut while the other stared glassy and unfocused at the ceiling. A tuft of her dark hair was matted with blood, sticking to the headboard like paint smeared by a cruel hand.

Across her stomach, the brand blistered raw, the flesh puckered and bubbled around the burned circle. It gleamed under the light, a wound carved to outlast her.

Thin cuts striped her thighs and breasts. Deliberate. Equidistant. Shallow enough not to kill, but deep enough to bleed. Not frenzied. Not rage. Punctuation marks. A signature flourish.

The sheets beneath her were soaked through, the blood already drying to a sticky brown. Her knees dug into the mattress hard enough to leave indents, as though he'd forced her into the pose and then stepped back to admire it.

Will's gut knotted, bile threatening to rise. This wasn't just killing. It was theater.

On the nightstand, a card leaned against the lamp. Its edges were smeared with a fingerprint of blood, pressed there deliberately.

Joe slid it into an evidence sleeve before reading, his voice low and hard:

*The lambs were given to me.*

*I will mark them.*

*I will cleanse them.*

*You do not stop His work.*

*You only delay His will.*

The words landed heavy, pressing on lungs, heavier than the stink in the room.

Lowe shifted, trying to keep his voice level, but it cracked anyway. "He's taunting us. Wants us to read it out loud."

Will's attention caught on the mirror across the room. At first, it appeared to be streaks of grime, but as he stepped closer, the truth revealed itself.

The surface was deeply gouged, with jagged letters carved into the glass using a blade. Shards littered the counter and floor, catching the sickly light in glittering fragments. The edges were raw, sharp enough to draw blood if touched.

YOU CANNOT SAVE THEM.

The words glared back at him, distorted by his own reflection staring through them.

Harris muttered, his voice breaking. "Holy Mother of..." He didn't finish.

The floor around the sink was dotted with smudges — bare footprints, smeared in what was either water or blood. The Prophet had stood here. Close enough to see himself as he carved. Close enough to admire his work.

Will stared until his reflection blurred, his own eyes framed inside the Prophet's declaration. *You cannot save them.* It was a taunt, yes. But it was also personal.

Joe broke the silence, his voice dark as stone. "This isn't escalation. This is war."

Rogers finally spoke from the corner, his tone flat, unreadable. "No. This is a sermon. And he's preaching straight to us."

The words hung heavy in the air.

The Prophet wasn't whispering anymore.

He was shouting.

And the interval between sermons was shrinking.

## Hannah

### Summit Falls PD – Records Division
**7:03 p.m.**

The fluorescents buzzed overhead, throwing pale light across the stacks of files and humming terminals. The air smelled of paper, toner, and the faint tang of stale coffee that clung to every corner of the task force's war room. Will sat hunched in front of a dusty monitor, sleeves rolled, the glow painting his face as his fingers tapped through the input fields.

Joe stood behind him, Styrofoam cup long gone cold in his hand, jacket carrying the scent of burnt coffee and cigarette smoke. He didn't move much, just shifted his weight, watching the screen with the still patience of a man who'd stared down far worse.

"Run the purse again," Joe said. His voice was rough, tired. "Start with the wallet."

Will keyed in the name, the cursor blinking in the task force's restricted login. A patchwork of databases bled together here—DMV, court filings, campus registrars—stitched into a portal the State Fusion Center had carved out for this case. Few departments had access, and even fewer had the necessary passwords. Will's current clearance let him slip past the outer wall.

The monitor flickered, the system dragging like it resented the work. A loading bar crawled, then finally blinked to life with a profile.

**Devereaux, Hannah Elise. Age 21. Ravenwood University.**

Enrollment history sat in a sidebar. Will clicked. The line item shifted:

**Active: Spring Semester. Status: Withdrawn. Effective: September 28.**

Will leaned closer, scrolling. Tuition refunds. Housing contract terminated. Loans deferred. It was all there, written in cold, bureaucratic language.

He muttered it under his breath, more to himself than to Joe. "Parents thought she was still enrolled."

Joe frowned. "Dropped out for what?"

Will clicked further. Financial records stacked across the screen—tuition refunds in September, then deposits from payment processors that had nothing to do with school or a part-time job. Each line is tagged by the system and flagged with usernames linked to the accounts.

One handle appeared again and again, repeating across three different platforms.

**Valentina Dawn.**

Will clicked it, and a profile bloomed onto the screen: neon lighting, lips painted deep crimson, the arch of her neck framed by a glittered backdrop. The smile was coy, calculated. Not Hannah Elise Devereaux, daughter and student. Valentina Dawn, commodity and brand.

Sub counts scrolled beside it in the thousands. Paywall tiers. Premium chats. Bookings. Private meetups were advertised in half-coded language that wasn't coded enough. A curated stage, one follower at a time.

Will sat back slightly, stomach tight. "Jesus."

Joe's expression didn't shift much, though the lines around his mouth hardened. He sipped his cold coffee anyway, like the bitterness grounded him. "She wasn't in school. She was surviving."

Will nodded faintly, eyes locked on the glow of the monitor. He could almost hear Maggie's voice in his head again—*it doesn't heal, not really*—and it cut deeper knowing Hannah had walked herself into this shadowed world, maybe thinking it was temporary, maybe thinking she could control it.

"Valentina Dawn," Will said quietly, as if saying it out loud could strip the mask from the girl beneath. "He knew her by this. Not as Hannah."

Joe finally set the cup down on the desk, the hollow sound loud in the quiet room. "Doesn't matter what name she put out there. He found her. He chose her. And now it's part of his sermon."

Will swallowed hard. On the screen, Hannah's painted lips smiled back at him, frozen in a pose she'd chosen—but twisted now into a kind of epitaph.

Joe let out a low whistle through his teeth. "Another online persona. Just like Howell."

Will printed the file, the machine coughing out a stack of warm pages. The first sheet bore Hannah's photo—bright-eyed in a Ravenwood ID headshot. The second showed the digital contrast: *Valentina Dawn*, posed and curated, her gaze coy and practiced.

Will flipped them side by side, the weight in his chest sinking heavier. "He's hunting women who make themselves visible. Who builds an audience. And then he rewrites the script."

Joe took the sheets, sliding them into a fresh file. "Ivy, Tammi, Avery, now Hannah. Doesn't matter if it's a street name or a website. He's not just picking victims—he's tearing down whatever identity they built for themselves."

The printer spat one last page. Will pulled it free: the image of her subscriber dashboard, numbers frozen like an audience waiting for a show that would never come.

He dropped it onto the pile. His voice came low. "Five women. Five sermons."

Joe muttered around his toothpick. "And he's cutting the pauses between verses."

The hum of the printer stopped. The silence after was louder.

**Next Morning, 10:12 a.m.**
The blinds cut harsh stripes across the table, one of them falling directly across Tessa Raymond's face. She

tilted her head as if it were a spotlight instead of an interrogation lamp.

Her name had come up the night before, buried in Hannah Devereaux's records. Lease agreements, utilities, and Wi-Fi bills all led back to a rented townhouse just off Ravenwood's campus. Tessa Raymond—same age, same dropout status, same digital fingerprints on subscription platforms. Roommate.

If Hannah had lived as Valentina Dawn, Tessa lived alongside her, sometimes in her shadow, riding the same wave.

She looked nothing like the girl in her old booking photos—back then, eyes sullen, hoodie swallowing her whole. Today, she had leaned into the image she sold: eyeliner sharp, lips glossed, nails tipped in glitter. The Ravenwood hoodie she wore was zipped tight, but the zipper dipped low, just enough to reveal her outfit underneath, suggesting she was always on stage, always on display.

Will sat across from her, notebook open. Joe leaned against the wall, arms crossed, toothpick rolling between his teeth.

Will sat across from her, notebook open. Joe leaned against the wall, arms crossed, toothpick rolling between his teeth.

Tessa smirked when she caught Joe watching her. "You know, if you're curious, I've got a promo running. The first thirty days are free. NoxieLuxe." She tapped her temple as if she were doing them a favor. "Might give you some context for what Hannah was about. It's... educational."

Joe's jaw flexed, but he didn't bite. "We're not here to subscribe. We're here to talk about Hannah Devereaux."

"She hated that name," Tessa said immediately. "Hannah. Sounded too vanilla. Valentina was better. She owned it." Her eyes glittered, proud by proxy. "She was pulling three times my numbers in half the time. If I could've bottled her brand, I would've. She was lightning."

Will pressed, his pen poised. "You said she had a client the night she disappeared."

"Yeah. Paid double for in-person." Tessa leaned forward like she was letting them in on a secret. "Wanted the full Valentina experience. Candlelight, lingerie, the whole kit. She thought she could handle it."

Joe asked, "Did she give you a name?"

"Ryan Miller." Tessa nodded, fast, eager. "Lives in Oakhaven. Forty-ish, plain guy. She showed me a pic— looked like somebody's boring accountant. We laughed about it. I told her it was sketch, but Hannah said boring was safe."

Will exchanged a look with Joe. Safe. None of them believed that anymore.

"You still have the picture?" Will asked.

"Yeah." Tessa dug through her phone, her thumbs moving with practiced speed. She turned the screen toward them—a grainy dating-app screenshot, Ryan Miller's face plain as drywall.

"Last thing she sent me," Tessa said. "Told me not to wait up."

She leaned back, crossing her arms smugly. "See? I'm helping. More than most. So... maybe drop my handle in your report? NoxieLuxe. Could use the publicity."

Will's pen froze over the page. He shut the notebook with a snap. She flinched at the sound.

Joe's voice came low and gravelly. "You don't get it, do you? Your friend's dead, and the guy who did it knew she thought boring was safe. You're sitting here selling subscriptions like it's a career fair."

Tessa blinked, unbothered. "It is my career. And if Valentina taught me anything, it's that you ride the wave while it's still warm. So maybe you should think about what she left behind instead of—"

Will stood, cutting her off. "Interview's over." His chair scraped sharply against the tile.

Joe lingered long enough to let the silence sink in. Then he spat the toothpick into the trash and followed.

Behind them, Tessa muttered under her breath, "Could've just signed up."

### Oakhaven – Miller Residence
**3:46 p.m.**

The Miller house was clean to the point of sterile—white siding, manicured lawn, and a wind chime tinkling above the porch. A stroller leaned against the wall, its wheels caked with mud from a recent walk.

Ryan Miller sat pale on the couch, his hands folded in his lap, knuckles bone-white. His wife hovered near the armrest, one hand on her swollen stomach, the other clutching his shoulder. She looked exhausted, wary of the detectives in her living room.

Will kept his tone steady. "Mr. Miller, we need to confirm your whereabouts on the night of April 6th."

"I already told the officer," Miller said, voice cracking. "I was here. All night. With her." His eyes flicked to his wife.

"Doorbell footage confirms he never left," she added quickly, defensive. "We ordered Thai at seven. I paid with my card. Our neighbor came by at nine to borrow a wrench. Ryan answered the door."

Joe leaned on the mantel, scanning the framed photos—wedding photos, ultrasound printouts, and a baby shower invitation stuck with a magnet. Normal life. "Have you ever met Hannah Devereaux? Or Valentina Dawn?"

Miller shook his head violently. "No. I don't know who that is. I never—" He broke off, voice strangled. "I swear to God, I've never met her."

The wife's eyes brimmed with angry tears. "He doesn't even leave me alone to get milk after dark. He hasn't been anywhere near that girl."

Will watched Miller's hands tremble, his leg bouncing despite the calm surface of his words. The man was terrified—not of being caught, but of being accused.

He snapped his notebook shut. Another dead end.

### Summit Falls PD – Task Force War Room
### 7:12 p.m.

The board loomed, five women pinned in a grim row. Hannah's bright Ravenwood headshot sat beside the sultry neon-lit Valentina Dawn, the contrast obscene.

Captain Archer braced both hands on the table, marker between his fingers like a weapon. "Intervals are shrinking from months to weeks to days. He's accelerating. Another girl could already be marked."

Kristen spoke first, her voice tight. "We interviewed Hannah's roommate, Tessa Raymond. She confirmed that Hannah went to meet Ryan Miller. Even showed us the picture. It lined up with Hannah's last message."

Joe slid the printout across the table. "But Miller's alibi is airtight. Doorbell cam, credit card receipts, neighbor testimony. Pregnant wife backing every second. No wiggle room."

Archer slammed the marker against the board hard enough to make it pop. "So he fed her a decoy. Either Hannah thought she was meeting Miller, or someone wanted her roommate to believe it. Either way, it's a dead trail."

Rogers spoke from the corner, voice flat. "He's steering us. Laughing while we chase our tails."

Lowe muttered, "Like he's writing us into his sermon too."

The silence that followed clung to the walls.

Will leaned forward, pen pressing deep into his notebook. Five women. Three counties. Street names, online personas, aliases. He's not just hunting them—he's dismantling what they built. Their stage names, their screens, their power. And every time, he's cutting the interval shorter."

Archer's jaw clenched. "Which means someone's already on deck. We don't sleep until we find her first."

The red threads glowed under the fluorescent light, cutting across the board like veins.

The Prophet wasn't slowing.

He was running faster.

## Breathe

### Kristen's Apartment – 8:03 p.m.

Kristen's apartment smelled of garlic and butter, the kind of comfort Will hadn't let himself notice in weeks. A pan sat drying in the sink, two mismatched candles burned low on the counter beside a vase of wilted daisies. Case files still crept onto the table, though—spilling into their plates like a third guest neither of them invited.

Will sat across from her, sleeves rolled, fork in hand, but untouched. Kristen curled into her chair, sweater loose at the collar, hair down around her shoulders. It softened her—less ADA Dalton, more Kristen. But the way her pen hovered over her legal pad said she wasn't letting the Prophet leave this room either.

She nudged her plate forward, gesturing at Hannah's photo pinned under a glass of wine. "It's not random. He's not just picking vulnerable women. He's picking women who build identities—Cherry, CandyCrush, HowellYouWantMe, and Valentina Dawn. Maggie, also known as Tonya. Each one of them had a brand. They all lived under more than one name."

Will twirled pasta, not eating. His eyes stayed on the photo. "And he strips that away. Inflicts pain as a repentance. Reduces them to sermons. To silence."

Kristen's gaze held on Hannah's neon-lit shot. "What if that's his obsession? Not just killing—erasing. Turning their personas into cautionary tales."

Will leaned back, jaw tight. "Then why leave notes? Why burn his symbol into their skin? That's not erasing. That's bragging. He's advertising."

She let out a breath, reaching for her glass. "Which brings us back to Maggie."

The weight of it pulled the room still.

Will finally looked up. "You still think it wasn't just him?"

Kristen's voice dropped, steady but sure. "Yes. I think he was reporting, checking in. He's not just killing for himself. He's performing. Feeding someone else."

Will stared at his wine, then past her, out the window where the city lights bled orange against the blinds. "If you're right, then we're not chasing a killer. We're chasing an audience."

The words clung like smoke.

Kristen broke it with a small laugh, too sharp to be light. "God. Dinner conversation, right?"

Will smirked, finally cutting into his pasta. "Better than talking about the weather."

They ate in silence for a few minutes. It wasn't heavy silence—more the kind that sits between people who've run out of defenses.

Kristen set her fork down, tilting her head as she studied him. "You know, I can't figure you out."

Will arched a brow. "That a compliment?"

"Maybe." Her lips curved. "You're this mix of soldier and cop. You stare down death scenes without flinching, but Maggie hugs you once, and you look like you don't know where to put your hands."

He chuckled, rubbing the back of his neck. "Not exactly trained for that."

Kristen leaned closer, elbows on the table, voice softer now. "It's why she trusted you. Why I trust you."

The words caught him off guard. His chest tightened, but he covered it with a sip of wine. "Careful, Counselor. Sounds like you're complimenting me."

She smirked. "Don't get used to it."

The candles guttered low, flickering shadows across the files they'd shoved to the side.

For a rare moment, the Prophet wasn't in the room. It was just them. And the silence wasn't about death.

Kristen picked up her glass again, her eyes not leaving his. "Eat before it's cold. Tomorrow we go back to war. Tonight... we breathe."

Will nodded slowly, holding her gaze longer than he meant to. "Yeah. Tonight we breathe."

Some time later, the food was nearly gone, but the wine bottle sat half-drained between them, two glasses catching the city's glow through the blinds. The files had been shoved to one end of the table, forgotten for once.

Kristen leaned back in her chair, her sweater slipping off one shoulder, her hair loose and curling around her face. She wasn't ADA Dalton in this light. She was just Kristen—tired, sharp-eyed, and human.

She let out a quiet laugh, shaking her head. "I don't know how you do it."

Will arched a brow. "Do what?"

"Walk into those rooms, see what we see, and not fall apart." Her gaze dropped to her glass, swirling the last of the wine. "I hold it together in front of everyone else, but when I'm alone? Sometimes I can't even look in the mirror without seeing..." She trailed off.

Will didn't press. He let the silence stretch, then said quietly, "Scars don't heal when you hide them. I've got more than I can count. Still carry 'em."

Kristen studied him, her mouth quirking into something that wasn't quite a smile. "You're not supposed to admit that."

"I'm not supposed to admit a lot of things," he said, a faint grin tugging at his mouth.

She laughed, soft and unguarded, then stood to clear the plates. Will moved to help, but she brushed his hand away, her fingers lingering on his for a second longer than necessary.

"Sit. I've got it."

When she came back, she didn't return to her chair. Instead, she sank onto the couch, tucking her legs under her, the sweater slipping further. She patted the cushion beside her without looking up.

Will hesitated only a moment before joining her. The air between them shifted, becoming less professional and more personal.

Kristen leaned back, her head tilting until it rested lightly against his shoulder. "Just for a minute," she murmured.

Will froze, unsure if he should move, but her voice came low, certain. "Relax, Anderson. You're safe here."

He let out a slow breath, the tension bleeding out of his shoulders. For the first time in weeks, he didn't feel like he had to brace for impact.

Kristen's eyes fluttered shut, her voice drifting. "You know... Maggie was right."

"About what?"

Her lips curved faintly, almost teasing. "Not letting you get away."

Will felt heat rise in his chest, his throat tight with something he couldn't name. He didn't answer, couldn't. But he didn't pull away either.

The city hummed outside. The Prophet's shadow still loomed over the board across town. But here, for one fragile moment, Kristen Dalton let down her guard.

And for a moment, Will Anderson let himself breathe.

Later that night, the city hummed outside, a low static through the window glass. Inside, the apartment was quiet except for the soft tick of the old wall clock and the occasional creak of pipes in the walls.

Kristen hadn't moved, her head still resting against Will's shoulder, her breath warm through his shirt. The weight of her there felt unfamiliar—lighter than the Kevlar of his days, heavier than any burden he'd carried in the war zone or the crime scenes.

"You know what I hate most?" she murmured, voice muffled.

Will glanced down at her, surprised she wasn't asleep. "What's that?"

"That every time I close my eyes, I see them staged— the beds, the burns, the ropes. And I don't see women anymore. I see evidence." She swallowed, her hand curling tighter into the knit of her sweater. "It scares me that I'll forget they were real."

Will's chest tightened. He wanted to tell her he understood—because he did—but he also knew she didn't need understanding. She needed something solid to anchor her.

"They're real," he said, his voice low. "And you're the reason they stay that way. You don't let them vanish into a file. That's the difference."

Kristen tilted her face just enough to meet his eyes. In the dim light, hers looked glassy, uncertain but steady on him. "You always know how to say the right thing."

He gave a small, humorless smile. "No. I just say the thing I wish someone had said to me."

That silence wasn't heavy—it was fragile, breakable if either of them pushed too hard.

Kristen shifted, the soft brush of her hair against his neck. "You're impossible, you know that?"

Will smirked faintly. "So I've heard."

She laughed under her breath, the sound small but real. Then, almost without realizing it, she let her head slide lower, her temple against his chest now. Her breathing slowed, steadier, settling into his rhythm.

Will stayed still, notebook forgotten on the table, his arm resting lightly along the back of the couch. He didn't move it, didn't dare.

Minutes stretched into an hour. Her glass tipped empty on the coffee table, her sweater slipped further off her shoulder, and eventually, her breath deepened into sleep.

Will stared at the ceiling, the weight of her against him, and for the first time in weeks, the war felt far away.

He didn't sleep. Couldn't. But he didn't mind.

For one night, Kristen Dalton let her guard down.

And Will Anderson kept his promise—to watch, to stay steady, to be there when someone needed him.

Tomorrow the Prophet would strike again.

But tonight, in this small apartment, they'd stolen something back from him.

### Kristen's Apartment – 6:22 a.m.

The first thing Will noticed was the light. Pale gray bleeding through the blinds, soft against the walls. The second was the weight—Kristen still curled against him, her hair spilling over his chest, the faint warmth of her breath against his shirt.

The clock on the wall ticked steadily. The city outside had already started to wake: muffled car horns, the distant rumble of a bus.

Kristen stirred, her hand brushing his arm as she shifted. For a heartbeat, she didn't move, as if she'd forgotten where she was. Then her eyes fluttered open.

She froze when she realized. "Oh God." She pushed herself upright, tugging the hem of her sweater back over her shoulder. "I didn't—"

Will sat up slower, rubbing the back of his neck. "You fell asleep. That's all."

Kristen's cheeks flushed faintly. She grabbed for the wineglasses on the table, setting them in the sink like the clink of glass could erase the quiet between them.

Will stood, stretching his back, the stiffness of the couch catching up to him. "Better than the motel beds we've been in."

Kristen glanced over her shoulder, one eyebrow arched. "Not the way I'd phrase it, Anderson."

That earned her a slight grin, and some of the tension broke.

They moved around each other easily in the kitchen. The coffee maker, prepped the night before, had filled the space with the warm promise of morning, and the elixir of the gods. Kristen moved through it like muscle memory, pouring into chipped mugs as he gathered the scattered files. For a moment, it felt almost ordinary, like the Prophet wasn't carving his sermons into women across the county.

Kristen slid a mug across the counter to him. "You know we can't talk about this at the war room."

Will nodded, sipping the coffee. "Doesn't mean it didn't happen."

Their eyes met over the rim of the cups—brief, steady, and then gone as she turned toward the sink.

By 7:30, Will had his jacket on, Kristen her case folder tucked under her arm. They stepped out into the sharp morning air together, the city already alive around them.

Side by side, their shoulders brushed as they headed for his cruiser. The Prophet was waiting. The board was waiting.

But the memory of the night—quiet laughter, unspoken truths, the feel of her head against his chest—lingered like an ember neither of them could put out.

## Nowhere

### Summit Falls PD – Task Force War Room
### 9:11 a.m.

The fluorescents buzzed overhead, a faint hum filling the silence between voices. The war room smelled of cold coffee and dry-erase ink. The board loomed across the wall—five women now, their faces stitched together by red thread like scars carved into the whiteboard.

Will sat at the table, notebook open, pen tapping slowly against the page. He kept his eyes on Hannah's two photos—bright-eyed Ravenwood student beside Valentina Dawn's neon-lit persona. Two lives. Two names. Both erased.

Archer stood at the head of the table, marker in hand, sleeves rolled, tie loosened, hair pressed flat on one side like he'd slept in his chair. He didn't waste time.

"Updates. Anderson. Donovan. Walk us through the roommate."

Will cleared his throat, flipping a page. "Tessa Raymond. Online handle NoxieLuxe. Roommate and part-time collaborator on Hannah's page. She admitted that Hannah left the apartment on April 6th to meet a client who'd paid double for an in-person meeting. Ryan Miller, Oakhaven. Hannah even showed her the dating app with his profile before she left."

Joe leaned forward, voice dry. "The girl was more worried about promo codes than her roommate. She tried to pitch us her subscription page during the interview. She called Hannah lightning in a bottle, said she wished she could've bottled her brand. Oblivious. Or greedy. Maybe both."

Kristen's brow furrowed. "She didn't realize she fits the same profile?"

Will shook his head. "Not even close. She thought boring was safe. She laughed at the guy's photo. Said he looked like an accountant. That's the bait he dangled."

Archer gestured with the marker. "And Miller?"

Joe tossed a printout onto the table. "Alibi locked. Doorbell cam, credit card receipts, pregnant wife, neighbor visit. The guy never left his house. He's clean."

The marker snapped against the board as Archer jabbed Hannah's photo. "So either she believed she was meeting Miller, or someone wanted Tessa to believe it. Either way, misdirection."

Rogers leaned back in his chair, arms folded, voice flat. "He's feeding us ghosts. While you're busy chasing Miller's receipts, he's already moved on to the next girl."

Kristen's jaw tightened. "That's not analysis, Rogers. That's defeatist bullshit."

He didn't flinch. "Call it what you want. I've seen men like him before. You don't catch them until they want to bleed. And by then, it's already too late."

Will's pen dug into his notebook. He wanted to call Rogers on the admiration buried in his tone. But some part of him wondered if there was truth in it.

Archer broke the tension with a sharp clap of the marker against the table. "We're not waiting for him to decide. We run every lead. NoxieLuxe's subscribers. Ravenwood dropouts. Anyone tied to Hannah. Knock on doors until someone slams one in your face. I don't care how thin it looks—we don't sit still."

Chairs scraped. Files shuffled. The hum of fluorescents filled the void where progress should've been.

Will lingered, staring at Hannah's photos until they blurred together. He thought of Maggie clutching her scar, saying she was his work. He thought of Tessa, still blind to the danger closing in on her.

Beside him, Kristen snapped her pad shut. Her voice was low, meant for only him. "Every road leads nowhere."

Will glanced at her. He wanted to assure her that she was wrong. But the truth weighed heavier.

"Not nowhere," he said finally, eyes fixed on the Prophet's circle scrawled on the board. "Exactly where he wants us."

The words clung in the air like smoke neither of them could clear.

The Prophet was already moving.

And they were still chasing ghosts.

**Summit Falls PD – Task Force War Room**
**Four Days Later**

The whiteboard looked the same. Five women. Five strings. Same burn marks. Same notes. Same silence. The only thing new was the mess: case files stacked like leaning towers, Styrofoam cups bleeding coffee rings into the wood, and the smell of sweat and exhaustion clinging to the air.

Archer stood with his jacket off, shirt wrinkled, marker in hand. "Walk me through it. One at a time. Anderson."

Will rubbed a hand across his face before flipping open his notebook. "We traced Hannah's crypto payments. Ran the top hundred subscribers through cyber. Ninety-eight were dead accounts or overseas. The two stateside accounts? One's a high school kid in Des Moines. The other's a sixty-two-year-old in Tampa who just wanted bikini photos. Neither has the profile."

Archer's jaw flexed. "Donovan."

Joe exhaled through his nose. "Hit Ivy Cole's old street again. Talked to neighbors. Nothing. The guy across the hall remembers hearing her laugh a lot. The woman downstairs remembers her heels on the stairs. That's it. Nobody saw who she left with, nobody saw her come back."

Kristen's pen tapped against her legal pad, quick and sharp. She lifted her gaze. "I reran Avery Howell's Ravenwood ties. Professors, classmates, former

212

roommates. She was quiet, disciplined. No red flags. The only hint is her website. But her subscribers? Same problem as Hannah's. Scrubbed, scattered, useless."

Rogers sat in the corner, arms folded, eyes hooded. "You're wasting time. He doesn't make mistakes."

Kristen snapped her head toward him. "Everyone makes mistakes."

"Not the kind you're hoping for," Rogers said, voice low, almost admiring. "The Prophet writes the sermon he wants you to hear. That's it. You're looking for verses that don't exist."

The tension snapped like static in the air. Archer slammed the marker against the board hard enough to splatter ink. "Enough. Lowe. Harris."

Lowe cleared his throat, voice flat with fatigue. "We pulled every motel registry within twenty miles of Summit Falls. Nothing overlaps. No repeat names, no reused addresses. Either he's using cash, or he's walking in invisible."

Harris added, "Checked pawn shops too. No jewelry, no clothing, nothing. If he's taking trophies, he's not leaving them in circulation."

Silence stretched. The board loomed over them, every photo staring back, every string connecting but not leading anywhere.

Will stared at Maggie's picture, the only survivor. Her scar, her voice, her words about the phone call echoing in his mind. He whispered to himself, too low for anyone else. *He's already planning the next one.*

Kristen caught it. Her voice was steady, but her pen dug so hard it nearly tore her pad. "And we're still three steps behind."

The room sat heavy in the fluorescent glow, the weight of failure pressing down on all of them.

The Prophet hadn't struck again. Not yet.

But he would. And they all knew it.

## Summit Falls – Riverside Greenbelt
### 7:03 a.m.

The morning air was sharp, the kind that stung the lungs and clung to skin. Mist clung low to the riverbank, silver light spilling through the trees. Police tape fluttered weakly in the breeze, cordoning off the clearing where joggers had stopped, pale and shaken, pointing to what they'd found.

Will ducked under the tape, boots crunching through damp grass. Joe was already there, jaw tight, coat collar up against the cold. Lowe and Harris hovered near the path, both looking like they wanted to be anywhere else. Rogers stood apart, hands buried in his jacket, eyes narrowed as if he were watching a stage.

At the center of the clearing, she lay in the grass.

Female, early twenties. Clothing neatly folded beside her like she'd set them there herself. Nude, pale in the mist-light, body arranged flat on her back with arms folded across her chest in mock repose.

No cuts. No bruises. No swollen lips or broken skin. Her face was peaceful—too peaceful, like she'd fallen asleep on the earth and never woken up.

Except for the brand.

The circle was seared into her stomach, the skin bubbled and blistered, angry red against pallor.

Will's pen scratched into his notebook, his throat tightening. This wasn't like the others. No ropes, no humiliation, no visible violence. Just the burn, the placement, the card resting like an offering on her folded shirt.

Joe crouched near the clothing, snapping on gloves. He picked up the card with care, sliding it into an evidence sleeve. His voice was gravelly when he read it.

*The flesh can be broken. The soul can be burned. The body is nothing. Only the mark remains.*

The words hung in the damp air.

"Same hand," Kristen murmured. She'd just arrived, hair pulled back, her coat brushing the grass as she crouched near Will. Her eyes stayed on the girl's face, soft but unyielding. "But the staging's different. No struggle. No restraint. Like he wanted her found whole."

Will's jaw worked. "Or like he wanted to remind us he doesn't need theatrics to preach."

The ME crew moved in carefully, preparing to bag the body. When they rolled her, the truth surfaced.

A second note.

Folded, pressed flat against her back, sticky with dew where her skin had cooled against the grass. The officer who found it swore under his breath as he slid it free and passed it to Joe.

He unfolded it carefully, eyes scanning the words. His mouth tightened. "Son of a bitch." He read aloud, slow:

*You hunt shadows. You chase noise. While you waste time, I decide who breathes. I am ahead of you. Always. Stop now—or watch them fall faster.*

Silence cut sharp across the clearing.

Kristen's breath steamed in the air. "He's not just taunting us. He's shifting. This isn't escalation—it's transformation. He's changing the sermon."

Will stared down at the girl, her face so deceptively calm, the mark on her stomach the only violation. His hand tightened on the notebook until the cardboard bent.

"He's telling us we're already too late."

Will watched as the ME slid a gloved hand beneath the folded pile of clothes with the care of someone unwrapping a fragile relic. The rain had left the grass bruised and dark; their breaths fogged as they leaned closer.

The stack was absurdly tidy—underwear, bra, T-shirt, shorts, socks, shoes—each item folded and laid on top of the next in the exact order they would have come off. Shoes on the bottom. Socks on top of them. Shorts folded neatly over the socks. A plain white tee. A bra, its cups nesting over the shirt. And between the bra and panties, tucked like a private note, a plastic school ID.

"Jesus," Joe said under his breath.

Will's throat went dry. He crouched until his knees ached and watched the photo: a wide, surprised smile, freckles dusting the cheeks, hair in a messy braid. The name printed beneath it hit him like a fist.

POPPY LANE

Ravenwood University — Freshman

"No persona," Lowe said, voice small. He touched the ID with two fingers, reverent and sick.

Kristen bent, eyes narrowing as she took the card. "She's a 19 year old student. Freshman." Her pen hovered uselessly over the page in her hand. "Not some professional profile. No subscriptions. No paid accounts." She scanned the ID again, then looked up at Will. "Check online. If she had anything, TikTok, Instagram—something."

Will pulled his phone out with fingers that weren't steady. The ME team eased back to give them space, boots whispering on wet grass. In the phone's glow, Poppy's social media came up fast: a small Instagram with a hundred-some followers, selfies threaded with captions about dorm life; a TikTok account—short clips, shot handheld, direct to camera: "Freshman hacks: how to survive eight a.m. classes," "Microwave ramen upgrades," little daily rants that were charming and goofy and utterly ordinary. No neon banners, no subscription links, no adult handles. Just a kid talking into the phone at 2 a.m. about laundry tips.

Will felt the world tilt. "She wasn't advertising herself," he said. "She was... living. Nothing curated beyond ordinary college stuff."

Kristen scrolled slowly, the videos looping in her peripheral vision. In one clip, Poppy laughed at a burnt mug and mouthed something like, "I'll be fine. You'll see." There was an earnestness there that made Kristen's throat tighten.

Joe crouched beside them, reading the ME's notes aloud. "No obvious trauma. No lacerations. Toxicology pending. Brand present. Sermon card same style—blood-smeared edges." He nodded toward the card still in evidence sleeve. "But different. He left her folded. Whole. Like a message."

Will closed his eyes for a second and felt Maggie's voice—You believe me?—like a memory with teeth. How many times had they mistaken theater for truth? "He staged her to look ordinary," he said. "Dressed her in order, like... like a mock undoing. He wanted her found that way."

Kristen's fingers tightened around the phone until the metal creaked. "That's the change," she said. "Before, he staged humiliation, display—rope, knives, exposure. Now he's arranging her like an offering. No visible fight. No signs he needed to force it to the same degree. Either he's got better at it... or he wants us to think she walked into it."

Will's gaze flicked to the brand on Poppy's stomach—angry, precise, the same circular scar that had been a throughline on the board for months. Up close, it pulsed with a cruelty that seemed to mock them. "If there's no overt trauma," he said softly, "then either he's using something subtle to finish them... or he's waiting until after. After we leave, after the scene cools."

Lowe leaned closer, voice flat as gravel. "ME says we didn't miss external blunt force. No defensive wounds. Could be strangulation, could be PO—positional asphyxia, could be something we don't see on gross exam. Toxic's inconclusive yet."

Joe shook his head. "And that note on her back—he only lets us see the joke after the ME flips her. He knew we'd have to handle her first. He's playing our process like an instrument."

Kristen closed her eyes for a breath. When she opened them again, she looked like someone who had decided to stop being gentle with the facts. "She's a freshman. A kid who does TikTok about ramen and memo pads. She wasn't looking for trouble. But he chose her and arranged her like a demonstration."

Will thought of Tessa's grin in the interview room, of subscription pitches and promo codes—small cruelties that suddenly seemed irrelevant against this scale of willful violence. Poppy's ordinary online life made her closeness to the public—her visibility—different from the sex-worker profile they'd been chasing. The Prophet's target set had shifted wider.

He opened his notebook and wrote Poppy's name in block letters, underlining it twice without meaning to. The pen left an impression on the paper that looked like a wound.

Kristen folded the school ID back into evidence plastic and slid it into a bag. "We'll run her contacts. Friends, classmates, anyone she DM'd. Pull the phone for messages—call logs, location. We need to know who she texted in the last twenty-four hours. The ME needs the tox back yesterday if possible." She looked up, met Will's eyes. "And put a request into cyber to pull her followers and anyone who interacted with her videos in the last week. Maybe someone reached out. Maybe it's nothing. But we check everything."

Will nodded. Internally, a new worry rose—if she was only a student with a modest online life, the Prophet's net was widening. "If he's choosing kids who aren't even part of that world we expected, then we're missing his criteria entirely."

Joe's voice cut through, practical and tired. "We canvass the greenbelt—anyone who jogged past, dog walkers, campers. Someone might've seen a truck, flash of taillights. We comb the area for camera footage. Doorbell cams, traffic cams on the route. He might be sloppy somewhere."

Rogers watched them with a slant in his mouth that never quite reached his eyes. "Or he's not sloppy. He's careful enough to choose girls who'll be overlooked—freshman, girls with school IDs, not profiles on subscription platforms. He's evolving the sermon to make us complicit."

Will closed his notebook, the paper whispering. He thought of Maggie's voice—You changed my life—and felt a sick pressure in his chest: a survivor's courage opening a new door; an offender's imagination widening the stage.

"We treat her like any other victim," Will said finally, and the steadiness of his voice drew the circle of men and women in. "But we don't ignore that she lived in a way that puts her in the public eye—TikTok, Instagram. He's adapted. So do we. Run her digital interactions, pull the ME's detailed exam, canvass the greenbelt, and get me every camera within a two-mile radius pinched now."

Kristen already had her phone out, fingers moving fast. "I'll take the digital. You take the canvass. Joe, coordinate with ME on expedited tox and the lab."

They moved like mechanics in a garage—efficient, practiced—while the clearing around them held its quiet. Poppy Lane lay still among the grass, folded and arranged, and the river moved on indifferent as ever.

Will walked to the edge of the tape and looked back at her one more time. Her smile in the ID looked almost insolent, as if life itself refused to be quieted into a story the Prophet could own.

He felt something like a vow settle in his chest. Not just to Maggie. Not just to the others on the board. To this girl who'd been folded into the earth like linen.

He couldn't let the Prophet's sermon end here.

## Vanished

The autopsy report lay open on the metal table beneath the fluorescence of the task force office — flat, sterile, final. Kristen stared at the toxicology results like they'd insulted her.

"No alcohol," she muttered. "No THC. No benzos, no GHB. Not even caffeine."

Will didn't look up from the file. He'd already read it twice. Three times. Maybe four.

"She was clean," he said flatly.

Kristen pushed away from the table and paced, arms folded tight across her ribs. "So she wasn't drugged. Wasn't drunk. She knew where she was, what she was doing—"

"And then she vanished."

The word hung there, unanswered.

The roommate said Poppy Lane had left her apartment at 7:15 p.m. sharp. Hair curled, lips glossed, hoodie zipped halfway to show just enough skin to say I'm casual, but I care. She was headed to a party off-campus — the kind of party where you bring your own drinks, and someone's couch becomes your sanctuary or your mistake.

"She was supposed to meet us at Shelly Wilson's place first," the roommate explained, her eyes red-rimmed but dry. "Just a quick pregame. That was the plan."

But before that, Poppy had said she needed to stop by the store. She was out of mixers — Sprite, maybe ginger ale. Something light. Something that wouldn't taste too much like vodka.

She never made it to Shelly's.

**7:28 p.m.** — Will watched the timestamp flicker at the bottom of the grainy security footage.

There she was.

Poppy Lane.

Real, in motion, alive.

Jeans snug on long legs, white sneakers, earbuds in. She tugged the sleeves of her cropped hoodie down as she stepped through the automatic doors of the grocery store, oblivious to the camera's indifferent eye.

The footage sped up.

She walked the soda aisle, plucked a bottle of Sprite off the shelf. Picked up a pack of gum from the impulse rack. Waited in line. Smiled at the cashier — a tight, polite curve of the mouth. The kind of smile you give when you know you're being looked at, but you're pretending you don't care.

Again at 7:41 p.m. — she stepped outside, Sprite in one hand, phone in the other. A glance down at the screen. A pause. Then she turned toward the parking lot and walked out of frame.

Will hit pause.

That was it.

"No one follows her," Kristen said. She stood behind him, arms folded, staring at the frozen image on the monitor. "No one brushes past her. She doesn't look scared. Doesn't look watched."

Will's eyes scanned the blacktop beyond the sliding doors. One row of parked cars. A cart return station. Nothing else.

"No contact in the lot. No commotion. No delay. Five minutes later, her phone dies."

Kristen leaned in closer. "Not just off. Dead."

Will nodded slowly. "Like someone ripped the battery out. Or crushed it."

"Can you still take the battery out of phones?" Kristen smirked.

"Figure of speech for reference," Will shot back.

They pulled footage from the exterior cameras. Nothing. The timestamp looped — 8:00 p.m. — and the system reset.

Gap.

A full twelve minutes overwritten automatically, per store policy. The night manager stated that the backups were not operational that day. Routine maintenance. Standard procedure.

Will didn't buy it. His gut stirred.

"She never made it back to her car," Kristen said, pinching the bridge of her nose. "Or if she did, she didn't drive it away. It was still there in the morning. Locked. Sprite is in the passenger seat. Unopened."

Will blinked. "Wait. The bottle was still there?"

"Yeah," Kristen said. "Untouched. She never got a sip."

They interviewed every friend, every girl Poppy was supposed to meet that night.

The dorm lounge smelled faintly of burnt popcorn and lavender dryer sheets, a half-dead floor lamp buzzing in the corner. The girls sat scattered across mismatched couches, faces pale, makeup smudged, a few still in pajama pants and slippers. Their voices trembled at first, overlapping nervously, then dwindled into rehearsed repetitions.

Every detail was the same.

She left at 7:15.

She said she'd stop for Sprite.

She texted the group at 7:35: *Grabbing Sprite, be there soon.*

And then—nothing.

"They called. They texted," Harris said, scrolling through one of the phones, his voice clipped and low. "No replies."

Eventually, they went to the party without her.

Will leaned forward, elbows resting on his knees, notebook open but ignored. His voice, when it came, was even—too even.

"No one thought it was strange she didn't show?"

A brunette with smudged eyeliner and chipped nail polish shrugged, eyes rimmed red. "She flaked sometimes. If a guy texted, or she didn't feel like it... It wasn't a huge deal."

Kristen's pen froze over her pad. Her voice cut in, sharper than she intended.

"She told you she was on the way."

The words landed like glass breaking.

The group fell into silence. A few shifted, eyes dropping to the floor. One twisted a friendship bracelet around her wrist until her skin turned pink. None of them looked like liars.

Just kids—guilty of assuming tomorrow was guaranteed.

Later, the task force conference room sat in near-darkness. Only the glow of the monitor lit the space, casting a jittering gray light on the walls.

Will sat forward, his face shadowed, watching the grainy footage on an endless loop. Poppy Lane.

Cropped hoodie. Sprite bottle. Gum at the checkout.

Alive, ordinary, real.

A ghost waiting to happen.

Kristen slipped into the chair beside him, her tablet tucked under her arm, her phone placed face-up on the table. She didn't speak at first. The footage kept rolling: Poppy smiling faintly at the cashier, stepping out into the night air, pausing to check her phone. Then—gone, swallowed by the darkness of the parking lot.

Finally, Kristen spoke, her voice soft but heavy.

"It doesn't fit. No sermon. No staging. No signature."

Will's jaw tightened. He kept watching, fingers curling against the edge of the table.

Kristen leaned in, eyes fixed on the frozen frame—Poppy's silhouette walking into the shadows beyond the sliding doors. "She wasn't a message," she said. "She was a test."

The room felt smaller. The silence pressed in.

Will drew in a breath, slow and controlled, but the sound betrayed the weight in his chest. His eyes stayed on the girl's last living image, a figure caught in grainy gray pixels, a Sprite bottle swinging from her hand as if she'd be back in five minutes.

When he spoke, his voice was low, gravel-edged.

"No." He shook his head once, still staring at the screen.

"She was a warning."

Kristen turned toward him, but he didn't meet her eyes.

On the screen, Poppy Lane kept walking, each replay dragging her into the dark again and again. No matter how many times Will watched, she never managed to escape.

## Burned

### Summit Falls PD
### Three Weeks After Poppy Lane

The break came at 2:16 p.m. on a Tuesday. Kristen was mid-sentence in the war room when the door slammed open and Lowe strode in, a DMV printout in one hand and his phone in the other.

"Got a hit," he said, voice tight. "DMV just confirmed the plate—dark green F-150, partial match from the Lane footage. Registered to Daniel Carrick. Died nine months ago. No next of kin, no stolen report filed. Just had Comms add it to the BOLO list; maybe one of the LPRs will pick it up. That's a License Plate Reader, Miss Dalton, sorry, cop lingo. We have a few around the city on poles."

Kristen sat up straighter. Archer looked up from the board. "Oh, really, how long ago?"

"Seconds," Lowe said, not even bothering to sit. "Maybe a minute. Just hung up with them on the way in here."

Before the air settled, the dispatch radio crackled.

"Dispatch to all units—BOLO alert ping just hit on Carrick's plate. The stationary LPR at 9th and Chamber picked up the truck in the westbound lane. Repeat, westbound on 9th."

Kristen froze, heart thudding, pen in her hand. She looked up at the board—Poppy's photo, the thread running from it, the old lead that had gone cold until now.

"Copy that," came Archer's voice through the open radio channel. "Visual confirmation pending. All nearby units redirect."

Will was already grabbing his gear.

"You coming?" Archer asked.

Kristen shook her head once. "Pass, I'll monitor from here. Go."

## Summit Falls – Downtown Grid, 3:02 p.m.

The chase wound through seven city blocks, the first patrol car catching sight of the green F-150 within minutes. But when the lights hit, the driver didn't even flinch. Sirens rose behind it, echoing off brick and glass as the city's arteries funneled the hunt forward. The truck slipped through it all like a ghost—too fast, too deliberate—threading traffic as if the streets themselves belonged to him, every blind corner another turn he'd already memorized.

Will's hands were white on the wheel, Archer in the seat beside him. Lowe reported from the unit behind. "Visual contact—suspect vehicle just passed 11th and Walker."

"Heading to the deck," Will muttered. "I see him."

The truck clipped a mailbox, scraped past two delivery vans, then disappeared into the yawning mouth of a parking deck beside the abandoned textiles plant.

Will's tires shrieked in pursuit. Over the radio, Archer's voice cut sharply: "Suspect vehicle just entered 11th and Walton—four-story garage. All units converge. Block every exit."

In the war room, Kristen bent over the console, knuckles pale against the edge of the desk. The fluorescents buzzed overhead, a brittle counterpoint to the radio's static. The air smelled of stale coffee and dry-erase ink.

Around her, the task force stood stiller than statues. Harris, Donovan, and Rogers watched the screens with jaws locked, arms folded tight. The fusion computer team techs hovered behind their terminals, eyes flicking between data streams that couldn't keep pace with the chase. Even the comms officer—normally a blur of clipped chatter—sat with his headset tilted, lips pressed thin as he relayed traffic updates in low, measured bursts.

The room felt suspended, the whole team listening with the same taut focus, every sound from the field carrying like a heartbeat over the radio—boots on concrete. Orders shouted and clipped—the ghost of breath over an open mic.

Kristen's pen slipped from her fingers, rattled once against a mug ring, then rolled away. No one moved to look.

The war room was silent, all of them waiting on the voices they couldn't reach. The hunt was alive—but it was happening out there, not here.

They entered the deck just as they could hear the truck's tires scream to a stop on the upper level.

"He's Trapped!" Archers' voice came over the radio.

Doors slammed open across the deck as Archer and Lowe flanked from the opposite side.

The F-150 sat idle. Windows tinted. Bed covered. No movement.

"Driver could still be inside," Archer warned. "Watch the cab."

They approached slowly, boots crunching on glass. The stench hit them first—chemical, acrid, almost sweet. Will's stomach turned.

"That smell," Archer murmured. "That's it. Maggie said that—like something sour under burnt rubber."

Will's hand stopped short of the door handle.

Something sat in the front seat.

Metal. Wires. A blinking red diode. Gas Canisters.

"Oh shit, move! Bomb!" Will shouted. "Get Back! Now!"

They dove behind the nearest pillar. A half-second later, the truck exploded.

The shockwave hit first. Then the fire—the sound didn't just echo, it pressed inward, collapsing the air around them like the world itself had drawn a breath and screamed.

The truck ignited in a geyser of heat, flames peeling upward as the windshield burst and the bed ruptured, sending a gout of fire into the concrete ceiling. Debris scattered like teeth.

They ducked, covered, ears ringing, the fire licking at their heels, black smoke filling the cavernous space.

Back in the war room, Kristen gripped the edge of the table, knuckles white as the explosion crackled through the radio feed. For a moment, all she could hear was static.

Then Will's voice came through, ragged. "Vehicle's gone. Incendiary rigged. The truck is totaled. We barely cleared. All units 10-4, send fire service."

Kristen closed her eyes, exhaled once, and looked at Poppy's photo.

## Parking Deck – Aftermath

The parking deck was sealed. Forensics combed the remains, but the heat had destroyed nearly everything. No prints. No DNA. No license plate left unscorched.

But the canisters—what remained of them—would be sent to the lab.

Lowe muttered from the corner, "Could've taken us all out. Whole floor."

Archer nodded grimly. "He doesn't just want to preach anymore. He wants to punish."

Kristen's voice came low when they regrouped. "That wasn't random. He wanted us there. The LPR wasn't a mistake. It was bait."

Will looked back at the scorched metal and the melted canisters, smoke still rising.

"He left the smell. He left the truck. He gave us the chase."

He looked up toward the ceiling, gone like a ghost, again.

"He gave us the illusion of a win."

### Later that night, Summit Falls PD

Kristen stood in front of the smartboard, arms folded, eyes locked on the burned-out outline of the truck's charred image.

Joe tossed the initial lab report from SLED on the table. "Those canisters? Traces of hydrogen sulfide mixed with industrial solvents. Not enough to kill you with exposure. But enough to smell... weird."

Kristen nodded slowly. "That's what Maggie smelled in the truck, what was on our suspect."

Will wrote two words on the whiteboard beneath Poppy's name:

**BURNING PROOF**

## Erased

**Summit Falls Conference Room – Six Weeks Later**

The war room felt colder than usual, not because of the AC, which hummed as tired and overworked as the people inside, but because something had shifted.

Nine weeks.

That's how long it had been since they found Poppy Lane.

Displayed. Branded. Silent.

And still, nothing.

The whiteboard hadn't changed.

Five faces. Five women. Five lives reduced to strings, timestamps, autopsy photos, and unanswered questions.

Poppy's image stared back from the center now—fresh-faced, eyes bright, that ridiculous braid half-falling from one shoulder. The ID photo that had once felt like a lead now felt like a monument.

Captain Archer stood at the head of the room, sleeves rolled up, arms crossed tight, watching status reports flicker across the smartboard like they might spontaneously evolve into answers. His silence wasn't passive—it radiated pressure.

The kind that made your chest tighten.

The kind that meant the subsequent explosion would be verbal and brutal.

Kristen sat beside Will, a tablet in her lap, dark circles carved under her eyes. Her coffee sat untouched beside her. Cold. Like everything else.

Lowe and Harris hunched over stacks of interview transcripts again, yellow highlighters clicking, margins marked and circled. Both of them looked like sleep had been a stranger for a while now.

Will didn't bother sitting.

He stood in the corner, arms folded, a statue with a pulse, eyes fixed on Poppy's photo. Something about her expression haunted him—not fear, not confusion. Just life. The kind of life that shouldn't end on the cold grass with a sermon on her back.

Then came the voice.

Lieutenant Dan Rogers, nursing a lukewarm coffee and that signature smirk he wore like armor.

Just enough sarcasm to crack the surface tension.

Too much to be harmless.

"Well," he said, stretching the word like a yawn, "I guess we can rule out suicide. Unless she arranged herself like origami."

The room stilled, collective patience wearing thin.

Kristen didn't even lift her head. Just cut a look sideways—lethal, low, and precise. "*Not now*, Dan."

He raised his coffee in mock salute, leaning back in his chair. "You said that nine weeks ago too."

Will clenched his jaw, the tendons twitching just under the skin. He didn't speak. Didn't need to. The silence felt sharper than any comeback.

Then—

Captain Archer's voice sliced through like a scalpel.

"I'm done asking nicely," he said, voice sharp. "We have nothing—no new leads, no suspect, no vehicle. The only truck we had went up in flames. No patterns. No press strategy. And the mayor's office is breathing down my neck. We're going to be on the front page by morning, and right now, it's going to say: *'Task Force Fails Again.'*"

He turned his gaze toward Will, sharp enough to pin. "You want to tell me what we *do* have?"

Will met the stare without blinking. "We know the unsub changed methodology: no overt trauma, no restraint. No theater. Poppy's body was handled differently—more care, less spectacle. But the brand was still present. Same position, same precision. The MO's still there, just wearing a different mask."

Lowe spoke without looking up from his notes. "And two messages. One philosophical—something about the soul and the mark. The other was a straight-up threat."

Kristen tapped her tablet screen to wake it, the reflection of Poppy's photo flickering across her pupils. "He's still speaking to us. He's just stopped quoting scripture. He's writing his own verses now."

Rogers leaned forward, elbows on the table, his expression unreadable except for the slight twitch at the corner of his mouth.

"Or," he said, voice low and needling, "he's done. And we're just too stubborn to admit we got outplayed. Maybe Poppy was his goodbye. One last chapter in a long, boring Bible."

Kristen looked at him as if he were mildew spreading on the foundation.

"He left a threat, Dan. That's not a goodbye. That's a dare."

Will's voice was quiet—more like the wind off cold stone than actual speech.

"Then what did he want?"

Rogers didn't answer. No one did. The question hung in the room like the sting of ammonia—too strong to ignore, too vague to name.

Captain Archer exhaled through his nose, a slow, controlled breath that said he was one metaphorical paper cut away from flipping the table.

"What's the word from cyber?"

Kristen didn't look up, fingers swiping across the tablet. "We pulled all digital interactions from Poppy's accounts. Instagram, TikTok, messaging apps—DMs are clean. No red flags. One weird reply on a ramen TikTok from an untraceable burner, but it reads more like a bad joke than anything else."

Archer didn't blink. "Weird how?"

Kristen scrolled, reading. "'I like mine extra soft.' That's it. No follow-up, no context. The account's dead now. Burner email. Proxy routing."

"Creepy," Lowe muttered. "But not actionable."

"And her physical connections?" Archer asked, eyes still on Kristen.

Harris stepped in, flipping through his notes. "Roommate's clean. No boyfriends. No record of stalking or harassment. No complaints to RA or housing. No medical visits. Nothing weird. She was just... a kid. A freshman who posted about dorm life and bad laundry detergent."

Will's jaw flexed again. "That's what scares me."

Captain Archer nodded slowly, his eyes now on the board—the strings, the names, the scarred symbols that might as well be a map they'd never learned to read.

"Let's talk about movement. Anything from neighboring jurisdictions? Cold hits? Similar bodies, tags, anything?"

Lowe shook his head, frustration flickering behind his eyes. "We pinged three states. Local agencies flagged four possibles, but none match the MO. No brands. No positioning. No messages."

"DNA?"

Kristen leaned back in her chair, arms crossed, expression brittle. "The scene was too clean. Again. No hair, no epithelial trace. No semen. No blood. Nothing but the body, the clothes, and those notes."

"TOX?" Archer asked.

Kristen's voice came sharper now. "Trace sedative in her system. Unidentified compound. Lab says either it was synthetic and undocumented, or it degraded past recognition before we found her."

Rogers gave a low whistle. "So... custom-made, or some chemistry-major special brewed in a dorm sink?"

"Could be environmental," Kristen said. "Could be misdirection."

"Could be we're still guessing," Rogers muttered, voice like gravel ground between molars.

The silence that followed was heavier than most. Not just quiet, but *weighted*. Like the room itself knew it was failing them.

The fluorescents buzzed, filling the spaces between the things they weren't saying.

Then Archer spoke, voice low but final.

"Press is circling. The mayor's office is pissed. All the brass is up in arms, DA's calling for results. If we don't give them something by the end of the week, this task force is getting split. They'll hand the case to some political committee and spin it as progress."

No one moved.

Will didn't speak.

Didn't blink.

Kristen finally broke the stillness, leaning forward, both palms braced on the table.

"He's still out there," she said. Her voice wasn't loud, but it cut like glass. "We just haven't seen the next girl yet."

Rogers scoffed, sipping his coffee like it might be whiskey. "And what makes you so sure?"

She met his eyes head-on. Steel against static.

"Because I still wake up in the middle of the night hoping she'll call her mom. And I know he built that."

She straightened, voice flat. "He's still writing."

Will's voice cut through the room like a cold wind.

"He's not done," he said. "He's watching. He's learning how we react when the sermon is silent, when there's no performance. Just death."

Captain Archer stared at the board.

At Poppy.

At the burnt circle etched in red around her photo.

Then he nodded, once.

"Then get me something," he said.

His voice had no volume.

Just weight.

"Now."

## One Week Later – Task Force

The war room was already half-empty when Will walked in.

Boxes stacked against the wall. Case files sealed in brown folders with evidence labels across their spines. The board still hung, white and glaring, but the photos had been stripped. Poppy's face was gone. Hannah's. Avery's. Ivy's. Valentina Dawn's.

Only faint tape outlines remained, like ghosts that had been erased but not forgotten.

Captain Archer stood at the head of the table one last time. His tie was knotted, jacket buttoned—formal, official, as if he'd already moved on to the next role the city wanted him to play. His voice carried the blunt force of an executioner.

"The mayor's office and the DA have made their decision," Archer said. "Effective immediately, the task force is disbanded. If new leads surface or another incident occurs, the unit may be reinstated. But as of today, all officers return to their original assignments."

The words dropped like stones. No protest. No appeal. Just policy.

Will stood beside Joe Donovan, both still in plain clothes but looking out of place without their patrol gear. Kristen sat two chairs down, tablet dark, her posture rigid, jaw tight. Lowe and Harris flipped closed their binders in unison, the sound sharp in the silence. Rogers wasn't even present. No surprise.

Archer's gaze moved across them, one by one. "Anderson. Donovan. You're back on patrol effective Monday. Harris, Lowe—return to your divisions. Rogers has already returned to Oakhaven." He paused, eyes finally landing on Kristen. "ADA Dalton, you're back to standard caseload. Arraignments, hearings, whatever comes across your desk, DA said he needed your expertise."

Kristen's voice came sharp, controlled, but brittle underneath. "So we box it up, pretend it never happened?"

Archer didn't flinch. "We box it up until something changes. That's the order."

Will felt his throat tighten, words pressing up but catching before they could form. He looked at the bare whiteboard—empty strings, faint marker stains. The hum of the fluorescents filled the silence where once there had been argument, strategy, and obsession.

Donovan shifted beside him, muttering under his breath. "Back to barking dogs and traffic stops. Hell of a fall."

Will's jaw worked. He didn't answer. He couldn't.

Kristen pushed back from the table abruptly, her chair screeching against tile. She gathered her tablet and case notes with tight, clipped motions. "He's still out there," she said flatly. Not loud. Not dramatic. Just fact. Then she left the room, the door swinging shut behind her.

No one followed.

Archer cleared his throat, breaking the static. "That's it. Thank you for your service. Dismissed."

One by one, chairs scraped back. Papers rustled. The war room emptied.

Will lingered at the edge of the board, staring at the faint circle where Poppy's photo had been taped. His reflection in the glossy white surface blurred until he couldn't tell if he was looking at himself or at one of the ghosts they hadn't caught.

Joe clapped him on the shoulder, heavy but not unkind. "C'mon. Patrol doesn't wait."

Will nodded once, but inside, something twisted. He knew he'd go back to the streets, the calls, the routine. But part of him wasn't leaving this room. Part of him would stay right here, waiting for the Prophet to write his next verse.

### Notebook Entry – Victims

*-Ivy Cole – "Cherry." Street name. Don't forget the girl under it.*

*-Tammi Warner – "CandyCrush." Online act. Still a victim.*

*-Maggie (Magnolia) Truelove – "Tonya." Locals knew her that way.*

*Remember her real name.*

*-Avery Howell – "HowellYouWantMe." Screen name. Trapped in it.*

*-Poppy Lane – No persona. Freshman. Just a kid.*

**Lesson:** *Names shift. People don't.*

*Remember the faces.*

## Slip

### Dinner – Will & Kristen

The restaurant wasn't fancy—brick walls, low lighting, tables tucked close enough to hear the hum of other conversations without having to speak over them. A place where people came to disappear for an hour without vanishing completely.

Will pushed his fork around the plate more than he ate, eyes flicking between the amber glow of the candle and Kristen across from him. She had her blazer draped over the back of her chair, sleeves rolled up, hair pulled back in a knot that was already starting to come loose. The circles under her eyes hadn't faded since the task force was shut down.

They sat in silence for a while. Not hostile. Just weighted.

Kristen finally spoke. "You ever think about how fast it all... evaporated? One minute we're buried in leads, chasing down threads until our hands bled, and then—" she snapped her fingers, "—poof. Boxed up. Cold file."

Will's voice came low. "Not closed. Just shelved."

Kristen studied him. "You don't think he's done?"

Will shook his head. "No. He's changed. Either a new method or someone helping him run interference. Could be both. But he's still out there."

Kristen's lips curved in something like a smile, but it didn't reach her eyes. "You always expect the worst."

"Someone has to."

She nodded slowly, then leaned back in her chair. Her glass of wine caught the light as she tilted it, watching the thin red cling to the glass. "When I look at those girls... Poppy, Avery, Hannah... I keep thinking about how their futures just vanished. No second chances. No families. No kids laughing in the kitchen. Just—gone."

She paused, frowning at the wine, then added without thinking, "Makes me think about ours. What kind of kids we'd even have, if..."

Her voice trailed off.

The silence that followed wasn't the comfortable kind. Her brow furrowed faintly, as if she hadn't even realized what she'd said. She took another sip, eyes fixed on the table, covering the moment with a quick pivot: "Anyway, he probably wants us doubting ourselves. That's the real sermon—make us question if we ever had him in our sights at all."

Will didn't respond. Didn't let the slip show on his face. But inside, it landed like a stone in still water, rippling outward.

*Our kids.*

She hadn't meant it. Hadn't even caught it. But he had.

And he wasn't about to forget.

He kept it to himself.

For now.

### Will's Apartment – Later That Night

The apartment was quiet, except for the hum of the fridge and the faint drip of the bathroom faucet, which he kept meaning to fix. Patrol boots by the door. Jacket thrown across the arm of the couch.

Will sat at the kitchen table with the case notebook still open in front of him, though the pages hadn't moved in twenty minutes. His pen rested idle across the paper.

He wasn't seeing the notes. Not the sketches of the Prophet's mark. Not the timelines or cross-references.

He was hearing her.

*"Makes me think about ours. What kind of kids we'd even have, if..."*

The words echoed like a misstep on a stairwell—unexpected, off-balance, leaving him suspended in the drop.

She hadn't meant to say it. He knew that. Kristen was too careful, too precise. She wielded words like scalpels, not slips. But there it was, bare and unguarded, a piece of her that had slipped out sideways while she was mourning the victims.

Kids. Their kids.

He pictured it without meaning to—Kristen in their kitchen, hair down, a laugh he didn't hear often enough. A child's toy in the corner. A life not built around autopsy photos and sermons carved into flesh.

He closed his eyes, exhaling through his nose. The image didn't feel real. Didn't feel safe. Because every time he let his guard down, he heard another voice layered over hers.

*The flesh can be broken. The soul can be burned.*

The Prophet wasn't finished. Will felt it in his bones, in the same marrow-deep certainty that told him Kristen's slip hadn't been just empty words.

He stared at the white page in front of him, then wrote in block letters across the margin:

**CHANGED METHOD**

**SECOND PLAYER?**

**WAITING FOR US TO SLIP**

The pen dug deep enough to dent the paper.

He set it down and leaned back, the kitchen light buzzing faintly overhead. The city outside his window kept moving—sirens in the distance, engines revving, the steady pulse of a place that never really slept.

Will sat in the middle of it, caught between two truths:

The Prophet was still out there.

And Kristen had just given him a glimpse of a future he didn't know he deserved.

Both scared him more than anything else.

### Kristen's Apartment – Later That Night

Kristen kicked her heels off at the door, let her bag drop where it fell, and padded barefoot into her kitchen. The clock on the stove blinked 11:47. She poured herself a glass of water she didn't want and leaned against the counter, staring at nothing.

Her tablet still sat in her bag, case notes and deposition prep waiting for her. She should have been reviewing them. She should have been outlining arguments for tomorrow's arraignments.

Instead, she was replaying dinner.

Not the food. Not the wine. Not the silence that had stretched too long between them.

The words.

Her words.

*"Makes me think about ours. What kind of kids we'd even have, if—"*

Kristen closed her eyes, groaned softly, and set the glass down too hard. Water sloshed over the rim.

She hadn't meant to say it. She wasn't even sure where it came from. One moment she'd been talking about the victims—about Poppy, Hannah, all the futures stolen from them. And the next moment... her own future had slipped into the sentence, with Will's name inked in invisible letters.

"Christ," she muttered, rubbing at her temples.

She wasn't built for that kind of life. She knew it. She'd spent years telling herself that—career first, control always, emotion at a safe distance. Families belonged to other people. Safer people. People who didn't drag monsters home in their thoughts every night.

And yet—She saw it. For half a second at that table, she saw it: Will across from her, not as a partner in a war room but as something else. A hand brushing hers, not over case files, but over the edge of a crib. A home instead of a crime scene.

The image startled her so much she almost laughed. Almost.

Kristen straightened, pressing her palms against the cool countertop until her arms ached. She shook her head once, sharply, as if she could jolt herself back into focus.

*No. Don't go there. That's not for you.*

She left the water on the counter, went to her desk, powered on her laptop, and buried herself in tomorrow's docket until the thought dulled. But beneath every sentence she typed, the slip lingered like a watermark she couldn't scrub away.

Will had heard it. She was sure of it.

She just didn't know what he'd do with it.

## Back on Assignment – One Week Later
## Summit Falls – Midnight Patrol

The cruiser idled at a red light, headlights stretching across an empty four-lane highway that looked like it hadn't seen life in hours. Neon from a twenty-four-hour laundromat flickered in the reflection on the windshield.

Will adjusted his grip on the wheel, his uniform collar biting at his neck. The city felt different now—too quiet, too thin—like the silence was mocking him.

Sergeant Donovan sat in the passenger seat, one boot propped against the dash despite the crease in his pants, coffee steaming in the cupholder. His stripes caught the glow of the dashboard light. Technically, he wasn't supposed to be here—he had his own work, the rest of his team to supervise—but tonight he'd shrugged it off.

"Figured I'd ride with you," Donovan said, sipping. "Patrol's patrol, but hell, I didn't feel like babysitting rookies. Thought we could keep each other awake."

Will glanced over, arching a brow. "Thought you liked babysitting."

Donovan smirked. "I like watching kids crash and burn. Different thing."

The radio cracked, dispatcher's voice thin and bored:

*"Unit 2-4, copy disturbance. Harbor View Apartments, building C. Caller reports yelling, possible domestic. No weapons mentioned."*

Will thumbed the mic. "Two-four, copy. En route. Also, be advised I am a two-man unit along with Two-zero."

The siren chirped once as he pulled the cruiser through the light.

Donovan stretched, settling deeper into his seat. "You miss it yet?"

"Miss what?"

"The Prophet," Donovan said casually, though his eyes stayed on the dark street. "The chase. The board. The war room. The late nights with Archer breathing down our necks."

Will's jaw flexed. "You don't miss a killer."

"That's not what I asked."

Will didn't answer. His hands tightened on the wheel instead. The truth itched inside him: he did miss it. The weight, the clarity of hunting something that mattered. Now he was driving toward a shouting match in an apartment complex that smelled like cat piss and mold.

Donovan let the silence hang. "Guy like him doesn't stop. Maybe he changed his song. Maybe he's got somebody else helping him write the verses."

Will shot him a look, startled by the echo of his own thoughts. "You don't think it's over."

Donovan shrugged, a bitter smile tugging at his mouth. "Do you?"

Will didn't answer because they both knew.

### Summit Falls – District Attorney's Office – Afternoon

Kristen sat at her desk with her hair pulled back in a tight knot, which gave her a headache. Her office was stacked with files—assaults, narcotics, arraignments— cases that blurred together in stale ink and plea deals.

She tried to read the motion in front of her, but the words slipped like oil. All she could hear was her own voice from dinner with Will.

*"Makes me think about ours. What kind of kids we'd even have, if—"*

Her stomach tightened. She'd said it without realizing, just let it spill into the air between wine and exhaustion. Will hadn't reacted, not then, but he'd heard. He always heard.

She pressed her palms against her eyes until stars bloomed. *Idiot. You don't get to think like that. Not with him. Not after everything you've seen.*

Her phone buzzed on the desk. A patrol report pinged her inbox—*Unit 2-4, disturbance at Harbor View Apartments. Anderson and Donovan.*

She stared at the screen longer than she should have. Not because the call mattered—routine domestic, most likely—but because of his name on the header.

Her reflection stared back at her in the glass of her monitor, eyes ringed with exhaustion. She muttered to herself, "You don't want that life, Kristen. You don't."

But a quiet part of her wondered if she was lying.

### Harbor View Apartments – 12:42 a.m.

The building smelled like fried onions and mildew. Voices carried down the stairwell as Will and Donovan climbed, the echoes sharp against peeling paint.

Third floor. Unit 3C. A door half-open, light spilling into the hall. A man and a woman arguing in tired voices, the kind that had repeated the same fight a hundred times before.

Donovan glanced at Will as they stopped in the doorway. "Ready for the big collar?"

Will gave him a flat look. "Try not to strain your back."

The couple froze at the sight of uniforms. The shouting deflated, replaced by sheepish mutters and crossed arms. No weapons. No danger. Just anger burned down to embers.

Routine. Pointless.

Will took names, filled out the incident card, and gave the talk he'd given a hundred times. "Cool off. Keep it down. Next time it's citations."

They left ten minutes later, boots heavy on the stairs. Outside, the cruiser waited, windshield catching the sodium glow of the streetlamp.

Donovan let out a low chuckle. "World saved again."

Will didn't laugh. His eyes scanned the street, as if the Prophet might be waiting in the shadows, watching them waste time.

### Back at the Station

The bullpen smelled like burned coffee and spent patience. Night lights hummed overhead; the clock above the squad room door counted seconds like a metronome. Will sat at the report terminal, the glow of the monitor throwing his face into hard planes. Paperwork blurred into checklist after checklist until the words meant nothing.

Joe slid into the chair across from him like he owned the place—because he almost did. He had the easy gait of a man who'd seen too much and learned to make jokes about it. He skewed his head and grinned.

"You and that pretty little ADA of yours need to wrap it up," Joe said, flat as a command and twice as casual.

Will blinked. The sentence landed oddly. For half a beat, he took it the way his gut wanted—wrap it up, end it, close the file. He felt an odd, sharp relief at the thought, like someone had offered him a way out. His shoulders eased, the knot in his chest loosening a fraction.

"Cut things off?" Will asked before he could stop himself, because his brain wanted the safety of distance. "You saying—keep it professional? Don't mix work with—" He trailed off, looking for the right word that wouldn't admit how much of his life had been absorbed by cases.

Joe's face broke into a laugh, loud and genuine, and Will's stomach dropped at the realization he'd misread everything.

"No, kid!" Joe slapped the desk, the sound sharp in the quiet room. "Not end it. I mean, wrap that left finger of hers, put a band on it before it's too late."

He leaned forward, grin crooked but eyes warmer than his tone. "You wait too long, and one of you is gonna do something you'll regret. That's what you avoid. Not the girl, not that girl, the hesitation."

Will blinked, the words hitting like a baton to the ribs. For a second, he couldn't tell if Joe was screwing with him or laying down gospel.

"You're telling me to marry her?" Will said. It came out small, half a question, half a laugh that didn't reach his eyes.

Joe's grin softened. "Telling you to decide. You tell me you and Dalton can't mix work and life because of the cases—well, sometimes the choice is to anchor each other, not to run. Life doesn't get easier, Will. It just gets fuller or lonelier depending on who's beside you. Would help her as well, I see the same fire in her as I do in you, kid."

Will's hand went to his left ring finger, the way the muscle memory of a reflex reaches for a wound. The skin there, bare, felt like a secret suddenly exposed. In his head, he saw Dalton at the dinner table—the slip, the offhand words about kids that had startled them both— and he felt the room tilt a little.

"You know what this job does," Will said, voice low. "You know what it takes. You think dragging someone into that—" He didn't finish. The Prophet's mark, the burned circle, the sermons carved into flesh all crowded the end of that sentence.

Joe's expression turned a shade more serious, the joke peeling back. "Yeah, I know, which is why you don't wait until 'yes' or 'no' gets decided for you. You need to choose before the world does it for you." He tapped the pad of his thumb against the desk like he was punctuating the point. "And if you think getting hitched is the kind of dumb thing you'll regret—do it anyway, or don't. But choose. Don't drift."

Will swallowed. He looked at the ring finger again as if he could will a band into being. In the fluorescent light, it was an island of plain skin. The thought of putting metal there felt both terrifying and quietly inevitable.

Joe stood, stretching, another cup of coffee in hand. He tossed a final grin over his shoulder. "I'm not your priest, Anderson. I'm a cop with a bad sense of timing and a worse taste in advice. But marry her, or don't—but for God's sake, don't wait on some phantom sermon to decide for you."

Will watched him go, the chair rocking slightly in the wake. The bullpen hummed on. The monitor blinked. In the low light, his left hand looked heavier than it had an hour before.

When the door shut behind Joe, Will didn't move for a long time. He thought of Dalton's words at dinner—*our kids*—and of the Prophet's quiet escalation. He thought of risk and love, of protection and the impossibility of promise.

Finally, he flexed his fingers slowly and rolled his knuckles one by one, as if testing what kind of future might fit them.

# Viral

## University Call – Midday

The call came over the radio just after noon:

*"Unit 2-4, campus security requesting assistance, intoxicated subject in the library, suspicious person complaint."*

Will shot Donovan a look. "Suspicious *and* drunk. Should be fun."

Joe sipped his coffee, the corner of his mouth twitching. "College town special. Let's go babysit."

The campus was alive with midday traffic—students hustling between classes, earbuds in, phones up, laughter bouncing off brick facades. Will guided the cruiser through the main quad toward the library, the green lawn dotted with backpacks and frisbee games like nothing bad ever happened in the world.

A campus officer flagged them down, already red in the face. "We've got an intox in custody inside," he said quickly, jerking a thumb toward the library doors. "But the suspicious male is out here—white hoodie, ballcap, lurking near the bike racks. Matches a student report."

Will spotted him easily: late twenties maybe, wiry, shifting on his feet like the pavement burned. Hoodie zipped high despite the warm day. Ballcap shadowing darting eyes.

Joe muttered, "He's practically wearing a neon sign that says *cop bait*."

They approached casually, hands loose, posture nonthreatening. Will started with the tone he used on traffic stops. "Afternoon, man. How are you doing? Got an ID on you?"

The guy froze. His eyes flicked between Will and Joe, sweat breaking along his temple.

Then he bolted.

*"Unit 2-4, foot pursuit!"* Will barked into the mic as he took off. Students scattered, squealing, phones already whipping up to record. The suspect sprinted down the brick walkway, weaving through bodies, shoving past a guy with a skateboard.

Will's boots pounded pavement, heart hammering. He closed the gap fast. The hoodie caught on the corner of a bench—just enough hesitation for Will to dive. He tackled the guy hard into the grass, momentum knocking the breath out of both of them.

The suspect flailed, yelling before Will even got cuffs on                                                                him. "Okay, okay—I got warrants, man! Don't tase me! I wasn't stalking Kelly, I promise! I wasn't!"

Will forced one wrist behind his back, knee on the guy's shoulder blade. Students ringed the scene in a half-circle, filming.

Joe strolled up, catching his breath like he'd run half the distance slower on purpose. "Hell of a catch, Anderson. Remind me to put you in for the NFL draft."

A girl with a dark red backpack had her phone out front and center, voice excited.

"Oh my God, I got it! I got it—y'all, look at this!" She flipped the camera, hair falling into her face as she grinned widely. "Coolest cops in Ravenwood County, y'all Hashtag HeroStopsPervert."

She swung the phone back to capture Will and Joe hauling the suspect to his feet in cuffs. The suspect was still rambling—"It wasn't stalking, she told me to text her! I just wanted to watch her walk to class!"—while students murmured and laughed around them.

An hour later, in the cruiser. The suspect sulked in the back seat, wrists tight in cuffs, hoodie stained with grass.

Will's phone buzzed. A message from Kristen.

**Kristen Dalton:** *You're a TikTok star.*

Will frowned at the screen. *What?*

A second later, a link came through.

He clicked.

There it was—shaky but clear enough: Will sprinting down the brick walkway, boots hammering the pavement, weaving through startled students. The camera caught the moment he dove, taking the hoodie guy down hard into the grass. The suspect flailed, yelling about warrants and Kelly, while Joe jogged into frame, looking more like backup in a movie than a cop on patrol.

The voice behind the camera was unmistakably thrilled. "Oh my God, I got it! I got it—y'all, look at this! Coolest cops in Ravenwood County!"

The clip cut to selfie mode. A girl in a Ravenwood hoodie filled the frame—round glasses, messy, wavy auburn ponytail, backpack strap across one shoulder. Her grin was wide, adrenaline still in her voice. "Casey Murphy here—@LawCaseyMurphy—and I just caught a Summit Falls PD officer taking down some perv outside the library. You cannot make this up, Ladies and gentlemen."

She swung the phone back around to capture Will and Joe hauling the guy up in cuffs. He was still rambling, swearing he hadn't stalked Kelly; he just wanted to watch her walk to class, saying she had taken a warrant out on him by mistake, while students gathered in the background, half amused, half filming for themselves.

The caption blared in bold text:

**#HeroStopsPervert @LawCaseyMurphy**
*Coolest cops in Ravenwood County, hands down.*

Within minutes, the view count ticked past a hundred, comments flooding in—

*"That tackle tho was lit"*

*"We have Officer NFL over here."*

*"Casey out here making true crime content live."*

Will scrolled, jaw tightening as he realized how fast the numbers were climbing.

The view count ticked upward in real time—hundreds already.

Joe leaned over, saw the screen, and barked a laugh that filled the cruiser. "Oh, that's rich. Look at you, rookie—famous already. Might need an autograph before the shift's over."

Will shook his head, cheeks hot. "Unbelievable."

From the back seat, the suspect piped up, "Hey, did she get a good angle of me? Tag me, man, I'll put it on my page. Get some followers outta this."

Without even glancing at each other, Will and Joe barked in unison:

"Shut up!" as Joe banged on the cage.

The suspect slumped against the partition, muttering, then leaned back in the seat.

Joe grinned, savoring the moment. "TikTok star, huh? Guess I'm riding with a celebrity."

Will groaned and drove on, the city rolling past like it hadn't just seen him turned into a hashtag.

### Family Dinner – Dalton House

A few days later, the Dalton home smelled like roasted turkey and cinnamon, warm light spilling across framed photos that lined the hall. The dining room table was already crowded—platters of stuffing, green beans, sweet potatoes, and the kind of rolls you could smell from the porch.

Kristen sat at the head of the table, cheeks flushed from wine and laughter. Beside her, Will was trying to keep pace with the rhythm of her family, a rhythm he'd never been invited into before tonight.

Her mom, Elaine Dalton, was the picture of Southern grace—silver streaking her dark hair, pearl earrings catching the light as she fussed over him. "Now, Will, you let me know if that turkey's too dry. I told Kristen we pulled it too early, but she never listens to her mother."

Will smiled. "It's perfect, ma'am."

Her dad, Robert Dalton, had a voice like gravel and a handshake that hadn't softened in sixty years. He'd already drawn Will into a long talk about the Army, nodding approvingly as Will spoke. Now he leaned back, sipping from a short glass of bourbon. "I'll say this, son— you've got the look of a man who knows how to keep steady in a storm. That's something I trust more than a résumé."

Across the table, Kristen's younger sister, Brittany Jo Dalton, had been grinning like a cat with cream all evening. Sharp, playful, and maybe a little too nosy, she leaned forward now, chin propped in her hand. "So, Officer Anderson... you gonna be writing family tickets too, or do we get a free pass?"

Kristen groaned. "Brittany—"

Will smirked. "Depends on whether the family brings pie."

Brittany Jo nearly choked on her wine, laughing. Elaine shook her head, smiling despite herself. Robert's chuckle rumbled low as he refilled his glass.

It felt... easy. Natural. The kind of dinner Will hadn't known he'd been missing until he was here.

Plates were cleared, and silver scraped into the sink. Elaine disappeared into the kitchen, promising pumpkin pie in ten minutes. Robert stood, working the cork out of another bottle of wine.

Will's heart kicked, hard and steady. He slid his hand into his pocket, feeling the velvet box there. He'd already sat with Robert earlier that afternoon, out on the porch, talking for nearly an hour. He'd spoken to Elaine too, careful but honest, telling her how much Kristen grounded him, how much he wanted to build a life with her. They'd been delighted. Thrilled, even.

Kristen leaned toward Will, brushing his hand under the table. "You've been awfully quiet tonight," she whispered, brow arched.

"Just waiting for the right moment," he said.

Then he pushed his chair back. The sound—sharp against the tile—cut through the hum of after-dinner chatter. Kristen blinked, confused.

"Will?"

Her dad glanced up, brows lifting. Elaine froze in the kitchen doorway with a pie knife in hand. Brittany Jo gasped, eyes going saucer-wide, and nearly squealed before clapping her hand over her mouth.

Will dropped to one knee beside Kristen's chair.

The velvet box opened.

"Kristen Dalton," he said, steady despite his racing heart, "from the first time you remembered me in that courthouse, you've grounded me. You've seen the worst parts of this job, the worst parts of me—and you never flinched. You make me better. You make me believe in something after the shift ends. I asked your mom and dad, and they gave me their blessing. Now I'm asking you: will you marry me?"

For a moment, Kristen just stared. Tears welled, but her lips trembled. She pulled her hands back from her face, shaking her head slightly like she couldn't catch her breath.

"Oh my God," she whispered. Her voice cracked. Her hands pressed against her chest. She looked down at him—eyes wide, overwhelmed. Her silence stretched too long. Long enough that Will's stomach dropped, his pulse roaring in his ears. Elaine's smile faltered. Robert leaned forward, jaw tight. Brittany Jo muttered under her breath, "Don't you dare—"

Then Kristen's chair screeched back, and she launched forward, throwing her arms around Will's neck. Her sobs burst out, wild and unrestrained. "Yes!" she cried. "Yes, yes, oh my God—yes!"

Will's relief came like a gut punch. He slid the ring onto her shaking hand, kissed her hard, and held her while she sobbed against his shoulder. Elaine was openly crying, Robert shaking his head but smiling as wide as Will had ever seen him, and Brittany Jo half out of her chair, clapping like a cheerleader.

When Kristen finally pulled back, laughing through her tears, Brittany Jo couldn't help herself. "Well, thank God," she said, wiping her eyes with a napkin. "For a second there, I thought you were about to be the first guy in Dalton history to get turned down *in front of the pie.*"

The room broke into laughter—Kristen swatting her sister with the napkin, Elaine scolding "Brittany Jo!" through her own tears, Robert raising his glass in a silent toast.

Will kissed Kristen's temple, whispering just for her: "Didn't want you to see it coming."

She laughed against him, still trembling, still crying. "You blindsided me, Anderson. But in the best way."

Pumpkin pie never stood a chance.

### Later – Dalton Porch Swing

The night air was cool and smelled faintly of woodsmoke. Crickets hummed in the grass beyond the porch. The swing creaked gently as Will and Kristen swayed together, her hand still tight in his, the new ring catching the moonlight like it had always belonged there.

Through the screen door behind them, laughter drifted from the dining room—her dad telling a story, her mom fussing about more coffee, Brittany Jo still giddy from almost spoiling the surprise.

Kristen leaned her head against Will's shoulder, her hair soft against his cheek. She exhaled, a sound that was half sigh, half laugh. "You nearly gave me a heart attack in there."

Will kissed the top of her head. "For a second, I thought you were gonna say no."

She turned her face up to him, eyes still rimmed red from crying. "Say no? To you?" Her voice cracked into a laugh. "Will, I think I was in shock. You blindsided me. My brain shut down before my heart could catch up."

"Had me sweating," he said, shaking his head. "I've faced down worse calls without nerves like that."

Kristen smirked through her tears. "Good. Means you care."

Silence stretched, comfortable this time. The swing rocked slowly. Will watched the ring glint again, the way her fingers tightened around his.

"You know," she whispered after a moment, "I wasn't sure I'd ever let someone in like this. With what I see at work, with what we've seen... it's easier to keep the walls up. But you—" she swallowed, her voice softening— "you make me feel like I don't have to carry it all alone. Like I get to have a life outside the job."

Will's chest tightened. He brushed his thumb across her hand, his words quiet but firm. "That's what you do for me, too. You keep me grounded. Even on the worst nights, I know I've got you to come back to."

Kristen shifted closer, her breath warm against his neck. "Good," she murmured. "Then promise me we'll keep it that way. No matter what the job throws at us."

Will turned, kissed her slowly and certainly. When he pulled back, he rested his forehead against hers. "Promise."

The swing creaked again, rocking steady as the two of them sat under the stars—inside, a family waiting, outside, a life ahead neither of them could have imagined two years ago.

## Transition

Back at his apartment, after a long shift, Will sat with the notebook open across his knees, the pages worn soft from two years of sweat and coffee stains. He flipped back to the first entries, the ones Donovan had barked into him like sermons.

*"You get one hesitation. That was yours."*

*"Patience and backup beat ego."*

*"Don't chase the chaos. Keep the beat."*

His own scrawls crowded the margins:

*Always the hands.*

*Stay alive, then do the job.*

*Listen longer than you talk.*

Then, on one page stained with rain, a line Joe had muttered during a dead-end midnight patrol. Will had written it down without thinking, not realizing how it would stick.

*"Don't let the noise fool you, kid. There are good cops out there fighting for justice. Not perfect, not saints—but men and women who show up, night after night, and don't quit. You'll never see them on the news. Doesn't matter. They're the ones holding the line."*

At the time, Will hadn't known what to make of it. But now—after Cherry, after Maggie—it hit different.

He traced the words with his thumb. Joe hadn't been talking about heroes. He'd been talking about survival. About showing up even when no one clapped, when the brass looked away, when the city forgot your name.

"Give it about a year and a half, kid, you'll then see what this job is all about, you'll understand what you are doing out here." Joe's words seemed like he was criticizing.

Two years of scribbles, mistakes, bruises, and lessons. And Will understood: Joe had been teaching him more than how to keep breathing, not criticizing. He'd been teaching him what kind of cop to be.

The kind who stayed in the fight.

Looking back, Will recalled, the first call on Drexel and Maple didn't end in blood. Not that night. But it reminded Will how quickly the rhythm could break—how routine turned to chaos with one radio call, one wrong step.

In the days that followed, his focus drifted—not because he wasn't doing the job, but because the job was shifting around him. The murder of Cherry. Tonya's attack, the others. The message carved into them all: pain, silence, degradation. And the system's answer? Indifference.

That was before the Prophet Task Force. Before Archer's war room, before the whiteboard of faces stared down at them like a jury that would never acquit. For nearly two years, Will had lived inside that case. Day after day of sermons carved into flesh, of chasing shadows through dead-end leads, of hoping one more interview, one more camera feed, would bring them closer. What he found instead was how heavy justice became when the city didn't want to look too closely at the women who were vanishing.

Will had seen death before, had worn a uniform in places where violence was expected. But this was different. In Summit Falls, violence hid behind routine. Behind locked motel doors. Behind a badge. There were no after-action reports here. No flags were folded neatly. Just the slow, suffocating weight of lives discarded because they didn't fit anyone's narrative of who mattered.

And still, there were good moments. Steady ones. Kristen's voice in the quiet, reminding him he didn't have to carry it all alone. Her hand in his, anchoring him when he wanted to come apart. She never flinched. Not when he talked about the body. Not when he admitted what it did to him. With her, he could bleed without breaking.

By the time his three months of field training ended, Will was officially cut loose—slotted into Joe Donovan's squad. Not by accident. Not by request. The brass liked pairing the green ones with Donovan. Said he broke them in right.

Will didn't argue.

The following two years, Will recalling blurred into streets, shifts, and off-duty hours spent slowly letting someone love him. Lessons carved into him one call at a time. Joe's voice never softened, but Will began to hear it differently. Not as a threat. As ballast.

The Army had taught him how to lock down fear. Police work taught him when to let it show. Combat had rules. This job had judgment.

The Prophet taught him something else entirely—that evil could be patient, that it could bleed into ordinary places: a motel bed, a dorm hallway, a quiet greenbelt at dawn. Will had carried Maggie out of that barn, had sat across from Poppy Lane's ghost in grainy security footage, and had stood in front of a truck that went up in flames before they could even open the door. Each moment etched itself into him the way Joe's lessons once had, only sharper, crueler.

He learned:

Some cops cut corners. Others froze. Some should never have pinned on a badge.

The shield didn't make them family. Not all of them could be trusted.

The job didn't end when the shift did. The weight came home with you—if you cared enough to carry it.

Joe didn't sugarcoat it. *"Trust no one,"* he'd say. *"Not the brass. Not the hotshots. Not even your partner sometimes. Keep your house clean, kid. That's how you survive."*

But Joe wasn't blind to those who did belong. Will recalled once again Joe's rant at least every six months or so, late night, under a flickering streetlight, he'd tell Will quietly:

*"Some of us are still in this for the right reasons. Men and women who'd bleed out before they let someone else get hurt. Don't let the bad ones poison the job for you. But remember—most of the public will never see the difference. And they won't care to."*

Will had wanted to believe the badge bound them together. That the public saw them for what they were trying to be. But he learned fast. The badge wasn't armor. It was weight.

By the end of his second year, he wasn't just wearing it.

He was carrying it.

And through it all—through the alleys, the bruises, the nights that wouldn't let him sleep—Kristen had been there. She'd grounded him in a way Joe never could. She listened when he couldn't put the job into words. She challenged him when he tried to wall off too much. Their chemistry was easy, electric, and steady all at once. For the first time since leaving the Army, he didn't feel like he was carrying the weight alone, his bride-to-be, the mother to his children.

Sometimes it was as simple as her laugh across a dinner table. Other times, it was her hand steadying his when the job left him raw. Either way, she had become part of the rhythm Joe always talked about—the beat that kept him going when the chaos tried to swallow him whole.

And still, even with her, the case lingered. Two years of chasing the Prophet had left him with more ghosts than answers, more lessons written in scars than in ink. The task force was gone now, boxed up and forgotten, but Will knew better. The Prophet wasn't finished. He'd spent two years learning how to be a cop, how to survive the shift. Now he had to learn something harder—how to live with the fact that survival might not be enough.

And then, two months later, everything shifted.

Sgt. Donovan was reassigned—transferred to Vice/Narcotics after the squad's longtime sergeant received a promotion. Soon after, within a week or so, two vacancies arose. One officer was gone for good, injured after a raid went sideways. Another moved on to a federal job.

The opening sat like a challenge.

Will applied the moment the posting went up. No hesitation. He'd been warned—Vice chewed up rookies. Too many blurred lines. Too much temptation. Too much looking the other way.

But if Joe was there, Will wanted to be there. To keep learning. To keep the beat—this time, where it mattered even more.

And now, with Kristen in his corner, he felt steadier than ever. He couldn't wait to see what the next chapter would hold—on the street, and with her.

His transfer came through faster than expected.

Just like that, patrol was in the rearview.

### Kristen's Apartment – Late Evening

The TV hummed in the background, some sitcom laugh track spilling into the room, but neither of them was really watching. Kristen curled up on the couch, oversized hoodie, legs tucked under her, hair loose now, her hand absently playing with the ring that still felt brand-new on her finger.

Will sat beside her, leaned back, his arm stretched along the cushion. He'd just finished telling her again—Vice had approved his transfer, it was official.

Kristen's lips curved, her eyes bright. "So that's it, huh? My fiancé, the detective, is getting to play undercover?" She tilted her head at him, mock serious. "I have to admit, I don't know how I feel about this."

Will frowned slightly. "You said you were okay with it."

"Oh, I *am*," she said quickly, smile widening. "But let's get one thing straight." She poked a finger into his chest. "I fell in love with a police officer. I'm not about to cheat on him with some made-up persona you're playing for the job."

Will blinked, then smirked. "Cheat on me... with me?"

"Exactly." Her laugh bubbled out, low and teasing. "If you come home one night pretending to be some drug runner named Snake or Ricky or whatever, don't think I'm going along with it."

He chuckled, shaking his head. "Snake?"

"I'm serious," she said, biting back another laugh. "I don't care how deep you go—Vice cop, undercover, whatever. You're still mine. And if you try to sell me some story about your alias—" She leaned closer, her lips brushing his ear. "—I'll arrest you myself."

Will felt his breath hitch as the heat rose quickly. "That a promise?"

"Mm-hm." Kristen slid off the couch, tugging his hand until he followed. She shot him a wicked grin over her shoulder as she pulled him down the hallway toward her bedroom. "Now come on, Officer Tom Hanson. Time for your cover to get blown."

The sitcom laugh track filled the empty couch as they disappeared down the hall, the glow of the TV painting the living room in flickers of light.

## Vice

The pool hall smelled like wet ashtrays and sweat. Neon beer signs flickered weakly in the windows, buzzing like dying insects. The felt on the pool tables was worn smooth in places, darker where years of chalk and grease had soaked in. Balls cracked lazily as a pair of hustlers played for pocket change, pretending not to notice the deals happening in the corners.

Will tugged at his collar. The wire hidden beneath rubbed against his skin, and the shirt clung too tightly under the heat of the overhead lights. Undercover work wasn't a uniform, wasn't crisp boots or polished brass—it was sweat-stained denim and a too-long stare at a bar mirror, pretending not to be what you were. He hated it already.

Joe stood near the jukebox, blending in without trying. Plainclothes, sleeves rolled, aviators reflecting the neon. He wasn't playing a part. He was just Joe. A wall of stone with a paper cup of black coffee he'd smuggled in. Nobody questioned him. Nobody ever did. Will reminded himself Joe had run vice once, before the stripes and the sergeant's shield. For him, this was old ground. For Will, it was quicksand.

Will shifted his stance, weight on his toes, a military habit.

"Relax your shoulders," Joe muttered without looking at him.

Will forced his posture to slacken. *This feels wrong. Soldiers stand tall. Cops should too. But tonight I'm supposed to be no one.*

At the bar, the mark leaned in close to his buddy, tattoos curling up his neck like spilled ink. His fingers toyed with a keychain, nervous ticks he probably thought no one saw. The buy was supposed to be simple: cash for product, backup staged a block away.

Will could already feel it unraveling.

The bartender slid a glass of flat soda toward him. "You gonna order something real, kid?"

Will forced a smirk. "Pacing myself."

The bartender snorted and moved on.

Joe's voice came low. "He's looking at you. Ease up."

Will turned slightly, not enough to break cover but enough to catch the mark's eyes on him—sharp, testing, the kind of look that cuts straight through the noise. The man whispered something into his buddy's ear, a low scrape of sound that didn't carry, then tugged at the hem of his jacket. Subtle, but not lost on Will. There was weight there. Metal, maybe.

The deal was slipping.

*Come on. Stick to the plan. Cash for product. Walk away clean.*

His pulse thudded against the wire under his shirt, every beat loud enough to give him away. He forced himself forward, shoulders loose the way Joe had told him, heart hammering all the same.

The cover story—his cover story—came out stiff, too polished, like reciting a report instead of leaning into the lie. Words arranged neatly in his mouth, nothing like the loose swagger he'd rehearsed in the mirror.

The mark's eyes narrowed, his mouth twisting into a humorless grin. He leaned in close, his breath sour with the smell of cheap beer and menthol.

"You sound like a cop."

Shit.

Will's throat went dry. He tried to swallow, but the air caught sharp, snagging on instinct. His fingers twitched at his side, wanting to reach for the badge that wasn't there, for the weight of the service weapon holstered under the denim. Every muscle screamed *do something.*

From across the room, Joe shifted—just slightly, just enough. He didn't step in, didn't break the scene. He didn't have to. A presence like stone, unmoving, watchful. The kind of man who'd worked vice long enough to know when a buy was about to turn bloody.

Will forced himself to breathe, to keep his eyes on the mark without flinching. His brain scrambled for an answer, a way to claw back control. The mark's buddy cracked his knuckles, grinning like a shark that smelled blood.

The whole room felt tighter. Smoke from the pool players' cigarettes hung in the air like a curtain, closing in.

Will's voice scraped out, lower, rougher, grasping at the kind of slang he'd only half-believed when practicing. "You think I'd be sittin' here in this dump if I was a cop? C'mon, man. Just hand it over. I ain't got time to play."

The mark didn't smile. He just stared, eyes flat, like he was deciding whether to sell or to pull.

He started to back toward the door, hand brushing his waistband.

Will moved too fast, blocking his way; every nerve screamed, 'Don't let him walk.'

He planted his feet in a military stance, his shoulders squared. Wrong move. Too aggressive. The room tensed. Pool balls stopped clattering. Cigarettes froze halfway to lips.

For a second, the air was gunpowder waiting for a spark.

Then Joe was there. Not loud, not rough, just a hand on the man's wrist, a whisper too soft for Will to catch. Whatever he said, it drained the fight from the suspect. The man sagged, his buddy cursed under his breath, and in the space of a heartbeat, backup flooded the hall. Cuffs clicked. Evidence bagged. Sting over.

Will stood frozen, adrenaline rushing hot, sweat running cold down his back.

Later, outside in the alley, he finally breathed. The neon glow bled onto the wet pavement, painting oil slicks in ugly rainbow streaks. Will leaned against the wall, hands trembling just enough to make him shove them in his pockets.

"This..." he muttered, shaking his head. "This isn't what I thought the job was, pretending in bars? Whisper deals? Feels like... feels like lying more than policing."

Joe lit a cigarette, flame briefly painting his lined face. He exhaled smoke in a steady stream. "You think the job's about how it looks?"

Will didn't answer. Didn't trust himself to.

Joe's tone stayed flat, almost bored, but his words cut clean. "Politics, Anderson. Brass wants stats. Arrests. Photos for the press release. That's noise. The job's the signal. You cut through the bullshit and protect the people who'd never walk into a place like that. That's the work."

Behind them, two vice cops joked as they loaded evidence into a cruiser. "Bagged another one for the monthly numbers," one said, smirking. "Brass will be happy."

The other laughed. "That's all that matters, right?"

Will's gut twisted. He glanced at Joe.

Joe didn't even turn his head. Just flicked ash into the gutter. "That's noise."

**Notebook Entry:**
*Vice. Pool hall sting. Sloppy but worked.*
*Brass wants stats. Street wants honesty.*
*Politics = noise. Job = signal.*

He paused. Added one more line beneath, smaller, like a question he wasn't ready to answer.

*Is this still policing?*

*Or just playing a part?*

He underlined it once, hard enough to tear the paper.

Then closed the book.

## Shoot

The tenement on Craven Street was a mausoleum masquerading as an apartment building. The air reeked of mold, cat piss, and fried onions that had seeped into the walls decades ago. The stairwell groaned beneath their boots, its steps slick with a film of grease that no mop had ever managed to touch.

A baby wailed on the second floor, thin and sharp, before a tired voice hushed it back into silence.

Will's vest felt heavier than usual, the straps biting into his shoulders like claws. His radio pressed into his ribs, sweat slicking the plastic. He adjusted it twice on the climb, then forced his hands still. He could hear Joe in his head: *Control the body, control the fear.*

Soldier first. Cop second.

Breathe steady.

Eyes up.

At the third-floor landing, Joe's fist went up. Stop. Wait.

Will froze mid-step, pulse slamming in his ears.

The door to 3C hung slightly open. Light spilled across the hall in jagged bands. Shadows shifted inside—voices—quick, sharp, too loud. Dealers spooked—guns likely drawn.

Joe leaned close, voice low enough to vanish under the hum of a dying fluorescent. "Hallway's a choke point. Don't linger. Corners clean. Eyes up."

Will nodded, throat sand-dry. He ran the scenarios in his head: advance, clear, secure. None ended quietly.

The door slammed open.

A man burst into the hall, wild-eyed, pistol already up.

"Police! Drop it," Joe barked—

Gunfire swallowed his voice.

The hallway erupted in a burst of sound and light. Muzzle flashes strobed against peeling wallpaper. Each burst was a white-hot snapshot of chaos. Plaster shredded. Bullets chewed the walls. A ceiling bulb popped overhead, showering glass in glowing fragments.

Will dropped low, weapon up, training screaming: *front sight, squeeze, return fire.*

But his body locked.

Half a second.

Too long.

The barrel swung toward Joe.

Joe barked two rounds, steady as a hammer. The gunman crumpled against the wall, blood painting the paper in a brutal bloom.

Another figure surged from the apartment—a sawed-off shotgun in hand, eyes wide with animal desperation.

Will's chest seized. His finger froze. MOVE, DAMN IT. MOVE.

Joe turned, but too slowly this time.

Will's body broke free. He squeezed off a round, two, the flashes ricocheting down the narrow hall. The suspect dropped, shotgun clattering across tile.

Silence crashed down. Smoke clung to the air like dirty curtains, thick enough to taste. Will's ears rang so sharply it swallowed the world—no shouts, no footsteps, not even the crack of the pool balls in the corner. He realized with a jolt that he hadn't even heard his own shots.

*Auditory exclusion.* The term flickered through his brain like training notes scrawled on a page—high-stress response. The body turns down sound to conserve energy and survive. It was why witnesses always swore different numbers—five shots, three shots, ten. Nobody could ever agree. Nobody could ever be sure.

Will blinked hard, chest heaving, trying to force the scene back into focus. The gunman was down. The guys buddy was gone too. Joe was already moving, stone-shouldered, voice cutting through the fog like it belonged to another world.

Joe stood still, chest rising, face cut from granite. His eyes found Will. Not grateful. Not angry. Just... measuring.

"You freeze, I die," Joe said, voice calm as if nothing had just happened. "Don't ever give me that half-second again."

Will nodded once, throat thick, ears buzzing. His hands trembled as he holstered. In the Army, you survived and moved on. Here, every bullet would be measured, written, and judged. Two worlds. Same fear.

Hours later, the precinct felt like another planet.

Two vice detectives laughed over paperwork at the end of the row.

"Hell of a bust," one said, slapping the folder. "Guns, dope, bodies on the floor. Command's gonna eat this up."

"Stat bump for sure," the other grinned. "Might even make the evening news. Good night's work, boys."

Joe turned to Will, "State boys will be back for more questions tomorrow. Go, get some rest." As the other half of the division carried on.

They grinned widely, like no one had almost died in that hallway. It was like a game.

Will sat apart at his desk, staring at his hands. They were still shaking. He balled them into fists, forcing them still, but the tremor worked its way up his arms, into his chest. The laughter around him blurred into noise.

Joe passed by, pausing just long enough to clap a heavy hand on Will's shoulder.

"You're still here," he murmured, quiet enough for only Will. "That's what matters."

No praise. No comfort. Just survival.

### Notebook Entry
*Craven Street. Hallway ambush.*
*Froze for half a second. Almost cost Joe his life.*

*Pulled the trigger. Suspect down.*
*Hands shaking.*
*Brass cheered the stats.*
*The squad laughed as if it were a scoreboard.*
*Joe said: You're still here. That's what matters.*
*Paid leave, state investigates.*

### Later – Will's Apartment

The glow of his phone lit the dark. He hadn't bothered with a lamp, just sat on the edge of the couch in cargo pants and a t-shirt, boots still by the door.

A message buzzed through:

**Kristen:** Heard about Craven Street. You okay?

Will stared at the screen, thumb heavy, before typing back.

**Will:** I froze. Almost got Joe killed.

Her reply came fast:

**Kristen:** You moved. You fired. You stopped him. That's what counts.

**Will:** Doesn't feel that way.

**Kristen:** Will, listen to me. That was a good shoot. Don't let IA or the state boys twist it. Don't let them spin you into something you're not.

**Will:** Easy for you to say.

**Kristen:** Easy?? Please. I argue with guys like that for a living. They love rewriting stories. Don't give them a pen.

He exhaled hard through his nose, almost a laugh.

**Will:** You always have an answer.

**Kristen:** That's why you keep me around.

**Kristen:** Well, that, and my cooking.

**Will:** You burned spaghetti once.

**Kristen:** It was ONE TIME. You never forget anything, do you?

**Will:** Not when it comes to you.

A pause. Three dots blinked, vanished, blinked again.

**Kristen:** ...you're lucky you're cute when you're brooding, but also, a smart cop would have told his fiancée in person, would have more than likely found some comfort from her.

Will shook his head, a smile tugging despite the ache in his chest. His hands finally stopped trembling.

**Will:** Thanks. For tonight. For knowing what to say.

**Kristen:** Always. Now eat something, soldier cop. Sleep. Tomorrow's another day.

**Kristen:** And if you tell anyone I called you, I'll deny it in court.

Will set the phone down, her words glowing back at him in the dark. For the first time since the hallway, he felt steady again.

# Trust

One week later, Will and Joe were back to full duty, cleared of the shooting. However, Joe called Will and told him to meet him outside the Internal Affairs Sergeant's office.

Will didn't want to believe it. Not her.

Officer Renee Vargas. The same cop who'd shared stale coffee on midnights, who laughed like smoke curling out of a barroom, who'd once ribbed him for writing his reports like he was gunning for a Pulitzer. She was sharp, street-smart, the kind who could talk down a drunk or charm a witness into remembering a plate.

But the intel leak pointed straight at her.

The raid had gone sideways—dealers waiting like they'd had the playbook in hand. The whispers around the squad room carried one name, the same name now echoing in Will's head. Vargas.

She'd run with half those dealers back before the academy. Everyone knew it. It was in the files. But she'd sworn she left it behind. Sworn the badge had cut her loose from that life.

Now, Internal Affairs closed in.

Will stood frozen in the hall as the IA agents led her out of the precinct in cuffs. Her eyes darted everywhere but his—dark, restless, burning with the look of someone caught but not broken.

"You can't prove shit," Vargas spat, jerking against their grip. "This is politics. Somebody needed a fall girl."

The IA agent recited her rights, voice flat. "You have the right to remain silent..."

Will's stomach churned. Hearing Miranda read to a fellow officer felt worse than gunfire. It was like watching the badge itself crack.

Renee's gaze cut to him once, sharp and fleeting. He remembered her leaning back in a squad car seat, smirking: *You cover me, rookie, I'll cover you. That's how it works.*

Now the only cover she'd get was a cell door.

Back in the car, Joe drove with his usual stillness, but the tension in his jaw said everything. The passing city lights carved trenches across his face.

Will stared out at the blur of neon and shuttered shops. His throat tightened. "So that's it? She was one of us. How the hell are we supposed to trust anyone?"

Joe flicked his eyes toward him, voice low and sharp. "You don't. You trust actions. Not the patch, not the past, not the words. The badge doesn't make family. Integrity does."

Will clenched his fists. "But if even Vargas—"

"Don't twist it," Joe cut in. "She made her choice. And yeah, it's a damn betrayal. But don't you dare let that

291

make you blind. There are still good cops out here. Men and women who'd bleed out in an alley before they let someone else take a hit. Don't let one sellout poison the whole well."

Later, they sat on a side street under a buzzing streetlamp, the moths batting themselves stupid against the glow. Joe rolled his cigarette between his fingers but didn't light it right away.

"You wanted brothers in blue, Anderson. Some are. Some aren't. A badge doesn't mean shit without the backbone to hold it up."

Will looked at him, voice tight. "Then why keep coming back? What's the point if it's all just...lies and politics?"

Joe finally sparked the cigarette, the tip flaring red in the dark. He exhaled slowly, smoke drifting out the cracked window.

"The point is somebody's gotta show up. Ain't the paycheck—you can make more flipping burgers. Ain't the brass—they don't care if you bleed out in a stairwell. Ain't the thank-yous—most folks won't even remember your name.

We come back because when the radio crackles, there has to be a car rolling.

We come back for the kid crying on the corner.

For the shopkeeper who opens after getting robbed three times.

For the partner sitting beside you—because if you don't, they're out here alone. For the Maggie's and Ivy's of the world.

That's why. Not for glory. Not for medals. Because if we don't, nobody will."

Joe's voice was gravelly, but steady, like he'd been carrying those words for years, saving them for the right night.

Will sat in silence, the betrayal still burning but softened by the truth in Joe's voice. Vargas had chosen wrong. But not everyone did. Not everyone would.

Hours later, in the locker room, Will sat on the bench, his vest half-off, staring at the floor. He could still see Vargas's face, hear the cuffs ratcheting down.

Joe sat across from him, coffee steaming in his hands. He let the silence linger before speaking.

"You see it now. Badge doesn't make a brother. Or a sister. Some of 'em never should've worn it."

Will swallowed. "So how do you know who to trust?"

Joe leaned forward, elbows on his knees, eyes steady. "You don't. Not at first. But you learn. You watch. And when you find the ones who bleed the right way? You hold onto them because the rest of the world won't see the difference. Hell, half the time they'll lump us all together with the worst of us. That's the burden. And the honor. Knowing the difference. Doing the job anyway."

Will nodded slowly, finally lifting his eyes from the floor. He thought of Kristen then—her steady presence, her fire in court, the way she believed him when the job chipped away at everything else. She was one of the ones who bled the right way, just not with a badge.

And for the first time that night, he felt like maybe Joe was right.

**Notebook Entry:**
*Fellow officer dirty. Sold us out. Brothers aren't automatic.*
*Lesson: Integrity isn't convenient.*
*You either have it or you don't.*
*Do the job anyway.*
*Badge doesn't make a brother.*
*Some cops shouldn't wear it.*
*But some damn good ones do.*
*Public won't see the difference.*
*They'll think they know better.*
*They don't.*
*Do the job anyway.*

*Why we come back:*
*Not brass.*
*Not paycheck.*
*Not medals.*
*Radio crackles = someone rolls.*
*People still need someone to show up.*
*Shopkeepers. Lost kids. Partners.*

*We come back for each other.*
*If we don't, nobody will.*

Later that night, Will found himself outside Kristen's apartment, the city gone still in the small hours. He hadn't planned to come—hadn't planned anything—but when she opened the door, he didn't have to explain.

They sat at her kitchen table, the only light coming from the hood lamp above the stove. She poured him coffee without asking, sliding the mug across the wood like she'd done a hundred times before.

Will wrapped his hands around it, but didn't drink. His voice was low, raw.

"Vargas was one of us. I thought I could trust her. I thought... the badge meant something."

Kristen's eyes softened, and she reached across the table, letting her fingers rest lightly over his. "Will, this wasn't you missing something. It wasn't the squad either." She hesitated, choosing her words carefully. "I probably shouldn't even say this, but... the DA's office already has proof. She wasn't just leaking. She'd been seeing one of the dealers—someone she knew way back, an old boyfriend from after high school. His phone had the texts, the photos, pretty graphic stuff. It wasn't a mistake in judgment—it was a choice she kept making. Long before the raid."

Will's shoulders sagged, the weight of it pressing harder. "Jesus."

Kristen squeezed his hand. "I know it feels like betrayal, and it is. But you need to hear me—this wasn't on you. You couldn't have fixed it, and you couldn't have stopped it. Vargas crossed her own line. And it caught up with her."

His throat tightened. "Joe says you trust actions, not the patch. But after tonight, I don't know how to tell the difference anymore."

Kristen held his gaze, steady but kind. "Then trust yourself. You already know who the good ones are—the ones who'd bleed the right way. Vargas showed you she wasn't one of them. But don't let her make you doubt the rest. Don't let her make you doubt you."

Her hand stayed over his, warm and certain. "You're one of the ones who can't walk away, Will. You don't need a badge to prove that. You've already proven it to yourself."

The silence that followed wasn't heavy like it had been in the locker room—it was lighter, steadier. For the first time since watching Vargas walk out in cuffs, Will felt something ease in his chest.

He didn't know if Joe was right about the job, about showing up because nobody else would. But he knew Kristen was right about him.

## Burns

The night had thinned into that uneasy quiet, the streets slick with the shine of neon and rain that hadn't fallen. Will rolled slowly down Eighth, window cracked just enough to catch the mix of exhaust, grease, and smoke that clung to the block.

That's when he saw her.

Young. Thin. Jacket hanging loose, skirt too short to be warm. But it wasn't the clothes that made him slow the car. It was the mark — a perfect, circular scar burned into the skin of her stomach by her navel, revealed each time her jacket slipped.

Will pulled to the curb and killed the engine. He got out, badge tucked but visible enough to show he wasn't there to hassle. "Hey," he said softly, hands loose at his sides. "Name's Will Anderson. Detective."

Her eyes narrowed, chin lifting in defiance. "Yeah? And I'm the fucking queen of England. You want a date, it costs extra if you stand there pretending you're a cop."

Will shook his head. "Not looking for that. Just... noticed your scar." He gestured faintly. "Looks like one I've seen before."

Her posture stiffened. Silence stretched.

He lowered his voice. "Tonya. Worked Seventh. She had one just like it. I helped her get out. I'm not here to burn you. You have a name?"

The girl shifted her weight, eyes darting. Her lips pressed tight, then trembled just slightly before she caught herself. Finally: "Why you care?"

"Because whoever gave you that mark doesn't stop at one," Will said. "And if he's still out there, I need to know what you remember. In case he comes back."

For a long moment, he thought she'd bolt. Then she exhaled sharply, her voice cutting like broken glass. "They call me Belle, three weeks ago. Oakhaven. Met some Joe-average at a bar. He slipped me something. Roofie, I guess. I don't remember shit until I woke up naked in a hotel room. Sore. Bruised. That burn screaming at me—he had his way with me for a long time. I mean, he must have because nothing on me wasn't hurting—everything ached, face, jaw, ass, legs, my cooch burned for days after. Nothing was off limits to him while I was passed out."

Will's jaw clenched. His pen moved across his notebook, but his eyes never left hers. "What else?"

Her gaze unfocused, like replaying a nightmare frame by frame. "Cuts. On my thighs, my tits. As if he were signing his name. See, look." She showed him the still-faint cuts on her thighs, which were in the late stages of healing.

"When I came to, he noticed—started on me again. Told me to scream while he—" She swallowed, hard, anger

298

and shame knotted in her throat. "I couldn't. Too doped. So he laughed. He finished, punched me in the gut. Got up. Said he'd be back for me soon. It was like I was lying on a cloud, all happy but getting reamed by some sicko who didn't pay up. I have seen some weird shit, but this guy. Fuck that. I was too messed up to be scared. But I remember."

Will's chest tightened. "You went to the hospital?"

"Yeah. Two days later. Couldn't stop bleeding." Her voice sharpened, defensive. "Told them my boyfriend got rough when he was drunk. Big cock, forgot to take it easy. They bought it. I hate hospitals. They don't help girls like me."

"Did you report it to the local police?" Will asked, even though he already knew the answer.

Her glare cut like a knife. "No. And I'm not going to. I need the money. So you can fuck off with your questions, Detective." She turned on her heel, tugging her jacket higher.

"Wait!" Will shouted.

She kept walking, middle finger popped up as she hurried across the intersection.

Will let her go. He stood in the glow of the streetlight, hand tight on the notebook, stomach burning with the weight of her words.

Back in his car, he punched Rogers' number into his phone.

"Rogers."

"It's Anderson. I just talked to a girl on Eighth. Fresh burn. Same as the Prophet's marks. Came from Oakhaven. She described... everything. Ghost in her memory, but it's him. It's still him."

Silence on the other end, broken only by Rogers' slow sigh. "You get her name?"

"She refused, but Belle is her street name. Wouldn't give me anything more. Won't cooperate."

Another pause, longer. "Alright. I'll put it upstairs."

Two hours later, the call came back. Rogers' voice was flat, resigned. "Brass says no cooperation, no investigation. Dead end."

Will gripped the wheel until his knuckles bleached. "She's not lying, Dan. He's still out there."

"I know," Rogers said quietly. "But without her, it's smoke. You tried."

The line clicked dead.

Will sat in the dark car, neon flickering across the windshield. His notebook lay open on the passenger seat, the latest entry scrawled jagged:

*False Prophet. Still breathing. Underground. Waiting. Changing tactics?*

He shut it, jaw tight. The city was quiet. Too quiet.

Will didn't go straight home. He parked in front of Kristen's apartment for nearly ten minutes, staring at the glow in her kitchen window, notebook open on his lap, the words scrawled there pulsing back at him.

*False Prophet. Still breathing. Underground. Waiting. Changing tactics?*

When he finally walked in, Kristen was at the counter in sweats, hair pulled back, briefs stacked beside her laptop. She looked up and read his face instantly. "What happened?"

Will dropped into the chair across from her, running a hand down his face. "Saw a girl on Eighth. Burned. Same mark as Tonya. Said she came from Oakhaven three weeks ago. Woke up in a hotel, drugged, cut, assaulted. Told me he laughed while—" He broke off, shaking his head. "She wouldn't give me her name. Won't cooperate. Rogers put it up the chain. Brass said no cooperation, no investigation."

Kristen's lips pressed into a hard line. Her voice stayed even, but her eyes burned. "So that's it? She's marked. She's bleeding. And because she won't put her name on a form, she doesn't count?"

"That's what they're saying," Will muttered.

Kristen shoved a hand through her hair, pacing. "Will, you know why victims like her don't report. No one believes them. They're humiliated. They're already carrying enough shame without a courtroom full of people picking them apart." Her voice cracked sharper. "And then brass has the nerve to say *no cooperation, no case*?"

Will looked down at the notebook, thumb running along the edge. "She remembered his cadence. His laugh.

That's all she could give me. He's still out there, Kris. Waiting. I can feel it."

She stopped pacing, came to stand behind him, her hands resting gently on his shoulders. Her voice softened, but the steel never left. "Then you keep writing it down. Keep chasing the edges. Because one day, someone's going to slip. And when they do, you'll be there."

Will closed his eyes briefly, the weight of her words easing just enough to breathe.

"You're an ADA," he said. "Doesn't this make you want to run for the hills? It's hopeless half the time."

Kristen leaned down, kissed his temple, whispering against his skin. "It makes me want to fight harder. For the ones who can't. Even if the system says they don't matter."

Will reached up, covering her hand with his. "That girl on Eighth... she mattered. Even if she told me to fuck off."

Kristen smiled faintly, though her eyes glistened. "That's why you're dangerous, Detective Anderson. Because you don't stop carrying them, even when they shove you away."

For the first time that night, Will's chest eased. She anchored him again — not with false hope, but with fire that matched his own.

**Notebook Entry**
*Eighth Street.*
*Burned. Same mark.*

*Came from Oakhaven. Drugged. Cut. Laughed while he broke her.*
*Wouldn't give a name.*
*Brass says no cooperation = no case.*
*Kristen says: Fight harder.*
*For the ones who can't.*
*She says I'm dangerous because I don't stop carrying them.*
*She's right. I can't.*
*She mattered. They all matter.*
*False Prophet still out there.*
*Waiting.*

# Brawl

The call came just after midnight: disturbance at The Rusty Nail, a dive two blocks off the river.

When Will shoved through the front door, the smell hit first—stale beer, cheap whiskey, wood soaked in sweat and regret. Cigarette smoke drifted under a ceiling fan that wobbled uselessly overhead, pushing nothing but warm air. In the corner, a battered jukebox flickered, its neon "PLAY ME" half-dead, pulsing sick light across the room.

Chaos inside.

Two men had each other by the shirts, fists hammering wild. A table flipped on its side, chairs scattered, bottles rolling, glass crunching under boots. Shouts stacked on shouts until the whole room felt like a fist ready to swing.

"Summit Falls PD!" Will barked, louder than he intended. "Break it up!"

No one heard. Or cared.

One fighter swung wide, missed, and slammed his opponent into the bar. The crowd roared like it was a prizefight.

Will moved. Training screamed: separate, control, cuff. Reality said: too close, too fast.

He grabbed the larger one by the collar and yanked—the man's breath stank of sour mash and rotgut. The guy spun with the momentum, fist already flying.

Impact.

Will's head snapped back. White light burst behind his eyes. Warmth spilled down his temple. Copper filled his mouth.

For half a second, the soldier in him roared—swing back, finish it, end this fast. But the cop in him ground down harder: control, not chaos.

He shoved forward, grip locked, slammed the man into the jukebox so hard the half-dead neon fizzled out with a sick pop. Gasps rippled through the crowd.

The second fighter lunged. Will pivoted, shoved him across the overturned table, wood splintering under the crash.

Then came the blur.

Arms. Fists. Boots skidding. Training took over. Muscle memory guided what his head couldn't track. Block, redirect, slam, cuff. His knuckles burned. His vest felt like it weighed a hundred pounds. Blood from his eyebrow dripped warm down his collar, sticky against his chest.

When the haze cleared, silence had fallen like someone had hit pause.

One man was cuffed to the bar, wheezing. The other groaning on the floor, blood and beer mixing under his cheek. The crowd stood frozen, wide-eyed.

And Will—chest heaving, shirt torn, blood dripping steadily from the cut above his eye.

That's when Joe stormed in, taking it all in with one flat glance. He didn't even flinch.

"You done redecorating?"

Will swiped his sleeve across his brow, smearing blood into a crimson streak. "They started it."

Joe gave him a look so flat it could've been a gravestone. "You finished it ugly."

### Outside – humid night

The air clung heavily, sweet with the scent of river rot and fried food from a diner down the block. Two older beat cops leaned against the cruiser, watching Will limp out. One gave him a long look, then a curt nod. The other muttered, almost grudgingly: "Not bad, Detective Anderson."

Will met their eyes. His jaw set, refusing to look away. The cut above his eye throbbed, but he held steady.

For the first time, no one called him rookie.

Respect. Hard-earned, bloody, and staring right back at him.

### In the car

Joe sipped his coffee, the steam fogging faintly against the window. Silence stretched so long that Will thought maybe the lecture wasn't coming.

Then Joe spoke, voice steady but sharp enough to cut.

"You're bloodied, sure. Got yourself a scar. Maybe even earned a nod from the peanut gallery."

Will straightened, bracing.

Joe didn't look at him, eyes locked on the dark street ahead. "But scars don't mean shit if you can't keep the beat after. Respect's fine. Rhythm's what keeps you alive."

Will sat back, pulse still drumming in his ears. He realized he wasn't just bleeding. He was learning.

### Notebook Entry:

*Dive bar. Blood on my shirt. Split eyebrow. First scar.*
*Finally, not "rookie."*

*Respect means nothing if you can't keep the beat after the chaos.*

### Kristen's Apartment – 2:14 a.m.

The knock at the door was soft but steady. Kristen padded across the darkened living room, bare feet silent against the hardwood, and pulled it open.

Will stood there in the hall, looking at Kristen, who stood in a short tank top and underwear, her shoulders squared but slouched with exhaustion. A white bandage cut across his eyebrow, tape tugging at the edges. His shirt was wrinkled, a faint smear of dried blood across the collar where the ER nurse hadn't quite cleaned him up.

Her chest clenched. "Oh my... What the hell, Will."

He tried to brush it off with a crooked half-smile. "Perks of plainclothes—you get to ruin your own shirt instead of city property."

"Don't joke," she snapped, sharper than she meant. Then her voice broke, softer. "You scared the hell out of me."

His face shifted, the weight of her words sinking in. "I didn't want to wake you. I just... didn't know where else to go."

Kristen stepped forward and wrapped her arms around him before he could say another word. The faint smell of antiseptic lingered around him, mingling with smoke and sweat. He stiffened, then collapsed against her, forehead resting on her shoulder.

"You came to the right place," she whispered.

She guided him to the couch, then disappeared down the hall. Will sat hunched forward, elbows on his knees, staring at his bloodstained hands. Joe's voice drifted through his head, gravelly and steady: *Keep your house clean, kid. That's how you survive.*

Back then, he'd thought Joe meant the job. The paperwork. The cases. Tonight, watching Kristen return with peroxide and a warm cloth, he realized Joe had meant more.

She knelt in front of him, gently pressing the cloth to his temple. He winced at the sting, and she steadied his chin with her free hand.

"Look at me," she said, eyes searching his. "I need to see you, not just the detective who walked into hell tonight. You."

His throat tightened. He let her wipe away the dried blood, her hands moving patiently and methodically. She worked the cloth down his neck, across his collar. When she was done, she pressed a towel to his cheek, holding it there like she could stop the bleeding by sheer will.

"You don't have to carry this back alone every time," she murmured. Her hand shifted, the engagement ring catching the lamp light. "That's what this means, Will. You come home broken, bruised, bleeding—I help make you whole again."

Will swallowed hard. The sting in his brow was nothing compared to the ache breaking open in his chest.

Kristen brushed his hair back gently, her thumb grazing the edge of the bandage. "And by the way?" she whispered. "I'm glad you finally took my advice."

His brows furrowed. "What advice?"

She gave him a small, knowing smile. "Seek your girl out for comfort when it gets bad. Don't keep it all inside."

Will leaned back, exhaling, her words settling like gravity. She was right. He had sought her out. Not the bar, not the bottle, not silence. Her.

For the first time that night, the tremor in his hands stilled.

Kristen eased down beside him, curling into his side, her hand finding his.

"There you go," she whispered. "Now, let me take it from here."

And for once, Will let her.

"You need a shower, Rocky!" she chirped, her smile faint but teasing. "But not right now. Just sit here for a minute."

Her head sank against his shoulder, her breathing slowing until it evened out completely. Will sat still, watching the way her lashes rested against her cheeks, the slight crease between her brows softening as sleep took hold.

When he was sure she was out, he shifted carefully, sliding out from beneath her. He caught her gently, lowering her onto the couch cushion without waking her. She murmured something, nuzzling into the pillow, and he smiled despite the ache in his body.

He pulled a blanket from the back of the couch and draped it over her, tucking it around her shoulders. For a moment, he stood there, just watching—this woman who saw past the badge, past the blood, to the man who kept showing up battered but still breathing.

The shower was quick, hot water stinging his split brow and washing the grime of the night down the drain. When he stepped out, steam curling in the mirror's corners, the bandage was fresh and his shirt was clean. But what he really needed wasn't in the bathroom.

He padded back into the living room and stooped low, sliding an arm beneath her knees and the other behind her back. Kristen stirred, her arms instinctively wrapping around his neck.

"Mmm," she whispered, half-dreaming. "There's my Rocky."

He carried her to the bedroom, the weight of her slight but grounding in his arms. He laid her down gently, pulled the covers up around her, and for a second just stood there—watching the steady rise and fall of her chest, the way peace clung to her in sleep.

Then he slid in beside her. Kristen shifted instantly, curling toward him, her head finding its place against his chest as if it had always belonged there.

Will closed his eyes, a vow forming in the quiet: he would never let anything happen to her. No matter what the job took from him, no matter what the city threw at them—she was the one thing he would guard above all else.

And with that silent promise, Will finally slept.

## Courthouse

### The Next Morning – Kristen's Apartment

The smell of coffee drifted through the kitchen, mingling with the faint crackle of eggs in the pan. Will stood barefoot at the stove, sleeves pushed up, moving with the kind of calm that only came after nights like last night. The bandage over his brow was fresh, but his posture was steady.

Behind him, footsteps padded across the hardwood. Kristen appeared in the doorway—hair damp from the shower, skirt on, but her blouse still abandoned somewhere in the bedroom. The soft morning light fell across her bare shoulders, catching on the engagement ring as she leaned against the frame.

She watched him for a beat, then said softly, "You know, I can't wait to marry you."

Will turned, spatula in hand, a crooked grin tugging at his mouth. "We could skip the waiting part. The courthouse is open today. Quick vows, signatures, done deal."

Kristen's smile didn't falter. Her eyes held his, serious and steady. "OK. Let's do it."

He froze, half thinking she was teasing, half knowing she wasn't. "Wait—are you...?"

"No, Will." She crossed the room until she was standing right in front of him, her hand brushing his wrist where he still held the spatula. "I'm serious. Let's do it. Soon."

He searched her face, still uncertain. "Why now?"

Kristen's voice softened, earnest. "Because it's us. Because after everything we've seen—the case, the nights you come home bleeding, the way we keep choosing each other—it's fitting. We don't need the show. We can throw a big reception later, have the family and friends, sure. But the vows? That can just be us. Close. Simple. Real."

Will set the spatula down, his chest tightening. "You really mean it."

"Yes, I mean it. What do you say, Will Anderson, ready to make me ADA Kristen Anderson?" she whispered up to his grinning face.

"Ok, I'm in, let's really do it then, your choice is law. So you really mean it, courthouse?" Will asked, smiling.

She nodded. "I do." Then, with a mischievous spark, she repeated, "OK, let's do it."

Will chuckled, shaking his head. "I already agreed. We'll do it."

Kristen reached for the side of her skirt, tugged the zipper down with deliberate slowness. The purr of the zipper echoed in the kitchen. The fabric slid to the floor around her ankles. She arched a brow. "No, dummy. Let's do it."

Will's grin widened. "Pretty sure your office has a policy against showing up in your underwear. Guess I'll have to help you change into something more... appropriate."

Kristen turned away, gathering her hair up in one hand, the line of her back bare and tempting. "Good idea. Why don't you start with the latches on this *very inappropriate* bra?"

Will stepped forward, hands already reaching—

She spun away at the last second, darting toward the bedroom, laughing.

The door slammed shut behind her. Her voice rang out through the wood, teasing and bright: "Hope you've got a search warrant, Officer!"

Will leaned against the doorframe, smiling despite himself, the sound of her laughter warming the air between them.

For the first time in days, the heaviness in his chest lifted.

### Summit Falls Courthouse – Late Morning

The courthouse lobby smelled faintly of lemon polish and old paper, fluorescent lights humming overhead. It wasn't grand, or romantic, or anything out of a movie. But Will thought it was perfect.

Kristen stood beside him in a pale cream dress that hit just above the knee, simple but stunning. No silk, no heels that made him sweat bullets — just Kristen, hair pinned back loosely, eyes sparking green in the sunlight that slanted through the tall windows. She could've been wearing her ADA blazer for all he cared. She still took his breath away.

Joe Donovan stood to Will's left, suit rumpled, tie crooked, smirk firmly in place. He looked more like he was waiting for a sentencing than a wedding. "This is it, kid," he muttered out of the corner of his mouth. "Say 'I do' before she sobers up and realizes what she's getting into."

On Kristen's side stood her younger sister, Brittany Jo, practically bouncing in place in a floral dress. She whispered loudly to Kristen, not bothering to hide her grin: "I can't believe you're actually doing this. Mom is going to *die* when she finds out."

Kristen shot her a look, but her lips twitched like she wanted to laugh.

The judge peered at them over his glasses, shuffling papers. "Alright, Detective Anderson, Assistant District Attorney Dalton — I understand you're keeping this brief?"

"Brief," Kristen confirmed, sliding her hand into Will's. Her palm was warm, steady.

The vows went quickly, but Will felt every word lodge deep in his chest. He slipped the ring onto her finger, the band small, simple, but shining brighter than anything he'd ever held. Kristen's hands lingered when she slid his into place, her eyes fixed on his like the rest of the room had fallen away.

"By the authority vested in me by the State of—" The judge droned on, but Will barely heard it. His heart was too loud in his ears.

"You may kiss the bride."

Kristen didn't wait. She rose on her toes and kissed him like the courthouse had just transformed into a cathedral. For once, Will forgot there was anyone else in the world.

Joe clapped twice, loud and slow, grin sharp. "Well, hell. Anderson, you just married up. Way up."

Brittany Jo squealed and hugged Kristen, then Will, before snapping a quick photo with her phone. "Okay, don't move, this one's going on the family thread *immediately.*"

Kristen leaned close to Will, her voice a whisper against his ear as they turned to leave. "See? Told you. We did it."

Will smiled, holding her hand like he'd never let go. For once, no ghosts were chasing him, no weight from the badge. Just Kristen, his wife, walking out of the courthouse beside him, his guiding star.

### Kristen's Apartment – Early Afternoon

The courthouse vows were still echoing in Will's head as they climbed the narrow stairs to Kristen's apartment, her hand tucked tightly in his. Joe and Brittany Jo had hugged them at the curb, Brittany nearly in tears and Joe muttering something about "rookies tying the knot before they even learn the dance."

Then it was just them., Kristen's hand again felt warm in his. At the door, she fumbled with the keys, nerves and excitement flickering across her face.

Before she could even fit the key in, Will swept her off her feet. Literally, she gave a startled gasp, then laughed, clinging to his shoulders as he carried her bridal-style across the threshold.

"Well," she teased breathlessly, "aren't you traditional."

He kissed her hair as the door clicked shut behind them. "Figured I'd start this marriage right."

Kristen's eyes glinted as she slid down just enough to whisper against his ear, "Good. Because now I want you to *officially* make me your wife."

She tugged at the zipper on her dress, silk slipping free and falling in a whisper to the floor. Standing barefoot, green eyes alive, she smirked and started backing toward the hallway.

"Better bring that search warrant with you, Officer."

Her laugh filled the apartment, light and reckless, as she disappeared toward the bedroom.

Will's pulse thundered. He followed, the world outside falling away.

## Missing

Recently, Will Anderson carried himself differently. The rookie sheen was long gone; the badge no longer felt like borrowed weight. He'd bled, stumbled, gotten back up, and each scar — inside and out — had carved lessons into him.

His notebook was thick now, its edges worn soft from years of being carried in his pocket. Every page a reminder: *hesitate once, survive, keep the beat, hold your integrity, do the job anyway.* It wasn't academy doctrine. It wasn't department policy. It was something more challenging, forged out of alleys, fire escapes, and gun smoke.

But somewhere along the line, a mantra had surfaced between the lines. One Joe never said, but Will lived by anyway:

*Everyone matters.*

Not just the shopkeepers who opened their doors each morning, not just the partners who had your back. The drunks in doorways. The kids caught stealing candy bars—even the lost ones who had already slipped too far. Every name in his notebook mattered, even if they never knew it.

Joe didn't share the sentiment. He didn't fight Will on it, either. He just called it "Anderson's curse" — the thing that kept him up nights while others slept soundly.

"You care too much, kid," Joe had told him once, watching him linger over a victim's photo long after the case was closed. "The job's already heavy. Don't drag it home with you."

The Mercer case started like too many others: a missing girl. Sixteen. Vanished overnight.

Sloane Mercer. Blond. Smile too big for her age. Rumors said she'd run off with her boyfriend — a coke dealer in his twenties, already known to Vice.

Will flipped through her photos in the file: a sweet sixteen party, a soccer game, laughing with friends. *She's just a kid.*

Joe glanced over his shoulder and scoffed. "You want the unvarnished version? Half these 'missing' girls are exactly where they want to be — in some shitty motel room with a loser boyfriend who promises them excitement and hands them a bump of coke." He tapped the folder with a nicotine-stained finger. "They call it love. We call it grooming. Either way, it doesn't end with a happy reunion."

Will bristled. "She's sixteen."

"Sixteen and dumb enough to think she's grown," Joe shot back. His tone wasn't cruel, just flat with experience. "That boyfriend? He won't be around when the money runs out. She'll be strung out, used up, and dropped on the curb like trash. That's the cycle. Don't romanticize it."

Will didn't answer. He couldn't. He kept staring at Sloane's smile in the photo — wide, innocent, hopeful. The kind of smile that didn't belong on a cold case board.

Sloane's bedroom looked like someone had pressed pause on her life.

The bedspread was patterned in faded flowers, one corner half-kicked onto the floor. A hairbrush with blond strands sat on the dresser, beside bottles of cheap perfume and a chipped jewelry box. Posters peeled from the walls: a boy band, a summer blockbuster, some quote about *dreaming big*.

The air was heavy with the sweet, cloying scent of body spray — teenage armor, trying too hard to smell older than sixteen. Underneath it, the faint musk of dust and stillness.

On the desk, a notebook lay open, doodles spiraling across the margins. Half a text message was scrawled in the corner: *"Don't wait up."*

Will crouched beside the bed, his hand brushing against a pink hoodie balled up on the floor. The fabric was still soft, still warm in its familiarity. He imagined her tugging it over her head, laughing, slamming the door behind her like she'd be back in ten minutes.

But she wasn't back. And maybe she never would be.

Joe lingered in the doorway, arms folded, expression flat. "Seen this scene a hundred times. Parents say missing. Rumors say she ran. Reality? She's holed up with that boyfriend of hers, getting fed dope and fairy tales."

Will glanced up sharply. "She's sixteen."

"Sixteen and dumb enough to think she's in love," Joe said, voice like gravel. "And he's old enough to know better, but scumbags like him never do. Give it a week, maybe two, she'll be another ghost we drag out of a motel bathtub. That's the math on cases like this."

Will's stomach tightened. He thought about the lessons already inked into his notebook:

*Don't hesitate.*

*Survival is the only win.*

*Keep the beat steady.*

*Integrity isn't convenient.*

All of them were true. All of them had saved his life.

But looking at Sloane's room, at the perfume bottles, the posters curling off the walls, the photo of her at the beach with a smile too big for her age, those lessons felt... thin. They kept you alive, sure. They didn't keep *her* alive.

"She still matters," he said quietly, almost to himself.

Joe sighed and shook his head. "Yeah, kid. They all do. But you don't get to carry her home. That's how you sink. You think you can save 'em all, and the ones you don't save, they haunt you."

Will's jaw tightened. *Maybe haunting was better than forgetting.*

He traced a thumb across the photo frame, locking her face into memory. *Everyone matters.*

Joe's eyes softened for just a moment, then hardened again. "Then do the job. Just don't fool yourself into thinking you can carry her across the finish line. She's gotta want to walk."

### Notebook Entry:
*Sloane Mercer. Sixteen. Gone.*
*The empty room smelled like perfume and dust.*
*Lessons so far: hesitation kills. Survival is the only win.*
*Keep the beat steady. Integrity is all you have.*
*But this one? She's more than a lesson.*
*Don't carry every victim home. Can't stop myself.*

### Kristen's Apartment – Night
Will dropped a thin file from Vice on the counter, rubbing the back of his neck. He looked like he hadn't slept — jacket off, sleeves rolled, tie hanging loose. Kristen was perched on a barstool with her laptop open, reviewing motions, her glasses sliding low on her nose.

"Got a name?" Will said, his voice flat. "Guy Sloane's been seen with. Eddie Markell."

Kristen's head snapped up. "Eddie Markell?"

Will frowned. "You know him?"

Her mouth tightened, eyes narrowing in a way Will had learned to recognize — prosecutor mode. "Yeah. I've seen him in court. Not on a case I handled, but I once sat in the gallery. Possession, solicitation, or some probation violation. Slime. The kind of guy who thinks slick hair and cologne can cover up the rot underneath." She closed her laptop with a sharp snap. "I got pedo vibes from him the moment he walked in. You don't forget that kind of presence."

Will's gut sank. "That's him." He slid the photo across the counter — grainy surveillance of Markell leaning against a gas station wall, cigarette dangling, hand on his phone like he owned the night. "Vice has been circling him for a while. Ties to low-level dope, rumored to be grooming girls barely old enough to drive. He knows how to keep them hooked — gifts, drugs, the whole cycle. Fits with Sloane."

Kristen stared at the photo, a look of disgust twisting across her face. "He doesn't just fit. He thrives on it. This is the guy your gut warns you about before you know why." She pushed the photo back with two fingers, as if it might burn her. "If she's with him, Will, she's not running away for fun. She's already in over her head."

Will exhaled, leaning his palms on the counter, head hanging for a beat. Joe's cynicism echoed in the back of his mind: *She's sixteen and dumb enough to think she's grown.* But Kristen's words were sharper, closer to the truth: *She's trapped, and he's the trap.*

"She still matters," Will muttered, mostly to himself.

Kristen reached across, curling her fingers over his wrist. "Then go prove it. Put Eddie Markell where he belongs. And don't let him charm his way out — guys like him count on the system underestimating the damage they do."

Will nodded slowly, jaw tightening, the mantra carving deeper: *Everyone matters. Especially her.*

## Underbelly

Four days.

That's how long Sloane Mercer had been gone.

Four days of leads that collapsed like wet paper. Four days of chasing ghosts down alleys that smelled of piss and burned foil. Four days of staring into the faces of girls who weren't Sloane, hollow-eyed, jittery, too old at twenty, bodies already broken by a city that chewed them up.

Will's notebook was filling with addresses, dead ends, fragments of names. None of it led to her.

Will recalled that his first stop during the last four days was another crack house on Craven Street. The place stank of ammonia and despair. Rotting food, piss-stained mattresses, spoons blackened from a hundred hits. A girl with no shoes rocked in the corner, her lips blistered, eyes darting to shadows only she could see.

Will crouched, voice low, trying. "You seen a girl? Blond. Sixteen. Name's Sloane."

She blinked through him. Whispered something about angels. Then started laughing, shrill and broken.

Will's stomach knotted. He pressed again: "Please. Just think—"

Joe tugged him back by the shoulder. Calm. Steady. Like this was just another beat on patrol. "She can't help you. Write the address. Move on."

Will wanted to shake her, wanted to force clarity out of her haze. But Joe was already walking out, lighting a cigarette, rhythm intact.

The next night, a tip sent them to a motel off the interstate. Room 207 smelled like mildew and Lysol sprayed too late. Cigarette burns cratered the carpet. A young woman, twenty, maybe twenty-one, sat on the bed with a towel around her shoulders, bruises blooming purple across her collarbone.

Will's gut twisted. He asked anyway. "You seen her? Sixteen, blond—"

The woman stared at the floor. "They come and go. Don't remember names. Don't want to."

Joe crouched down, eye-level, voice even. "Are you safe here? You need medical?"

She shook her head once, tiny. Joe left it at that. Stood, nodded to Will. "We're done."

Out in the hall, Will's voice was tight. "That was it? You're just gonna let her—"

Joe cut him off, steady as always. "She gave what she could. You keep pushing, and she shuts down. You can't save them all in one night, kid. Don't try."

By day four, the rhythm was gone, at least for Will. He slammed a locker door hard enough to rattle the hinges. Snapped at another detective for dragging his feet. His hands shook as he poured the coffee, and the dark circles under his eyes made him look ten years older.

Joe cornered him outside the squad room, cigarette tucked behind his ear. His tone hadn't changed a decibel since day one. "You're running hot, Anderson. Frustration makes you sloppy. Sloppy gets you killed."

Will glared at him. "She matters."

Joe lit up, exhaled smoke through his nose. "Yeah, kid. They all do. But you gotta keep the beat. Or you're no good to her, or anyone else."

That night, parked under a flickering streetlamp, Will flipped open his notebook. The words came jagged, the ink pressed deep into the page.

**Notebook Entry:**
*Four days. Dead ends. Crack houses, motels, strip clubs, abandoned buildings.*
*Faces that weren't hers.*
*Joe keeps the beat. I can't. Not this time.*
*The streets eat girls like her alive.*
*Lesson: frustration = sloppy.*
*But I can't slow down.*
*Not when she's still out there.*

### Kristen's Apartment – Night

The coffee table was a crime scene of its own — Sloane Mercer's file spread wide, half-drained cups of coffee, Will's notebook flipped open with his cramped handwriting filling the pages. He hadn't been home in days. He looked it, too — stubble rough, shirt rumpled, bandage still across his brow from a scrape on a warrant the night before.

Kristen padded out of the kitchen barefoot, wine glass in hand. She stopped, looking at the photos again: Sloane in a soccer uniform, Sloane at her sweet sixteen, Sloane smiling too wide for sixteen. Kristen let out a soft breath. "Four days."

"Four days," Will echoed. His voice was gravelly. He dragged a hand down his face. "Every lead we get is trash. Every girl we talk to is either too high to remember her own name or too scared to speak up. And Markell—"

Kristen's mouth tightened at the name. "I told you the first night, Will. I've seen him in court. Sleazebag. Thought he was slick in front of the judge, but he gave me pedo vibes from the start."

Will's jaw flexed. "He's older, he's got her strung out on coke, and he knows exactly what he's doing. And I can't get a clean angle on him. He's slippery. He hides behind girls like her." He slammed the notebook shut, too hard. "She's sixteen, Kristen. She doesn't even know what she's walking into."

Kristen lowered herself onto the couch beside him, setting her glass down. She studied him, then the photos. "Will, that's the problem. She *thinks* she does. To Sloane, Markell isn't a predator. He's excitement. Freedom. He's telling her she's grown, that she's in control, that she's not just somebody's little girl. That's intoxicating when you're sixteen and desperate to matter to somebody."

Will shook his head, voice sharp. "It's poison. He's killing her."

"Of course it is," Kristen said, firm but calm. "But she doesn't see it that way yet. To her, the danger feels like power. That's how guys like Markell keep them close." She leaned in, catching his eyes. "You want to save her? You have to remember she doesn't think she needs saving."

Will slumped back against the couch, staring up at the ceiling. His chest rose and fell like he was holding back an avalanche. "She matters, Kris. More than just another runaway on the board. She *matters*."

Kristen slid her hand over his, squeezing hard. "Then hold on to that. You'll need it because Markell counts on people like you burning out. He wants her forgotten. Don't give him that win."

Will's throat worked, tight. For the first time in days, he let his fingers lace through hers, the grip firm, steady.

## Deliverance

The tip came from a junkie who hadn't slept in three days, teeth ground to nubs, twitching in the back of the cruiser. He swore Sloane was in a rowhouse off Craven, locked up by her boyfriend, high as a kite.

Will wanted to believe him so badly that it ached in his teeth. Joe gave him the side-eye over the rim of his coffee. "Half these guys would sell their own mothers for a cheeseburger."

"Then why tip us?" Will asked, too sharply.

"Maybe he wants the boyfriend out of the way. Maybe he wants a fix. Doesn't matter. You check it anyway. Just don't let your heart write checks your gun hand can't cash."

The rowhouse leaned into its neighbors, windows dark, door sagging off rusted hinges. Paint peeled like dead skin. The street outside was silent except for a dog barking two blocks away.

Will's pulse was already running ahead of him. He wanted to kick the door in, tear the place apart. Joe's hand landed on his arm before he moved.

"You breathe. You go steady. You don't freeze. And you don't lose your head."

Will nodded, but his body was already thrumming like a live wire.

The door gave way on the second hit. The smell rolled out first: piss, mildew, and something acrid, chemical. Their flashlights cut through dust.

The first floor was empty—just broken furniture, bottles, needles glinting like glass teeth.

Then, upstairs: a locked door. A muffled sound.

Joe's look was enough. He braced. Will kicked. Wood splintered.

Inside—

Sloane.

Sixteen years old, curled up on a filthy mattress, knees to her chest. Wearing only an oversized t-shirt, bare from the hips down, her hair matted and her lips cracked. A crust of powder lined her nostrils. Her eyes flickered, trying to focus, but she couldn't hold steady.

Will froze. His heart cracked in his chest.

Then the movement.

The boyfriend. Skinny, rat-eyed, jaw twitching. He lurched out of the shadows, a knife in his hand, yelling something Will didn't hear.

Will didn't hesitate. His gun was up before he thought. "DROP IT!"

The boyfriend smirked, knife flashing. "She's mine, man. You don't get it. You can't have her."

Something broke inside Will. All the late nights, the dead ends, the stink of motels, the empty looks of girls already too far gone — all of it roared to the surface.

He didn't fire. He lunged.

The gun clattered to the floorboards as Will's shoulder drove the boyfriend into the wall. The knife slipped from his hand. Then Will's fists were flying — one, two, three, bone-jarring cracks. Blood spattered across the peeling wallpaper.

"You think she's yours?" Another punch. The boyfriend's teeth clattered against the floor. "You think she's trash you can use up?"

The kid tried to cover his head, but Will's rage broke through his arms. His knuckles split, pain shooting through his hand, but he didn't stop. Not when the memory of Sloane's perfume-sweet room pressed against his mind. Not when he pictured her smile turning into another face on a cold case board.

By the fifth blow, the boyfriend was a heap, gasping wetly, face unrecognizable.

A hand clamped his shoulder.

"Enough!" Joe's voice was iron, but tight.

Will froze mid-swing, chest heaving. His fist trembled inches above the kid's jaw.

Joe's eyes bored into him — sharp, unsettled. For the first time, the veteran looked like he wasn't sure what Will would do next. "You beat him to death, Anderson, you lose everything. Not just the badge. You. He's already nothing — don't make yourself nothing too."

The words cut through the red haze. Will staggered back, fists lowering. His breath came in ragged gasps.

Joe dropped to a knee, cuffing the boyfriend with rough efficiency, one knee grinding between his shoulder blades. The kid moaned weakly, blood smearing the floor.

Will's eyes tracked down, finding his service weapon lying on the boards where he'd dropped it. His hand shook as he bent to pick it up. He wiped blood from the grip with the hem of his sleeve, the act grounding him, reminding him who he was supposed to be.

Only then did he look back.

Sloane lay on the filthy mattress, knees drawn to her chest, drowning in nothing but an oversized t-shirt. Her hair was matted, her lips cracked, her pupils blown wide from whatever she'd been given. She tried to lift her head, dazed, confused, rolled over, exposing herself as if two strange men were not even in the room with her, sixteen years old, and already broken in ways no one her age should be.

Will's throat closed. His rage drained into something worse: a cold, sick hollowness.

She was alive. That was all that mattered.

Outside, red and blue lights painted the cracked brick walls. Will carried the limp girl down the stairs and out the front door. Her head was leaning against his outer carrier; he could hear her labored, slow breathing, her eyes partially open, staring up at him as if she was trying to look at the world but couldn't yet see. Waiting paramedics helped Will ease Sloane onto a stretcher. She whimpered when the IV went in, too weak to fight it.

"She's been drugged," he told them, "have them run a full tox screen for narcotics, she's probably also been sexually assaulted, I'll be by later to check on her, what ER are you guys headed to?" Will questioned the EMT who was headed for the driver's seat.

"Midlands General," she barked back to him as she wrenched open the door and hopped inside. "I'll let them know you are coming. I'll tell them to look for Tony Stark in battle mode coming in the emergency entrance."

Will stood in the street, jaw tight, watching. His reflection warped in the cruiser's side mirror. Eyes wild. Lip trembling. He looked like someone he didn't recognize. Hands and knuckles, bloodied, shirt and carrier splattered with specks of blood, not his.

Joe came up beside him, cigarette glowing in the dark. "Still breathing, kid. That's the win. Don't you forget it."

Will didn't answer. Couldn't. His throat felt raw.

### Midlands General – ER

The automatic doors slid open with a hiss, and the antiseptic smell hit Will harder than the blood and sweat still clinging to him. Nurses moved fast between curtained bays, monitors beeped in uneven rhythms, and voices overlapped in clipped orders.

At the desk, a young resident glanced up. His eyes flicked over Will's blood-spattered shirt before settling on his badge clipped to his belt. "Mercer? Room seven. Still stabilizing."

Will pushed through the curtain.

Sloane lay on the bed, IV taped to her arm, monitors tracking each fragile breath. Her blond hair was matted, and her skin was pale beneath the bruises. The broad smile from her photos was gone — lips dry, face slack in exhaustion. A blanket was pulled to her chin, but nothing could hide the smallness of her frame, the way life had been drained out of her in just four days.

A nurse adjusted the drip. "She's conscious in flashes. Mostly out. We ran the tox — benzos, opioids, traces of coke. High doses, mixed. She's lucky she's alive."

Will's hand curled around the rail, knuckles whitening. "And...?"

The nurse hesitated, then kept her voice low. "Signs of assault. We've already paged the SANE nurse. Evidence kit is being prepped."

Will swallowed hard, the words like shards in his throat. He forced himself to nod. "She's going to make it?"

"She's fighting," the nurse said. "And she's young. That helps."

Will stayed a long minute, just listening to the steady beep of the monitor, the proof she was still here. He leaned down slightly, voice quiet. "You matter, Sloane. You're not a ghost. Not tonight."

For the first time since Craven Street, the weight in his chest shifted — not lighter, but bearable.

The steady beep of the monitor kept pace with Will's heartbeat. He stood at the bedside, eyes locked on the girl he'd carried out of hell only an hour earlier. IV lines, oxygen cannula, bruises blooming across her arms. Sixteen years old, and already marked by too much.

For a moment, he thought she was still out cold. Then her lashes fluttered. Her eyes cracked open, hazy, unfocused — until they found him.

Her lips trembled. A tear slipped sideways into her hairline. "I... saw you..." Her voice was a rasp, broken glass against her throat.

Will leaned in, carefully and steadily. "You're safe now. Just breathe. Let them take care of you."

Her fingers twitched against the blanket, searching. Will hesitated only a heartbeat before sliding his battered hand into hers. Her grip was weak, trembling, but fierce in its intent. She tugged, desperate, her arm shifting the blanket down off her shoulder. For a moment, the blanket slipped askew, exposing the bruises and scratches scattered across her collarbone and down her side to her hip.

Will's breath caught, not from the glimpse, but from what it meant. Her body, so slight, so marked, was a reminder of how close she'd come to being erased. She wasn't reaching for comfort like a child clutches a blanket — she was clawing for life itself, and he was the only anchor in the room.

He steadied her, pulling the blanket back up, covering her again. But she clutched his hand tighter, pressed it to her torso like it tethered her to the world. "Thank you," she whispered, voice cracking, tears streaking down her temples.

Her eyes closed again, exhaustion winning. She didn't release him until her body lost the strength to hold on, her fingers slipping away one by one. Will stayed a moment longer, jaw tight, throat thick. He smoothed the blanket up over her shoulders, covering the fragile shape beneath.

Then, with hands still shaking, he pulled a card from his pocket — the standard Summit Falls PD contact card. He flipped it over and pressed his pen hard to the cardboard, the words cutting deep into the surface.

**You matter.**

**Call me when you're ready.**

— Will

[personal cell number scrawled underneath]

He set it gently on the counter beside the tray of gauze and syringes, angled where she'd see it when she woke again.

Then he turned, pulling the curtain closed behind him, and walked out into the antiseptic hum of the ER —

carrying the weight of her thank you like it was heavier than any evidence bag.

That night, in the locker room, he sat with the notebook open on his lap, blood smudges still drying on his cuffs.

### Notebook Entry:
*Found her. Alive. Barely.*
*Almost lost it. Almost crossed the line.*
*Lesson: Survival isn't just mine. It's hers too.*
*Rage is not survival.*
*She is a fighter. She is ALIVE.*

### Kristen's Apartment – Just Before Dawn
Kristen was still half-asleep when the knock came. She opened the door in an oversized tee, hair a mess, eyes squinting against the hall light.

Will stood there, hooded jacket slung over his shoulder, the exhaustion in his face deeper than usual. He didn't say a word at first — just stepped inside, and she knew. She shut the door behind him and let him drop onto the couch.

"What happened?" she asked quietly, settling beside him.

Will scrubbed a hand across his face, fingers skittering over dried grit and the sting of fresh tears he refused to let show. His knuckles were raw, the skin split in places from the fight. "We found her," he said, voice rough. "Sloane Mercer. She's alive... barely. Drugged. Bruised. Clinging to anything she could find." His throat tightened; the words scraped out. *I almost killed that lowlife,* he thought, the image of the dealer's knife flashing across his mind. *He came at me with a blade. I could've shot him. I could've ended it.*

He swallowed hard, the confession falling out in a rush. "Something in me snapped, Kris. I— I tell you, all I wanted to do was pummel the life out of him and watch it drain from his face. I don't know what came over me. If it hadn't been for Joe, I don't know if I'd still be standing here."

Kristen watched him, the table light cutting soft planes across his jaw. She'd seen this side of him before— the afterglow of a fight, when adrenaline thinned out into something raw and dangerous—but tonight there was more: a frightened honesty he rarely allowed himself. *He's carrying it like it's going to crush him,* she thought. *He's not just replaying the fight. He's carrying the part of himself that wanted to stay in it.*

He buckled forward a little, as if the motion could force the image out of his chest. "Then at the hospital—" He paused, voice dropping until it was nearly a whisper. "She reached for me, Kris. Pulled so hard the blanket slipped down. She didn't care if she was exposed. She just... needed to hold on to something that wasn't going to let go."

Kristen's throat tightened. Her hand found his without thinking, fingers curling around the same palm Sloane had clutched hours ago. The skin there was callused and warm. She felt the tremor beneath his grip—the aftershocks of doing what needed doing, and the guilt that came after. *He's an anchor for other people, and he forgets to anchor himself,* she thought, then corrected herself: *He's never forgotten; he just bears the load alone until he can't.*

"You were that anchor," she said out loud, because someone had to make it true for him. Her voice was steady, but inside she felt a fierce protectiveness flare up—anger at what had been done to Sloane and at how close Will had come to being swallowed by his own rage. *He kept her from vanishing. He kept her hand in his until they could get her safe. That matters.*

Will looked down at their joined hands and the tautness in his jaw eased a fraction. "She thanked me," he said, the memory raw and small in his chest. "Whispered it like she was afraid it wouldn't last." He closed his eyes for a beat. "Then she passed out. I covered her. Left her a card with my cell—wrote 'You matter' on the back." His voice was almost unreadable now, stripped of bravado. "She's sixteen, Kris. Sixteen. And she almost slipped through the cracks like she was nothing."

Kristen's fingers tightened around his knuckles, a simple squeeze that carried everything she couldn't say: that Sloane was not nothing, that Will had not been foolish to risk himself, that anger had a place but so did restraint. *He thinks he should be ashamed for what he almost became,* she thought. *But this—that he brought her back—this is what will count.*

She let the silence stretch just long enough for him to breathe into it, then met his eyes. "You did the right thing," she said, plain and sure. "You came for her. You stayed. You told the doctors what to check for. You didn't let him win. That's what matters."

Will let out a ragged laugh that was almost a sob. Relief and exhaustion and a little of the old, stubborn pride flickered across his face. He squeezed her hand back, a private thanks. *She gives me the words I don't have,* he thought. *She keeps me from turning into what I fear.*

They sat like that for a minute—two quiet people holding the thin rope between what the job stole and what they could still keep. Outside, the city carried on. Inside, Kristen's certainty and Will's worn honesty braided into something steadier than either had alone.

Kristen pressed closer, her voice steady, sure. "She didn't slip because you were there. Because you believe what too many people forget: that she matters. And now she knows it, too. Even if she forgets again, she has proof in her hand that someone told her otherwise."

Will let out a long breath, some of the tension easing from his shoulders.

Kristen laid her head against him, her words soft but fierce. "That's why I said yes to you, Will. Because you carry people, even when it breaks you down. You matter to me. And you'll matter to her. Don't doubt it."

For the first time since carrying Sloane out of that house, Will's chest loosened enough to let in air. He held Kristen tighter, knowing she was the only reason the weight didn't crush him completely.

### Notebook Entry –

*Carried Sloane out. Alive. Barely.*
*Pulled at me like she was drowning.*
*Blanket slipped. Didn't care. Just wanted to hold on.*
*Fragile. So damn fragile.*
*Whispered thank you. Faded out.*
*Covered her. Left my card.*
*Back of it: **You matter. Call when you're ready.***
*Joe says: keep the beat. Don't carry it home.*
*Kristen says: she didn't slip because I was there.*
*She matters because I made her matter.*
*Two voices. Same truth.*
*One keeps me alive.*
*One keeps me human.*

### *Kristen's Apartment – Morning*

Steam hissed behind the bathroom door. The faint sound of running water, Will's shadow shifting under the frosted glass.

Kristen moved through the living room, blazer draped over one arm, coffee cooling in the other. She paused at the table — his notebook sat there, open just a sliver, a pen slid sideways between the pages like a bookmark.

Curiosity tugged. She set her cup down, thumbed the cover open. The ink cut hard into the paper, words pressed deep. his notes, raw, jagged.

*Carried Sloane out. Alive. Barely.*
*Pulled at me like she was drowning.*
*Fragile. So damn fragile.*
*Whispered thank you. Faded out.*
*Covered her. Left my card.*
*Back of it: You matter. Call when ready.*
*Joe says: keep the beat. Don't carry it home.*
*Kristen says: she didn't slip because I was there.*
*She matters because I made her matter.*
*Two voices. Same truth.*
*One keeps me alive.*
*One keeps me human.*

Kristen's breath caught. Her hand pressed over her mouth, eyes burning.

The shower cut off. Silence, then the squeak of the door. She blinked fast, snapping the notebook shut, sliding the pen back across the cover like she hadn't touched it.

She grabbed her blazer, straightened. Her heart pounded — not from guilt, but from the weight of what she'd just read.

He hadn't told her. He'd written it and written her into the pages where he bled the job out.

From the bathroom, Will's voice carried, casual, unaware. "You heading out already?"

Kristen swallowed hard, forcing her voice steady. "Yeah. Court docket's full."

She glanced once more at the notebook before turning to the door. The words echoed in her chest as she left for work: One keeps me alive. One keeps me human.

## Ghost

The squad room was quieter than usual the next morning. Paperwork hummed through the typewriters, phones buzzed, but voices stayed low. Everyone had heard about the raid on Craven Street. Everyone knew Will Anderson had found the Mercer girl alive.

Alive. Barely.

Will sat at his desk, hand wrapped around a paper cup of coffee gone cold. His knuckles were swollen, and his skin was split across two fingers. Every time he flexed them, he felt the ghost of bone meeting bone.

Joe dropped into the chair across from him, cigarette dangling from his lips. For a long minute, he said nothing. Just watched the smoke curl toward the ceiling.

Finally: "You scared the hell out of me last night."

Will looked up, surprised. "Me?"

Joe's eyes were steady, bloodshot but sharp. "Yeah, you. I've seen rookies freeze. I've seen vets cut corners. I've seen plenty lose their nerve. But you? You almost lost yourself. That's worse."

Will said nothing. The memory of his fists crashing into the boyfriend's face replayed behind his eyes. He could still feel the cartilage give, still hear the wet rattle of breath.

345

"I told you once — don't carry them home," Joe continued. "But you carried that girl before we even found her. And last night? It damn near carried you into the ground with her."

Will stared down at his notebook, open on the desk. The last entry glared back at him in blocky ink: *Rage is not survival.*

"She's alive," Will muttered. "That's what matters."

Joe leaned forward, voice gravelly. "Yeah. And if I hadn't pulled you off him, you'd be in a holding cell right now instead of writing that report. You care, Anderson. That's good. But you let that care turn to rage, and you're done. Badge or no badge."

The silence stretched. Will clenched his jaw, forcing himself not to snap back.

Then Joe leaned back, exhaled smoke toward the ceiling. "You're better than that. Don't prove me wrong."

The door opened, and silence rolled through the squad room like someone had cut the power. Even the typewriters stilled mid-stroke. A man stepped inside. Not rushed. Not hesitant. Just deliberate — every motion controlled, as if he'd measured the distance between the door and Will's desk before he even entered.

His suit was black, perfectly cut, the kind of cloth that didn't exist in Summit Falls unless it was imported. Not flashy — just *expensive enough to whisper.*

Two men followed at his shoulders, not speaking. Their eyes swept exits, hands hovering near their jackets. Military haircuts, crisp posture. Not bodyguards in name, but anyone watching would know better.

The man at their center didn't need them. He carried a presence that made space bend around him — something heavy, practiced, and absolute. He didn't project danger. He *embodied* it. When he looked at people, it wasn't curiosity. It was evaluation. Measurement.

Will felt it immediately. Not fear, not even threat — something deeper. Recognition. This was a man who'd seen the same kind of ugliness Will had... but had *learned to use it.*

The man stopped in front of Will's desk. "Detective Anderson," he said. His voice was even, every syllable precise — like a blade honed to cut without effort.

Will straightened automatically, chair legs scraping the floor. "Sir," he began, already halfway to standing.

"Please," the man said, one hand lifting slightly, palm outward. "Don't get up. You've done enough already."

Will froze mid-motion, then eased back down. The air between them tightened. He glanced around — half the squad room was still pretending not to stare.

The man studied him for a long moment. The bruised knuckles. The blood ground into the cuff. The exhaustion in his eyes.

Then, almost softly: "You found my daughter."

Will blinked. The words landed with weight, but it was the pronoun that struck harder — *my daughter*.

"Yes, sir," Will said carefully. "She's at Midlands General. Stable, last I heard."

The man nodded once, slow. "Sloane." He said the name like it was a secret, or a reminder. His gaze drifted, just for a breath, before snapping back to Will. "You went into that house knowing you might not walk out."

"It's the job," Will said, voice tighter than he meant. "She needed help."

"She needed a savior," the man corrected softly. "And you were it."

Will opened his mouth to reply, but the man was already reaching into his jacket. The movement was unhurried, deliberate. The two men behind him tensed anyway, scanning the room. He withdrew a small white card and held it out between two fingers.

Will hesitated, then took it. Plain card. No logo, no title. Just a phone number written in clean black print.

"If you ever need anything," the man said. "Anything at all, no matter how small — call me."

Will turned the card over once, then looked up. "I didn't do it for thanks."

"I know," the man replied. His faint smile never reached his eyes. "That's why I trust you enough to offer it."

The silence that followed pressed hard enough to hum.

Finally, the man extended his hand. "Orin Mercer," he said.

Will took it. The handshake was firm — not aggressive, just heavy, like it carried the weight of too many unspoken things.

Mercer's grip lingered a fraction longer than polite, his gaze holding steady. "You gave me back my blood," he said quietly. "That makes us... connected."

Before Will could respond, Mercer released him and turned. His two men fell in step, and the squad room seemed to breathe again.

Will looked down at the card still in his palm. The number was ordinary. The paper, not. It felt heavier than it                                              should.
The weight of the card sat wrong, heavier than the paper should.

Mercer turned without waiting for thanks. His two shadows fell in behind him, and just like that, the squad room exhaled again.

Will stared down at the card, throat dry.

From the corner, Joe's voice came, quiet but hard enough to cut glass. "That man's not your friend."

Will looked over. "You know him?"

Joe didn't blink. "Don't need to. I know his kind. You know those men, the ones who live in shadows. Who never leave fingerprints. You think the dealers on Craven Street are dangerous? They're toddlers playing with plastic knives compared to Orin Mercer."

Will slipped the card into his wallet, telling himself it was just a courtesy. But Joe's words dug deeper than the ink on the page.

Notebook Entry:
*Orin Mercer. Thanked me. Gave me a card.*
*Power behind the smile.*
*Poison in the paper.*
*Integrity = no shortcuts. Hide it. Forget it.*
*Unless the world's on fire.*

# Closed

The radio crackled, sharp against the still night: *"All Units, be advised, strong-arm robbery in progress, suspect is now fleeing on foot. Any car in the area?"*

Will's hand was already on the wheel. *"David 1-3, I'm close."*

By the time he spotted the suspect—a wiry kid in a gray sweatshirt that flapped behind him like torn wings—adrenaline had already had his body moving before thought could catch up. Will yanked the wheel, slammed the shifter into park, and was out the door.

"Police! Stop!"

The kid didn't stop. He bolted harder, sneakers smacking the pavement with desperate rhythm.

They cut down an alley where the air stank of grease and old garbage. A dumpster overflowed, rats scattering as they passed. The boy's breath wheezed in the narrow space, a high, frantic sound swallowed by the echo of boots behind him.

The fire escape loomed ahead. Metal clanged as the kid scrambled up. Will followed without hesitation, his vest catching the railing, boots hammering steel steps. His lungs burned, but he kept his pace steady. *Soldier first, cop second. Control the breath. Keep the rhythm.*

The rooftops opened wide at the top: tar paper, gravel, rusted satellite dishes tilting like broken teeth. The neon from a pawn shop below painted everything in sick green and red.

The kid glanced back once, wild-eyed, and nearly slipped. Will surged closer, his voice cutting across the night. "Don't be stupid—you can't win!"

The only answer was the scrape of sneakers digging for speed.

The city stretched out on all sides, a pulse of noise and light—sirens in the distance, horns blaring, laughter spilling from bars. Will's stomach lurched at the height, but training held him steady. And beneath that training, Joe's voice hummed like a second heartbeat: *Don't freeze. Keep the beat. Finish the chase.*

The kid hit the edge of the roof, launched across a gap. His foot clipped the far ledge. He stumbled, arms flailing. That half-second of imbalance was all Will needed.

He dove, shoulder first, the impact jarring through bone. They hit hard, gravel scraping Will's cheek raw, tearing open his palm. The kid bucked under him, a mess of fists and elbows, but Will bore down, weight and discipline pinning him.

"Get off me! I didn't mean it!" the boy cried, voice cracking, lip bleeding from the fall. "I just—I was desperate!"

Will's breath tore in and out, sweat dripping into his eyes. His hands worked the cuffs on instinct, the final *click* sounding louder than the sirens below.

The kid sagged, chest heaving, tears streaking grime down his face.

By the time backup arrived, lights bouncing blue across the rooftops, Will already had him up on his feet, one hand locked on the chain between the cuffs. The boy stumbled as they moved toward the fire escape, whispering through broken sobs, "Didn't mean it... swear to God, I didn't mean it..."

Will didn't answer. He just walked him off the roof, the night air sharp in his lungs, his mind already writing the words he knew he'd scribble later:

**Notebook Entry:**
*Don't freeze. Keep the beat. Finish the chase.*
*The kid cried about desperation. Lip split. Eyes scared, not evil.*
*Rage is easy. Control is harder.*
*Desperate doesn't mean harmless.*

Two days later, Will stood in the precinct's briefing room, cameras flashing, brass lined shoulder to shoulder. The captain clipped a commendation to his chest, voice carrying through the room:

"Quick thinking, fast response, excellent police work."

The applause rose politely and practiced. Will forced a smile, shook hands, and nodded where he was supposed to. The medal felt cold against his uniform, light and hollow at the same time.

Kristen stood near the back wall, pressed suit, legal pad clutched more like armor than necessity. She didn't clap the loudest, didn't cheer like the brass expected. But her eyes—when they found his—softened with something real. Pride, yes, but also understanding. She knew this ribbon wasn't the victory. The victory was Sloane Mercer, still breathing in a hospital bed.

When it was over, she found him just outside the briefing room, away from the flashbulbs. Her hand brushed his sleeve where the medal sat. "I'm proud of you," she said quietly, her voice pitched for him alone. Then, softer still: "But don't let them cheapen what you did. She's the reason it matters, not the ribbon."

Will felt something unclench in his chest. He nodded, unable to say more than, "I know."

That night, the city blurred past the windshield of an unmarked Ford Taurus, the kind Vice liked—paint dull, antenna bent, invisible by design. Joe sat in the passenger seat, coffee steaming, eyes fixed on the streetlights carving the dark.

He didn't even glance at the ribbon still clipped to Will's chest. Just muttered, "Don't let them feed you scraps and call it a feast."

Will's hands tightened on the wheel. "It was a good arrest."

Joe shrugged, smoke in his tone. "Sure. But the brass hand out medals like poker chips. They pin 'em on whoever makes them look good that week. You think the street gives a damn about your ribbon?"

The hum of the engine filled the silence.

Joe finally turned, eyes catching the passing glow of neon. "Don't chase medals, Anderson. Chase truth. That's the only thing that lasts."

Will flicked his gaze to the rearview, caught the glint of the ribbon under the dashboard light. Kristen's words replayed: *Don't let them cheapen what you did.* Joe followed close behind: *Chase truth.*

He drove on through the dark, feeling the ribbon grow heavier than it had all day.

**Notebook Entry**
*Closed robbery. Rooftop chase.*
*Commendation pinned. Felt nothing.*
*Don't chase medals.*
*Chase truth.*

## Promotion

The briefing room had been scrubbed into something unrecognizable. The cracked blinds were pulled straight, the podium gleamed like someone had buffed it with nervous energy, and even the flag in the corner stood crisp and square instead of sagging. Rows of folding chairs filled the space, creaking as family members and press wedged shoulder-to-shoulder. The smell of polish and fresh coffee hung thick in the air.

Will stood in the front row, dress blues sharp, shoes gleaming like mirrors under the fluorescents. His collar itched, but he didn't move to fix it. In the second row, he spotted Kristen's mother, her hands clasped, her smile trembling as if she might break into tears at the slightest excuse.

The brass droned through speeches—duty, honor, sacrifice—the exact words Will had heard since academy orientation. He nodded at the right beats, but the words slid off him like rain on glass. His eyes kept drifting to the small black box on the table. The one that held the detective's shield.

When his name was finally called, his boots clicked against the tile. Applause rose—polite, scattered, enough to echo but not enough to fill the room.

The captain gave him a handshake, a pat on the shoulder, then turned. "Sergeant Donovan, if you would do the honors."

Joe walked up slowly, his uniform pressed but creased from years of real use, not ceremony. His expression didn't shift. No grandstanding, no grin for the cameras. Just steady hands opening the box, lifting the gleaming shield as if it weighed a hundred pounds.

He pinned it onto Will's chest with deliberate precision. For a moment, his hand lingered there, heavy, pressing the badge into the fabric like he was fixing it in place for more than one reason. His eyes lifted, sharp and bloodshot, searching Will's face.

"Congratulations, kid," Joe said, low enough that the microphones wouldn't catch it. Then the corner of his mouth twitched. "Commendation and a promotion in the same damn week. Keep this up, you'll be chief by the end of the month."

Will let out the smallest laugh, nerves cracking through his chest. "Not likely."

Joe gave the slightest nod, then stepped back. The applause swelled again, louder this time, as if the crowd had caught some weight in the moment.

From the second row, Kristen's eyes caught his. She was in a charcoal skirt suit, hair pinned neatly, hands folded in her lap like the consummate ADA. But her smile—it wasn't polite or ceremonial. It was private. The

357

kind that reached her eyes and sharpened into something mischievous when no one else was looking.

Later, after the photos, the shaking of hands, the polite chatter—when the crowd thinned and the echo of applause faded—Will caught Joe in the hallway.

"You've called me kid since the first day," Will said, leaning against the wall, the new shield cool against his chest. "Guess that's over now."

Joe cracked the door open for smoke, lit his cigarette, and let the smoke curl out into the night. "You'll always be someone's kid in this job. Just means you're not a rookie anymore."

Will touched the badge unconsciously. It gleamed too bright, too clean, and for the first time, he felt its weight press down instead of lift him up.

Joe studied him for a long beat. Then, with that same gravel tone, he said, "Listen closely. The badge doesn't get lighter. Ever. The brass'll try to use it. The public'll try to judge it. Some nights it'll feel like it's dragging you under. But it's not about them. It's about how you carry it. You carry it straight, even when it costs you. That's the job."

Ash flicked off the cigarette, his hand trembling just slightly. Will caught it—caught the new lines around his eyes, the way his shoulders slumped when he thought no one was watching. For the first time, the years looked heavier on Joe than the badge did.

Joe's gaze cut back sharply. "Don't forget that, and you'll do fine. Forget it, and the shield will own you instead of the other way around."

Then he clapped Will on the shoulder once—firm, final—and walked down the hall, his limp more pronounced, his figure folding into shadow. Will stood there, the hum of the fluorescents buzzing in his chest.

For the first time, he wondered what the squad would look like without Joe Donovan in it.

A soft voice broke the thought. "Hey."

Kristen leaned against the wall opposite, heels dangling from her hand now, her professional armor softened by the long day. She tilted her head, eyes sliding down to the badge. "Looks good on you," she said.

Will managed a tight smile. "Feels heavy."

"Good," she replied, stepping close enough to adjust his tie like she was smoothing the weight into place. "Means you understand it." Then, with that wicked glint she reserved just for him, she added, "We'll celebrate later."

Her grin sharpened, devilish, a promise she didn't need to spell out.

Will's chest eased, the knot loosening just a little. He could already see her later, without the crowd, without the brass—just them, just real. He nodded, voice low. "Looking forward to it."

## Notebook Entry

*New shield. Joe pinned it.*
*Still called me kid.*
*Commendation and a promotion in the same week—Joe says I'll be chief by next month.*
*Badge feels heavier.*
*Carry it straight, even when it costs you.*
*Joe's shoulders looked heavier too.*
*Kristen said it looks good on me.*
*Said we'll celebrate later—smiled like she meant it.*

## Kristen's Apartment – That Evening

Will knocked softly, shifting the weight of his dress blues across his shoulders. He'd come straight from the ceremony, the commendation ribbon still clipped neatly and precisely to his uniform. His shoes clicked against the hallway tile, the polish already dulled from a long day.

Inside, the apartment glowed low and warm. The faint scent of candles drifted through the air—vanilla and something floral, carried by the hum of quiet music that played from the speaker in the corner. When he stepped in, he saw the table. Two place settings. White china. Folded napkins. Candles in glass votives cast golden light across the surface. Simple, but intimate in a way that made his chest tighten.

From the back of the apartment came her voice. "Dinner's ready."

Kristen appeared from the hallway, and Will's breath caught in his throat.

She had shed the professional armor she'd worn all day—no more pressed charcoal suit, no more ADA mask. Instead, she wore a green silk dress that seemed to have been poured onto her frame. The fabric shimmered like wet paint under the candlelight, hugging every curve, low at the neckline in a way that left no room for imagination, cut to the thigh so that every step flashed bare skin. There were no lines of straps, no seams that betrayed anything beneath it. Just silk, skin, and the certainty that nothing interrupted the two.

The green deepened and shifted with the light, clinging to her as if it had been stitched in place just for her body alone. Thin straps framed her shoulders, the silk plunging in a deep V that showed the delicate rise of her collarbones and more. The hem hovered just high enough that when she moved, the suggestion of her leg carried the threat of revealing more than it already was; nothing was hidden, if it wasn't skin, it was expressed outwardly as if she were not wearing a thing.

Will froze, his throat bone-dry, eyes tracing her as if he'd never seen her before. He had words somewhere, but none that survived the trip from chest to mouth. *God,* he thought, *she's... she's beyond stunning. She's the definition of unfair.*

Kristen's mouth curved in a slow, knowing smile as she closed the space between them. Without a word, she slid her hands over his shoulders, eased the formal coat off him, and laid it across the back of a chair. "Relax," she said softly, her voice velvet. "Tonight isn't about brass speeches or ribbons."

Will could only nod, his pulse hammering.

She pulled out a chair for him, guiding him down as if he were the guest of honor. When he sat, the medal tugged lightly against his shirt with the motion, a sharp reminder of the day's weight. Kristen brushed her hand against it once before retreating to the kitchen.

A moment later, she returned with plates—something simple, yet elegant. Seared chicken breast with a delicate glaze, roasted vegetables charred just right at the edges, small red potatoes glistening with butter and herbs. Not extravagant but crafted. Careful. Something made with her hands.

She set the plate before him, then put her own, and poured two glasses of wine. The crimson shimmer of it caught the candlelight as she filled his glass, then poured just a little in hers, setting the bottle aside.

Kristen eased into the chair across from him, green silk catching the flicker of the flame, eyes bright in the low light. "Eat," she said, a half-smile tugging at her lips. "Before I start thinking you only showed up to stare."

Will let out a breathless laugh, shaking his head. "You make it... difficult to do anything else."

Kristen lifted her glass, tapping the rim gently against his. "Good. Then you're right where I want you."

## Human

The candles burned low, casting a soft gold glow across the table. Kristen's green silk dress shimmered with every subtle movement, the candlelight sketching shadows where the silk dipped and clung. Wine glasses stood half full, the plates mostly cleared, and the faint hum of jazz filled the silence between words.

Kristen leaned back in her chair, eyes fixed on him, her smile unguarded in a way that would never appear in a courtroom. "You know," she began softly, "I was proud of you today. Not just because of the badge or the ceremony. Because of the man standing there. The one I got to marry." Her voice caught slightly, but she pressed through, steadily. "You filled me with so much joy, Will. Watching you... it wasn't just pride. It was... knowing I chose right."

Will blinked, his throat tight. For a man used to command, to fire and chaos, her words hit deeper than the medal still pinned to his chest. "Kris," he said, shaking his head, "I stood there thinking the same about you. You in that courtroom, cutting through lies like they're paper, holding your ground no matter who tries to shake it. I've watched you win when it wasn't popular, fight when no one else would. You're stronger than I'll ever be."

She smirked, leaning in over her glass. "You're a terrible liar for someone who writes reports for a living."

"Not lying," he countered, eyes locked on hers. "Just finally saying it out loud."

Her gaze softened. Then she hesitated, her hand brushing the rim of her glass. "I need to tell you something," she murmured, voice quieter now. "The other morning, when you were in the shower... I saw your notebook. The page you marked."

Will stiffened, the word *notebook* snapping his pulse like a tripwire. His jaw flexed, ready to defend the private weight scrawled there. But she kept going.

"You wrote about me," Kristen said, her eyes steady, her voice trembling just slightly. "How I make you feel... human." She emphasized the word, her lips shaping it carefully. "Will, do you know what it means to hear that from you? That I'm not just some piece of your world, or a person you lean on when you're bleeding—but that I make you human? You make me want to be better every day, but that..." Her eyes glistened. "That undid me."

The room seemed smaller suddenly, the candlelight warmer, the air thicker.

Will set his fork down, his hand reaching across the table to cover hers. His thumb brushed the back of her hand, steady, grounding. "Kris," he said, his voice low and raw. "You don't just make me human. You remind me why I need to stay that way because it's too damn easy to lose it out there. To let rage or fear take over. But with you..." He exhaled, shaking his head. "With you, I feel like a man, not just a badge. Not just a cop. A man who still deserves you."

Her lips parted, her breath catching. She turned her hand under his, weaving their fingers together tight.

"That's all I ever want," she whispered. "To keep you human."

For a moment, neither moved. Just hands clasped across the table, the weight of their confessions binding them closer than any medal, any badge, any case ever could.

Then Kristen's mouth curved into a familiar, wicked smile. She leaned in, whispering like a secret meant only for him: "And I fully intend to celebrate making you human tonight."

Will laughed softly, shaking his head. "You already have."

A short time later, the wine glasses sat abandoned on the table, the candles guttering low. Will barely remembered moving from the table, only that Kristen had taken his hand, the green silk catching the light as she rose. She led him down the hall, barefoot, laughing softly when his shoulder brushed the doorway too wide in his dress blues.

Her apartment was hushed except for the sound of their breaths, the occasional soft clink of a button, the whisper of silk sliding away. Every line of her body pressed into his, every curve exactly as it had looked when the dress had clung to her like paint. But now there was nothing between them.

Kristen's hands found his face, pulled him down into a kiss that tasted of wine and candle smoke. The world outside fell away. There was no badge, no squad room, no city. Just them—skin to skin, confessions turning to touch, vows spoken without words.

Later, tangled in sheets, the dim glow of the last candle casting her profile in gold, Kristen traced her fingers over his chest, following the lines of muscle and the scar near his collarbone. Her voice was soft, but her words carried weight.

"When you wrote *human,*" she said, almost whispering, "it scared me."

Will turned his head, eyes meeting hers. "Scared you?"

She nodded, fingers still moving slowly across his chest. "Because I realized how close you are to losing that, every day. Out there, with the badge, with the darkness you carry. And if I make you human... it means I could lose you if I ever fail at that. If you forget." She swallowed, her throat tight. "It means I matter that much."

Will caught her hand, pressed it flat against his chest where his heart hammered steadily beneath her palm. His voice was low, but every word steady. "You don't make me human because I'd fall apart without you. You make me human because you remind me I'm still worth being that, even when I can't see it. Even when the job tries to strip it away."

Her eyes shimmered, lips trembling into a small smile. She leaned closer, her forehead resting against his.

"Then promise me," she whispered. "Promise you'll always fight to stay human. For us."

Will kissed her, slow and sure, the vow sinking deeper than anything he'd ever written in his notebook. "I promise."

Kristen curled into him, her body molding against his, her hand still pressed to his chest. The last candle went out, but the word lingered in the dark between them—*human.*

### Kristen's Apartment – Early Morning

The bedroom was quiet except for the steady hum of the city outside the window. Pale light slipped through the blinds, striping the sheets across their tangled bodies. The candles had burned themselves out hours ago, leaving only the faint scent of smoke and melted wax.

Kristen lay pressed against Will, her leg thrown over his hip, her arm wrapped tight across his chest. It wasn't just closeness; it was possession, as if she were holding him in place, daring the world to pry him from her.

Will's fingers traced lazy patterns down her spine, the rhythm soothing, steady. He was half-awake, content in the stillness, when her voice broke the quiet.

"You keep saying I make you human," she murmured, her lips brushing against his chest. "But I've been keeping something from you."

Will blinked, the words cutting through the haze of sleep. His body tensed just slightly. "Kris?"

She shifted, her eyes lifting to his, green and glinting with nerves and something brighter. Her voice was soft, but deliberate. "The truth is... I already made us more human." She smiled faintly, the corner of her mouth trembling as she said it. "I'm pregnant, Will."

For a second, the air stalled in his lungs. His pulse roared in his ears. Pregnant. The word hit him harder than any gunfire ever had.

Kristen's grip tightened, her arm locking across him like she was anchoring herself as much as him. "I wasn't sure how to tell you. But last night—when we talked about *human*—I couldn't hold it in any longer. Because this little life... It's proof. Proof that what we're building isn't just surviving the badge or the job. It's more. It's *us*."

Will's throat worked, words stuck behind the weight in his chest. His hand slid down to her stomach, resting there gently, reverently, like it might break if he pressed too hard. His eyes burned, and for once, he didn't fight it.

"Kris," he whispered, voice raw. "You—you gave me everything. Everything I never thought I'd have again."

She smiled, tears slipping free as she pressed her forehead to his. "You said I keep you human. Now we've got someone else who'll make sure you never forget it."

Will kissed her, fierce and unsteady, his palm never leaving her stomach. And for the first time since he'd pinned on a badge, the word *human* didn't feel like something fragile he had to protect. It felt like a future.

## Cost

Six months had passed since the courthouse vows were exchanged. Six months since Kristen leaned across the sheets with that quiet, trembling smile and told him she was pregnant.

Six months of the city grinding on.

Will sat alone in his apartment long after midnight, blinds half-shut against the orange city glow. The radiator hissed, the hum of traffic bled through the window glass, but inside it was quiet enough that the silence pressed harder than any siren ever had.

His dress shirt — the one he only wore when testifying or dragged into command's dog-and-pony shows — hung off the back of a chair. Tonight it wasn't just wrinkled. The collar was sweat-stained, the cuffs stiff with dried blood. Not his blood. Not this time.

The smell of iron clung no matter how many times he scrubbed his hands. He could still feel the tacky smear against his palms.

Hours earlier, he hadn't been prowling Vice shadows in plainclothes. He'd been shoved into full blues. Command wanted bodies visible. "Community operation," they called it — neighborhood safety, cameras rolling, the press tipped off.

But nothing about the street stayed neat for long.

A suspect bolted in the middle of the staged meet-and-greet. Barreled straight into the crowd. His shoulder caught an older woman square in the chest, sending her tumbling backward.

She would've cracked her skull on the pavement. Will's hands got there first.

The hit split her nose wide, blood gushing bright down her face. She gasped, clawing for something solid as Will pressed his shirt against the wound. His sleeve soaked instantly, blood streaking into the cuff and spreading across his chest. Her hand gripped his forearm with surprising strength, fingers digging into his skin as if she'd drown if she let go.

Her eyes — wide, terrified, disbelieving. Not just fear of falling. Fear that the city itself had finally reached her doorstep.

The cameras caught it all. Hero cop in pressed blues, saving a civilian. He could already hear the chief spinning it: *Community trust. Quick action. Another win for the department.*

But that wasn't what stuck. What stuck was the frail weight of her clutch, the way her body trembled against his, the raw proof that even someone that far removed could be crushed in seconds. He'd left her with the paramedics, her blood still wet in the weave of his shirt.

Now, hours later, he poured two fingers of whiskey but didn't drink. Just stared at it, the glass heavy in his palm, his reflection warped in the window.

Split eyebrow that never healed smoothly. A fading slash along his ribs from a broken bottle in an alley — a reminder of the last time a dealer thought a corner was worth bleeding for. Shadows carved into his eyes so deep they looked permanent.

He looked older than his years. Felt older, too.

The job wasn't just carving him down. It was carving everyone. Vargas' betrayal, then O'Riley was gunned down on a traffic stop gone bad. Torres, gutted by IA after a questionable call, was stripped of his badge and benched for good. Men he'd trained beside scattered like ashes, remembered only by dust-caked plaques in City Hall.

Funerals stacked in his memory: the wail of bagpipes, the cold precision of rifles firing in salute, folded flags placed into the hands of widows whose eyes had gone hollow long before the graveside service. Each one left a mark deeper than fists, knives, or bullets. The False Prophet still out there, needing to be caught.

Sleep came jagged when it came at all. Phantom radio static jolting him awake. Gunshots echoing in his dreams that weren't really there. Sloane Mercer's face, pale and fragile, whispering *thank you* as her grip clung to his hand with more strength than her body should've had.

He'd jolt upright, sweat-soaked, the notebook already open on the nightstand — a shield he wrote into like it could keep the dark at bay.

Kristen noticed. She always did. She anchored him with her touch, with her laugh, with her words. But he saw it — the worry behind her eyes when she thought he wasn't looking. The way her smile sometimes trembled before she forced it steady.

She carried not just their unborn child, but the weight of his nights.

And he hated that.

His phone buzzed across the table. Joe.

**Joe Donovan [23:42]:** Heard you were out in blues tonight. Blood on the collar? Not your style, Anderson. Vice wears shadows, not parade gear. What the hell happened?

Will stared at the message, jaw tight. He hadn't answered Joe's last two either. How did he explain? That brass wanted him on display. That blood wasn't his; the street didn't care about uniforms, optics, or ribbon-cutting photo ops.

That no matter what they called it — community outreach, officer presence, neighborhood trust — the city always had a way of spilling blood across his hands.

He leaned back, staring at the ceiling, remembering the first day he'd put on the uniform. Collar stiff. The badge gleamed too brightly. Hope whispering that maybe the job was about justice.

Now he knew better. The street didn't care about justice. It carved you down, slice by slice, until all you could carry was whatever didn't break you.

And still, Joe's voice cut through the cracks.

*Don't freeze. Keep the beat. Integrity isn't convenient. Don't chase medals. Carry it straight, even when it costs you.*

The words were heavier than the badge itself.

Will set the whiskey down, untouched. He flipped open his notebook, pressed the pen deep enough into the paper that it almost tore.

### Notebook Entry
*The street takes its cut. Friends. Time. Sleep.*
*You keep going, or you drown.*
*Badge is heavy. Carry it anyway.*
*Even when it costs her. Even when it costs me.*

Will thumbed open his phone, the screen too bright in the dark apartment. His shirt still hung off the chair like an accusation, the blood crusted into the cuff catching the edge of the lamplight. He didn't want Kristen to see that, not while she was already carrying so much. But silence felt worse.

**Will [00:08]:** *You alright? Didn't mean to be out so late. I just wanted to check in on you and the baby.*

He stared at the three pulsing dots that appeared almost instantly. She was awake. She always was when he couldn't sleep.

Across town, Kristen lay propped on her pillows, the glow of her phone lighting the curve of her cheek. The apartment smelled faintly of chamomile tea she hadn't finished. She'd kept the news muted after the 11 p.m.

374

segment replayed for the third time, but his face had been burned into her mind anyway — Will, kneeling on the pavement, steady hands cradling an older woman as blood poured from her nose. He looked so solid on-screen, but she knew better.

**Kristen [00:11]:** *We're fine. I saw you on the 11 o'clock news. You didn't tell me you were starring in a press piece tonight.*

He exhaled through his nose, rubbing at the bridge of it with two fingers. He could already hear Joe's voice if he'd seen the footage: *Command's golden boy, huh? It's time to start practicing your smile for the cameras.* He hated the way the brass paraded them.

**Will [00:12]:** *Not my choice. Brass wanted blues out front.*

Kristen's fingers hovered over the keyboard, her pulse soft in her throat. She wanted to tell him how proud she was, how she'd felt her heart ache when she saw him steady that woman like the rest of the world didn't exist. Instead, she typed what she knew he'd allow himself to hear.

**Kristen [00:13]:** *They showed you kneeling with that older lady, holding her hand. You looked... steady like the one thing keeping the world together.*

His chest tightened. He remembered the woman's grip, frail but desperate, nails biting into his forearm as if she'd drown without him. He hadn't felt steady — he'd felt seconds away from unraveling.

**Will [00:15]:** *She was scared. Blood everywhere. Didn't feel steady. Just did what I had to.*

Kristen's eyes blurred. She brushed a hand across her belly, small but already firm, grounding herself in the reminder of what they'd made together.

**Kristen [00:16]:** *That's exactly why you're the man I married. And why I know our kid is going to have the best dad in the world.*

Will swallowed hard, throat raw. He leaned back in his chair, phone trembling in his hand as he typed.

**Will [00:17]:** *Don't know about that. But I do know I love you. Both of you.*

Kristen smiled through her tears. For all the darkness the job carried home with him, for all the weight in his notebook, she knew this was the truth that anchored him.

**Kristen [00:18]:** *We love you too. Now get some sleep, Will. Goodnight.*

He let his head rest against the back of the chair, the knot in his chest loosening just a fraction.

**Will [00:19]:** *Goodnight, Kris.*

The phone dimmed in his hand. He didn't finish the whiskey. Instead, he reached for the notebook, not to write, but to slide it back into the drawer. Tonight, her words would have to be the shield.

## Shift

The burglaries had started quietly. A liquor store on the west end, back door pried with a crowbar. A pawnshop on Market, glass spiderwebbed, cash drawer empty. Then a string of corner stores uptown — always the side entrance, always fast, consistently sloppy.

At first, Vice wouldn't have touched it. Property crimes belonged to the uniformed squads. But then the reports started stacking in with overlaps too ugly to ignore — electronics dumped at the same fence, pawn slips linked to names already on Vice's watchlists. Every petty burglary tied back to the same drug corners.

The brass tossed it their way. "Handle it," the captain had said, like dropping a shovel into their hands and pointing at a mountain.

So they did.

For weeks, Will and Joe sat in unmarked cars with bad shocks and worse heat. Drinking coffee that tasted like cardboard. Listening to radios buzz with chatter that never seemed to give enough. Writing plate numbers, mapping patterns, waiting for the same dented van to circle again.

Each time, Will found himself growing sharper. His notebook filled with plate numbers, descriptions, and half-heard names mumbled through pawnshop doors. Joe never praised him, but the silence was telling. It meant Will was pulling his weight.

One night, parked outside a rundown convenience store with a busted neon sign, Will had murmured, "They're not even good at this. They keep hitting the same fences. Same tools. It's like they want to get caught."

Joe had lit a cigarette, the glow briefly outlining his scarred jaw. "That's the thing about amateurs. They think sloppy means lucky. But sloppy leaves crumbs. Follow the crumbs, Anderson. Don't chase the rats."

Weeks blurred into each other. Rain slicked the windshield. Frost crept around the edges of the glass. Spring broke through, bringing the scent of thawed garbage in the alleys.

Finally, the pattern tightened. A corner house in the east ward, stripped before dawn. A pawn slip dated the same day. The van was spotted twice within a three-block radius.

That was the break.

Tonight, it came together.

The van rolled up slowly, headlights cut, paint dull as rust. Four men inside, masks tugged low, crowbars glinting as they spilled out.

The suspects rolled up in a dented Econoline van that looked like it had lived three lives too long. The paint had faded to primer in spots, and the muffler was coughing every time they slowed. The headlights cut a block early.

Inside, silhouettes shifted, masks tugged low, crowbars glinting under the sodium glow of the streetlight.

From across the street, Will adjusted his earpiece, heart rate steady. He and Joe sat in the unmarked, windows cracked, the stale smoke of Joe's last cigarette lingering in the upholstery.

"They're late," Will murmured, eyes on the van.

Joe's lip twitched. "Criminals don't own watches. Just bad habits."

The side door slid open with a metallic scrape. Four men spilled out, shoulders hunched, moving fast toward the side of the house. Their voices were hushed, but not enough to hide the nerves in them.

Joe flicked his chin toward the house. "There's our window. Let's go."

They moved—no wasted motion, no chatter. Two shadows breaking from the car, slipping across the street with the precision of men who'd done this a hundred times. Will felt the same rush he'd felt in combat years ago — not panic, but the sharp clarity that narrowed everything to angles, steps, breath.

The suspects were at the side door, crowbar wedged against the frame. One gave a low grunt as the wood splintered. That was when Joe's voice cut sharp across the dark.

"Police! Hands where we can see 'em!"

The crew froze, one with his knee half-bent, another twisting back with eyes wide above his mask.

Will came in from the other side, weapon up but steady. "Don't do it. Don't even think about it."

The leader hesitated, crowbar still wedged in the frame, eyes darting like a cornered animal. Will took a half step closer, voice even. "It's over. Drop it. Cuffs are the only way this ends clean."

A long breath. Then the metal clattered to the ground.

The rest followed. Hands went up, backs pressed against peeling siding as Joe and Will worked in tandem. Joe cuffed with the same economy he used lighting a cigarette — fast, practiced, no hesitation. Will read Miranda, steady, the words crisp against the night air.

Backup units swept in with flashing lights that painted the houses red and blue. Neighbors peeked from the curtains. Radios squawked as the suspects were loaded into cruisers, heads ducked, wrists cinched tight.

And then it was over, just like that. No blood. No shots. No scramble.

Will stood on the curb, chest rising steadily in the cool night air. For the first time in years, he realized Joe hadn't said a single word to correct him. No barked reminder. No quiet rebuke. He'd carried his side without faltering.

Joe struck a match, the flare carving deep lines into his face, making him look older in the glow. He lit his cigarette, took a drag, and exhaled toward the empty sky.

"Smooth," he muttered, smoke curling from his lips. "Damn near clean."

Will allowed himself the ghost of a smile. "We make a good team."

Joe's eyes narrowed through the smoke. "Don't get cocky, Anderson. Tonight we were Crockett and Tubbs. Tomorrow? Tomorrow's never promised."

Will huffed a short laugh, shaking his head. But deep down, he knew Joe was right.

Joe cupped the lighter against the breeze, the flare briefly painting the lines carved into his face. Deep grooves, darker shadows — he looked older than he had that first day in the squad car, older than he'd admit. Worn down by years of smoke, steel, and silence.

He drew in, exhaled a steady ribbon of smoke that curled skyward like something escaping. "Smooth," he muttered, voice gravel and fatigue. "Damn near clean."

Will let himself breathe out, a small smile tugging at the corner of his mouth. "We make a good team."

Joe's eyes didn't find him. They stayed on the smoke as it vanished into the night, his gaze far away. "Yeah. But this is it for me, kid."

The words landed harder than gunfire. Will had felt the signs creeping in — the limp getting worse, the pauses growing longer between movements, the way Joe's eyes lingered on the younger uniforms, as if he were measuring the world he was leaving behind. But hearing it out loud was different. It tightened something in Will's chest, sharp and immediate.

"You're retiring," Will said, voice quieter than he meant.

Joe didn't answer right away. He just watched the smoke curl upward until it disappeared. Then he flicked the cigarette butt into the gutter, sparks scattering and dying on wet asphalt.

"It's not the cases that break you," Joe said finally, voice low. "It's the silence after. That's the part I can't carry anymore."

The block was quiet, except for the faint crackle of radios and the occasional murmur from the uniforms hauling evidence. A siren wailed three streets over, but here it was hollow. Empty.

Will wanted to speak — to thank him, to acknowledge what Joe had been, the ballast he'd leaned on when the badge first felt too heavy. But the words jammed in his throat. Joe had never been one for speeches.

Instead, Joe reached out and clapped him once on the shoulder. The same way he had the day Will got his shield. Solid. Final.

"You'll do fine, Anderson. Just remember — the badge is heavy. But you're the kind of man who can carry it right."

His hand lingered just long enough to mean what words didn't, then slipped away. Joe turned, walking toward his car. Shoulders stooped, steps slower than Will had ever seen, his limp stark under the streetlight glow.

Will watched until Joe's silhouette vanished into the dark. For the first time since his rookie year, the silence pressed down without a buffer.

Will lingered on the curb long after the vans pulled away and the radios quieted. The night pressed down heavily, like the air itself had thickened after Joe's words.

He slid into the unmarked, hands still gripping the wheel even though he hadn't turned the key. The seat beside him was empty — the first time in years. Empty in a way that felt permanent.

Will pulled his notebook from the center console, the leather cover worn smooth from constant use in his pocket. He flipped past old pages: Craven Street, The Prophet, Sloane Mercer, all the ghosts still whispering through ink. He stopped on a clean sheet.

The pen hovered, then scratched hard against the paper:

**Notebook Entry**
*Last case with Joe.*
*Smooth. Clean.*
*He said: It's not the cases that break you. It's the silence after.*
*He's right.*
*The badge is heavy.*
*Carry it straight.*
*Carry it right.*

*Carry it alone, if I have to.*

Will sat back, pen tapping against the page, jaw tight. The silence Joe spoke about was already there, filling the car.

For the first time, he understood what it meant to lose the buffer, to feel the full weight without someone else to steady it. He closed the notebook, slid it back into his pocket, and started the car.

The engine turned over, but the seat beside him stayed empty. And he knew it always would.

## Apartment

The apartment was dark except for the glow of the lamp in the living room. Kristen was curled up on the couch, case files spread across the coffee table, a pen tucked behind her ear. She looked up as soon as the door clicked shut.

"You're late," she said softly. No accusation, just observation.

Will dropped his keys in the bowl by the door, the sound louder than it should've been. "Case wrapped. Burglaries. Clean arrests."

She studied his face, the tension in his shoulders, the way his tie hung loose like he'd forgotten about it halfway through the night. "But?"

He didn't answer right away. He just sat down beside her, elbows on his knees, head in his hands. Silence stretched — the exact silence Joe had spoken about.

Kristen slid closer, her hand resting lightly on his back. "Joe?"

Will lifted his head and met her eyes. His voice was low, rough. "He's done. Said this was it for him. No more cases. No more beat."

Her eyes softened, though her jaw tightened like she was holding the weight for him. "I knew it was coming.

He's been limping worse every time I've seen him. But hearing it..." She shook her head. "That's different."

Will leaned back into the couch, staring at the ceiling. "He said it's not the cases that break you. It's the silence after."

Kristen reached for his hand, threading her fingers through his, grounding him. "Then don't sit in it alone."

He turned to her, eyes burning, throat tight. "Feels like the floor just dropped out. Like the beat won't sound the same without him."

She squeezed his hand, her voice firm. "It won't. But you're not him. You're you. And you don't have to carry that silence by yourself."

Will let out a shaky breath, the words hitting something deeper than the whiskey he hadn't touched. He leaned into her shoulder, her hair brushing his cheek, the warmth of her presence anchoring him in a way no notebook ever could.

Kristen whispered against his temple, steady as stone: "You've still got me. Always."

For the first time that night, the silence didn't feel so crushing.

Kristen shifted closer, her hand resting on his chest, feeling the tension beneath his shirt. "You know," she murmured, "your lease is up in three weeks."

Will gave a humorless snort. "Yeah. Not like I've been living there anyway."

She smiled faintly. "Exactly. Most of your stuff's already here. The baby doesn't need to come home to two addresses."

He turned his head toward her, brow furrowed. "You saying you're tired of me crashing at my place on late nights?"

"I'm saying you don't need to hide over there just because you're worried about waking me up. This—" she squeezed his hand, pressed it to her stomach "—this is home now. Both of us. All three of us."

Will's eyes softened. He let his palm linger on the curve of her belly, the swell that seemed to grow more real every day. "Feels like he's been in there forever," he muttered. "Why hasn't he popped out yet? You sure it's not an alien?"

Kristen laughed, the sound warm and unguarded in the dim room. "If he kicks through my ribs tonight, I'll let you know." She tilted her head, eyes shining. "But no, Will. He's just... taking his time. Coming when he's ready."

Will stared at her, the weight of Joe's words still heavy in his chest, but the sight of her — of them — anchored him. The silence didn't feel like an empty space anymore. It felt like room being made for something new.

"You anchor me," he said quietly, almost to himself.

Kristen kissed his temple, her whisper threading into the air between them. "Good. Because you're not carrying this alone anymore. Not the badge. Not the silence. Not him." She guided his hand back against her belly, pressing it close. "Never alone."

For the first time that night, Will let himself believe it as he fell asleep in her arms.

The morning started the way so many had before. Sunlight slanted in through the blinds, stripes of gold cutting across the bed. Will stirred awake at the sound of Kristen shifting beside him, her groan a mix of exhaustion and humor.

"Your son is using my ribs as a punching bag," she muttered.

Will rolled toward her, brushing her hair from her forehead. "He gets that from your side."

Kristen's laugh was soft but tired. She pushed herself upright, hands braced on her belly. "Help me in the shower? I'm not sure I can bend enough even to reach my own ankles anymore."

"Yes, ma'am." Will climbed out of bed, stretching the stiffness out of his shoulders. He caught sight of her in the mirror as they moved into the bathroom — her curves fuller, her body radiant even as she groaned at the effort. He steadied her as she stepped into the tub, his hands gentle but sure.

Kristen leaned into him as the water warmed, her forehead against his chest. "Promise me something?"

"Anything."

"Promise me we'll always do mornings like this, even when we're running late. Even when he's screaming the house down."

Will kissed the crown of her damp hair. "Deal."

They dressed slowly, Kristen pausing to catch her breath more than once. Will scrambled eggs while she buttered toast, the normalcy of breakfast grounding them both.

By eight-thirty, Kristen was out the door in a navy skirt suit, her files tucked under one arm as she headed toward the Ravenwood County courthouse. Will buttoned into his plainclothes, shoulder holster snug beneath his jacket, on his way to Summit Falls PD. They kissed quickly at the door, a routine that still felt like a promise every time.

Two hours later, Will was flooring the unmarked down Main, siren wailing.

"David 1-3 in pursuit," he barked into the radio. "Southbound on Pike. Suspect vehicle is a silver Honda, confirmed narcotics warrants."

The Honda clipped a trash can and swerved to the side. Patrol fell in behind him, tires shrieking against the asphalt. Will's pulse hammered steady, training and instinct keeping the beat.

"Summit Falls PD!" he shouted on the PA system. "Pull over now!"

The driver didn't.

In his rearview, a marked unit closed the gap, sliding into the two-car position. Will's radio crackled: *"Anderson, we've got it. You're free to peel."*

Almost simultaneously, dispatch's voice cut in. *"David One-Three, priority message. Contact home immediately. Repeat, contact home."*

Will's gut dropped. His hand fumbled for the phone already buzzing against the dash. Kristen's assistant's voice spilled out, panicked but controlled. "Detective Anderson? It's happening. She's in labor. They're taking her by ambulance to Midlands."

Will's heart jackknifed. He pressed the mic. "Dispatch, David One-Three peeling off, less than a mile out from Midlands. Repeat, I'm en route to meet my child."

He cut hard at the next light, siren blaring, the unmarked weaving through traffic like it was cutting through water. His throat was dry, his palms slick, but the thought pounding louder than the engine was simple: *don't miss this.*

The ambulance was backing into the bay when Will skidded into the ER lot. He bailed out of the unmarked before it stopped rocking, sprinting to the double doors. Kristen was on the gurney, her assistant Kim clutching her hand, wide-eyed.

"Will," Kristen gasped, sweat streaking her temples. "You made it."

He caught her hand and squeezed it tightly. "Wouldn't be anywhere else."

Hours blurred into heart monitors, shouted vitals, nurses moving like a tide. And then — a cry. Sharp. Fierce. Alive.

The doctor held him up, tiny and wriggling, lungs announcing his arrival to the world. "William Robert Anderson," the nurse said, wrapping him tight before placing him in Kristen's arms. Named after Will and Kristen's fathers.

Tears streaked Kristen's face. She kissed the crown of their son's head, then looked at Will, laughing through the exhaustion. "Promise me one thing."

"What's that?" His voice was already breaking.

"We are not calling him Billy Bob."

Despite the tears, Will barked a laugh. "Deal."

Her parents arrived not long after, Brittany Jo in tow. The room filled with laughter and relief, stories and photos already being snapped.

Kristen's assistant, Kim, lingered in the corner, pale and shaken. Finally, she pulled out her phone. "I... I think I'll call my doctor. Renew my birth control. I'm not ready for that."

The room erupted with laughter, Kristen's even through the sweat and exhaustion.

Will leaned in close, brushing his thumb across Kristen's temple, eyes fixed on their son nestled against her.

"You did it," he whispered.

Kristen's eyes softened, shining. "No, we did it. Together."

For the first time in months, Will felt the silence in his chest replaced — not by weight, but by life.

## Epilogue: Direction

Three years later

The house in Oakhaven was warm with light spilling from the windows, the kind of glow Will never thought he'd call his own. Toys were scattered across the living room floor — blocks, plastic trucks, a half-dressed action figure propped against the couch like it was standing guard.

Billy's laugh carried through the open doorway, high and wild, Kristen chasing him with a mock growl as he tore down the hallway in mismatched socks. He rounded the corner, hair sticking up like a storm cloud, and collided square into Will's leg.

"Daddy!" Billy squealed, his little arms wrapping tight around him. "Mommy says you were chasing bad guys again!"

Will bent, scooping him up into one arm, kissing the top of his head. "Only the nasty ones," he said. "And only when they run slower than me."

Kristen appeared behind him, flushed from the chase, hair falling loose from the bun she'd worn to court. Her smile softened when she saw him — the same smile that had steadied him through years of weight and silence. She tugged at his tie. "Late again, Detective Anderson. Lucky for you, we saved dinner."

"Detective Anderson," he repeated with mock gravity, setting Billy down. "Still sounds strange."

But it wasn't strange anymore. Not here. Not after Lt. Dan Rogers had put in a word with the Oakhaven chief, calling him *one of the few who'll carry the badge straight, even when it costs him.* Not after Will had built a reputation in Summit Falls that stretched further than the precinct walls. Not after he realized the schools here, the quiet streets, the steadier nights, were what Billy deserved.

Kristen smoothed a strand of hair behind her ear, her eyes flickering with a fire he'd come to know well. "Speaking of titles... You realize I'm announcing next week, right?"

Will cocked his head. "Announcing?"

She arched a brow, daring him. "For District Attorney. Sinclair's stepping down, and this city's not going to hand itself over to someone who thinks justice is a bargaining chip. I'm running."

Will let out a low whistle, then smiled slowly. "So my wife's going to be the DA."

"Your wife already is," Kristen corrected, lips quirking. "The voters just don't know it yet."

Billy tugged at Will's sleeve, whispering loud enough for both of them to hear. "Does that mean Mommy's boss of all the police?"

Kristen crouched, pulling him close. "It means Mommy gets to help make sure Daddy and his friends put the bad guys away for good."

Will's chest tightened, pride and awe mixing like it always did when he looked at her — at them. Oakhaven wasn't Summit Falls. The cases weren't fewer, nor were they always cleaner, but the weight felt different. Manageable. Balanced.

He watched Kristen gather Billy into her lap, her hand resting absentmindedly on the boy's back, the fire in her eyes tempered by something steadier now.

For the first time, Will didn't feel like he was caught between the silence and the badge.

For the first time, he felt like he was exactly where he was supposed to be.

Billy leaned against Kristen, already fighting sleep even as his toy car rattled in his small hands. Kristen caught Will's gaze over their son's head, a silent question — *You okay?*

He nodded once, slowly. But when he carried the empty plates into the kitchen, the past caught up to him the way it always did in quiet moments.

The badge clipped to his belt gleamed in the kitchen light, Oakhaven PD etched fresh into the shield. Different city. Different rhythm. Same weight.

He thought of Joe then, unbidden — the stoop in his shoulders, the gravel in his voice, the way he'd clapped a hand on Will's chest and said, *The badge is heavy. But you're the kind of man who can carry it right.*

Joe never saw Billy. Never knew Kristen's grin when she told Will he was going to be a father. Never knew laughter and warmth instead of ghosts had filled the silence he left behind.

But Joe was in this kitchen all the same. In every case, Will worked. In every page of the notebook, it was still tucked in the drawer upstairs. In the scar over his eyebrow that Kristen kissed when she thought he was half asleep.

Rogers had helped him get here — put his name in the chief's ear, vouched for him when Oakhaven opened the homicide slot. "Anderson doesn't flinch," Rogers had told them. "Not even when it costs him."

But Joe had built him. Carved him out of hesitation and silence. Made sure that when the day came, he could carry the badge straight. And it wasn't just Joe—every officer Will had fought beside in the trenches left their mark. Blood, sweat, and the stubborn determination to make the world better, one shift at a time.

He'd learned what to do from those he was privileged to work alongside. And from others, he'd learned what *not* to do—the shortcuts, the callousness, the rot that everyone else tried to push out. The bad apples.

Through it all, Joe remained the cornerstone of his time in Summit Falls. The one steady weight that shaped him into the cop he was becoming.

Will rinsed the plates, water hissing against porcelain, and whispered under his breath like Joe could hear him across the years: "Still carrying it, Sarge. Just like you said."

When he returned to the living room, Kristen and Billy were curled together on the couch, both half-asleep. The quiet wasn't crushing anymore. It was steady. Safe.

For the first time, Will didn't fear the silence.

Will poured two fingers of Eagle Rare into a heavy glass, the bottle a parting gift from his old squad in Summit Falls. The amber caught the patio light as he eased into a chair by the pool, the night humming with cicadas. Beyond the water, the city of Oakhaven glowed faintly, a softer horizon than Summit Falls ever offered.

He let himself breathe. The whiskey warmed his hand before it touched his lips. The silence wasn't jagged anymore; it was steady, tempered by the sound of Billy's soft snores drifting faintly through the open slider.

The door clicked again. Bare feet padded across the stone. Kristen slipped behind him, her arms sliding over his shoulders, her chin resting lightly against his temple. She smelled of lavender and courtroom resolve.

"Celebrating without me?" she teased, her voice low, warm.

He started to answer, but she laid something flat across the rim of his glass. A white, glossy square.

Will frowned, set the whiskey down, and flipped it over.

The grainy black-and-white shapes resolved slowly in the glow of the patio light. Two small forms. Two labels. Baby A. Baby B.

His chest tightened, breath caught like he'd taken a hit of cold air. He looked up at her, eyes wide, throat thick. "Twins?"

Kristen's smile grew, her nod quick and sure. "Good observation, Detective."

He barked out a laugh, half disbelieving, half euphoric. "What are we going to do with twins?"

Kristen glanced toward the sliding door, where Billy lay sprawled across the couch, one sock kicked off, toy car still clutched in his hand. Her voice softened, steady. "Same thing we did with that one. Just twice as much."

Something in Will's chest cracked open, the kind of weight Joe used to warn him about — only this wasn't the badge, or the scars, or the silence. This was joy, fierce and undeniable.

He stood, scooped Kristen up into his arms, her laugh echoing across the still water. He kissed her hard, deep, the photo still pinched between his fingers.

For that moment, with whiskey warm on the table, his son safe inside, and the future multiplying in Kristen's smile, Will Anderson felt like a king of the world.

Kristen kissed his cheek before slipping inside, barefoot and glowing, off to tuck Billy in for the third time tonight. Will watched her go, her silhouette briefly framed by the glow of the hallway light before the slider clicked shut behind her.

The night pressed in again, softer now. Oakhaven breathed quieter than Summit Falls ever had — but he knew better than to let the silence fool him.

He took another sip of whiskey, eyes tracing the skyline.

The future stretched out like a road half-lit — clean on one side, shadowed on the other. Oakhaven wasn't without its darkness: different street names, different uniforms, same sickness under the skin. The badge hadn't gotten lighter in the move, just shifted where it pressed.

He'd traded rookie nerves for calloused instincts. And now, he'd traded patrol for vice, vice for homicide, chasing what most cops turned away from. The aftermaths. The silence after screams. The sermons carved in blood.

Some nights would be worse than Summit. Worse than Cherry. Worse than Maggie.

Because now, it was his case. His victims. His beat.

He knew the cost. The job would keep cutting — carving out pieces of his time, his sleep, his soul. It always did. Evil didn't sleep, didn't flinch, didn't take weekends.

But neither did he.

Not anymore.

He'd chase the worst of the world to the ends of it — not for revenge, not even for justice, but because someone had to. And he could. That mattered. That still mattered.

Inside, Billy's laughter sparked once more before fading into the hush of bedtime. Soon there would be two more voices, two more hearts beating under the same roof.

Will exhaled.

He'd face monsters by day, come home to chaos by night, and hold onto whatever pieces were left in between. Because now he knew what he was fighting for.

Not just the case files. Not just the badge.

But for everything inside that house.

**Final Notebook Entry**

*Summit Falls to Oakhaven.*

*Some cases are closed, while others remain open.*

*Evil wins when good men do nothing.*

*Badge still heavy. Always will be.*

*Everyone matters.*

*Billy = 3 years of laughter, fire, chaos.*

*Now: Baby A. Baby B.*

*Twins.*

*Didn't freeze. Didn't break.*

*Not carrying this alone anymore.*

*Kristen anchors me.*

*They all do.*

*The job takes its cut.*

*But tonight, I feel whole.*

## About the Author

Mark Harrington spent more than two decades in law enforcement before trading reports for novels. His stories draw from the reality of true crime behind the badge—the split-second choices, the moral gray area, and the cost of carrying the job home.

A lifelong Southerner, Harrington writes from his roots in small-town Carolina, where loyalty runs deep and darkness hides in plain sight. His fiction explores what courage looks like when the rules no longer apply and what it truly means to hold the line.

*Blood and Silence* is the prequel to his acclaimed Will Anderson series, which continues with *The Demon of Oakhaven* and *The Devil at Rocky Pointe.*

Both are available in print and online at your local book retailer.

## Blood and Silence

*The Origins of Will Anderson*

Before Summit Falls had a task force. Before Oakhaven had its killer called a demon.
There was just a rookie cop learning what the badge really meant.

When Will Anderson first pinned it on, he thought the job was about law and order. He learned fast that it was about blood and silence. Blood from the alleys, the victims, and sometimes your own hands. Silence from the brass, the politics, and the betrayal that rotted from within.

Mentored by a hard-bitten sergeant, tested by corruption in his own squad, and haunted by a killer who preached sermons in flesh, Will was forged in nights that didn't end and cases that wouldn't close.

This is where it began.
The making of a detective.
The weight of a badge.
And the silence that never really lifts.

Before Oakhaven had its demon, Will Anderson was just a rookie cop in Summit Falls, learning that the badge comes with weight you can't shake. Mentored by a sergeant who carved lessons in grit and silence, tested by corruption inside his own squad, and scarred by a predator who left sermons written in flesh, Will discovers that survival on the job isn't about glory—it's about blood, silence, and the choices that shape the kind of cop you become.